Welcome to a strange, not-so-distant future . . .

In Brian W. Aldiss's "Old Hundredth," a muted, autumnal future thousands of years after Singularity has forever changed Earth into an ancient and ruinous planet devoid of humankind . . .

In Charles Stross's "Rogue Farm," visit a deceptively bucolic future on the far side of Singularity where nothing is as simple—or as harmless—as it seems . . .

Pasco County Library System
Overdue notices are a courtesy of the Library System.
Failure to receive an overdue notice does not absolve the borrower of the obligation to return the materials on time.

D1598297

Edited by Jack Dann & Gardner Dozois

UNICORNS!
MAGICATS!
BESTIARY!
MERMAIDS!
SORCERERS!
DEMONS!
DOGTALES!
SEASERPENTS!
DINOSAURS!
LITTLE PEOPLE!
MAGICATS II
UNICORNS II
DRAGONS!
INVADERS!
HORSES!
ANGELS!
HACKERS
TIMEGATES
CLONES
IMMORTALS
NANOTECH
FUTURE WAR
GENOMETRY
SPACE SOLDIERS
FUTURE SPORTS
BEYOND FLESH
FUTURE CRIMES
A.I.s
ROBOTS
BEYOND SINGULARITY

BEYOND SINGULARITY

EDITED BY
JACK DANN & GARDNER DOZOIS

ACE BOOKS, NEW YORK

HUDSON BRANCH

THE BERKLEY PUBLISHING GROUP
Published by the Penguin Group
Penguin Group (USA) Inc.
375 Hudson Street, New York, New York 10014, USA
Penguin Group (Canada), 90 Eglinton Avenue East, Suite 700, Toronto, Ontario M4P 2Y3, Canada
(a division of Pearson Penguin Canada Inc.)
Penguin Books Ltd., 80 Strand, London WC2R 0RL, England
Penguin Group Ireland, 25 St. Stephen's Green, Dublin 2, Ireland (a division of Penguin Books Ltd.)
Penguin Group (Australia), 250 Camberwell Road, Camberwell, Victoria 3124, Australia
(a division of Pearson Australia Group Pty. Ltd.)
Penguin Books India Pvt. Ltd., 11 Community Centre, Panchsheel Park, New Delhi—110 017, India
Penguin Group (NZ), Cnr. Airborne and Rosedale Roads, Albany, Auckland 1310, New Zealand
(a division of Pearson New Zealand Ltd.)
Penguin Books (South Africa) (Pty.) Ltd., 24 Sturdee Avenue, Rosebank, Johannesburg 2196, South Africa

Penguin Books Ltd., Registered Offices: 80 Strand, London WC2R 0RL, England

This is a work of fiction. Names, characters, places, and incidents either are the product of the authors' imaginations or are used fictitiously, and any resemblance to actual persons, living or dead, business establishments, events, or locales is entirely coincidental. The publisher does not have any control over and does not assume any responsibility for author or third-party websites or their content.

BEYOND SINGULARITY

An Ace Book / published by arrangement with the editors

PRINTING HISTORY
Ace edition / December 2005

Copyright © 2005 by Jack Dann and Gardner Dozois.
A complete listing of individual copyrights can be found on page v.
Cover art by Ben Gibson.
Cover design by Rita Frangie.

All rights reserved.
No part of this book may be reproduced, scanned, or distributed in any printed or electronic form without permission. Please do not participate in or encourage piracy of copyrighted materials in violation of the authors' rights. Purchase only authorized editions.
For information address: The Berkley Publishing Group,
a division of Penguin Group (USA) Inc.,
375 Hudson Street, New York, New York 10014.

ISBN: 0-441-01363-5

ACE
Ace Books are published by The Berkley Publishing Group,
a division of Penguin Group (USA) Inc.,
375 Hudson Street, New York, New York 10014.
ACE and the "A" design are trademarks belonging to Penguin Group (USA) Inc.

PRINTED IN THE UNITED STATES OF AMERICA

10 9 8 7 6 5 4 3 2 1

If you purchased this book without a cover, you should be aware that this book is stolen property. It was reported as "unsold and destroyed" to the publisher, and neither the author nor the publisher has received any payment for this "stripped book."

ACKNOWLEDGMENT IS MADE FOR PERMISSION
TO REPRINT THE FOLLOWING MATERIAL:

"Old Hundredth" by Brian W. Aldiss. Copyright © 1960 by Brian W. Aldiss. First published in *New Worlds*, November 1960. Reprinted by permission of the author.

"Border Guards" by Greg Egan. Copyright © 1999 by *Interzone*. First published in *Interzone*, October 1999. Reprinted by permission of the author.

"Rogue Farm" by Charles Stross. Copyright © 2003 by Charles Stross. First published in *Live Without a Net* (Roc), edited by Lou Anders. Reprinted by permission of the author.

"All Tomorrow's Parties" by Paul J. McAuley. Copyright © 1997 by *Interzone*. First published in *Interzone*, April 1997. Published by permission of the author.

"Naturals" by Gregory Benford. Copyright © 2003 by *Interzone*. First published in *Interzone*, September 2003. Reprinted by permission of the author.

"Osmund Considers" by Timons Esaias. Copyright © 2002 by *Interzone*. First published in *Interzone*, May 2002. Reprinted by permission of the author.

"Coelacanths" by Robert Reed. Copyright © 2002 by Spilogale, Inc. Published in *The Magazine of Fantasy & Science Fiction*, March 2002. Reprinted by permission of the author.

"The Dog Said Bow-Wow" by Michael Swanwick. Copyright © 2001 by Dell Magazines. First published in *Asimov's Science Fiction Magazine*, October/November 2001. Reprinted by permission of the author.

"Barry Westphall Crashes the Singularity" by James Patrick Kelly. Copyright © 2002 by James Patrick Kelly. First published electronically on *The Infinite Matrix*, September 30, 2002. Reprinted by permission of the author.

"Flowers From Alice" by Cory Doctorow and Charles Stross. Copyright © 2003 by Cory Doctorow and Charles Stross. First published in *New Voices in Science Fiction* (DAW). Reprinted by permission of the authors.

"Tracker" by Mary Rosenblum. Copyright © 2004 by Dell Magazines. First published in *Asimov's Science Fiction Magazine*, April/May 2004. Reprinted by permission of the author.

"Steps Along the Way" by Eric Brown. Copyright © 1999 by Eric Brown. First published in *Moon Shots* (DAW), 1999. Reprinted by permission of the author.

"The Millennium Party" by Walter Jon Williams. Copyright © 2002 by Walter Jon Williams. First published electronically on *The Infinite Matrix*, May 8, 2002. Reprinted by permission of the author.

"The Voluntary State" by Christopher Rowe. Copyright © 2004 by Scifi.com. First published electronically on SCI Fiction, May 5, 2004. Reprinted by permission of the author.

CONTENTS

Preface

"Within thirty years, we will have the technological means to create superhuman intelligence. Shortly after, the human era will be ended."

With these provocative words, Vernor Vinge began his presentation on the future at the VISION-21 Symposium sponsored by the NASA Lewis Research Center in 1993, and so launched into popular culture the idea of the Singularity: that point in the future where humans are no longer the dominant species on Earth and where the rate of technological change becomes so great that predicting what the future will be like becomes nearly impossible, a tipping point beyond which "societal, scientific, and economic change is so fast we cannot even imagine what will happen from our present perspective, and when humanity will become posthumanity"—*if* it survives at all. A world as different from today's world as our world is from the world of the Australopithecus. A world in which humans may gain godlike powers or be wiped from existence altogether . . . might be rendered obsolete and relegated to the equivalent of zoos or nature reserves, or *merge* with machines in strange ways to produce creatures few people alive today would even recognize as human. A world that is, in a literal sense, *unimaginable*—beyond the powers of our imaginations to conceive.

The Singularity had been envisioned before—Stan Ulam mentions a conversation with scientist John Von Neumann in the 1950s in which "our conversation centered on the ever accelerating progress of technology and changes in the mode of human life, which gives the appearance of approaching some essential Singularity in the history of the race beyond which human affairs, as we know them, could not continue," and the idea is sounded in a somewhat different key in Arthur C. Clarke's 1948 novel *Against the Fall of Night*—but Vinge's paper changed the Singularity from a vague speculation about something that might happen in the very distant future to something that probably would happen within the lifetimes of many of the people sitting in the audience. In Vinge's words: "From the human point of view this change will be a throwing away of all the previous rules, perhaps in the blink of an eye, an exponential runaway beyond any hope of control. Developments that before were thought might only happen in 'a million years' (if ever) will likely happen in the next century." (For the entire text of Vinge's ground-breaking paper—plus links to other speculation and commentary about the Singularity—see www.ugcs.caltech .edu/~phoenix/vinge/vingesing.html. A discussion about the Singularity featuring Charles Stross and gory Doctorow titled "Is Science Fiction About to Go Blind?" can also be found at www.popsci.com/popsci/science/ article/0,20967,676265,00.html.)

The idea of a technological Singularity, plus the related ideas of posthumanity and superintelligent Artificial Intelligences, have had an enormous impact on science fiction throughout the '90s and the Oughts to date, challenging and changing the genre's vision of what the future is going to be like. Here, over a third of the way to the date Vinge predicts for its arrival, some of the best science fiction being written grapples with the implications of the Coming of the Singularity and attempts the incredibly difficult task of peering ahead, beyond Singularity, to see what the posthuman world might be like.

Of course, today's authors can't *really* give us the view from a posthuman intelligence, from the far side of a Singularity, any more than an Australopithecus could have written a story seen through the eyes of a contemporary twenty-first-century human; after all, the stories are being written by people on this side of the Singularity, and no matter how lavish and radical the imaginations of the authors, they remain of necessity limited to being the *human* perspective on *post*humanity. The idea of Singularity is so new that relatively few stories dealing with the world *beyond* the Singularity have been written. Yet although the task is perhaps by definition impossible, SF writers such as

Greg Egan, Michael Swanwick, Charles Stross (whose Accelerando stories, taken as a unit, may be the most complete vision yet of life beyond the Singularity), Cory Doctorow, Robert Reed, Brian Stableford, Stephen Baxter, Bruce Sterling, Greg Bear, Iain Banks, Nancy Kress, Alastair Reynolds, Peter F. Hamilton, Walter Jon Williams, Gregory Benford, Paul J. McAuley, James Patrick Kelly, Ian McDonald, Vernor Vinge himself, and the rest of the authors in this anthology, as well as a dozen others, continue to give it their best shot, producing work that dances right at the cutting edge of the genre—and which may be the best that mere humans on this side of the Singularity can do to predict the mysterious and perhaps incomprehensible future that may await us only a few decades down the line.

So before the Singularity swallows us and whisks us off to our unknown and perhaps unknowable fates, while we're still recognizably human, open the pages of this book to find fourteen visions of what *might* happen to us in the not-so-distant future—and, while you still *can* process such a primitive, meatbrain, mainframe-human emotion, enjoy!

(For further speculations on this and related themes, check out our Ace anthologies *A.I.s*, *Beyond Flesh*, *Robots*, *Nanotech*, *Genometry*, *Hackers*, *Immortals*, and *Future War*, and Gardner Dozois's *Supermen: Tales of the Posthuman Future*.)

Old Hundredth

Brian W. Aldiss

*The far future seems to hold a special fascination and al-
lure for Brian W. Aldiss, and in a field where such stories
are relatively rare, he has almost made a specialty out of
writing about it. The Long Afternoon of Earth (also known
as the Hothouse series, under which title it won a special
Hugo Award in 1962) remains one of the classic visions of
the distant future of Earth, as well as being a foundation-
stone of the subgenre of science-fantasy. Aldiss has also
handled the theme with grace and a wealth of poetic imagination in many other stories, including classics such as
"The Worm That Flies" and "Full Sun," as well as the novels of the Helliconia trilogy (and handles a closely related
theme with similar excellence in The Malacia Tapestry as
well).*

*Never has he envisioned the far future more vividly than
in the story that follows, though, which takes us to a muted,
autumnal future thousands of years after a Singularity has
forever changed all life on Earth; a future full of echoes
and old ghosts; an ancient and ruinous Earth from which
humankind has forever departed; a strange world of Involutes and Impures and musicolumns, with Venus for a
moon, and hogs as big as hippos; a world of stately, living
music under dusty umbrella trees ...*

*One of the true giants of the field, Brian W. Aldiss has
been publishing science fiction for more than a quarter
century and has more than two dozen books to his credit.
The Long Afternoon of Earth won a Hugo Award in 1962.
"The Saliva Tree" won a Nebula Award in 1965, and
Aldiss's novel Starship won the Prix Jules Verne in 1977.
He took another Hugo Award in 1987 for his critical study
of science fiction Trillion Year Spree, written with David
Wingrove. His other books include An Island Called*

Moreau, Graybeard, Enemies of the System, A Rude Awakening, Life in the West, Forgotten Life, Dracula Unbound, *and* Remembrance Day, *and a memoir,* Bury My Heart at W. H. Smith's, *and an autobiography,* The Twinkling of an Eye, or, My Life as an Englishman. *His short fiction has been collected in* Space, Time, and Nathaniel, Who Can Replace a Man?, New Arrivals, Old Encounters, Galaxies Like Grains of Sand, Seasons in Flight, *and* Common Clay, *and he's published a collection of poems,* Home Life With Cats. *His many anthologies include* The Penguin Science Fiction Omnibus *and, with Harry Harrison,* Decade: The 1940s, Decade: The 1950s, *and* Decade: The 1960s. *His latest books are the novels* Affairs at Hampden Ferrers *and* Jocasta. *He lives in Oxford, England.*

The road climbed dustily down between trees as symmetrical as umbrellas. Its length was punctuated at one point by a musicolumn standing on the verge. From a distance, the column was only a stain in the air. As sentient creatures neared it, their psyches activated it, it drew on their vitalities, and then it could be heard as well as seen. Their presence made it flower into pleasant sound, instrumental or chant.

All this region was called Ghinomon, for no one lived here now, not even the odd hermit Impure. It was given over to grass and the weight of time. Only a wild goat or two activated the musicolumn nowadays, or a scampering vole wrung a chord from it in passing.

When old Dandi Lashadusa came riding on her baluchitherium, the column began to intone. It was no more than an indigo trace in the air, hardly visible, for it represented only a bonded pattern of music locked into the fabric of that particular area of space. It was also a transubstantio-spatial shrine, the eternal part of a being that had dematerialized itself into music.

The baluchitherium whinnied, lowered its head, and sneezed onto the gritty road.

"Gently, Lass," Dandi told her mare, savoring the growth of the chords that increased in volume as she approached. Her long nose twitched with pleasure as if she could feel the melody along her olfactory nerves.

Obediently, the baluchitherium slowed, turning aside to crop fern, although it kept an eye on the indigo stain. It liked things to have being or not to have being; these half-and-half objects disturbed it, though they could not impair its immense appetite.

Dandi climbed down her ladder onto the ground, glad to feel the ancient dust under her feet. She smoothed her hair and stretched as she listened to the music.

She spoke aloud to her mentor, half a world away, but he was not listening. His mind closed to her thoughts, and he muttered an obscure exposition that darkened what it sought to clarify.

". . . useless to deny that it is well-nigh impossible to improve anything, however faulty, that has so much tradition behind it. And the origins of your bit of metricism are indeed embedded in such an antiquity that we must needs—"

"Tush, Mentor, come out of your black box and forget your hatred of my 'metricism' a moment," Dandi Lashadusa said, cutting her thought into his. "Listen to the bit of 'metricism' I've found here; look at where I have come to; let your argument rest."

She turned her eyes around, scanning the tawny rocks near at hand, the brown line of the road, the distant black-and-white magnificence of ancient Oldorajo's town, doing this all for him, tiresome old fellow. Her mentor was blind, never left his cell in Aeterbroe to go farther than the sandy courtyard, hadn't physically left that green cathedral pile for over a century. Womanlike, she thought he needed change. Soul, how he rambled on! Even now, he was managing to ignore her and refute her.

". . . for consider, Lashadusa woman, nobody can be found to father it. Nobody wrought or thought it, phases of it merely *came* together. Even the old nations of men could not own it. None of them know who composed it. An element here from a Spanish pavan, an influence there of a French psalm tune, a flavor here of early English carol, a savor there of later German chorale. All primitive—ancient beyond ken. Nor are the faults of your bit of metricism confined to bastardy—"

"Stay in your black box then, if you won't see or listen," Dandi said. She could not get into his mind; it was the mentor's privilege to lodge in her mind, and in the minds of those few other wards he had, scattered around Earth. Only the mentors had the power to inhabit another's mind—which made them rather tiring on occasions like this, when they would not get out. For over seventy centuries, Dandi's mentor had been persuading her to die into a dirge of his choosing (and composing). Let her die, yes, let her transubstantio-spatialize herself a thousand times! His quarrel was not with her decision but with her taste, which he considered execrable.

Leaving the baluchitherium to crop, Dandi walked away from the musicolumn toward a hillock. Still fed by her steed's psyche, the column continued to play. Its music was of a simplicity, with a dominant-tonic recurrent bass part suggesting pessimism. To Dandi, a savant in musicolumnology, it yielded other data. She could tell to within a few years when its founder had died and also what sort of creature, generally speaking, he had been.

Climbing the hillock, Dandi looked about. To the south where the road led were low hills, lilac in the poor light. There lay her home. At last she was returning, after wanderings covering three hundred centuries and most of the globe.

Apart from the blind beauty of Oldorajo's town lying to the west, there was only one landmark she recognized. That was the Involute. It seemed to hang iridial above the ground a few leagues ahead; just to look on it made her feel she must go nearer.

Before summoning the baluchitherium, Dandi listened once more to the sounds of the musicolumn, making sure

she had them fixed in her head. The pity was that her old
fool wise man would not share it. She could still feel his
sulks floating like sediment through her mind.

"Are you listening now, Mentor?"

"Eh? An interesting point is that back in 1556 Pre-
Involutary, your same little tune may be discovered lurking
in Knox's Anglo-Genevan Psalter, where it espoused the
cause of the third psalm—"

"You dreary old fish! Wake yourself! How can you crit-
icize my intended way of dying when you have such a fus-
tian way of living?"

This time he heard her words. So close did he seem that
his peevish pinching at the bridge of his snuffy old nose
tickled hers, too.

"What are you doing *now*, Dandi?" he inquired.

"If you had been listening, you'd know. Here's where I
am, on the last Ghinomon plain before Crotheria and
home." She swept the landscape again and he took it in,
drank it almost greedily. Many mentors went blind early in
life shut in their monastic underwater life; their most ef-
fective vision was conducted through the eyes of their
wards.

His view of what she saw enriched hers. He knew the
history, the myth behind this forsaken land. He could stock
the tired old landscape with pageantry, delighting her and
surprising her. Back and forward he went, painting her pictures: the Youdicans, the Lombards, the Ex-Europa Emis-
sary, the Grites, the Risorgimento, the Involuters—and
catchwords, costumes, customs, courtesans, pelted briefly
through Dandi Lashadusa's mind. Ah, she thought admir-
ingly, who could truly live without these priestly, beastly,
erudite, erratic mentors?

"Erratic?" he inquired, snatching at her lick of thought.
"A thousand years I live, for all that time to absent myself
from the world, to eat mashed fish here with my brothers,
learning history, studying rapport, sleeping with my bones
on stones—a humble being, a being in a million, a mentor
in a myriad, and your standards of judgment are so

mundane you find no stronger label for me than erratic?!
Fie, Lashadusa, bother me no more for fifty years!"

The words squeaked in her head as if she spoke herself.
She felt his old chops work phantomlike in hers, and half
in anger half in laughter called aloud, "I'll be dead by
then!"

He snicked back hot and holy to reply, "And another
thing about your footloose swan song—in Marot and
Beza's Genevan Psalter of 1551, Old Time, it was musical
midwife to the one hundred and thirty-fourth psalm. Like
you, it never seemed to settle!" Then he was gone.

"Pooh!" Dandi said. She whistled. "Lass."

Obediently her great rhinolike creature, eighteen feet
high at the shoulder, ambled over. The musicolumn died as
the mare left it, faded, sank to a whisper, silenced: only the
purple stain remained, noiseless, in the lonely air. Lowering its great Oligocene head, Lass nuzzled its mistress's
hand. She climbed the ladder onto the ridged plateau of its
back.

They made toward the Involute, lulled by the simple
and intricate feeling of being alive.

Night was settling in now. Hidden behind banks of mist,
the sun prepared to set. But Venus was high, a gallant half-
crescent four times as big as the moon had been before the
moon, spiraling farther and farther from Earth, had shaken
off its parent's clutch to go dance around the sun, a second
Mercury. Even by that time Venus had been moved by
gravitotraction into Earth's orbit, so that the two sister
worlds circled each other as they circled the sun.

The stamp of that great event still lay everywhere, its
tokens not only in the crescent in the sky. For Venus placed
a strange spell on the hearts of man, and a more penetrating displacement in his genes. Even when its atmosphere
was transformed into a muffled breathability, it remained
an alien world; against logic, its opportunities, its possibilities, were its own. It shaped men, just as Earth had shaped
them.

On Venus, men bred themselves anew.

And they bred the so-called Impures. They bred new plants, new fruits, new creatures—original ones, and duplications of creatures not seen on Earth for eons past. From one line of these familiar strangers Dandi's baluchitherium was descended. So, for that matter, was Dandi.

The huge creature came now to the Involute, or as near as it cared to get. Again it began to crop at thistles, thrusting its nose through dewy spiders' webs and ground mist.

"Like you, I'm a vegetarian," Dandi said, climbing down to the ground. A grove of low fruit trees grew nearby; she reached up Into the branches, gathered, and ate, before turning to inspect the Involute. Already her spine tingled at the nearness of it; awe, loathing, and love made a part-pleasant sensation near her heart.

The Involute was not beautiful. True, its colors changed with the changing light, yet the colors were fish-cold, for they belonged to another dimension. Though they reacted to dusk and dawn, Earth had no stronger power over them. They pricked the eyes. Perhaps, too, they were painful because they were the last signs of materialist man. Even Lass moved uneasily before that ill-defined lattice, the upper limits of which were lost in thickening gloom.

"Don't fear," Dandi said. "There's an explanation for this, old girl." She added, "There's an explanation for everything, if we can find it."

She could feel all the personalities in the Involute. It was a frozen screen of personality. All over the old planet the structures stood, to shed their awe on those who were left behind. They were the essence of man. They were man—all that remained of him on Earth.

When the first flint, the first shell, was shaped into a weapon, that action shaped man. As he molded and complicated his tools, so they molded and complicated him. He became the first scientific animal. And at last, via information theory and great computers, he gained knowledge of all his parts. He formed the Laws of Integration, which reveal all beings as part of a pattern and show them their part in the pattern. There is only the pattern; the pattern is all the universe, creator and created. For the first time it became possible to duplicate that pattern artificially—the transubstantio-spatializers were built.

Men left their strange hobbies on Earth and Venus and projected themselves into the pattern. Their entire personalities were merged with the texture of space itself. Through science, they reached immortality.

It was a one-way passage.

They did not return. Each Involute carried thousands or even millions of people. There they were, not dead, not living. How they exulted or wept in their transubstantiation, no one left could say. Only this could be said: man had gone, and a great emptiness was fallen over Earth.

"Your thoughts are heavy, Dandi Lashadusa. Get you home." Her mentor was back in her mind. She caught the feeling of him moving around and around in his coral-formed cell.

"I must think of man," she said.

"Your thoughts mean nothing, do nothing."

"Man created us: I want to consider him in peace."

"He only shaped a stream of life that was always entirely out of his control. Forget him. Get onto your mare and ride home."

"Mentor—"

"Get home, woman. Moping does not become you, I want to hear no more of your swan song, for I've given you my final word on that. Use a theme of your own, not of man's. I've said it a million times, and I say it again."

"I wasn't going to mention my music. I was only going to tell you that—"

"What then?" His thought was querulous. She felt his powerful tail tremble, disturbing the quiet water of his cell.

"I don't know—"

"Get home then."

"I'm lonely."

He shot her a picture from another of his wards before

leaving her. Dandi had seen this ward before in similar, dreamlike glimpses. It was a huge mole creature, still boring underground as it had been for the last hundred years. Occasionally it crawled through vast caves; once it swam in a subterranean lake; most of the time it just bored through rock. Its motivations were obscure to Dandi, although her mentor referred to it as "a geologer." Doubtless if the mole was vouchsafed occasional glimpses of Dandi and her musicolumnology, it would find her as baffling. At least the mentor's point was made: loneliness was psychological, not statistical.

Why, a million personalities glittered almost before her eyes!

She mounted the great baluchitherium mare and headed for home. Time and old monuments made glum company.

Twilight now, with just one streak of antique gold left in the sky, Venus sweetly bright, and stars peppering the purple. A fine evening in which to be alive, particularly with one's last bedtime close at hand.

And yes, for all her mentor said, she was going to turn into that old little piece derived from one of the tunes in the 1540 *Souter Liedekens*, that splendid source of Netherlands folk music. For a moment, Dandi Lashadusa chuckled almost as eruditely as her mentor. The sixteenth century, with the virtual death of plainsong and virtual birth of the violin, was most interesting to her. Ah, the richness of facts, the texture of man's brief history on Earth! Pure joy! Then she remembered herself.

After all, she was only a megatherium, a sloth as big as a small elephant, whose kind had been extinct for millions of years until man reconstituted a few of them in the Venusian experiments. Her modifications in the way of fingers and enlarged brain gave her no real qualification to think up to man's level.

Early next morning, they arrived at the ramparts of the town Crotheria, where Dandi lived. The ubiquitous goats

thronged about them, some no bigger than hedgehogs,
some almost as big as hippos—what madness in his last
days had provoked man to so many variations on one
undistinguished theme?—as Lass and her mistress moved
up the last slope and under the archway.

It was good to be back, to push among the trails fringed
with bracken, among the palms, oaks, and treeferns. Almost all the town was deeply green and private from the
sun, curtained by swathes of Spanish moss. Here and there
were houses—caves, pits, crude piles of boulders, or even
genuine man-type buildings, grand in ruin. Dandi climbed
down, walking ahead of her mount, her long hair curling in
pleasure. The air was cool with the coo of doves or the occasional bleat of a merino.

As she explored familiar ways, though, disappointment
overcame her. Her friends were all away, even the dreamy
bison whose wallow lay at the corner of the street in which
Dandi lived. Only pure animals were here, rooting happily
and mindlessly in the lanes, beggars who owned the Earth.
The Impures—descendants of the Venusian experimental
stock—were all absent from Crotheria.

That was understandable. For obvious reasons man had
increased the abilities of herbivores rather than carnivores.
After the Involution, with man gone, these Impures had
taken to his towns as they took to his ways, as far as this
was possible to their natures. Both Dandi and Lass, and
many of the others, consumed massive amounts of vegetable matter every day. Gradually a wider and wider circle of desolation grew about each town (the greenery in the
town itself was sacrosanct), forcing a semi-nomadic life
onto its vegetarian inhabitants.

This thinning in its turn led to a decline in the birthrate.
The travelers grew fewer, the towns greener and emptier;
in time they had become little oases of forest studding the
grassless plains.

"Rest here, Lass," Dandi said at last, pausing by a bank
of brightly flowering cycads. "I'm going into my house."

A giant beech grew before the stone façade of her home,

so close that it was hard to determine whether it did not help support the ancient building. A crumbling balcony jutted from the first floor; reaching up, Dandi seized the balustrade and hauled herself onto it.

This was her normal way of entering her home, for the ground floor was taken over by goats and hogs, just as the third floor had been appropriated by doves and parakeets. Trampling over the greenery self-sown on the balcony, she moved into the front room. Dandi smiled. Here were her old things, the broken furniture on which she liked to sleep, the vision screens on which nothing could be seen, the heavy manuscript books in which, guided by her know-all mentor, she wrote down the outpourings of the musi-columns she had visited all over the world.

She ambled through to the next room.

She paused, her peace of mind suddenly broken.

A brown bear stood there. One of its heavy hands was clenched over the hilt of a knife.

"I am no vulgar thief," it said, curling its thick black lips over the syllables. "I am an archaeologer. If this is your place, you must grant me permission to remove the man things. Obviously you have no idea of the worth of some of the equipment here. We bears require it. We must have it."

It came toward her, panting doggy fashion, its jaws open. From under bristling eyebrows gleamed the lust to. kill.

Dandi was frightened. Peaceful by nature, she feared the bears above all creatures for their fierceness and their ability to organize. The bears were few: they were the only creatures to show signs of wishing to emulate man's old aggressiveness.

She knew what the bears did. They hurled themselves through the Involutes to increase their power; by penetrating those patterns, they nourished their psychic drive, so the mentor said. It was forbidden. They were transgressors. They were killers.

"Mentor!" she screamed.

The bear hesitated. As far as he was concerned, the hulking creature before him was merely an obstacle in the way of progress, something to be thrust aside without hate. Killing would be pleasant but irrelevant; more important items remained to be done. Much of the equipment housed here could be used in the rebuilding of the world, the world of which bears had such high, haphazard dreams. Holding the knife threateningly, he moved forward.

The mentor was in Dandi's head, answering her cry, seeing through her eyes, though he had no sight of his own. He scanned the bear and took over her mind instantly, knifing himself into place like a guillotine.

No longer was he a blind old dolphin lurking in one cell of a cathedral pile of coral under tropical seas, a theologer, an inculcator of wisdom into feebler-minded beings. He was a killer more savage than the bear, keen to kill anything that might covet the vacant throne once held by men. The mere thought of men could send this mentor into sharklike fury at times.

Caught up in his fury, Dandi found herself advancing. For all the bear's strength, she could vanquish it. In the open, where she could have brought her heavy tail into action, it would have been an easy matter. Here her weighty forearms must come into play. She felt them lift to her mentor's command as he planned for her to clout the bear to death.

The bear stepped back, awed by an opponent twice its size, suddenly unsure.

She advanced.

"No! Stop!" Dandi cried.

Instead of fighting the bear, she fought her mentor, hating his hate. Her mind twisted, her dim mind full of that steely, fishy one, as she blocked his resolution.

"I'm for peace!" she cried.

"Then kill the bear!"

"I'm for peace, not killing!"

She rocked back and forth. When she staggered into a wall, it shook; dust spread in the old room. The mentor's fury was terrible to feel.

"Get out quickly!" Dandi called to the bear.

Hesitating, it stared at her. Then it turned and made for the window. For a moment it hung with its shaggy hind-quarters in the room. Momentarily she saw it for what it was, an old animal in an old world, without direction. It jumped. It was gone. Goats blared confusion on its retreat.

The mentor screamed. Insane with frustration, he hurled Dandi against the doorway with all the force of his mind.

Wood cracked and splintered. The lintel came crashing down. Brick and stone shifted, grumbled, fell. Powdered filth billowed up. With a great roar, one wall collapsed. Dandi struggled to get free. Her house was tumbling about her. It had never been intended to carry so much weight, so many centuries.

She reached the balcony and jumped clumsily to safety, just as the building avalanched in on itself, sending a cloud of plaster and powdered mortar into the overhanging trees.

For a horribly long while the world was full of dust, goat bleats, and panic-stricken parakeets.

H*eavily astride her* baluchitherium once more, Dandi Lashadusa headed back to the empty region called Ghi-nomon. She fought her bitterness, trying to urge herself to-ward resignation.

All she had was destroyed—not that she set store by possessions: that was a man trait. Much more terrible was the knowledge that her mentor had left her forever; she had transgressed too badly to be forgiven this time.

Suddenly she was lonely for his persnickety voice in her head, for the wisdom he fed her, for the scraps of dead knowledge he tossed her—yes, even for the love he gave her. She had never seen him, never could: yet no two be-ings could have been more intimate.

She also missed those other wards of his she would glimpse no more: the mole creature tunneling in Earth's depths, the seal family that barked with laughter on a des-olate coast, a senile gorilla that endlessly collected and classified spiders, an aurochs—seen only once, but then unforgettably—that lived with smaller creatures in an Arctic city it had helped build in the ice.

She was excommunicated.

Well, it was time for her to change, to disintegrate, to transubstantiate into a pattern not of flesh but music. That discipline at least the mentor had taught and could not take away.

"This will do, Lass," she said.

Her gigantic mount stopped obediently. Lovingly, she patted its neck. It was young; it would be free.

Following the dusty trail, she went ahead, alone. Somewhere afar a bird called. Coming to a mound of boulders, Dandi squatted among gorse, the points of which could not prick through her thick old coat. Already her selected music poured through her head, already it seemed to loosen the chemical bonds of her being.

Why should she not choose an old human tune? She was an antiquarian. Things that were gone solaced her for things that were to come. In her dim way, she had always stood out against her mentor's absolute hatred of men. The thing to hate was hatred. Men in their finer moments had risen above hate. Her death psalm was an instance of that—a multiple instance, for it had been fingered and changed over the ages, as the mentor himself insisted, by men of a variety of races, all with their minds directed to worship rather than hate.

Locking herself into thought disciplines, Dandi began to dissolve. Man had needed machines to help him do it, to fit into the Involutes. She was a lesser animal: she could change herself into the humbler shape of a musicolumn. It was just a matter of *rearranging*—and without pain she formed into a pattern that was not a shaggy megatherium body, but an indigo column, hardly visible. . . .

For a long while Lass cropped thistle and cacti. Then she ambled forward to seek the hairy creature she fondly— and a little condescendingly—regarded as her equal. But of the sloth there was no sign.

Almost the only landmark was a violet-blue dye in the air. As the baluchitherium mare approached, a sweet old music grew in volume from the dye. It was a music almost as ancient as the landscape itself, and certainly as much traveled, a tune once known to men as Old Hundredth. And there were voices singing: "All creatures that on Earth do dwell. . . ."

Border Guards

Greg Egan

*Looking back at the century that's just ended, it's obvious
that Australian writer Greg Egan was one of the Big New
Names to emerge in SF in the nineties and is probably one
of the most significant talents to enter the field in the last
several decades. Already one of the most widely known of
all Australian genre writers, Egan may well be the best
new hard-science writer to enter the field since Greg Bear,
and he is still growing in range, power, and sophistication.
In the last few years, he has become a frequent contributor
to* Interzone *and* Asimov's Science Fiction Magazine *and
has made sales to* Pulphouse, Analog, Aurealis, Eidolon,
*and elsewhere; many of his stories have also appeared in
various Best of the Year series, and he was on the Hugo
Final Ballot in 1995 for his story "Cocoon," which won the
Ditmar Award and the Asimov's Readers Award. He won
the Hugo Award in 1999 for his novella "Oceanic." His
first novel,* Quarantine, *appeared in 1992; his second
novel,* Permutation City, *won the John W. Campbell
Memorial Award in 1994. His other books include the novels* Distress, Diaspora, *and* Teranesia, *and three collections
of his short fiction,* Axiomatic, Luminous, *and* Our Lady
of Chernobyl. *His most recent book is a novel called*
Schild's Ladder. *He has a website at www.netspace
.netau/^gregegan/.*

*Almost any story by Egan would have served perfectly
well for this anthology; in fact, with the possible excep-
tions of Brian Stableford and Charles Stross, Egan has
probably written more about the posthuman future than
any other writer of the last decade—being one of the key
players in shaping current ideas about that future—and
there were more than a dozen possibilities to choose from,
including stories such as "Learning to Be Me," "Dust,"*

"Fidelity," "Reasons to Be Cheerful," "The Planck Dive," "Tap," "Oceanic," and "Wang's Carpets."

I finally settled on the dazzlingly imaginative story that follows, as it takes us as deep into that posthuman future, as far beyond Singularity, as anything that Egan has yet written, for a compelling study of old loyalties and new possibilities.

In the early afternoon of his fourth day out of sadness, Jamil was wandering home from the gardens at the center of Noether when he heard shouts from the playing field behind the library. On the spur of the moment, without even asking the city what game was in progress, he decided to join in.

As he rounded the corner and the field came into view, it was clear from the movements of the players that they were in the middle of a quantum soccer match. At Jamil's request, the city painted the wave function of the hypothetical ball across his vision, and tweaked him to recognize the players as the members of two teams without changing their appearance at all. Maria had once told him that she always chose a literal perception of color-coded clothing instead; she had no desire to use pathways that had evolved for the sake of sorting people into those you defended and those you slaughtered. But almost everything that had been bequeathed to them was stained with blood, and to Jamil it seemed a far sweeter victory to adapt the worst relics to his own ends than to discard them as irretrievably tainted.

The wave function appeared as a vivid auroral light, a quicksilver plasma bright enough to be distinct in the afternoon sunlight, yet unable to dazzle the eye or conceal the players running through it. Bands of color representing the complex phase of the wave swept across the field, parting to wash over separate rising lobes of probability before hitting the boundary and bouncing back again, inverted.

The match was being played by the oldest, simplest rules:
semiclassical, nonrelativistic. The ball was confined to the
field by an infinitely high barrier, so there was no question
of it tunneling out, leaking away as the match progressed.
The players were treated classically: their movements
pumped energy into the wave, enabling transitions from
the game's opening state—with the ball spread thinly
across the entire field—into the range of higher-energy
modes needed to localize it. But localization was fleeting;
there was no point forming a nice sharp wave packet in the
middle of the field in the hope of kicking it around like a
classical object. You had to shape the wave in such a way
that all of its modes—cycling at different frequencies,
traveling with different velocities—would come into phase
with each other, for a fraction of a second, within the goal
itself. Achieving that was a matter of energy levels, and
timing.

Jamil had noticed that one team was under-strength.
The umpire would be skewing the field's potential to keep
the match fair; but a new participant would be especially
welcome for the sake of restoring symmetry. He watched
the faces of the players, most of them old friends. They
were frowning with concentration, but breaking now and
then into smiles of delight at their small successes, or their
opponents' ingenuity.

He was badly out of practice, but if he turned out to be
dead weight he could always withdraw. And if he misjudged his skills, and lost the match with his incompe-
tence? No one would care. The score was nil all; he could
wait for a goal, but that might be an hour or more in coming. Jamil communed with the umpire and discovered that
the players had decided in advance to allow new entries at
any time.

Before he could change his mind, he announced himself. The wave froze, and he ran onto the field. People
nodded greetings, mostly making no fuss, though Ezequiel
shouted, "Welcome back!" Jamil suddenly felt fragile
again; though he'd ended his long seclusion four days be-

fore, it was well within his power, still, to be dismayed by everything the game would involve. His recovery felt like a finely balanced optical illusion, a figure and ground that could change roles in an instant, a solid cube that could evert into a hollow.

The umpire guided him to his allotted starting position, opposite a woman he hadn't seen before. He offered her a formal bow, and she returned the gesture. This was no time for introductions, but he asked the city if she'd published a name. She had: Margit.

The umpire counted down in their heads. Jamil tensed, regretting his impulsiveness. For seven years he'd been dead to the world. After four days back, what was he good for? His muscles were incapable of atrophy, his reflexes could never be dulled, but he'd chosen to live with an unconstrained will, and at any moment his wavering resolve could desert him.

The umpire said, "Play." The frozen light around Jamil came to life, and he sprang into motion.

Each player was responsible for a set of modes, particular harmonics of the wave that were theirs to fill, guard, or deplete as necessary. Jamil's twelve modes cycled at between 1,000 and 1,250 milliHertz. The rules of the game endowed his body with a small, fixed potential energy, which repelled the ball slightly and allowed different modes to push and pull on each other through him, but if he stayed in one spot as the modes cycled, every influence he exerted would eventually be replaced by its opposite, and the effect would simply cancel itself out.

To drive the wave from one mode to another, you needed to move, and to drive it efficiently, you needed to exploit the way the modes fell in and out of phase with each other: to take from a 1,000-milliHertz mode and give to a 1,250, you had to act in synch with the quarter-Hertz beat between them. It was like pushing a child's swing at its natural frequency, but rather than setting a single child in motion, you were standing between two swings and acting more as an intermediary: trying to time your interventions in such a way as to speed up one child at the other's expense. The way you pushed on the wave at a given time and place was out of your hands completely, but by changing location in just the right way, you could gain control over the interaction. Every pair of modes had a spatial beat between them—like the moiré pattern formed by two sheets of woven fabric held up to the light together, shifting from transparent to opaque as the gaps between the threads fell in and out of alignment. Slicing through this cyclic landscape offered the perfect means to match the accompanying chronological beat.

Jamil sprinted across the field at a speed and angle calculated to drive two favorable transitions at once. He'd gauged the current spectrum of the wave instinctively, watching from the sidelines, and he knew which of the modes in his charge would contribute to a goal and which would detract from the probability. As he cut through the shimmering bands of color, the umpire gave him tactile feedback to supplement his visual estimates and calculations, allowing him to sense the difference between a cyclic tug, a to and fro that came to nothing, and the gentle but persistent force that meant he was successfully riding the beat.

Chusok called out to him urgently, "Take, take! Two-ten!" Everyone's spectral territory overlapped with someone else's, and you needed to pass amplitude from player to player as well as trying to manage it within your own range. *Two-ten*—a harmonic with two peaks across the width of the field and ten along its length, cycling at 1,160 milliHertz—was filling up as Chusok drove unwanted amplitude from various lower-energy modes into it. It was Jamil's role to empty it, putting the amplitude somewhere useful. Any mode with an even number of peaks across the field was unfavorable for scoring, because it had a node—a zero point between the peaks—smack in the middle of both goals.

Jamil acknowledged the request with a hand signal and shifted his trajectory. It was almost a decade since he'd last played the game, but he still knew the intricate web of possibilities by heart; he could drain the two-ten harmonic into the three-ten, five-two, and five-six modes—all with "good parity," peaks along the center-line—in a single action.

As he pounded across the grass, carefully judging the correct angle by sight, increasing his speed until he felt the destructive beats give way to a steady force like a constant breeze, he suddenly recalled a time—centuries before, in another city—when he'd played with one team, week after week, for forty years. Faces and voices swam in his head. Hashim, Jamil's ninety-eighth child, and Hashim's granddaughter Laila had played beside him. But he'd burned his house and moved on, and when that era touched him at all now, it was like an unexpected gift. The scent of the grass, the shouts of the players, the soles of his feet striking the ground, resonated with every other moment he'd spent the same way, bridging the centuries, binding his life together. He never truly felt the scale of it when he sought it out deliberately; it was always small things, tightly focused moments like this, that burst the horizon of his everyday concerns and confronted him with the astonishing vista.

The two-ten mode was draining faster than he'd expected; the seesawing center-line dip in the wave was vanishing before his eyes. He looked around, and saw Margit performing an elaborate Lissajous maneuver smoothly orchestrating a dozen transitions at once. Jamil froze and watched her, admiring her virtuosity while he tried to decide what to do next; there was no point competing with her when she was doing such a good job of completing the task Chusok had set him.

Margit was his opponent, but they were both aiming for exactly the same kind of spectrum. The symmetry of the field meant that any scoring wave would work equally well for either side—but only one team could be the first to reap the benefit, the first to have more than half the wave's probability packed into their goal. So the two teams were obliged to cooperate at first, and it was only as the

wave took shape from their combined efforts that it gradually became apparent which side would gain by sculpting
it to perfection as rapidly as possible, and which would
gain by spoiling it for the first chance, then honing it for
the rebound.

Penina chided him over her shoulder as she jogged past,
"You want to leave her to clean up four-six, as well?" She
was smiling, but Jamil was stung; he'd been motionless for
ten or fifteen seconds. It was not forbidden to drag your
feet and rely on your opponents to do all the work, but it
was regarded as a shamefully impoverished strategy. It
was also very risky, handing them the opportunity to set up
a wave that was almost impossible to exploit yourself.

He reassessed the spectrum, and quickly sorted through
the alternatives. Whatever he did would have unwanted
side effects; there was no magic way to avoid influencing
modes in other players' territory, and any action that would
drive the transitions he needed would also trigger a multitude of others, up and down the spectrum. Finally, he made
a choice that would weaken the offending mode while
causing as little disruption as possible.

Jamil immersed himself in the game, planning each
transition two steps in advance, switching strategy halfway
through a run if he had to, but staying in motion until the
sweat dripped from his body, until his calves burned, until
his blood sang. He wasn't blinded to the raw pleasures of
the moment, or to memories of games past, but he let them
wash over him, like the breeze that rose up and cooled his
skin with no need for acknowledgment. Familiar voices
shouted terse commands at him; as the wave came closer
to a scoring spectrum, every trace of superfluous conversation vanished, every idle glance gave way to frantic, pur-
poseful gestures. To a bystander, this might have seemed
like the height of dehumanization: twenty-two people reduced to grunting cogs in a pointless machine. Jamil
smiled at the thought but refused to be distracted into a
complicated imaginary rebuttal. Every step he took was
the answer to that, every hoarse plea to Yann or Joracy,

Chusok or Maria, Eudore or Halide. These were his friends, and he was back among them. Back in the world.

The first chance of a goal was thirty seconds away, and the opportunity would fall to Jamil's team; a few tiny shifts in amplitude would clinch it. Margit kept her distance, but Jamil could sense her eyes on him constantly—and literally feel her at work through his skin as she slackened his contact with the wave. In theory, by mirroring your opponent's movements at the correct position on the field, you could undermine everything they did, though in practice, not even the most skillful team could keep the spectrum completely frozen. Going further and spoiling was a tug of war you didn't want to win too well: if you degraded the wave too much, your opponent's task—spoiling your own subsequent chance at a goal—became far easier.

Jamil still had two bad-parity modes that he was hoping to weaken, but every time he changed velocity to try a new transition, Margit responded in an instant, blocking him. He gestured to Chusok for help; Chusok had his own problems with Ezequiel, but he could still make trouble for Margit by choosing where he placed unwanted amplitude. Jamil shook sweat out of his eyes; he could see the characteristic "stepping stone" pattern of lobes forming, a sign that the wave would soon converge on the goal, but from the middle of the field it was impossible to judge their shape accurately enough to know what, if anything, remained to be done.

Suddenly, Jamil felt the wave push against him. He didn't waste time looking around for Margit; Chusok must have succeeded in distracting her. He was almost at the boundary line, but he managed to reverse smoothly, continuing to drive both the transitions he'd been aiming for.

Two long lobes of probability, each modulated by a series of oscillating mounds, raced along the sides of the field. A third, shorter lobe running along the center-line melted away, reappeared, then merged with the others as they touched the end of the field, forming an almost rectangular plateau encompassing the goal.

The plateau became a pillar of light, growing narrower

and higher as dozens of modes, all finally in phase, crashed together against the impenetrable barrier of the field's boundary. A shallow residue was still spread across the entire field, and a diminishing sequence of elliptical lobes trailed away from the goal like a staircase, but most of the wave that had started out lapping around their waists was now concentrated in a single peak that towered above their heads, nine or ten meters tall.

For an instant, it was motionless.

Then it began to fall.

The umpire said, "Forty-nine point eight."

The wave packet had not been tight enough.

Jamil struggled to shrug off his disappointment and throw his instincts into reverse. The other team had fifty seconds, now, to fine-tune the spectrum and ensure that the reflected packet was just a fraction narrower when it reformed, at the opposite end of the field.

As the pillar collapsed, replaying its synthesis in reverse, Jamil caught sight of Margit. She smiled at him calmly, and it suddenly struck him: *She'd known they couldn't make the goal. That was why she'd stopped opposing him.* She'd let him work toward sharpening the wave for a few seconds, knowing that it was already too late for him, knowing that her own team would gain from the slight improvement.

Jamil was impressed; it took an extraordinary level of skill and confidence to do what she'd just done. For all the time he'd spent away, he knew exactly what to expect from the rest of the players, and in Margit's absence he would probably have been wishing out loud for a talented newcomer to make the game interesting again. Still, it was hard not to feel a slight sting of resentment. Someone should have warned him just how good she was.

With the modes slipping out of phase, the wave undulated all over the field again, but its reconvergence was inevitable: unlike a wave of water or sound, it possessed no hidden degrees of freedom to grind its precision into entropy. Jamil decided to ignore Margit; there were cruder strategies than mirror-blocking that worked almost as well. Chusok was filling the two-ten mode now; Jamil chose the four-six as his spoiler. All they had to do was keep the wave from growing much sharper, and it didn't matter whether they achieved this by preserving the status quo, or by nudging it from one kind of bluntness to another.

The steady resistance he felt as he ran told Jamil that he was driving the transition, unblocked, but he searched in vain for some visible sign of success. When he reached a vantage point where he could take in enough of the field in one glance to judge the spectrum properly, he noticed a rapidly vibrating shimmer across the width of the wave. He counted nine peaks: good parity. Margit had pulled most of the amplitude straight out of his spoiler mode and fed it into *this*. It was a mad waste of energy to aim for such an elevated harmonic, but no one had been looking there, no one had stopped her.

The scoring pattern was forming again, he only had nine or ten seconds left to make up for all the time he'd wasted. Jamil chose the strongest good-parity mode in his territory, and the emptiest bad one, computed the velocity that would link them, and ran.

He didn't dare turn to watch the opposition goal; he didn't want to break his concentration. The wave retreated around his feet, less like an Earthly ebb tide than an ocean drawn into the sky by a passing black hole. The city diligently portrayed the shadow that his body would have cast, shrinking in front of him as the tower of light rose.

The verdict was announced. "Fifty point one."

The air was filled with shouts of triumph—Ezequiel's the loudest, as always. Jamil sagged to his knees, laughing. It was a curious feeling, familiar as it was: he cared, and he didn't. If he'd been wholly indifferent to the outcome of the game, there would have been no pleasure in it, but obsessing over every defeat—or every victory—could ruin it just as thoroughly. He could almost see himself walking the line, orchestrating his response as carefully as any action in the game itself.

He lay down on the grass to catch his breath before play
resumed. The outer face of the microsun that orbited
Laplace was shielded with rock, but light reflected skyward
from the land beneath it crossed the 100,000-kilometer
width of the 3-toroidal universe to give a faint glow to the
planet's nightside. Though only a sliver was lit directly,
Jamil could discern the full disc of the opposite hemisphere in the primary image at the zenith: continents and
oceans that lay, by a shorter route, 12,000 or so kilometers
beneath him. Other views in the lattice of images spread
across the sky were from different angles, and showed substantial crescents of the dayside itself. The one thing you
couldn't find in any of these images, even with a telescope,
was your own city. The topology of this universe let you
see the back of your head, but never your reflection.

Jamil's team lost, three nil. He staggered over to the fountains at the edge of the field and slaked his thirst, shocked
by the pleasure of the simple act. Just to be alive was glorious now, but once he felt this way, anything seemed possible. He was back in synch, back in phase, and he was
going to make the most of it, for however long it lasted.

He caught up with the others, who'd headed down toward the river. Ezequiel hooked an arm around his neck,
laughing. "Bad luck, Sleeping Beauty! You picked the
wrong time to wake. With Margit, we're invincible."

Jamil ducked free of him. "I won't argue with that." He
looked around. "Speaking of whom—"

Penina said, "Gone home. She plays, that's all. No friv-
olous socializing after the match."

Chusok added, "Or any other time." Penina shot Jamil
a glance that meant not for want of trying on Chusok's
part.

Jamil pondered this, wondering why it annoyed him so
much. On the field, she hadn't come across as aloof and
superior. Just unashamedly good.

He queried the city, but she'd published nothing beside

her name. Nobody expected—or wished—to hear more than the tiniest fraction of another person's history, but it was rare for anyone to start a new life without carrying through something from the old as a kind of calling card, some incident or achievement from which your new neighbors could form an impression of you.

They'd reached the riverbank. Jamil pulled his shirt over his head. "So what's her story? She must have told you something."

Ezequiel said, "Only that she learned to play a long time ago; she won't say where or when. She arrived in Noether at the end of last year, and grew a house on the southern outskirts. No one sees her around much. No one even knows what she studies."

Jamil shrugged, and waded in. "Ah well. It's a challenge to rise to." Penina laughed and splashed him teasingly. He protested, "I *meant* beating her at the game."

Chusok said wryly, "When you turned up, I thought you'd be our secret weapon. The one player she didn't know inside-out already."

"I'm glad you didn't tell me that. I would have turned around and fled straight back into hibernation."

"I know. That's why we all kept quiet." Chusok smiled. "Welcome back."

Penina said, "Yeah, welcome back, Jamil."

Sunlight shone on the surface of the river. Jamil ached all over, but the cool water was the perfect place to be. If he wished, he could build a partition in his mind at the point where he stood right now, and never fall beneath it. Other people lived that way, and it seemed to cost them nothing. Contrast was overrated; no sane person spent half their time driving spikes into their flesh for the sake of feeling better when they stopped. Ezequiel lived every day with the happy boisterousness of a five-year-old; Jamil sometimes found this annoying, but then any kind of disposition would irritate someone. His own stretches of meaningless somberness weren't exactly a boon to his friends.

Chusok said, "I've invited everyone to a meal at my house tonight. Will you come?"

Jamil thought it over, then shook his head. He still wasn't ready. He couldn't force-feed himself with normality; it didn't speed his recovery, it just drove him backward.

Chusok looked disappointed, but there was nothing to be done about that. Jamil promised him, "Next time. OK?"

Ezequiel sighed. "What are we going to do with you? You're worse than Margit!" Jamil started backing away, but it was too late. Ezequiel reached him in two casual strides, bent down and grabbed him around the waist, hoisted him effortlessly onto one shoulder, then flung him through the air into the depths of the river.

Jamil was woken by the scent of wood smoke. His room was still filled with the night's grey shadows, but when he propped himself up on one elbow and the window obliged him with transparency, the city was etched clearly in the predawn light.

He dressed and left the house, surprised at the coolness of the dew on his feet. No one else in his street seemed to be up; had they failed to notice the smell, or did they already know to expect it? He turned a corner and saw the rising column of soot, faintly lit with red from below. The flames and the ruins were still hidden from him, but he knew whose house it was.

When he reached the dying blaze, he crouched in the heat-withered garden, cursing himself. Chusok had offered him the chance to join him for his last meal in Noether. Whatever hints you dropped, it was customary to tell no one that you were moving on. If you still had a lover, if you still had young children, you never deserted them. But friends, you warned in subtle ways. Before vanishing.

Jamil covered his head with his arms. He'd lived through this countless times before, but it never became easier. If anything, it grew worse, as every departure was

weighted with the memories of others. His brothers and
sisters had scattered across the branches of the New Territories. He'd walked away from his father and mother when
he was too young and confident to realize how much it
would hurt him, decades later. His own children had all
abandoned him eventually, far more often than he'd left
them. It was easier to leave an ex-lover than a grown child:
something burned itself out in a couple, almost naturally,
as if ancestral biology had prepared them for at least that
one rift.

Jamil stopped fighting the tears. But as he brushed them
away, he caught sight of someone standing beside him, He
looked up. It was Margit.

He felt a need to explain. He rose to his feet and addressed her. "This was Chusok's house. We were good
friends. I'd known him for ninety-six years."

Margit gazed back at him neutrally. "Boo hoo. Poor
baby. You'll never see your friend again."

Jamil almost laughed, her rudeness was so surreal. He
pushed on, as if the only conceivable, polite response was
to pretend that he hadn't heard her. "No one is the kindest,
the most generous, the most loyal. It doesn't matter. That's
not the point. Everyone's unique. Chusok was Chusok."
He banged a fist against his chest, utterly heedless now of
her contemptuous words. "There's a hole in me, and it will
never be filled." That was the truth, even though he'd grow
around it. *He should have gone to the meal, it would have
cost him nothing.*

"You must be a real emotional Swiss cheese," observed
Margit tartly.

Jamil came to his senses. "Why don't you fuck off to
some other universe? No one wants you in Noether."

Margit was amused. "You *are* a bad loser."

Jamil gazed at her, honestly confused for a moment; the
game had slipped his mind completely. He gestured at the
embers. "What are you doing here? Why did you follow
the smoke, if it wasn't regret at not saying goodbye to him
when you had the chance?" He wasn't sure how seriously

to take Penina's lighthearted insinuation, but if Chusok had
fallen for Margit, and it had not been reciprocated, that
might even have been the reason he'd left.

She shook her head calmly. "He was nothing to me. I
barely spoke to him."

"Well, that's your loss."

"From the look of things, I'd say the loss was all
yours."

He had no reply. Margit turned and walked away. Jamil
crouched on the ground again, rocking back and forth,
waiting for the pain to subside.

Jamil *spent the* next week preparing to resume his studies.
The library had near-instantaneous contact with every artificial universe in the New Territories, and the additional
lightspeed lag between Earth and the point in space from
which the whole tree-structure blossomed was only a few
hours. Jamil had been to Earth, but only as a tourist; land
was scarce, they accepted no migrants. There were remote
planets you could live on, in the home universe, but you
had to be a certain kind of masochistic purist to want that.
The precise reasons why his ancestors had entered the
New Territories had been forgotten generations before—
and it would have been presumptuous to track them down
and ask them in person—but given a choice between the
then even-more-crowded Earth, the horrifying reality of
interstellar distances, and an endlessly extensible branch-
ing chain of worlds which could be traversed within a matter of weeks, the decision wasn't exactly baffling.

Jamil had devoted most of his time in Noether to studying the category of representations of Lie groups on complex vector spaces—a fitting choice, since Emmy Noether
had been a pioneer of group theory, and if she'd lived to
see this field blossom, she would probably have been in
the thick of it herself. Representations of Lie groups lay
behind most of physics: each kind of subatomic particle
was really nothing but a particular way of representing the

universal symmetry group as a set of rotations of complex vectors. Organizing this kind of structure with category theory was ancient knowledge, but Jamil didn't care; he'd long ago reconciled himself to being a student, not a discoverer. The greatest gift of consciousness was the ability to take the patterns of the world inside you, and for all that he would have relished the thrill of being the first at anything; with ten-to-the-sixteenth people alive that was a futile ambition for most.

In the library, he spoke with fellow students of his chosen field on other worlds, or read their latest works. Though they were not researchers, they could still put a new pedagogical spin on old material, enriching the connections with other fields, finding ways to make the complex, subtle truth easier to assimilate without sacrificing the depth and detail that made it worth knowing in the first place. They would not advance the frontiers of knowledge. They would not discover new principles of nature, or invent new technologies. But to Jamil, understanding was an end in itself.

He rarely thought about the prospect of playing another match, and when he did, the idea was not appealing. With Chusok gone, the same group could play ten-to-a-side without Jamil to skew the numbers. Margit might even choose to swap teams, if only for the sake of proving that her current team's monotonous string of victories really had been entirely down to her.

When the day arrived, though, he found himself unable to stay away. He turned up intending to remain a spectator, but Ryuichi had deserted Ezequiel's team, and everyone begged Jamil to join in.

As he took his place opposite Margit, there was nothing in her demeanor to acknowledge their previous encounter: no lingering contempt, but no hint of shame either. Jamil resolved to put it out of his mind; he owed it to his fellow players to concentrate on the game.

They lost, five nil.

Jamil forced himself to follow everyone to Eudore's

house, to celebrate, commiserate, or, as it turned out, to
forget the whole thing. After they'd eaten, Jamil wandered
from room to room, enjoying Eudore's choice of music but
unable to settle into any conversation. No one mentioned
Chusok in his hearing.

He left just after midnight. Laplace's near-full primary
image and its eight brightest gibbous companions lit the
streets so well that there was no need for anything more.
Jamil thought: Chusok might have merely traveled to another city, one beneath his gaze right now. And wherever
he'd gone, he might yet choose to stay in touch with his
friends from Noether.

And his friends from the next town, and the next?
Century after century?

Margit was sitting on Jamil's doorstep, holding a bunch
of white flowers in one hand.

Jamil was irritated. "What are you doing here?"

"I came to apologize."

He shrugged. "There's no need. We feel differently
about certain things. That's fine. I can still face you on the
playing field."

"I'm not apologizing for a difference of opinion. I
wasn't honest with you. I was cruel." She shaded her eyes
against the glare of the planet and looked up at him. "You
were right: it was my loss. I wish I'd known your friend."

He laughed curtly. "Well, it's too late for that."

She said simply, "I know."

Jamil relented. "Do you want to come in?" Margit nodded, and he instructed the door to open for her. As he followed her inside, he said, "How long have you been here?
Have you eaten?"

"No."

"I'll cook something for you."

"You don't have to do that."

He called out to her from the kitchen, "Think of it as a
peace offering. I don't have any flowers."

Margit replied, "They're not for you. They're for Chusok's house."

Jamil stopped rummaging through his vegetable bins and walked back into the living room. "People don't usually do that in Noether."

Margit was sitting on the couch, staring at the floor. She said, "I'm so lonely here. I can't bear it anymore."

He sat beside her. "Then why did you rebuff him? You could at least have been friends."

She shook her head. "Don't ask me to explain."

Jamil took her hand. She turned and embraced him, trembling miserably. He stroked her hair. "Sssh."

She said, "Just sex. I don't want anything more."

He groaned softly. "There's no such thing as that."

"I just need someone to touch me again."

"I understand." He confessed, "So do I. But that won't be all. So don't ask me to promise there'll be nothing more."

Margit took his face in her hands and kissed him. Her mouth tasted of wood smoke.

Jamil said, "I don't even know you."

"No one knows anyone anymore."

"That's not true."

"No, it's not," she conceded gloomily. She ran a hand lightly along his arm. Jamil wanted badly to see her smile, so he made each dark hair thicken and blossom into a violet flower as it passed beneath her fingers.

She did smile, but she said, "I've seen that trick before."

Jamil was annoyed. "I'm sure to be a disappointment all round, then. I expect you'd be happier with some kind of novelty. A unicorn, or an amoeba."

She laughed. "I don't think so." She took his hand and placed it against her breast. "Do you ever get tired of sex?"

"Do you ever get tired of breathing?"

"I can go for a long time without thinking about it."

He nodded. "But then one day you stop and fill your lungs with air, and it's still as sweet as ever."

Jamil didn't know what he was feeling anymore. Lust. Compassion. Spite. She'd come to him hurting, and he wanted to help her, but he wasn't sure that either of them really believed this would work.

Margit inhaled the scent of the flowers on his arm. "Are
they the same color? Everywhere else?"

He said, "There's only one way to find out."

Jamil *woke in* the early hours of the morning, alone. He'd
half-expected Margit to flee like this, but she could have
waited till dawn. He would have obligingly feigned sleep
while she dressed and tiptoed out.

Then he heard her. It was not a sound he would normally have associated with a human being, but it could not
have been anything else.

He found her in the kitchen, curled around a table leg,
wailing rhythmically. He stood back and watched her, afraid
that anything he did would only make things worse. She met
his gaze in the half-light, but kept up the mechanical whimper. Her eyes weren't blank; she was not delirious, or hallu-
cinating. She knew exactly who, and where, she was.

Finally, Jamil knelt in the doorway. He said, "Whatever
it is, you can tell me. And we'll fix it. We'll find a way."

She bared her teeth. "You can't *fix it*, you stupid child."
She resumed the awful noise.

"Then just tell me. Please?" He stretched out a hand toward her. He hadn't felt quite so helpless since his very
first daughter, Aminata, had come to him as an incon-
solable six-year-old, rejected by the boy to whom she'd
declared her undying love. He'd been twenty-four years
old; a child himself. More than a thousand years ago.
Where are you now, Nata?

Margit said, "I promised I'd never tell."

"Promised who?"

"Myself."

"Good. They're the easiest kind to break."

She started weeping. It was a more ordinary sound, but
it was even more chilling. She was not a wounded animal
now, an alien being suffering some incomprehensible pain.
Jamil approached her cautiously; she let him wrap his arms
around her shoulders.

He whispered, "Come to bed. The warmth will help. Just being held will help."

She spat at him derisively, "It won't bring her back."

"Who?"

Margit stared at him in silence, as if he'd said something shocking.

Jamil insisted gently, "Who won't it bring back?" She'd lost a friend, badly, the way he'd lost Chusok. That was why she'd sought him out. He could help her through it. They could help each other through it.

She said, "It won't bring back the dead."

Margit *was seven* thousand five hundred and ninety-four years old. Jamil persuaded her to sit at the kitchen table. He wrapped her in blankets, then fed her tomatoes and rice, as she told him how she'd witnessed the birth of his world.

The promise had shimmered just beyond reach for decades. Almost none of her contemporaries had believed it would happen, though the truth should have been plain for centuries: *the human body was a material thing.* In time, with enough knowledge and effort, it would become possible to safeguard it from any kind of deterioration, any kind of harm. Stellar evolution and cosmic entropy might or might not prove insurmountable, but there'd be aeons to confront those challenges. In the middle of the twenty-first century, the hurdles were aging, disease, violence, and an overcrowded planet.

"Grace was my best friend. We were students." Margit smiled. "Before everyone was a student. We'd talk about it, but we didn't believe we'd see it happen. It would come in another century. It would come for our great-great-grandchildren. We'd hold infants on our knees in our twilight years and tell ourselves: *this one will never die.*

"When we were both twenty-two, something happened. To both of us." She lowered her eyes. "We were kidnapped. We were raped. We were tortured."

Jamil didn't know how to respond. These were just words to him: he knew their meaning, he knew these acts would have hurt her, but she might as well have been describing a mathematical theorem. He stretched a hand across the table, but Margit ignored it. He said awkwardly, "This was . . . the Holocaust?"

She looked up at him, shaking her head, almost laughing at his naïveté. "Not even one of them. Not a war, not a pogrom. Just one psychopathic man. He locked us in his basement, for six months. He'd killed seven women." Tears began spilling down her cheeks. "He showed us the bodies. They were buried right where we slept. He showed us how we'd end up, when he was through with us."

Jamil was numb. He'd known all his adult life what had once been possible—what had once happened, to real people—but it had all been consigned to history long before his birth. In retrospect, it seemed almost inconceivably stupid, but he'd always imagined that the changes had come in such a way that no one still living had experienced these horrors. There'd been no escaping the bare minimum, the logical necessity: his oldest living ancestors must have watched their parents fall peacefully into eternal sleep. But not this. Not a flesh-and-blood woman, sitting in front of him, who'd been forced to sleep in a killer's graveyard.

He put his hand over hers, and choked out the words. "This man . . . *killed* Grace? He killed your friend?"

Margit began sobbing, but she shook her head. "No, no. We got out!" She twisted her mouth into a smile. "Someone stabbed the stupid fucker in a barroom brawl. We dug our way out while he was in hospital." She put her face down on the table and wept, but she held Jamil's hand against her cheek. He couldn't understand what she'd lived through, but that couldn't mean he wouldn't console her. Hadn't he touched his mother's face the same way, when she was sad beyond his childish comprehension?

She composed herself and continued. "We made a resolution, while we were in there. If we survived, there'd be no more empty promises. No more daydreams. What he'd done to those seven women—and what he'd done to us—would become impossible."

And it had. Whatever harm befell your body, you had the power to shut off your senses and decline to experience it. If the flesh was damaged, it could always be repaired or replaced. In the unlikely event that your jewel itself was destroyed, everyone had backups, scattered across universes. No human being could inflict physical pain on another. In theory, you could still be killed, but it would take the same kind of resources as destroying a galaxy. The only people who seriously contemplated either were the villains in very bad operas.

Jamil's eyes narrowed in wonder. She'd spoken those last words with such fierce pride that there was no question of her having failed.

"*You* are Ndoli? You invented the jewel?" As a child, he'd been told that the machine in his skull had been designed by a man who'd died long ago.

Margit stroked his hand, amused. "In those days, very few Hungarian women could be mistaken for Nigerian men. I've never changed my body that much, Jamil. I've always looked much as you see me."

Jamil was relieved; if she'd been Ndoli himself, he might have succumbed to sheer awe and started babbling idolatrous nonsense. "But you worked with Ndoli? You and Grace?"

She shook her head. "We made the resolution, and then we floundered. We were mathematicians, not neurologists. There were a thousand things going on at once: tissue engineering, brain imaging, molecular computers. We had no real idea where to put our efforts, which problems we should bring our strengths to bear upon. Ndoli's work didn't come out of the blue for us, but we played no part in it.

"For a while, almost everyone was nervous about switching from the brain to the jewel. In the early days, the jewel was a separate device that learned its task by mimicking the brain, and it had to be handed control of the body at one chosen moment. It took another fifty years before it could be engineered to replace the brain incrementally, neuron by neuron, in a seamless transition throughout adolescence."

So Grace had lived to see the jewel invented, but held back, and died before she could use it? Jamil kept himself from blurting out this conclusion, all his guesses had proved wrong so far.

Margit continued. "Some people weren't just nervous, though. You'd be amazed how vehemently Ndoli was denounced in certain quarters. And I don't just mean the fanatics who churned out paranoid tracts about 'the machines' taking over, with their evil, inhuman agendas. Some people's antagonism had nothing to do with the specifics of the technology. They were opposed to immortality, in principle."

Jamil laughed. *"Why?"*

"Ten thousand years' worth of sophistry doesn't vanish overnight," Margit observed dryly. "Every human culture had expended vast amounts of intellectual effort on the problem of coming to terms with death. Most religions had constructed elaborate lies about it, making it out to be something other than it was—though a few were dishonest about life, instead. But even most secular philosophies were warped by the need to pretend that *death was for the best*.

"It was the naturalistic fallacy at its most extreme—and its most transparent, but that didn't stop anyone. Since any child could tell you that death was meaningless, contingent, unjust, and abhorrent beyond words, it was a hallmark of sophistication to believe otherwise. Writers had consoled themselves for centuries with smug, puritanical fables about immortals who'd long for death—who'd *beg* for death. It would have been too much to expect all those who were suddenly faced with the reality of its banishment to confess that they'd been whistling in the dark. And would-be moral philosophers—mostly those who'd experienced no greater inconvenience in their lives than a late train or a surly waiter—began wailing about the destruction of the human spirit by this hideous blight. We needed death and suffering to put steel into our souls! Not horrible, horrible *freedom and safety!*"

Jamil smiled. "So there were buffoons. But in the end, surely they swallowed their pride? If we're walking in a desert and I tell you that the lake you see ahead is a mirage, I might cling stubbornly to my own belief, to save myself from disappointment. But when we arrive, and I'm proven wrong, I *will* drink from the lake."

Margit nodded. "Most of the loudest of these people went quiet in the end. But there were subtler arguments, too. Like it or not, all our biology and all of our culture had evolved in the presence of death. And almost every righteous struggle in history, every worthwhile sacrifice, had been against suffering, against violence, against death. Now, that struggle would become impossible."

"Yes." Jamil was mystified. "But only because it had triumphed."

Margit said gently, "I know. There was no sense to it. And it was always my belief that anything worth fighting for—over centuries, over millennia—was worth attaining. It can't be noble to toil for a cause, and even to die for it, unless it's also noble to succeed. To claim otherwise isn't sophistication, it's just a kind of hypocrisy. If it's better to travel than arrive, you shouldn't start the voyage in the first place.

"I told Grace as much, and she agreed. We laughed together at what we called the *tragedians*: the people who denounced the coming age as the age without martyrs, the age without saints, the age without revolutionaries. There would never be another Gandhi, another Mandela, another Aung San Suu Kyi—and yes, that was a kind of loss, but would any great leader have sentenced humanity to eternal misery for the sake of providing a suitable backdrop for eternal heroism? Well, some of them would have. But the downtrodden themselves had better things to do."

Margit fell silent. Jamil cleared her plate away, then sat opposite her again. It was almost dawn.

"Of course, the jewel was not enough," Margit continued.

"With care, Earth could support forty billion people, but where would the rest go? The jewel made virtual reality the easiest escape route: for a fraction of the space, a fraction of the energy, it could survive without a body attached. Grace and I weren't horrified by that prospect, the way some people were. But it was not the best outcome, it was not what most people wanted, the way they wanted freedom from death.

"So we studied gravity, we studied the vacuum."

Jamil feared making a fool of himself again, but from the expression on her face he knew he wasn't wrong this time. *M. Osvát and G. Füst.* Co-authors of the seminal paper, but no more was known about them than those abbreviated names. "You gave us the New Territories?"

Margit nodded slightly. "Grace and I."

Jamil was overwhelmed with love for her. He went to her and knelt down to put his arms around her waist. Margit touched his shoulder. "Come on, get up. Don't treat me like a god, it just makes me feel old."

He stood, smiling abashedly. Anyone in pain deserved his help—but if he was not in her debt, the word had no meaning.

"And Grace?" he asked.

Margit looked away. "Grace completed her work, and then decided that she was a tragedian, after all. Rape was impossible. Torture was impossible. Poverty was vanishing. Death was receding into cosmology, into metaphysics. It was everything she'd hoped would come to pass. And for her, suddenly faced with that fulfillment, everything that remained seemed trivial.

"One night she climbed into the furnace in the basement of her building. Her jewel survived the flames, but she'd erased it from within."

I*t was morning* now. Jamil was beginning to feel disoriented; Margit should have vanished in daylight, an apparition unable to persist in the mundane world.

"I'd lost other people who were close to me," she said. "My parents. My brother. Friends. And so had everyone around me, then. I wasn't special; grief was still common-place. But decade by decade, century by century, we shrank into insignificance, those of us who knew what it meant to lose someone forever. We're less than one in a million, now.

"For a long time, I clung to my own generation. There were enclaves, there were ghettos, where everyone under-stood the old days. I spent two hundred years married to a man who wrote a play called *We Who Have Known the Dead*—which was every bit as pretentious and self-pitying as you'd guess from the title." She smiled at the memory. "It was a horrible, self-devouring world. If I'd stayed in it much longer, I would have followed Grace. I would have begged for death."

She looked up at Jamil. "It's people like you I want to be with: *people who don't understand.* Your lives aren't trivial any more than the best parts of our own were: all the tranquility, all the beauty, all the happiness that made the sacrifices and the life-and-death struggles worthwhile.

"The tragedians were wrong. They had everything upside-down. Death never gave meaning to life; it was always the other way round. All of its gravitas, all of its significance, was stolen from the things it ended. But the value of life always lay entirely in itself—not in its loss, not in its fragility.

"Grace should have lived to see that. She should have lived long enough to understand that the world hadn't turned to ash."

Jamil sat in silence, turning the whole confession over in his mind, trying to absorb it well enough not to add to her distress with a misjudged question. Finally, he ventured, "Why do you hold back from friendship with us, though? Because we're just children to you? Children who can't understand what you've lost?"

Margit shook her head vehemently. "I *don't want you* to understand! People like me are the only blight on this world, the only poison." She smiled at Jamil's expression of anguish, and rushed to silence him before he could swear that she was nothing of the kind. "Not in everything we do and say, or everyone we touch; I'm not claiming that we're tainted, in some fatuous mythological sense. But when I left the ghettos, I promised myself that I wouldn't bring the past with me. Sometimes that's an easy vow to keep. Sometimes it's not."

"You've broken it tonight," Jamil said plainly. "And neither of us have been struck down by lightning."

"I know." She took his hand. "But I was wrong to tell you what I have, and I'll fight to regain the strength to stay silent. I stand at the border between two worlds, Jamil. I remember death, and I always will. But my job now is to guard that border. To keep that knowledge from invading your world."

"We're not as fragile as you think," he protested. "We all know something about loss."

Margit nodded soberly. "Your friend Chusok has vanished into the crowd. That's how things work now: how you keep yourselves from suffocating in a jungle of endlessly growing connections, or fragmenting into isolated troupes of repertory players, endlessly churning out the same lines.

"You have your little deaths—and I don't call them that to deride you. But I've seen both. And I promise you, they're not the same."

In the weeks that followed, Jamil resumed in full the life he'd made for himself in Noether. Five days in seven were for the difficult beauty of mathematics. The rest were for his friends.

He kept playing matches, and Margit's team kept winning. In the sixth game, though, Jamil's team finally scored against her. Their defeat was only three to one.

Each night, Jamil struggled with the question. What exactly did he owe her? Eternal loyalty, eternal silence, eternal obedience? She hadn't sworn him to secrecy; she'd extracted no promises at all. But he knew she was trusting him to comply with her wishes, so what right did he have to do otherwise?

Eight weeks after the night he'd spent with Margit, Jamil found himself alone with Penina in a room in Joracy's house. They'd been talking about the old days. Talking about Chusok.

Jamil said, "Margit lost someone very close to her."

Penina nodded matter-of-factly, but curled into a comfortable position on the couch and prepared to take in every word.

"Not in the way we've lost Chusok. Not in the way you think at all."

Jamil approached the others, one by one. His confidence ebbed and flowed. He'd glimpsed the old world, but he couldn't pretend to have fathomed its inhabitants. What if Margit saw this as worse than betrayal—as a further torture, a further rape?

But he couldn't stand by and leave her to the torture she'd inflicted on herself.

Ezequiel was the hardest to face. Jamil spent a sick and sleepless night beforehand, wondering if this would make him a monster, a corrupter of children, the epitome of everything Margit believed she was fighting.

Ezequiel wept freely, but he was not a child. He was older than Jamil, and he had more steel in his soul than any of them.

He said, "I guessed it might be that. I guessed she might have seen the bad times. But I never found a way to ask her."

The three lobes of probability converged, melted into a plateau, rose into a pillar of light.

The umpire said, "Fifty-five point nine." It was Margit's most impressive goal yet.

Ezequiel whooped joyfully and ran toward her. When he scooped her up in his arms and threw her across his shoulders, she laughed and indulged him. When Jamil stood beside him and they made a joint throne for her with their arms, she frowned down at him and said, "You shouldn't be doing this. You're on the losing side."

The rest of the players converged on them, cheering, and they started down toward the river. Margit looked around nervously. "What is this? We haven't finished playing."

Penina said, "The game's over early, just this once. Think of this as an invitation. We want you to swim with us. We want you to talk to us. We want to hear everything about your life."

Margit's composure began to crack. She squeezed Jamil's shoulder. He whispered, "Say the word, and we'll put you down."

Margit didn't whisper back; she shouted miserably, "What do you want from me, you parasites? I've won your fucking game for you! What more do you want?"

Jamil was mortified. He stopped and prepared to lower her, prepared to retreat, but Ezequiel caught his arm.

Ezequiel said, "We want to be your border guards. We want to stand beside you."

Christa added, "We can't face what you've faced, but we want to understand. As much as we can."

Joracy spoke, then Yann, Narcyza, Maria, Halide. Margit looked down on them, weeping, confused.

Jamil burned with shame. He'd hijacked her, humiliated her. He'd made everything worse. She'd flee Noether, flee into a new exile, more alone than ever.

When everyone had spoken, silence descended. Margit trembled on her throne.

Jamil faced the ground. He couldn't undo what he'd done. He said quietly, "Now you know our wishes. Will you tell us yours?"

"Put me down."

Jamil and Ezequiel complied.

Margit looked around at her teammates and opponents, her children, her creation, her would-be friends.

She said, "I want to go to the river with you. I'm seven thousand years old, and I want to learn to swim."

Rogue Farm

Charles Stross

Although he made his first sale back in 1987, it's only recently that British writer Charles Stross has begun to make a name for himself as a Writer to Watch in the new century ahead (in fact, as one of the key Writers to Watch in the Oughts), with a sudden burst in the last few years of quirky, inventive, high-bit-rate stories such as "Antibodies," "A Colder War," "Bear Trap," "Dechlorinating the Moderator," "Toast: A Con Report," and others in markets such as Interzone, Spectrum SF, Asimov's Science Fiction Magazine, Odyssey, Strange Plasma, *and* New Worlds. *A sequence of frenetic, densely packed stories in what's come to be known as his Accelerando series—"Lobsters," "Troubadour," "Tourist," "Halo," "Router," "Nightfall," "Curator," "Elector," and "Survivor," each story taking us a jump further into an acceleratingly strange future, and eventually through a Vingian Singularity and out the other side—really cranked up the buzz about him to high volume, as well as getting him on the Hugo Final Ballot several times. Taken together, the Accelerado stories represent one of the most dazzling feats of sustained imagination in science fiction history, and radically up the Imagination Ante for every other writer who wants to sit down at the Future History table and credibly deal themselves into the game.*

Recently, Stross has become prolific at novel length as well. He'd already published a novel online, Scratch Monkey, *available to be read on his website (www .antipope.org/charlie/), and saw his first commercially published novel,* Singularity Sky, *released in 2003, but he had three novels come out in 2004,* Iron Sunrise, A Family Trade, *and* The Atrocity Archives *(formerly serialized in the British magazine* Spectrum SF*), with another new novel,* The Clan Corporate, *hard on their heels in early*

2005 . . . and, of course, an Accelerando novel and its sequel are already on the way as well. His first collection, Toast, and Other Burned Out Futures, *was released in 2002. He lives with his wife in Edinburgh, Scotland.*

Here he gives us a fast, funny, and highly inventive look at a deceptively bucolic future on the far side of Singularity where nothing is quite as simple—or as harmless—as it seems . . .

It was a bright, cool March morning: mare's tails trailed across the southeastern sky toward the rising sun. Joe shivered slightly in the driver's seat as he twisted the starter handle on the old front loader he used to muck out the barn. Like its owner, the ancient Massey Ferguson had seen better days; but it had survived worse abuse than Joe routinely handed out. The diesel clattered, spat out a gobbet of thick blue smoke, and chattered to itself dyspeptically. His mind as blank as the sky above, Joe slid the tractor into gear, raised the front scoop, and began turning it toward the open doors of the barn—just in time to see an itinerant farm coming down the road.

"Bugger," swore Joe. The tractor engine made a hideous grinding noise and died. He took a second glance, eyes wide, then climbed down from the tractor and trotted over to the kitchen door at the side of the farmhouse. "Maddie!" he called, forgetting the two-way radio clipped to his sweater hem. "Maddie! There's a farm coming!"

"Joe? Is that you? Where are you?" Her voice wafted vaguely from the bowels of the house.

"Where are you?" he yelled back.

"I'm in the bathroom."

"Bugger," he said again. "If it's the one we had round the end last month . . ."

The sound of a toilet sluiced through his worry. It was followed by a drumming of feet on the staircase; then Maddie erupted into the kitchen. "Where is it?" she demanded.

"Out front, about a quarter mile up the lane."

"Right." Hair wild and eyes angry about having her morning ablutions cut short, Maddie yanked a heavy green coat on over her shirt. "Opened the cupboard yet?"

"I was thinking you'd want to talk to it first."

"Too right I want to talk to it. If it's that one that's been lurking in the copse near Edgar's pond, I got some *issues* to discuss with it." Joe shook his head at her anger and went to unlock the cupboard in the back room. "You take the shotgun and keep it off our property," she called after him. "I'll be out in a minute."

Joe nodded to himself, then carefully picked out the twelve-gauge and a preloaded magazine. The gun's power-on self-test lights flickered erratically, but it seemed to have a full charge. Slinging it, he locked the cupboard carefully and went back out into the farmyard to warn off their unwelcome visitor.

The farm squatted, buzzing and clicking to itself, in the road outside Armitage End. Joe eyed it warily from behind the wooden gate, shotgun under his arm. It was a medium-size one, probably with half a dozen human components subsumed into it—a formidable collective. Already it was deep into farm-fugue, no longer relating very clearly to people outside its own communion of mind. Beneath its leathery black skin he could see hints of internal structure, cytocellular macroassemblies flexing and glooping in disturbing motions. Even though it was only a young adolescent, it was already the size of an antique heavy tank, and it blocked the road just as efficiently as an Apatosaurus would have. It smelled of yeast and gasoline.

Joe had an uneasy feeling that it was watching him. "Buggerit, I don't have time for this," he muttered. The stable waiting for the small herd of cloned spidercows cluttering up the north paddock was still knee-deep in manure, and the tractor seat wasn't getting any warmer while he shivered out here, waiting for Maddie to come and sort this thing out. It wasn't a big herd but it was as big as his land and his labor could manage—the big

biofabricator in the shed could assemble mammalian
livestock faster than he could feed them up and sell them
with an honest HAND-RAISED NOT VAT-GROWN label. "What
do you want with us?" he yelled up at the gently buzzing
farm.

"Brains, fresh brains for Baby Jesus," crooned the farm
in a warm contralto, startling Joe half out of his skin. "Buy
my brains!" Half a dozen disturbing cauliflower shapes
poked suggestively out of the farm's back and then re-
tracted again, coyly.

"Don't want no brains around here," Joe said stubbornly, his fingers whitening on the stock of the shotgun.
"Don't want your kind round here, neither. Go away."

"I'm a nine-legged semiautomatic groove machine!"
crooned the farm. "I'm on my way to Jupiter on a mission
for love! Won't you buy my brains?" Three curious eyes
on stalks extruded from its upper glacis.

"Uh—" Joe was saved from having to dream up any
more ways of saying "fuck off" by Maddie's arrival. She'd
managed to sneak her old battle dress home after a stint
keeping the peace in Mesopotamia twenty ago, and she'd
managed to keep herself in shape enough to squeeze inside. Its left knee squealed ominously when she walked it
about, which wasn't often, but it still worked well enough
to manage its main task—intimidating trespassers.

"You." She raised one translucent arm, pointed at the
farm. "Get off my land. *Now.*"

Taking his cue, Joe raised his shotgun and thumbed the
selector to full auto. It wasn't a patch on the hardware riding Maddie's shoulders, but it underlined the point.

The farm hooted. "Why don't you love me?" it asked
plaintively

"*Get orf my land,*" Maddie amplified, volume cranked
up so high that Joe winced. "*Ten seconds! Nine! Eight—*"
Thin rings sprang out from the sides of her arms, whining
with the stress of long disuse as the Gauss gun powered up.

"I'm going! I'm going!" The farm lifted itself slightly,
shuffling backwards. "Don't understand. I only wanted to

set you free to explore the universe. Nobody wants to buy my fresh fruit and brains. What's wrong with the world?"

They waited until the farm had retreated round the bend at the top of the hill. Maddie was the first to relax, the rings retracting back into the arms of her battle dress, which solidified from ethereal translucency to neutral olive drab as it powered down. Joe safed his shotgun. "Bastard," he said.

"Fucking-A." Maddie looked haggard. "That was a bold one." Her face was white and pinched-looking, Joe noted. Her fists were clenched. She had the shakes, he realized without surprise. Tonight was going to be another major nightmare night, and no mistake.

"The fence." On again and off again for the past year, they'd discussed wiring up an outer wire to the CHP baseload from their little methane plant.

"Maybe this time. Maybe." Maddie wasn't keen on the idea of frying passers-by without warning, but if anything might bring her around, it would be the prospect of being overrun by a bunch of rogue farms. "Help me out of this, and I'll cook breakfast," she said.

"Got to muck out the barn," Joe protested.

"It can wait on breakfast," Maddie said shakily "I need you."

"Okay." Joe nodded. She was looking bad; it had been a few years since her last fatal breakdown, but when Maddie said "I need you," it was a bad idea to ignore her. That way led to backbreaking labor on the biofab and loading her backup tapes into the new body; always a messy business. He took her arm and steered her toward the back porch. They were nearly there when he paused.

"What is it?" asked Maddie.

"Haven't seen Bob for a while," he said slowly. "Sent him to let the cows into the north paddock after milking. Do you think—?"

"We can check from the control room," she said tiredly. "Are you really worried? . . ."

"With that thing blundering around? What do *you* think?"

"He's a good working dog," Maddie said uncertainly. "It won't hurt him. He'll be all right; just you page him."

A*fter Joe helped* her out of her battle dress, and after Maddie spent a good long while calming down, they breakfasted on eggs from their own hens, homemade cheese, and toasted bread made with rye from the hippie commune on the other side of the valley. The stone-floored kitchen in the dilapidated house they'd squatted and rebuilt together over the past twenty years was warm and homely. The only purchase from outside the valley was the coffee, beans from a hardy GM strain that grew like a straggling teenager's beard all along the Cumbrian hilltops. They didn't say much: Joe, because he never did, and Maddie, because there wasn't anything that she wanted to discuss. Silence kept her personal demons down. They'd known each other for many years, and even when there wasn't anything to discuss, they could cope with each other's silence. The voice radio on the windowsill opposite the cast-iron stove stayed off, along with the TV set hanging on the wall next to the fridge. Breakfast was a quiet time of day.

"Dog's not answering," Joe commented over the dregs of his coffee.

"He's a good dog." Maddie glanced at the yard gate uncertainly. "You afraid he's going to run away to Jupiter?"

"He was with me in the shed." Joe picked up his plate and carried it to the sink, began running hot water onto the dishes. "After I cleaned the lines I told him to go take the herd up the paddock while I did the barn." He glanced up, looking out the window with a worried expression. The Massey Ferguson was parked right in front of the open barn doors as if holding at bay the mountain of dung, straw, and silage that mounded up inside like an invading odorous enemy, relic of a frosty winter past.

Maddie shoved him aside gently and picked up one of the walkie-talkies from the charge point on the windowsill.

It bleeped and chuckled at her. "Bob, come in. Over." She frowned. "He's probably lost his headset again."

Joe racked the wet plates to dry. "I'll move the midden. You want to go find him?"

"I'll do that." Maddie's frown promised a talking-to in store for the dog when she caught up with him. Not that Bob would mind: words ran off him like water off a duck's back. "Cameras first." She prodded the battered TV set to life, and grainy bisected views flickered across the screen, garden, yard, Dutch barn, north paddock, east paddock, main field, copse. "Hmm."

She was still fiddling with the smallholding surveillance system when Joe clambered back into the driver's seat of the tractor and fired it up once more. This time there was no cough of black smoke, and as he hauled the mess of manure out of the barn and piled it into a three-meter-high midden, a quarter of a ton at a time, he almost managed to forget about the morning's unwelcome visitor. Almost.

By late morning, the midden was humming with flies and producing a remarkable stench, but the barn was clean enough to flush out with a hose and broom. Joe was about to begin hauling the midden over to the fermentation tanks buried round the far side of the house when he saw Maddie coming back up the path, shaking her head. He knew at once what was wrong.

"Bob,"he said, expectantly.

"Bob's fine. I left him riding shotgun on the goats." Her expression was peculiar. "But that *farm*—"

"Where?" he asked, hurrying after her.

"Squatting in the woods down by the stream," she said tersely "Just over our fence."

"It's not trespassing, then."

"It's put down feeder roots! Do you have any idea what that means?"

"I don't—" Joe's face wrinkled in puzzlement. "Oh."

"Yes. *Oh*." She stared back at the outbuildings between their home and the woods at the bottom of their small-

holding, and if looks could kill, the intruder would be dead
a thousand times over. "It's going to estivate, Joe, then it's
going to grow to maturity on our patch. And do you know
where it said it was going to go when it finishes growing?
Jupiter!"

"Bugger," Joe said faintly, as the true gravity of their
situation began to sink in. "We'll have to deal with it first."

"That wasn't what I meant," Maddie finished. But Joe
was already on his way out the door. She watched him
crossing the yard, then shook her head. "Why am I stuck
here?" she asked, but the cooker wasn't answering.

The hamlet of Outer Cheswick lay four kilometers down the
road from Armitage End, four kilometers past mostly derelict
houses and broken-down barns, fields given over to weeds
and walls damaged by trees. The first half of the twenty-first
century had been cruel years for the British agrobusiness sec-
tor; even harsher if taken in combination with the decline in
population and the consequent housing surplus. As a result,
the dropouts of the forties and fifties were able to take their
pick from among the gutted shells of once fine farmhouses.
They chose the best and moved in, squatted in the derelict
outbuildings, planted their seeds and tended their flocks and
practiced their DIY skills, until a generation later a mansion
fit for a squire stood in lonely isolation alongside a decaying
road where no more cars drove. Or rather, it would have
taken a generation had there been any children against whose
lives it could be measured; these were the latter decades of
the population crash, and what a previous century would
have labeled downshifter DINK couples were now in the ma-
jority, far outnumbering any breeder colonies. In this aspect
of their life, Joe and Maddie were boringly conventional. In
other respects they weren't: Maddie's nightmares, her aver-
sion to alcohol, and her withdrawal from society were all
relics of her time in Peaceforce. As for Joe, he liked it here.
Hated cities, hated the Net, hated the burn of the new. Anything for a quiet life . . .

The Pig and Pizzle, on the outskirts of Outer Cheswick, was the only pub within about ten kilometers—certainly the only one within staggering distance for Joe when he'd had a skinful of mild—and it was naturally a seething den of local gossip, not least because Ole Brenda refused to allow electricity, much less bandwidth, into the premises. (This was not out of any sense of misplaced technophobia, but a side effect of Brenda's previous life as an attack hacker with the European Defense Forces.)

Joe paused at the bar. "Pint of bitter?" he asked tentatively. Brenda glanced at him and nodded, then went back to loading the antique washing machine. Presently she pulled a clean glass down from the shelf and held it under the tap.

"Hear you've got farm trouble," she said noncommitally as she worked the hand pump on the beer engine.

"Uh-huh." Joe focused on the glass. "Where'd you hear that?"

"Never you mind." She put the glass down to give the head time to settle. "You want to talk to Arthur and Wendy-the-Rat about farms. They had one the other year."

"Happens." Joe took his pint. "Thanks, Brenda. The usual?"

"Yeah." She turned back to the washer. Joe headed over to the far corner where a pair of huge leather sofas, their arms and backs ripped and scarred by generations of Brenda's semiferal cats, sat facing each other on either side of a cold hearth. "Art, Rats. What's up?"

"Fine, thanks." Wendy-the-Rat was well over seventy, one of those older folks who had taken the p53 chromosome hack and seemed to wither into timelessness: white dreadlocks, nose and ear studs dangling loosely from leathery holes, skin like a desert wind. Art had been her boy-toy once, back before middle age set its teeth into him. He hadn't had the hack, and looked older than she did. Together they ran a smallholding, mostly pharming vaccine chicks but also doing a brisk trade in high-nitrate fertilizer that came in on the nod and went out in sacks by moonlight.

"Heard you had a spot of bother?"

"'S true." Joe took a cautious mouthful. "Mm, good. You ever had farm trouble?"

"Maybe." Wendy looked at him askance, slitty-eyed. "What kinda trouble you got in mind?"

"Got a farm collective. Says it's going to Jupiter or something. Bastard's homesteading the woods down by Old Jack's stream. Listen . . . Jupiter?"

"Aye, well, that's one of the destinations, sure enough." Art nodded wisely, as if he knew anything.

"Naah, that's bad." Wendy-the-Rat frowned. "Is it growing trees, do you know?"

"Trees?" Joe shook his head. "Haven't gone and looked, tell the truth. What the fuck makes people do that to themselves, anyway?"

"Who the fuck cares?" Wendy's face split in a broad grin. "Such as don't think they're human anymore, meself."

"It tried to sweet-talk us," Joe said.

"Aye, they do that," said Arthur, nodding emphatically. "Read somewhere they're the ones as think we aren't fully human. Tools an' clothes and farmyard machines, like? Sustaining a pre-post-industrial lifestyle instead of updating our genome and living off the land like God intended?"

"'Ow the hell can something with nine legs and eye stalks call itself human?" Joe demanded, chugging back half his pint in one angry swallow.

"It used to be, once. Maybe used to be a bunch of people." Wendy got a weird and witchy look in her eye. "'Ad a boyfriend back thirty, forty years ago, joined a Lamarckian clade. Swapping genes an' all, the way you or me'd swap us underwear. Used to be a 'viromentalist back when antiglobalization was about big corporations pissing on us all for profits. Got into gene hackery and self-sufficiency big time. I slung his fucking ass when he turned green and started photosynthesizmg.

"Bastards," Joe muttered. It was deep green folk like that who'd killed off the agricultural-industrial complex in the early years of the century, turning large portions of the countryside into ecologically devastated wilderness gone to rack and ruin. Bad enough that they'd set millions of countryfolk out of work—but that they'd gone on to turn green, grow extra limbs, and emigrate to Jupiter orbit was adding insult to injury. And having a good time in the process, by all accounts. "Din't you 'ave a farm problem, coupla years back?"

"Aye, did that," said Art. He clutched his pint mug protectively.

"It went away," Joe mused aloud.

"Yeah, well." Wendy stared at him cautiously.

"No fireworks, like." Joe caught her eye. "And no body. Huh."

"Metabolism," said Wendy, apparently coming to some kind of decision. "That's where it's at."

"Meat—" Joe, no biogeek, rolled the unfamiliar word around his mouth irritably. "I used to be a software dude before I burned, Rats. You'll have to 'splain the jargon 'fore using it."

"You ever wondered how those farms *get* to Jupiter?" Wendy probed.

"Well." Joe shook his head. "They, like, grow stage trees? Rocket logs? An' then they est-ee-vate and you are fucked if they do it next door 'cause when those trees go up they toast about a hundred hectares?"

"Very good," Wendy said heavily. She picked up her mug in both hands and gnawed on the rim, edgily glancing around as if hunting for police gnats. "Let's you and me take a hike."

Pausing at the bar for Ole Brenda to refill her mug, Wendy led Joe out past Spiffy Buerke—throwback in green wellingtons and Barbour jacket—and her latest femme, out into what had once been a car park and was now a tattered wasteground out back behind the pub. It was dark, and no residual light pollution stained the sky: the Milky Way was visible overhead, along with the pea-size red cloud of orbitals that had gradually swallowed

Jupiter over the past few years. "You wired?" asked
Wendy.

"No, why?"

She pulled out a fist-size box and pushed a button on
the side of it, waited for a light on its side to blink green,
and nodded. "Fuckin' polis bugs."

"Isn't that a—?"

"Ask me no questions, an' I'll tell you no fibs." Wendy
grinned.

"Uh-huh." Joe took a deep breath: he'd guessed Wendy
had some dodgy connections, and this—a portable local
jammer—was proof: any police bugs within two or three
meters would be blind and dumb, unable to relay their chat
to the keyword-trawling subsentient coppers whose job it
was to prevent conspiracy-to-commit offenses before they
happened. It was a relic of the Internet Age, when enthusiastic legislators had accidentally demolished the right of
free speech in public by demanding keyword monitoring
of everything within range of a network terminal—not re-
alizing that in another few decades 'network terminals'
would be self-replicating 'bots the size of fleas and about
as common as dirt. (The Net itself had collapsed shortly
thereafter, under the weight of self-replicating viral libel
lawsuits, but the legacy of public surveillance remained.)
"Okay. Tell me about metal, meta—"

"Metabolism." Wendy began walking toward the field
behind the pub. "And stage trees. Stage trees started out as
science fiction, like? Some guy called Niven—anyway.
What you do is, you take a pine tree and you hack it. The
xylem vessels running up the heartwood, usually they just
lignify and die, in a normal tree. Stage trees go one better,
and before the cells die, they *nitrate* the cellulose in their
walls. Takes one fuckin' crazy bunch of hacked 'zymes to
do it, right? And lots of energy, more energy than trees'd
normally have to waste. Anyways, by the time the tree's
dead, it's like ninety percent nitrocellulose, plus built-in
stiffeners and baffles and microstructures. It's not, like,
straight explosive—it detonates cell by cell, and *some* of

the xylem tubes are, eh, well, the farm grows custom-
hacked fungal hyphae with a depolarizing membrane
nicked from human axons down them to trigger the reaction. It's about efficient as 'at old-time Ariane or Atlas
rocket. Not very, but enough."

"Uh." Joe blinked. "That meant to mean something to
me?"

"Oh 'eck, Joe." Wendy shook her head. "Think I'd bend
your ear if it wasn't?"

"Okay." He nodded, seriously. "What can I do?"

"Well." Wendy stopped and stared at the sky. High
above them, a belt of faint light sparkled with a multitude
of tiny pinpricks; a deep green wagon train making its orbital transfer window, self-sufficient posthuman Lamarckian colonists, space-adapted, embarking on the long, slow
transfer to Jupiter.

"Well?" He waited expectantly.

"You're wondering where all that fertilizer's from,"
Wendy said elliptically.

"Fertilizer." His mind blanked for a moment.

"Nitrates."

He glanced down, saw her grinning at him. Her perfect
fifth set of teeth glowed alarmingly in the greenish over-
spill from the light on her jammer box.

"Tha' knows it makes sense," she added, then cut the
jammer.

When Joe finally staggered home in the small hours, a thin
plume of smoke was rising from Bob's kennel. Joe paused
in front of the kitchen door and sniffed anxiously, then re-
laxed. Letting go of the door handle, he walked over to the
kennel and sat down outside. Bob was most particular
about his den—even his own humans didn't go in there
without an invitation. So Joe waited.

A moment later there was an interrogative cough from inside. A dark, pointed snout came out, dribbling smoke from
its nostrils like a particularly vulpine dragon. "Rrrrrrr?"

"'S'me."

"Uuurgh." A metallic click. "Smoke good smoke joke cough tickle funny arf arf?"

"Yeah, don't mind if I do."

The snout pulled back into the kennel; a moment later it reappeared, teeth clutching a length of hose with a mouthpiece on one end. Joe accepted it graciously, wiped off the mouthpiece, leaned against the side of the kennel, and inhaled. The weed was potent and smooth: within a few seconds the uneasy dialogue in his head was still.

"Wow, tha's a good turnup."

"Arf-arf-ayup."

Joe felt himself relaxing. Maddie would be upstairs, snoring quietly in their decrepit bed: waiting for him, maybe. But sometimes a man just had to be alone with his dog and a good joint, doing man-and-dog stuff. Maddie understood this and left him his space. Still . . .

"'At farm been buggering around the pond?"

"Growl exclaim fuck-fuck yup! Sheep-shagger."

"If it's been at our lambs—"

"Nawwwwrr. Buggrit."

"So whassup?"

"Grrrr, Maddie yap-yap farmtalk! Sheep-shagger."

"Maddie's been *talking* to it?"

"Grrr yes-yes!"

"Oh, shit. Do you remember when she did her last backup?"

The dog coughed fragrant blue smoke. "Tank thump-thump full cow moo beef clone."

"Yeah, I think so, too. Better muck it out tomorrow. Just in case."

"Yurrrrrp." But while Joe was wondering whether this was agreement or just a canine eructation a lean paw stole out of the kennel mouth and yanked the hookah back inside. The resulting slobbering noises and clouds of aromatic blue smoke left Joe feeling a little queasy: so he went inside.

•   •   •

The next morning, over breakfast, Maddie was even quieter than usual. Almost meditative.

"Bob said you'd been talking to that farm," Joe commented over his eggs.

"Bob—" Maddie's expression was unreadable. "Bloody dog." She lifted the Rayburn's hot plate lid and peered at the toast browning underneath. "Talks too much."

"Did you?"

"Ayup." She turned the toast and put the lid back down on it.

"Said much?"

"It's a farm." She looked out the window. "Not a fuckin' worry in the world 'cept making its launch window for Jupiter."

"It—"

"Him. Her. They." Maddie sat down heavily in the other kitchen chair. "It's a collective. Usedta be six people. Old, young, whatever, they's decided ter go to Jupiter. One of 'em was telling me how it happened. How she'd been living like an accountant in Bradford, had a nervous breakdown. Wanted *out*. Self-sufficiency." For a moment her expression turned bleak. "Felt herself growing older but not bigger, if you follow."

"So how's turning into a bioborg an improvement?" Joe grunted, forking up the last of his scrambled eggs.

"They're still separate people: bodies are overrated, anyway. Think of the advantages: not growing older, being able to go places and survive anything, never being on your own, not bein' trapped—" Maddie sniffed. "Fuckin' toast's on fire!"

Smoke began to trickle out from under the hot plate lid. Maddie yanked the wire toasting rack out from under it and dunked it into the sink, waited for waterlogged black crumbs to float to the surface before taking it out, opening it, and loading it with fresh bread.

"Bugger," she remarked.

"You feel trapped?" Joe asked. *Again?* He wondered.

Maddie grunted evasively. "Not your fault, love. Just life."

"Life." Joe sniffed, then sneezed violently as the acrid smoke tickled his nose. "Life!"

"Horizon's closing in," she said quietly. "Need a change of horizons."

"Ayup, well, rust never sleeps, right? Got to clean out the winter stables, haven't I?" said Joe. He grinned uncertainly at her as he turned away. "Got a shipment of fertilizer coming in."

In between milking the herd, feeding the sheep, mucking out the winter stables, and surreptitiously EMPing every police 'bot on the farm into the silicon afterlife, it took Joe a couple of days to get round to running up his toy on the household fabricator. It clicked and whirred to itself like a demented knitting machine as it ran up the gadgets he'd ordered—a modified crop sprayer with double-walled tanks and hoses, an air rifle with a dart loaded with a potent cocktail of tubocurarine and etorphine, and a breathing mask with its own oxygen supply.

Maddie made herself scarce, puttering around the control room but mostly disappearing during the daytime, coming back to the house after dark to crawl, exhausted, into bed. She didn't seem to be having nightmares, which was a good sign. Joe kept his questions to himself.

It took another five days for the smallholding's power field to concentrate enough juice to begin fueling up his murder weapons. During this time, Joe took the house off-Net in the most deniable and surreptitiously plausible way, a bastard coincidence of squirrel-induced cable fade and a badly shielded alternator on the backhoe to do for the wireless chitchat. He'd half expected Maddie to complain, but she didn't say anything—just spent more time away in Outer Cheswick or Lower Gruntlingthorpe or wherever she'd taken to holing up.

Finally, the tank was filled. So Joe girded his loins,

donned his armor, picked up his weapons, and went to do battle with the dragon by the pond.

The woods around the pond had once been enclosed by a wooden fence, a charming copse of old-growth deciduous trees, elm and oak and beech growing uphill, smaller shrubs nestling at their ankles in a green skirt that reached all the way to the almost-stagnant waters. A little stream fed into it during rainy months, under the feet of a weeping willow; children had played here, pretending to explore the wilderness beneath the benevolent gaze of their parental control cameras.

That had been long ago. Today the woods really *were* wild. No kids, no picnicking city folks, no cars. Badgers and wild coypu and small, frightened wallabies roamed the parching English countryside during the summer dry season. The water drew back to expose an apron of cracked mud, planted with abandoned tin cans and a supermarket trolley of Precambrian vintage, its GPS tracker long since shorted out. The bones of the technological epoch, poking from the treacherous surface of a fossil mud bath. And around the edge of the mimsy puddle, the stage trees grew.

Joe switched on his jammer and walked in among the spear-shaped conifers. Their needles were matte black and fuzzy at the edges, fractally divided, the better to soak up all the available light: a network of taproots and fuzzy black grasslike stuff covered the ground densely around them. Joe's breath wheezed noisily in his ears, and he sweated into the airtight suit as he worked, pumping a stream of colorless smoking liquid at the roots of each ballistic trunk. The liquid fizzed and evaporated on contact: it seemed to bleach the wood where it touched. Joe carefully avoided the stream: this stuff made him uneasy. As did the trees, but liquid nitrogen was about the one thing he'd been able to think of that was guaranteed to kill the trees stone dead without igniting them. After all, they had cores that were basically made of gun cotton—highly explosive, liable to go off if you subjected them to a sudden sharp impact or the friction of a chainsaw. The tree he'd hit on creaked ominously, threatening to fall sideways, and Joe stepped round it, efficiently squirting at the remaining roots. Right into the path of a distraught farm.

"My holy garden of earthly delights! My forest of the imaginative future! My delight, my trees, my trees!" Eye stalks shot out and over, blinking down at him in horror as the farm reared up on six or seven legs and pawed the air in front of him. "Destroyer of saplings! Earth mother rapist! Bunny-strangling vivisectionist!"

"Back off," said Joe, dropping his cryogenic squirter and fumbling for his air gun.

The farm came down with a ground-shaking thump in front of him and stretched eyes out to glare at him from both sides. They blinked, long black eyelashes fluttering across angry blue irises. "How *dare* you?" demanded the farm. "My treasured seedlings!"

"Shut the fuck up," Joe grunted, shouldering his gun. "Think I'd let you burn my holding when tha' rocket launched? Stay the *fuck* away," he added as a tentacle began to extend from the farm's back.

"My crop," it moaned quietly. "My exile! Six more years around the sun chained to this well of sorrowful gravity before next the window opens! No brains for Baby Jesus! Defenestrator! We could have been so happy together if you hadn't fucked up! Who set you up to this? Rat Lady?" It began to gather itself, muscles rippling under the leathery mantle atop its leg cluster.

So Joe shot it.

Tubocurarine is a muscle relaxant: it paralyzes skeletal muscles, the kind over which human nervous systems typically exert conscious control. Etorphine is an insanely strong opiate—twelve hundred times as potent as heroin. Given time, a farm, with its alien adaptive metabolism and consciously controlled proteome might engineer a defense against the etorphine—but Joe dosed his dart with enough to stun a blue whale, and he had no intention of giving the farm enough time.

It shuddered and went down on one knee as he closed in on it, a Syrette raised. "Why?" it asked plaintively in a voice that almost made him wish he hadn't pulled the trigger. "We could have gone together!"

"Together?" he asked. Already the eye stalks were drooping; the great lungs wheezed effortfully as it struggled to frame a reply.

"I was going to ask you," said the farm, and half its legs collapsed under it, with a thud like a baby earthquake. Oh, Joe, if only—"

"Joe? *Maddie?*" he demanded, nerveless fingers dropping the tranquilizer gun.

A mouth appeared in the farm's front, slurred words at him from familiar seeming lips, words about Jupiter and promises. Appalled, Joe backed away from the farm. Passing the first dead tree, he dropped the nitrogen tank: then an impulse he couldn't articulate made him turn and run, back to the house, eyes almost blinded by sweat or tears. But he was too slow, and when he dropped to his knees next to the farm, pharmacopoeia clicking and whirring to itself in his arms, he found it was already dead.

"Bugger," said Joe, and he stood up, shaking his head. "*Bugger.*" He keyed his walkie-talkie: "Bob, come in, Bob!"

"Rrrrowl?"

"Momma's had another break-down. Is the tank clean, like I asked?"

"Yap!"

"Okay. I got 'er backup tapes in t'office safe. Let's get t' tank warmed up for er an' then shift t' tractor down 'ere to muck out this mess."

That autumn, the weeds grew unnaturally rich and green down in the north paddock of Armitage End.

All Tomorrow's
Parties

Paul J. McAuley

Born in Oxford, England, in 1955, Paul J. McAuley now makes his home in London. A professional biologist for many years, he sold his first story in 1984 and has gone on to be a frequent contributor to Interzone, *as well as to markets such as* Asimov's Science Fiction Magazine, SCI Fiction, Amazing, The Magazine of Fantasy & Science Fiction, Skylife, The Third Alternative, When the Music's Over, *and elsewhere.*

McAuley is at the forefront of several of the most important subgenres in SF today, producing both "radical hard science fiction" and the revamped and retooled widescreen Space Opera that has sometimes been called The New Space Opera, as well as Dystopian sociological speculations about the very near future. He also writes fantasy and horror. His first novel, Four Hundred Billion Stars, *won the Philip K. Dick Award, and his novel* Fairyland *won both the Arthur C. Clarke Award and the John W. Campbell Award in 1996. His other books include the novels* Of The Fall, Eternal Light, Pasquale's Angel, Confluence—*a major trilogy of ambitious scope and scale set ten million years in the future, comprised of the novels* Child of the River, Ancient of Days, *and* Shrine of Stars—Life on Mars, The Secret of Life, *and* Whole Wide World. *His short fiction has been collected in* The King of the Hill and Other Stories *and* The Invisible Country, *and he is the coeditor, with Kim Newman, of an original anthology,* In Dreams. *His most recent books include the novel* White Devils *and a collection called* Little Machines.

A wide range of influences can be seen in McAuley's

*work, from Cordwainer Smith and Brian Aldiss to Roger
Zelazny and Larry Niven, topped off with a dash of Samuel
R. Delany, with perhaps some H. G. Wells to give a bottom
to the mixture. All of which and more are evident in the
evocative, supercharged, and intense little story that follows, packed with enough new ideas to fuel many another
author's six-hundred-page novel, that takes us far into the
future and thousands of light-years from home for a very
odd sort of family reunion . . .*

And with exactly a year left before the end of the century-
long gathering of her clade, she went to Paris with her current lover, racing ahead of midnight and the beginning of
the New Year. Paris! The Premier Quartier: the early
Twentieth Century Fireworks bursting in great flowers
above the night-black Seine, and a brawling carnival
which under a multicolored rain of confetti filled every
street from the Quai du Louvre to the Arc de Triomphe.

Escorted by her lover (they had been hunting big game
in the Pleistocene–era taiga of Siberia; he still wore his sa-
fari suit, and a Springfield rifle was slung over his shoulder), she crossed to the Paleolithic oak woods of the Ile de
la Cité. In the middle of the great stone circle naked druids
with blue-stained skins beat huge drums under flaring
torches, while holographic ghosts swung above the electric
lights of the Twentieth Century shore, a fleet of luminous
clouds dancing in the sky. Her attentive lover identified
them for her, leaning against her shoulder so she could
sight along his arm. He was exactly her height, with piercing blue eyes and a salt-and-pepper beard.

An astronaut. A gene pirate. Emperor Victoria. Mickey
Mouse.

"What is a mouse?"

He pointed. "That one, the black-skinned creature with
the circular ears."

She leaned against his solid human warmth. "For an

animal, it seems very much like a person. Was it a product of the gene wars?"

"It is a famous icon of the country where I was born. My countrymen preferred creatures of the imagination to those of the real world. It is why they produced so few good authors."

"But you were a good author."

"I was not bad, except at the end. Something bad always happened to all good writers from my country. Sometimes slowly, sometimes quickly, but without exception."

"What is it carrying?"

"A light saber. It is an imaginary weapon that is authentic for the period. They were obsessed with weapons and divisions. They saw the world as a struggle of good against evil. That was how wars could be called good, except by those who fought in them."

She didn't argue. Her lover, a partial, had been modelled on a particular Twentieth Century writer, and had direct access to the appropriate records in the Library. Although she had been born just at the end of the Twentieth Century, she had long ago forgotten everything about it.

Behind them, the drums reached a frenzied climax and fell silent. The sacrificial victim writhed on the heel stone and the chief druid lifted the still beating heart above his head in triumph. Blood that looked black in the torchlight ran down his arms.

The spectators beyond the circle clapped or toasted each other. One man was trying to persuade his companion to fuck on the altar. They were invisible to the druids, who were merely puppets lending local color to the scene.

"I'm getting tired of this," she said.

"Of course. We could go to Cuba. The ocean fishing there is good. Or to Afrique, to hunt lions. I think I liked that best, but after a while I could no longer do it. That was one of the things that destroyed my writing."

"I'm getting tired of you," she said, and her lover bowed and walked away.

●　　　●　　　●

She was getting tired of everything.

She had been getting tired of everything for longer than she could remember. What was the point of living forever if you did nothing new? Despite all her hopes, this *faux* Earth, populated by two billion puppets and partials, and ten million of her clade, had failed to revive her.

In one more year, the fleet of spaceships would disperse; the sun, an ordinary G2 star she had moved by the pressure of its own light upon gravity tethered reflective sails, would go supernova; nothing would be saved but the store of information which the Library had collected and collated. She had not yet accessed any of that. Perhaps that would save her.

She returned to the carnival, stayed there three days. But despite use of various intoxicants she could not quite lose herself in it, could not escape the feeling that she had failed after all. This was supposed to be a great congress of her own selves, a place to share and exchange memories that spanned five million years and the entire Galaxy. But it seemed to her that the millions of her selves simply wanted to forget what they were, to lose themselves in the pleasures of the flesh. Of course, many had assumed bodies for the first time to attend the gathering; one could perhaps excuse them, for this carnival was to them a genuine farewell to flesh they would abandon at the end of the year.

On the third day she was sitting in cold dawn light at a green café table in the Jardin des Tuileries, by the great fountain. Someone was sculpting the clouds through which the sun was rising. The café was crowded with guests, partials and puppets, androids and animals—even a silver gynoid, its face a smooth oval mirror. The air buzzed with the tiny machines which attended the guests; in one case, a swirling cloud of gnat-sized beads *was* a guest. After almost a century in costume, the guests were reverting to type.

She sipped a *citron pressé*, listened to the idle chatter.

The party in Paris would break up soon. The revelers
would disperse to other parts of the Earth. Except for a
clean-up crew, the puppets, partials and all the rest would
be returned to store. At another table, a youthful version of
her erstwhile lover was talking to an older man with brown
hair brushed back from his high forehead and pale blue
eyes magnified by the thick lenses of his spectacles.

"The lions, Jim. Go to Afrique and listen to the lions
roar at night. There is no sound like it."

"Ah, and I would love that, but Nora would not stand it.
She needs the comforts of civilization. Besides, the thing
we must not forget is that I would not be able to see the
lions. Instead I think we will drink some more of this fine
white wine and you will tell me about them."

"Aw hell, I could bring you a living lion if you like," the
younger man said. "I could describe him to you and you
could touch him and smell him until you got the idea." He
was quite unaware that there were two lions right there in
the park, accompanying a naked girl child whose feet, with
pigeon's wings at the ankles, did not quite touch the
ground.

Did these puppets come here every day, and recreate a
conversation millions of years dead for the delectation of
the guests? Was each day to them the same day? Suddenly,
she felt as if a cold wind was blowing through her, as if she
was raised up high and naked upon the pinnacle of the
mountain of her millions of years.

"You confuse the true and the real," someone said. A
man's voice, soft, lisping. She looked around but could not
see who amongst the amazing people and creatures might
have said such a thing, the truest realest thing she had heard
for . . . how long? She could not remember how long.

She left, and went to New Orleans.

Where it was night, and raining, a soft warm rain falling
in the lamplit streets. It was the Twentieth Century here,
too. They were cooking crawfish under the mimosa trees at

every intersection of the brick-paved streets, and burning the Maid of New Orleans over Lake Pontchartrain. The Maid hung up there in the black night sky—wrapped in oiled silks and shining like a star, with the blue-white wheel of the Galaxy a backdrop that spanned the horizon—then flamed like a comet and plunged into the black water while cornet bands played "*Laissez le Bon Temps Rouler.*"

She fell in with a trio of guests whose originals were all less than a thousand years old. They were students of the Rediscovery, they said, although it was not quite clear what the Rediscovery was. They wore green ("For Earth," one said, although she thought that odd because most of the Earth was blue), and drank a mild psychotropic called absinthe, bitter white stuff poured into water over a sugar cube held in silver tongs. They were interested in the origins of the clade, which amused her gteatly, because of course she was its origin, going amongst the copies and clones disguised as her own self. But even if they made her feel every one of her five million years, she liked their innocence, their energy, their openness.

She strolled with her new friends through the great orrery at the waterfront. Its display of the lost natural wonders of the Galaxy was derived from records and memories guests had deposited in the Library, and changed every day. She was listening to the three students discuss the possibility that humans had not originally come from the Earth when someone went past and said loudly, looking right at her, "None of them look like you, but they are just like you all the same. All obsessed with the past because they are trapped in it."

A tall man with a black, spade-shaped beard and black eyes that looked at her with infinite amusement. The same soft, lisping voice she had heard in the café in Paris. He winked and plunged into the heart of the white-hot whirlpool of the accretion disc of the black hole of Sigma Draconis 2, which drew matter from the photosphere of its companion blue-white giant—before the reconstruction, it had been one of the wonders of the Galaxy. She followed, but he was gone.

She looked for him everywhere in New Orleans, and fell in with a woman who before the gathering had lived in the water vapor zone of a gas giant, running a tourist business for those who could afford to download themselves into the ganglia of living blimps a kilometer across. The woman's name was Rapha; she had ruled the worlds of a hundred stars once, but had given that up long before she had answered the call for the gathering.

"I was a man when I had my empire," Rapha said, "but I gave that up too. When you've done everything, what's left but to party?"

She had always been a woman, she thought. And for two million years she had ruled an empire of a million worlds—for all she knew, the copy she had left behind ruled there still. But she didn't tell Rapha that. No one knew who she was, on all the Earth. She said, "Then let's party until the end of the world."

She knew that it wouldn't work—she had already tried everything, in every combination—but because she didn't care if it worked or not, perhaps this time it would.

They raised hell in New Orleans, and went to Antarctica.

It was raining in Antarctica, too.

It had been raining for a century, ever since the world had been made.

Statite sails hung in stationary orbit, reflecting sunlight so that the swamps and cycad forests and volcanic mountain ranges of the South Pole were in perpetual day. The hunting lodge was on a floating island a hundred meters above the tops of the giant ferns, close to the edge of a shallow viridescent lake. A flock of delicate, dappled *Dromiceiomimus* squealed and splashed in the shallows; great dragonflies flitted through the rainy middle air; at the misty horizon the perfect cones of three volcanoes sent up threads of smoke into the sagging clouds.

She and Rapha rode bubbles in wild loops above the forests, chasing dinosaurs or goading dinosaurs to chase them. Then they plunged into one of the volcanoes and caused it to erupt, and one of the hunters overrode the bubbles and brought them back and politely asked them to stop.

The lake and the forest were covered in a mantle of volcanic ash. The sky was milky with ash.

"The guests are amused, but they will not be amused forever. It is the hunting that is important here. If I may suggest other areas where you might find enjoyment . . ."

He was a slightly younger version of her last lover. A little less salt in his beard; a little more spring in his step.

She said, "How many of you have I made?"

But he didn't understand the question.

They went to Thebes (and some of the hunting party went with them), where they ran naked and screaming through the streets, toppling the statues of the gods. They went to Greenland, and broke the rainbow bridge of Valhalla and fought the trolls and ran again, laughing, with Odin's thunder about their ears. Went to Troy, and set fire to the wooden horse before the Greeks could climb inside it.

None of it mattered. The machines would repair everything; the puppets would resume their roles. Troy would fall again the next night, on schedule.

"Let's go to Golgotha," Rapha said, wild-eyed, very drunk.

This was in a bar of some Christian–era American town. Outside, a couple of the men were roaring up and down the main street on motorcycles, weaving in and out of the slow-moving, candy-colored cars. Two cops watched indulgently.

"Or Afrique," Rapha said. "We could hunt man-apes."

"I've done it before," someone said. He didn't have a name, but some kind of number. He was part of a clone. His shaved head was horribly scarred; one of his eyes was mechanical. He said, "You hunt them with spears or slings. They're pretty smart, for man-apes. I got killed twice."

Someone came into the bar. Tall, saturnine, black eyes, a spade-shaped beard. At once, she asked her machines if he was a partial or a guest, but the question confused them. She asked them if there were any strangers in the world, and at once they told her that there were the servants and those of her clade, but no strangers.

He said softly, "Are you having a good time?"

"Who are you?"

"Perhaps I'm the one who whispers in your ear, 'Remember that you are mortal.' Are you mortal, Angel?"

No one in the world should know her name. Her true name.

Danger, danger, someone sang in the background of the song that was playing on the jukebox. *Danger*, burbled the coffee pot on the heater behind the counter of the bar.

She said, "I made you, then."

"Oh no. Not me. You made all of this. Even all of the guests, in one way or another. But not me. We can't talk here. Try the one place which has any use in this *faux* world. There's something there I'm going to take, and when I've done that I'll wait for you."

"Who are you? What do you want?"

"Perhaps I want to kill you." He smiled. "And perhaps you want to die. It's one thing you have not tried yet."

He walked away, and when she started after him Rapha got in the way. Rapha hadn't seen the man. She said the others wanted to go to Hy Brasil.

"The gene wars," Rapha said. "That's where we started to become what we are. And then—I don't know, but it doesn't matter. We're going to party to the end of the world. When the sun explodes, I'm going to ride the shock wave as far as I can. I'm not going back. There's a lot of us who aren't going back. Why should we? We went to get copied and woke up here, thousands of years later, thousands of light-years away. What's to go back for? Wait! Where are you going?"

"I don't know," she said, and walked out.

•   •   •

The man had scared her. He had touched the doubt which had made her organize the gathering. She wanted a place to hide so that she could think about that before she confronted him.

Most of the North American continent was, in one form or another, modeled after the Third Millennium of the Christian Era. She took a car (a red Dodge as big as a boat, with fins and chrome trim) and drove to Dallas, where she was attacked by tribes of horsemen near the glittering slag of the wrecked city. She took up with a warlord for a while, poisoned all his wives, grew bored and seduced his son, who murdered his father and began a civil war. She went south on horseback through the alien flower jungles which had conquered Earth after humanity had more or less abandoned it, then caught a *pneumatique* all the way down the spine of Florida to Key West.

A version of her last lover lived there, too. She saw him in a bar by the beach two weeks later. There were three main drugs in Key West: cigarettes, heroin, and alcohol. She had tried them all, decided she liked alcohol best. It helped you forget yourself in an odd, dissociative way that was both pleasant and disturbing. Perhaps she should have spent more of her long life drunk.

This version of her lover liked alcohol, too. He was both lumbering but shy, pretending not to notice the people who looked at him while he drank several complicated cocktails. He had thickened at the waist; his beard was white and full. His eyes, webbed by wrinkles, were still piercingly blue, but his gaze was vague and troubled. She eavesdropped while he talked with the barkeep. She wanted to find out how the brash man who had to constantly prove himself against the world had turned out.

Badly, it seemed. The world was unforgiving, and his powers were fading

"I lost her, Carlos," he told the barkeep. He meant his muse. "She's run out on me, the bitch."

"Now, Papa, you know that is not true," the young bar-keep said. "I read your article in *Life* just last week."

"It was shit, Carlos. I can fake it well enough, but I can't do the good stuff any more. I need some quiet, and all day I get tourists trying to take my picture and spooking the cats. When I was younger I could work all day in a café, but now I need . . . hell, I don't know what I need. She's a bitch, Car-los. She only loves the young." Later, he said, "I keep dream-ing of lions. One of the long white beaches in Afrique where the lions come down at dusk. They play there like cats, and I want to get to them, but I can't."

But Carlos was attending to another customer. Only she heard the old man. Later, after he had gone, she talked with Carlos herself. He was a puppet, and couldn't understand, but it didn't matter.

"All this was a bad idea," she said. She meant the bar, Key West, the Pacific Ocean, the world. "Do you want to know how it started?"

"Of course, ma'am. And may I bring you another drink?"

"I think I have had enough. You stay there and listen. Millions of years ago, while all of what would become hu-manity lived on the nine worlds and thousand worldlets around a single star in the Sky Hunter arm of the Galaxy, there was a religion which taught that individuals need never die. It was this religion which first drove humanity from star to star in the Galaxy. Individuals copied their personalities into computers, or cloned themselves, or spread their personalities through flocks of birds, or fish, or amongst hive insects. But there was one flaw in this re-ligion. After millions of years, many of its followers were no longer human in form or in thought, except that they could trace back, generation upon generation, their descent from a single human ancestor. They had become transcen-dents, and each individual transcendent had become a clade, or an alliance, of millions of different minds. Mine is merely one of many, but it is one of the oldest, and one of the largest.

"I brought us here to unite us all in shared experiences.

It isn't possible that one of us could have seen every wonder in the Galaxy, visit every world. There are a hundred billion stars in the Galaxy. It takes a year or two to explore the worlds of each star, and then there is the travel between the stars. But there are ten million of us here. Clones, copies, descendants of clones and copies. Many of us have done nothing but explore. We have not seen everything, but we have seen most of it. I thought that we could pool all our information, that it would result in . . . something. A new religion, godhead. Something new, something *different*. But it seems that most just want to party, and I wonder how much I have changed, for they are so little like me. Many of them say that they will not return, that they will stay here until the sun ends it all. Some have joined in the war in China—a few even refuse regeneration. Mostly, though, they want to party."

"There are parties every night, ma'am," the barkeep said. "That's Key West for you."

"Someone was following me, but I lost him. I think he was tracing me through the travel net, but I used contemporary transport to get here. He frightened me and I ran away, but perhaps he is what I need. I think I will find him. What month is this?"

"June, ma'am. Very hot, even for June. It means a bad hurricane season."

"It will get hotter," she said, thinking of the machine ticking away in the core of the sun.

And went to Tibet, where the Library was.

For some reason, the high plateau had been constructed as a replica of part of Mars. She had given her servants a lot of discretion when building the Earth; it pleased her to be surprised, although it did not happen very often.

She had arrived at the top of one of the rugged massifs that defined the edge of the vast basin. There was a shrine here, a mani eye painted on a stone pillar, a heap of stones swamped with skeins of red and blue and white and yellow

prayer flags raveling in the cold wind. The scarp dropped
away steeply to talus slopes and the flood lava of the
basin's floor, a smooth, lightly cratered red plain mantled
with fleets of barchan dunes. Directly below, nestling
amongst birches at the foot of the scarp's sheer cliff, was
the bone-white Library.

She took a day to descend the winding path. Now and
then pilgrims climbed past her. Many shuffled on their
knees, eyes lifted to the sky; a few fell face-forward at
each step, standing up and starting again at the point where
their hands touched the ground. All whirled prayer wheels
and muttered their personal mantra as they climbed, and
few spared her more than a glance, although at noon while
she sat under a gnarled juniper one old man came to her
and shared his heel of dry black bread and stringy dried
yak meat. She learned from him that the pilgrims were not
puppets, as she had thought, but were guests searching for
enlightenment. That was so funny and so sad she did not
know what to think about it.

The Library was a replica of the White Palace of the
Potala. It had been a place of quiet order and contempla-
tion, where all the stories that the clade had told each other,
all the memories that they had downloaded or exchanged,
had been collected and collated.

Now it was a battleground.

Saffron-robed monks armed with weaponry from a
thousand different eras were fighting against man-shaped
black androids. Bodies of men and machines were
sprawled on the great steps; smoke billowed from the top-
most ranks of the narrow windows; red and green energy
beams flickered against the pink sky.

She walked through the carnage untouched. Nothing in
this world could touch her. Only perhaps the man who was
waiting for her, sitting cross-legged beneath the great
golden Buddha, which a stray shot from some energy
weapon had decapitated and half-melted to slag. On either
side, hundreds of candles floated in great bowls filled with

water; their lights shivered and flickered from the vibration of heavy weaponry.

The man did not open his eyes as she approached, but he said softly, "I already have what I need. These foolish monks are defending a lost cause. You should stop them."

"It is what they have to do. They can't destroy us, of course, but I could destroy you."

"Guests can't harm other guests," he said calmly. "It is one of the rules."

"I am not a guest. Nor, I think, are you."

She told her machines to remove him. Nothing happened.

He opened his eyes. He said, "Your machines are invisible to the puppets and partials you created to populate this fantasy world. I am invisible to the machines. I do not draw my energy from the world grid, but from elsewhere."

And then he leaped at her, striking with formal moves millions of years old. The Angry Grasshopper, the Rearing Horse, the Snapping Mantis. Each move, magnified by convergent energies, could have killed her, evaporated her body, melted her machines.

But she allowed her body to respond, countering his attacks. She had thought that she might welcome death; instead, she was amused and exhilarated by the fury of her response. The habit of living was deeply ingrained; now it had found a focus.

Striking attitudes, tangling in a flurry of blows and counterblows, they moved through the battleground of the Library, through its gardens, moved down the long talus slope at the foot of the massif in a storm of dust and shattered stones.

At the edge of a lake which filled a small, perfectly circular crater, she finally tired of defensive moves and went on the attack. The Striking Eagle, the Plunging Dragon, the Springing Tiger Who Defends Her Cubs. He countered in turn. Stray energies boiled the lake dry. The dry ground shook, split open in a mosaic of plates. Gradually, a curtain of dust was raised above the land, obscuring the setting sun

and the green face of the Moon, which was rising above
the mountains.

They broke apart at last. They stood in the center of a
vast crater of vitrified rock. Their clothes hung in tatters
about their bodies. It was night, now. Halfway up the scarp
of the massif, small lightnings flashed where the monks
still defended the Library.

"Who are you?" she said again. "Did I create you?"

"I'm closer to you than anyone else in this strange mad
world," he said.

That gave her pause. All the guests, clones or copies or
replicants, were of her direct genetic lineage.

She said, "Are you my death?"

As if in answer, he attacked again. But she fought back
as forcefully as before, and when he broke off, she saw that
he was sweating.

"I am stronger than you thought," she said.

He took out a small black cube from his tattered tunic.
He said, "I have what I need. I have the memory core of
the Library. Everything anyone who came here placed on
record is here."

"Then why do you want to kill me?"

"Because you are the original. I thought it would be fitting, after I stole this."

She laughed. "You foolish man! Do you think we rely
on a single physical location, a single master copy? It is the
right of everyone in the clade to carry away the memories
of everyone else. Why else are we gathered here?"

"I am not of your clade." He tossed the cube into the air,
caught it, tucked it away. "I will use this knowledge
against you. Against all of you. I have all your secrets."

"You say you are closer to me than a brother, yet you do
not belong to the clade. You want to use our memories to
destroy us." She had a sudden insight. "Is this war, then?"

He bowed. He was nearly naked, lit by the green light
of the Moon and the dimming glow of the slag that
stretched away in every direction. "Bravo," he said. "But it
has already begun. Perhaps it is even over by now; after

all, we are twenty thousand light-years above the plane of
the Galactic disc, thirty-five thousand light-years from the
hub of your Empire. It will take you that long to return.
And if the war is not over, then this will finish it."

She was astonished. Then she laughed. "What an imagination I have!"

He bowed again, and said softly, "You made this world
from your imagination, but you did not imagine me."

And he went somewhere else.

H*er machines could* not tell her where he had gone; she
called upon all the machines in the world, but he was no
longer on the Earth. Nor was he amongst the fleet of ships
which had carried the guests—in suspended animation, as
frozen embryos, as codes triply engraved in gold—to the
world she had created for the gathering.

There were only two other places he could be, and she
did not think he could have gone to the sun. If he had, then
he would have triggered the machine at the core, and destroyed her and everyone else in the subsequent supernova.

So she went to the Moon.

She arrived on the farside. The energies he had used
against her suggested that he had his own machines, and
she did not think that he would have hidden them in full
view of the Earth.

The machines which she had instructed to recreate the
Earth for the one hundred years of the gathering had recreated the Moon, too, so that the oceans of the Earth would
have the necessary tides; it had been easier than tangling
gravithic resonances to produce the same effect. It had
taken little extra effort to recreate the forests which had
cloaked the Moon for a million years, between the first fal-
tering footsteps and the abandonment of the Earth.

It was towards the end of the long Lunar night. All
around, blue firs soared up for hundreds of meters, cloaked
in wide fans of needles that in the cold and the dark had
drooped down to protect the scaly trunks. The gray rocks

were coated in thin snow, and frozen lichens crunched underfoot. Her machines scattered in every direction, quick as thought. She sat down on top of a big rough boulder and waited.

It was very quiet. The sky was dominated by the triple-armed pinwheel of the Galaxy. It was so big that when she looked at one edge she could not see the other. The Arm of the Warrior rose high above the arch of the Arm of the Hunter; the Arm of the Archer curved in the opposite direction, below the close horizon. Star clusters made long chains of concentrated light through the milky haze of the galactic arms. There were lines and threads and globes and clouds of stars, all fading into a general misty radiance dissected by dark lanes which barred the arms at regular intervals. The core was knitted from thin shells of stars in tidy orbits concentrically packed around the great globular clusters of the heart stars, like layers of glittering tissue wrapped around a heap of jewels.

Every star had been touched by humankind. Existing stars had been moved or destroyed; millions of new stars and planetary systems had been created by collapsing dust clouds. A garden of stars, regulated, ordered, tidied. The Library held memories of every star, every planet, every wonder of the old untamed Galaxy. She was beginning to realize that the gathering was not the start of something new, but the end of five million years of Galactic colonization.

After a long time, the machines came back, and she went where they told her.

It was hidden within a steep-sided crater, a castle or maze of crystal vanes that rose in serried ranks from deep roots within the crust, where they collected and focused tidal energy. He was at its heart, busily folding together a small spacecraft. The energy of the vanes had been greatly depleted by the fight, and he was trying to concentrate the remainder in the motor of the spacecraft. He was preparing to leave.

Her machines rose up and began to spin, locking in resonance with the vanes and bleeding off their store of energy. The machines began to glow as she bounded down the steep smooth slope towards the floor of the crater, red-hot, white-hot, as hot as the core of the sun, for that was where they were diverting the energy stored in the vanes.

Violet threads flicked up, but the machines simply absorbed that energy too. Their stark white light flooded the crater, bleaching the ranks of crystal vanes.

She walked through the traps and tricks of the defenses, pulled him from his fragile craft and took him up in a bubble of air to the neutral point between the Moon and the Earth.

"Tell me," she said. "Tell me why you came here. Tell me about the war."

He was surprisingly calm. He said, "I am a first generation clone, but I am on the side of humanity, not the transcendents. Transcendent clades are a danger to all of the variety within and between the civilizations in the Galaxy. At last the merely human races have risen against them. I am just one weapon in the greatest war ever fought."

"You are my flesh. You are of my clade."

"I am a secret agent. I was made from a single cell stolen from you several hundred years before you set off for this fake Earth and the gathering of your clade. I arrived only two years ago, grew my power source, came down to steal the memory core and kill you. Although I failed to kill you before, we are no longer in the place where you draw your power. Now—"

After a moment in which nothing happened, he screamed in frustration and despair. She pitied him. Pitied all those who had bent their lives to produce this poor vessel, this failed moment, although all the power, the intrigues and desperate schemes his presence implied were as remote from her as the politics of a termite nest.

She said, "Your power source is not destroyed, but my machines take all its energy. Why did your masters think us dangerous?"

"Because you would fill the Galaxy with your own kind. Because you would end human evolution. Because you will not accept that the Universe is greater than you can ever be. Because you refuse to die, and death is a necessary part of evolution."

She laughed. "Silly little man! Why would we accept limits? We are only doing what humanity has always done. We use science to master nature just as man-apes changed their way of thinking by making tools and using fire. Humanity has always striven to become more than it is, to grow spiritually and morally and intellectually, to go up to the edge and step over it."

For the first time in a million years, those sentiments did not taste of ashes. By trying to destroy her, he had shown her what her life was worth.

He said, "But you do not change. That is why you are so dangerous. You and the other clades of transhumans have stopped humanity evolving. You would fill the Galaxy with copies of a dozen individuals who are so scared of physical death that they will do any strange and terrible thing to themselves to survive"

He gestured at the blue-white globe that hung beneath their feet, small and vulnerable against the vast blackness between galaxies.

"Look at your Earth! Humanity left it four million years ago, yet you chose to recreate it for this gathering. You had a million years of human history on Earth to choose from, and four and a half billion years of the history of the planet itself, and yet almost half of your creation is given over to a single century."

"It is the century where we became what we are," she said, remembering Rapha. "It is the century when it became possible to become transhuman, when humanity made the first steps beyond the surface of a single planet."

"It is the century you were born in. You would freeze all history if you could, an eternity of the same thoughts thought by the same people. You deny all possibilities but your own self."

He drew himself up, defiant to the last. He said, "My ship will carry the memory core home without me. You take all, and give nothing. I give my life, and I give you this."

He held up something as complex and infolded as the throat of an orchid. It was a vacuum fluctuation, a hole in reality that when inflated would remove them from the Universe. She looked away at once—the image was already burned in her brain—and threw him into the core of the sun. He did not even have a chance to scream.

Alone in her bubble of air, she studied the wheel of the Galaxy, the ordered pattern of braids and clusters. Light was so slow. It took a hundred thousand years to cross from one edge of the Galaxy to the other. Had the war against her empire, and the empires of all the other transcendents, already ended? Had it already changed the Galaxy, stirred the stars into new patterns? She would not know until she returned, and that would take thirty-five thousand years.

But she did not have to return. In the other direction was the limitless Universe, a hundred billion galaxies. She hung there a long time, watching little smudges of ancient light resolve out of the darkness. Empires of stars wherever she looked, wonders without end.

We will fight the war, she thought, and we shall win, and we will go on forever and ever.

And went down, found the bar near the beach. She would wait until the old man came in, and buy him a drink, and talk to him about his dream of the lions.

Naturals

Gregory Benford

The last few stories have shown rather optimistic scenarios for the Post-Singularity future, including those in which humans have been gifted with vast new powers and abilities and lead lives of wealth and abundance. But, of course, there are more pessimistic scenarios for the fate of humanity on the far side of Singularity as well, including the one that follows, in which human beings as we know them today have become obsolete, and their immensely superior successors don't intend to cut them any slack . . .

Gregory Benford is one of the modern giants of the field. His 1980 novel, Timescape, *won the Nebula Award, the John W. Campbell Memorial Award, the British Science Fiction Association Award, and the Australian Ditmar Award and is widely considered to be one of the classic SF novels of the last two decades. His other novels include* Beyond Jupiter, The Stars in Shroud, In the Ocean of Night, Against Infinity, Artifact, Across the Sea of Suns, Great Sky River, Tides of Light, Furious Gulf, Sailing Bright Eternity, Cosm, Foundation's Fear, *and* The Martian Race. *His short work has been collected in* Matter's End, Worlds Vast and Various, *and* Immersion and Other Short Novels; *his essays have been assembled in a nonfiction collection,* Deep Time. *His most recent book is the novel* Beyond Infinity. *Coming up is another novel,* The Sunborn. *Benford is a professor of physics at the University of California, Irvine.*

At times Dawn thought that she was, well, a bit too intense. She seemed to have too much personality for one person and yet not enough for two.

Perhaps the cause lay in her upbringing? She had been most attentively raised by her Meta, an ancient term for the meta-family of loosely related people clustered around her biological father and mother. A Meta provided an overview, a larger vision of how to grow up.

The Meta had spotted her as a wild card, early on. It made no difference. Though hers, the Hard River Meta, was entirely, deliberately populated by Naturals—those without deep-seated connections to external machine intelligences—not many were Originals. Dawn was an Original of particularly primordial type, based on genes that had great vintage. Other Originals carried genes that had passed through revisions so many times that, in comparison, Dawn's suite was a fossil.

This gave her a kind of status. Not many Originals walked the Earth, though the historians who pestered her early education said there had once been billions of them afoot.

Billions! There were hardly a tenth that many now in all Earthly humanity. Not that she cared much about such numbers; few in her time bothered to scale the heights of analysis that the ancient civilizations had climbed, marked as their own, and finally abandoned as too chilly, remote and inhuman.

She cared far more for things close by, not abstractions. That was the gift of living in Hard River Meta—the natural world, custom-made for Naturals. They had enough technology to be comfortable, but did not waste time tending to it. Nobody much cared about events beyond their horizon. She had dozens of good friends and saw them daily. Children had jobs that meant something and nobody lorded it over others. Leadership rotated. Her life was one of small, steady delights.

She was happy, but. The filling in of the rest of that sentence would, she knew quite early, occupy the rest of her life. And she knew even then that the things she sought in life could disappear even as she reached for them, the way a fist went away when she opened her hand.

She suspected her antic energy came from a heavy genetic legacy. As an Original, she knew herself to be something of a hothouse plant, and not an orchid, either. More like a cactus, feverishly flowering under the occasional passing shower. Anyone who showered her with attention got her one-plus-some personality, ready or not. She wore people out.

Especially, she tired her fellow Originals, in their orderly oatmeal lives. She suspected that she carried some Supra genes, or maybe some of the intermediate breeds of human that had been in vogue through the last several hundred million years. She tried to find out if this might be so, and hit the stone wall of Meta security, whose motto in most matters genetic was Best Not to Know.

So she watched herself for telltale signs of intermediate forms. Nobody would help her, and she was too close to herself to be objective—and who wasn't? A stutter she developed at age nine—could that be a telltale? She worried endlessly. Bit off fingernails, even when they were part of her extendible tools. Then the stutter went away. Another telltale?

She felt as though she might very well spend the rest of her life with her button nose pressed against the glass of a room where she should be, only she couldn't find the door.

Her Meta never told her exactly who her parents were. She only knew that some pair among the 60 or so in her Meta had given birth to her, genetically. Just which pair? She sometimes wondered. It was usually reassuring that the genetic parents often did not themselves recall—and sometimes, not reassuring at all.

But then, growing up was not supposed to be easy. A woman in her Meta once said to her, "It's the toughest work you'll ever do." For a long while Dawn had thought this an exaggeration. Now she was not so sure she could even do it.

The troubling question was, when was growing up over? Maybe never.

Supras were around as (unneeded) reminders that some

people really were better than you. Worse, better in ways
that were not even easy to put a finger on—a feature she
had noted in adults, when she was just a kid. Even the
Supra children of her age were daunting. They ignored her,
of course.

The means of making a fresh person were so complex
that old ideas like simple parenting, with strictly assigna-
ble designer DNA, were useless. The Meta loved her,
brought her to the verge of first maturity, and so fell heir to
the usual blame for the traumas everyone suffered just in
getting that far.

Many women in her Meta mothered Dawn, as time
came available and their interest allowed. Some years it
would be smiling, big-breasted Andramana, and other
years it would be lean, cool, analytical Iratain. Others,
too—maybe half a dozen, each fine in their moments, then
receding into the background as others came to the fore.

The Meta's men provided fathering, too, but here the
usual Meta scheme went awry. She was supposed to gain
from multiple fatherings, to see what men were like in general, and work on her attachment strategies in light of this.
So much for theory.

By accident she learned that her genetic father had left
the Meta for undisclosed reasons when she was three years
old. She remembered some dim sensations of him—a dark
musk, deeply resonant voice, and whiskers (an affectation,
apparently quite ancient). That was all, but it was enough.

So, thinking it absolutely natural, she awaited his return. She dreamed about it—a weighty presence descending from the sky, usually, like angry thunderheads
brimming with ribbed light. So she made herself wonderful for him, anticipating his grand return. Occasionally a
new male would join the Meta, and she always wondered
if maybe this new set of smells and sounds was her One
True Father.

She could not be sure, of course, because the Meta kept
fatherhood and motherhood secret. Not so much because it
was hugely significant, though. Just policy. People would

put too much weight on those old, simple connections, so best be done with them.

The Meta felt that such genetic details were totally beside the point. What mattered, truly, was the Meta and its work. Humans did not reproduce like animals, after all, anchored in primordial musk.

Dawn wasn't having any of this, though she never said so. Her gut feelings won out over all inherited wisdom. She simply kept making herself wonderful for him, sure he would show up. And of course, when he did, she would know.

Her true mother might be within an arm's reach at any moment, in the milling Meta culture, but that had no claim on her attention. Her mother's identity was a conventional puzzle, dulled by overuse. Father, now there was true singing mystery.

He grew daily in her imagination. She loved him, she worshipped him, she built whole stories around his exploits. *Dad's Dangerous Days*, Chapter 37.

By this time, no man who ever came into the Meta ever matched the specifications of Her Father, so she was quite sure that he had never returned. She sat dutifully through the ritual experiences of a Meta upbringing, honestly enjoying them but knowing deep down that they were preliminaries to the moment when she would really know, down deep—when her Father returned.

Somehow, as her years stacked up, this yearning never fastened upon her Mother. She did wonder still which of the women of the Meta might be her Mother, but the issue did not have heft, did not wrap itself in the shadowy shroud of the Father. Obviously. Though she sometimes wondered why this was so.

When she spoke about it with any of the adults in her Meta, they carefully reasoned with her and it all seemed straightened out, crystal clear until she left the room. Then she would run free again, down the hallways of her mind, banging on doors, ready with her Father Story to tell.

She had noticed early on that everyone had a story to

tell, and not about Fathers. So she got one, too. She was just another Original, a genetic form roughly close to the variety that had started civilization off, so long ago that to express it took an exponential notation.

Her story was about the Father, of course, only cloaked in Meta language. Her life story did not quite seem to belong to her, though. She used it to get close to people, and she did care about them . . . but relating ostensibly personal sub-stories about herself seemed to be like offering them for barter. In return for . . . what? She was not sure.

So people—first from her Meta, then from allied Metas—came into her life, shaped it, and departed, their bags already packed. She wondered if everyone experienced life this way—that others came in, introduced themselves, exchanged confidences, and then milled around in her life until they found an exit. She valued them terribly at the time, but they left only smudged memories.

After a while she started dining out on the delightful details of people she knew, things they did. Other people were so much easier to talk about. She had sharpened her powers of observation, looking for her Father. The step from Watcher to Critic was easy, fun. People were the most complex things in the world, ready-made for stories. Exotica like the slow-walking croucher trees and skin-winged floater birds were fun, but in the end had no stories. The natural world didn't, usually. She suspected that civilization had been invented to make more stories.

And after a while, she came to feel that most others deserved her implied tribute: they really were more interesting than she was. Sometimes she felt like saying to strangers, "Hello, and welcome to my anecdote."

The electric leer of artfully crafted memory guided her. People remembered each other because they recalled stories, for stories made the person. With the myriad ways to remember, from embedded inboards to external agent-selves, there were endless fertile ways to sort and filter and rewrite the stories that were other people's lives. At times, she soon noticed, people constructed stories that were

missing parts, as if the business of being themselves did
not hold their full attention. Shoddy work. She was much,
much better at it.

She was intent upon the sliding scale that people
showed her. Boys her age would ooze from arrogant to impressive in the span of a single sentence, and then back
down that slope again—and she was never sure just why.

At times she was not quite certain who she was. When
she was with the boys she knew growing up, she often
thought that she was more alive for being with them. He
thinks, therefore I am. Afterward, she would enjoy the
feeling of having been with a boy and come through it all
right, free of awful embarrassing moments, and most especially, without seeing in them The Father.

Instead, she had the odd feeling of being disconnected:
This will be fun to remember. Not: *This is fun now.*

She had the usual sexual adventures. Kissing was sometimes like devouring the other person, savouring the sweet,
swarthy head meat, no sauce. Bright grins, dark excesses.
Even then, though, she came to feel that lust lacked, well,
depth. Amid the mad moment, she would sometimes think,
This reminds me of the time I felt déjà vu.

But if you couldn't learn from experience, what was
left? She talked about this with one of the older women in
her Meta, who said dryly, "The best definition of intelligence is the ability to learn not from your mistakes, but
from others'." Dawn went away puzzled. She needed not
advice, but a Road Map of Life.

So she resolved: until she knew where she stood, she
would continue lying down. It certainly beat running away.
That way she had tried, too: hard him, hesitant her.

There was no cure for such injuries. Dawn endured
them because she assumed that, after the ordeals of adolescence were done, she would get her reward—the clear,
smooth calm and blithe confidence that adults surely had.
After all, they looked self-assured, didn't they? Especially
the Supras, who were more than adults.

The few moments when she could tell an adult was un-

easy, or awkward, or embarrassed, were excruciating. She
made it a point to avoid the fallen adult after that happened; just spending time with them would bring the memory into foreground, risking even more of the same.

So she persisted in her faith, which was, of course, not
a dry slate of dictates, but A Story: that, first thing of all,
she would pass through schools, then find something she
loved doing, meet men and mate with them (no genetic
contracts implied, though), experience raptures and delights unknown to mere young people, survive those and
learn from them, and then generally move with growing
serenity through the ever-expanding world.

She did manage to finish school. That was as far as her
Life Game Plan worked.

Adolescence came upon Dawn unannounced.

The various shades of humanity above Naturals had dispensed with such sudden advents and halts in the body's
evolution. Nature's unwanted punctuations, they sniffed.
They could orchestrate their tides and rhythms, like an artfully managed story. So she had little warning of the Natural progressions, especially the firm events of an Original
such as she. Menstruation arrived with startling, well,
frankness. She had senso'd about it, of course, but the sudden flow made her think of a wound, not a grand overture
to heart-stopping romance.

When it first happened, she dipped her head as if in
prayer to natural forces, knees knocked together to hold in
the embarrassment. As if this were not a blossoming, but
punishment for a transgression. She fell to her knees,
hands linking fingers, head tilted up to a God she did not
believe in. Whatever God made of this, He/She/It did not
help. The dark hot leaden burn refused to go away.

There was a simple pharmaceutical cure for all this, of
course, and one of the Meta women offered it. Dawn automatically rejected it without knowing why.

One Original frontier crossed, she awaited the Virginity

Event. The Meta was easy-going about sex. With nearby other Metas it gave scrupulously clear classes and instructional aids. These were carefully not erotic, but in their clinical cheer also did not give any good reason to do The Thing at all. Abstraction prevailed.

At this time she invented her own, interior Theory of Virginity. In her model, virginity was not a single thing, abolished by a single act, but a continuum. She could give away parts of it. After all, wasn't she a many-sided person, even if a mere Natural?

With other Naturals she had tussled quite agreeably on lounging chairs and in cars, preferring the outdoors. But she had not dispensed any of the fractions in her V Inventory, as she termed it to her girl friends.

She had avoided the company of most young women in her Meta, who seemed more attached to the trappings of the world, most of them on their way to being trapped into an attachment, already ordained by the Meta. For Meta-reasons, of course: types Naturally attracted each other, as the conventional wisdom had it. But Dawn never got much of a buzz from the men of her supposed type. Nor from those in the nearby classes of human. She had an arranged meeting with a man of the Sigmas, once, which stood in her mind for the whole round-Dawn-square-men puzzle. Sigmas were usually nude, and as she bandied nonsense with this one, she could not help but notice that he had no apparent genitalia. There was nothing there at all, not even hair.

He saw her glance and said blandly, "It's inside."

"It?"

"The ancient apparatus had several parts, true, but ours is integrated into one shaft." He smiled, as if describing a mildly interesting toy. "The Original design was not elegant. And the danger!" His eyebrows shot up.

"I thought the, uh, older gadget had at least two uses."

"Of course, but we do not excrete through ours."

"Uh, you . . ."

"Use the rear exit for both."

"And the machinery comes out to play only at recess?"

He laughed quite easily. She was blushing and wished she could stop it, but such control was not available to Originals. "Only as needed, to prevent damage. The shaft generates the semen as well."

She kept her eyes resolutely on his. "No need to have those messy add-ons dangling out in the air?"

"In you Originals that was a design feature to keep the semen cool. We simply adjust our blood flow, lowering the internal temperature in their vicinity."

She kept a purely dispassionate expression on her face, afraid to let her lips move for fear they would lapse into a deranged leer, an O of astonishment, or something even worse. Shouting, *Show me your plumage!* for example. Or *Design feature? Seems more like a bug.* But firmly fixing her face, she said instead, "Is it the same . . . otherwise?"

For the first time he displayed a knowing grin. "Larger."

"Where have I heard that before?" Though in fact she hadn't.

"To give us an advantage."

"At?"

"Social and biological." His tone was bland but the grin stayed put.

"I'm just all a-twitter."

Absolutely flat: "You should be."

"You're too sure of yourself."

"And you, too unsure." With that he evaporated, turning away and into the spongelike crowd. She felt put down and also lucky, to not know what his next line was.

So it was with the other classes and orders of greater-than-thou humans. They were almost jaunty in their arid certainty that their variation on the grand theme was the best, or at least better than the first. Their men plainly felt that she should be bowled over by the chance to enjoy their obliquely-referred-to talents, endowments, or superior wiring diagrams. Their women twisted luscious true-red mouths (no cosmetics!) in sour amusement, sure that she

was an upstart tart who had wandered out of her rightful
level.

Even if they were all scrupulously correct, and they did
have pots of advanced abilities, charm was not one of
them. The best aspect of their company was that at least it
was not addictive.

For a long time she was terribly aware that everyone knew.
They knew—that she, as an Original, was going through
the primordial fever-pitch of oncoming sexual urges, and
could do nothing about it. Helpless, swept down hormonal
river.

Other times, she was proud of it. She wanted to shout in
crowded rooms, "I'm following Nature! Watch!"—and then
do nothing, just stand there brimming with primitive life.

She never did that, of course.

What she did was an intellectual version, in a way, of
declaring her Naturalness. Her Originality. She sought out
and took an underling position at the Library of Life. In the
Vaults.

They deserved the capital letter—vast, forbidding underground repositories of human history. Though the continents continued to grind and shove away at each other,
the Ancients (a collective noun covering more time than
linear thinking coul. encompass) had chosen below-
ground burial for their legacies. An unconscious repetition
of the habit of burying the dead, probably. Primitive.

And there, amid the claustro-corridors far from sunlight, she met Kurani.

He loomed large. Their first job was to unearth a slab
that carried intricate data encoded in nuclear spins, a
method Kurani termed "savage nouveaux." They trained
bright beams upon the flinty surface and machines tracked
across the slab, clicking, measuring, sucking up history.

As Kurani's shadow passed before one of the spotlights
she felt herself momentarily eclipsed, a chill stealing over
her suddenly prickly skin. They had just opened a new

Vault and technology hovered in the air like flies. These micro-readers would snap up any data-dust that escaped the slab. Amid the buzz he skated on rippling legs, the Supra carriage gliding smooth and sure. Level, hydraulic, supple.

"Are the indices notified?" he asked of the air.

Nobody seemed sure who was addressed, so she said, "Done already. Dates unclear—"

"A specialty scheme?"

"It seems so," she managed.

He orbited toward her, his size bringing full night to shroud her. "Why did so many of the Ancients think they should redate everything? That some birth or death or collapse of a civilization was so important."

She ventured, adding to his sentence, "That, of course, all human history would ever after be marked from that time."

"Exactly" His smile brought the sun back to her shadowed self.

"So what all those eras have in common is the automatic assumption that they are special."

"Our fault as well." He smiled slightly, turning his fullbore gaze upon her and it was like a second spotlight in the narrow Vault.

"You think time begins with you?" It was not a very bright comment but she had to say something, his eyes were not letting her slide away from them.

"When we meet people we can't see them because we are so busy looking at ourselves to be sure we look all right, in case this should be an important somebody we are just meeting."

To this avalanche of astonishing self-revelation (or was it, with the "we"?) she shot back, "Me too. I'm thinking that I really suddenly see this person, when what I'm seeing is me reflected in their eyes. Me, proving yet again that I am quick and fascinating and that I *can*."

—and then, of course, she saw that he had been speaking aloud what he read in her. Very Supra. But still—

He laughed, sunrise again. "So you almost envy people who are meeting you? Because they're getting the full you?"

She nodded furiously, not giving herself enough time to see that she was sledding downhill without a clue. And picking up speed. "I keep wanting to meet somebody who is completely on, the way I can be maybe five minutes in a year."

He turned just slightly, as if a shot had nearly winged him. "The way you are right now."

How could he know so much? "Oh, this is just warming up."

A lie, and his quizzical lift of a lip conveyed that he knew it. She was not just downsloping now, but plunging. Skiing on the moment. Maybe big black rocks up ahead, but—it felt glorious.

Still, she couldn't let him have the last word, even an unspoken one. "I always wanted to be somebody," she said. A pause. "Maybe I should have been more specific."

To his credit—even if he did have a huge account with her already—he laughed. Loudly. Big.

The trick, she saw, was to have anything to talk about that was wholly hers. To make the dumb stuff she had believed or done seem at least ardent and naïve, not just boneheaded and Original.

Then, too, there was the toiling, earnest quality to even conversation. Some Supras, far over the horizon somewhere, might spend their vast days on haute fluff, but here all was earnest. Even laughter had a purpose: relieving stress.

From him, weirdly, she learned to relax. To smooth the stress, at least. An Original working among Supras was a mouse foraging for seeds among elephant feet.

(And there still were elephants. They supervised a lot of the heavy manual work. More supple than machines, savvy in the ways living things carried in their guts, they worked

joyously, singing, dancing late into the night. She thought
they were an excellent, unlikely idea and was astonished to
find that they were more ancient than humans, and not invented at all.)

He had methods of soothing the jangled nerveworks.
Technical ones—inboards, flex triggers to the neuromus-
culars, tricks even the Supras found necessary. She was
shocked to find he did not even know the chemical Original methods, some as strange as alcohol. Their molecules
locked agreeably into his receptors, he found, with a sizzle
and a shake.

This broke the ice between them, and then the pattern
was straightforward. The inevitable came. Between breeds
and castes there is always a certain fascination, longing
looks cast both up and down the staircase of genetic gradi-
ent. He was the primary, she the satellite. He knew centuries, she was not full grown. She learned to relax even
more.

Right away he took command of the situation, of her. A
Supra utterly at ease, a king. Deep-bass words that rang
like bells in her hollow heart. His face, a smile in it somewhere. So many nuances crowded into that classic expression, it was hard for her to make out the significance of a
slightly arched eyebrow, the flashing of his earlobes as
they recorded her image, smell, glandular secretions—all
for a processor sitting somewhere maybe on the other side
of the world, but feeding Kurani all he needed to know to
assess the situation. To assess her.

He had her. They both knew it. So they then filled the
rest of their first intimate meeting, and then a drink, and
then a meal, with fodder-talk. Facts, data, life trajectories
sketched out in names of cities and schools and Meta-
connections. Sniffing.

All through it she felt as if he were saying something
else, or rather more, that subtext flitted through his words
like birds, lofty and quick, beings of the moment, gone if
not glimpsed.

Uneasily and yet, she supposed, quite Naturally, she

sensed that he had arranged all this. Had stalked her, maybe. But in offhand fashion, seemingly without effort, invisibly—and she knew then that he would have her.

In that moment she felt another fraction of her Virginity Inventory vanish, though there had been not a jot of the physical, no act beyond a lifted corner of his ample mouth. She could not take her eyes off that mouth.

He knew it, too. He reached across the table to take her hand. "Simple fingers." His voice resonated deep notes down to her toes.

She blushed—another Natural response she made a note to get edited out immediately. (Could it be?) She extended three of her tool augmentations through her two shortest fingers, saying lightly, "Not entirely." The web-sensors that wrapped around her thumbs went without saying.

"Do they feel as supple?" He watched her eyes, not the finger display.

"As —? How would I know?"

"You could try a recant, you know. Experience what the higher adaptations are like."

Yes, he had actually said "higher" even though it was very rude. Or maybe because it was.

After the meal they walked the suddenly narrow corridors. Chiselled from rock, the walls gave back everything enhanced. Their boots rang against the walls like snapped fingers, calling her to attention. The Library air hung clammy with time beyond knowing, humid with the pungent breath that she couldn't quite get enough of. With him beside her the long avenues shrank, seen down the wrong end of a telescope. When he stopped and drew her to him it was entirely like being gathered up. She felt herself blown up a mountainside, driven by an overpowering wind.

"Wait," she said, and instantly disliked herself.

So much of him, so little of her. With a rich velvety sound he slid his hand down her back. He asked where she lived but it was a formality, of course. He could get it in an

eye-flick from his inboards. But she whispered the truth
back to him in words gone moist. When they got to her
spare, scrupulous room she was paralyzed with dread and
hope and fever dreams.

She sent a quick spurt to turn on the lights, dim, and he
caught it, said "No," and countered her signal to the room
with an electromagnetic tweak. A command from the king.

His pushing through the door into the next room, into
private spaces, sent her fever rising thick and warm into
her throat. He reached down and unslipped the side of her
suit. It peeled off and she said, "Prehistoric," hoping it
would come over as a joke, but as the word left her, she
meant it.

"So you are," he answered, moving all over her.

Stress fell away like her negligée. As if she had one on.

The next thing she felt was his hot breath between her
legs and an answering O from inside her. O, oh, oh yes,
yearning to be a zero. I'll be O and you be . . .

A fraction, soon gone. Well spent.

S*he went to* work in his division. Her days passed in an
aura of sultry air, short of breath, high excited trills echoing in her. The work was good. At meals she ate with many
varieties of humans, though here they were mostly Supras.
She enjoyed the food and the talk and sometimes she was
allowed to speak herself.

She caught fragments of the unspoken, which seemed
to comprise most of what was getting said. Someone referred to herself in the unspoken and she caught the phrase
"—manages to be naked with her clothes on—" About her,
the verb-signifier said. It came with clear Supra uptones
but was obliquely a compliment. Or she took it so.

So she worked to fit in. This was easier than she had
expected.

The essential trait all types of humans relied on was
time-binding. To work in the Library meant labouring in
the shadow of Time Itself, after all. So to get a grasp at all

took knowing how humans saw the world. Humans of
whatever vintage.

The span of a single life was quite great, taking into account the contacts with the old and young, who extended
one's reach fore and aft in time. Even among the ancients,
in fragile bodies unaided by technology, the span was a
few centuries.

Now it was many millennia. Prehistory back when life
was astonishingly short—a few decades!—still had
spanned 10,000 generations. In years that was not much. In
generations, it was respectable, comparable to the lifetimes
of the advanced societies, when people lived aeons and
had plenty of time to get bored with their relatives. With
their friends. With, sometimes, everything—exit stage left,
in haste.

Prehistory had been the great shaping time of primordial, first-form humanity—the Naturals. No surprise, then,
that Naturals' own opinions about what was important in
life were moulded far more by prehistory than by their trivial experience of early, simple civilization.

From that vast era Naturals got their basic perceptions.
Their leaders who understood this went far. Naturals felt
best in groups of a hundred or so, and even better if only a
few dozen were involved. Hunting parties had been about
that size, even for the big, long-extinct game. Many important institutions were of the same rough scale—the ancient village, governing councils of nations, commanding
élites of vast armies, teams playing games, orchestras,
family fests. All human enterprises that worked were of
that size, and nearly everything that failed was not.

So the Library had to be organized using this bedrock
wisdom. Otherwise, it would fail.

Civilization had long maintained the appearance of
such communal closeness, in small units people could
manage. Societies had evolved that could stack such social
nuggets into vaster larger arrays. A squad of ten worked
well together, and united with ten other squads could do far
more. Those ten who commanded squads could then meet

in a room and make up a squad themselves, and so on up a pyramid that could sum the labours of billions.

All this was built on the firm foundation of primate bonding patterns. If the pattern broke down at the bottom, it gave a rabble. Loss of scale at the top led to dictators, who always fell in the long run. Democracy emerged and worked because it let people form groups they could actually manage and like.

The Library was democratic, but. After all, there were dozens of variations on the Great Human Theme in the staff. The Library needed them all because their forms had all contributed to the Library. Fathoming what Library records meant demanded intense co-operation. Every form of human had to be respected. Acknowledged.

Democratic, but. The Supras were still, everybody agreed, the very best.

She started working in serial languages. Easy stuff, suitable for Originals. She could almost hear Kurani thinking that, in her hyperactive imagination.

Serial writings were a persistent human tradition. Many Library workers felt them to be somehow more authentic than the later methods that directly integrated with the nervous system. Dawn had little experience with serials, though. How quaint, she thought at first, even for a Library: to set down symbols one after another and make the eyes (or in one case, the fingers, and another, the nose) manufacture meaning from them, seen one at a time. Piecework.

Nobody did that any more, though of course speech was still serial. No subspecies had ever tried to make the throat and vocal chords perform in the way the eyes could, ferrying vast gouts of information at a glance. Making sound waves do that faced both a bandwidth problem and a fleshy one.

The throat was a string instrument, resonant but limited. Humans could not drink and speak at the same time, a

design flaw not shared by the other ancient primates. Yet it
was one that nobody had ever overcome. People still
strangled at banquets, appropriately dressed in formal gear
for their funerals—all due to a faulty collaboration between eating and speaking.

She got interested in serial methods and delved back
into the very earliest. The most ancient, the "Arbic" notation, had a shrunken 26 letters, whereas even the ancients
knew that something around 40 speech-sounds and
phonemes were optimum. The earliest forms even used
something she had to struggle to understand—letters with
two cases, big and small, with almost no value added to the
doubling of symbols.

Later languages dropped these cultural carbuncles.
Down through the myriad millennia, letters assumed
shapes to show the position taken by the vocal organs
(which varied) in articulating the sounds. Those quickest
to draw evoked the most frequent sounds.

She got the idea of serial writing right away. Humans
liked the step-by-step nature of stories, narrative momentum,
and sentences carried one forward in a pleasurable way

Still, she was glad to get back into the hohlraum. It was
a wondrous tool that shaped itself to her (in-)abilities. Supple, subtle, sly. Deftly it brought her intense, layered
knowledge. After reading the serial languages, the
hohlraum was like the experience of having read. The
memories of the serial texts were there, but reachable instantly at many levels.

The hohlraum flew like a bird over a rumpled landscape, spying all. It could see the geological layers beneath
that bore in massive strata the assumptions, histories, and
worldviews that slumbered beneath the surface text. It
could sense the warp and weave of time, as well. Like conceptual lava, information flowed up to the surface, seeping
hot and new, there to cool and congeal into ravines of reasoning and mountains of conclusion. In the long sweep of
time those peaks and valleys would in turn crumble, their
continental wisdoms collide, rumbling into dust.

All this came into her mind in the slow pace of gravid change, its majesty impressing her. This was the lot of being human over the long eras, in which whole grand cultures were mere mayflies.

She taught herself to not mind when he vanished for days.

Supras did that. They had other concerns, matters lying well beyond her conceptual horizons, yes, yes, she understood that.

It was as if, leaving, he turned out the light. Sex, having come rushing to her out of nowhere, rushed back. She worked.

Then he would return, send her a quirky smile. His tide came roaring back in. Her world blazed.

And when he appeared, it was always first things first. First, as in Original.

She liked his taste, and not merely his skin. He had kept the Original cock, a handsome wick indeed. No efficient Supra rig for him, no. She had seen it all before, of course, and there was to the entire act, up close, the quality of being attacked by a giant, remorseless snail. The whole arrangement seemed on the face of it unlikely, a temporary design that had gotten legislated into concrete. But it worked. Somehow. Wisdom of the ancients. Snail and swamp, who could have guessed?

Nothing was more Original than what humans of all brands called, with unthinking arrogance, *the out of doors*—as if all creation were defined by its location just outside where We lived. Kurani never used the term, but he certainly used the feelings.

He liked weather—the more, the better. They always slept outside when a storm of swollen, angry purple clouds came muscling over the horizon. As the heavens tore at each other, so did the humans. One powerful night, the thunder and lightning came closer and closer together, each booming roar like a commandment, which they followed to the letter. Afterward they lay exhausted and warm

and delightfully sweaty, listening to the storm shoulder its
way off into the mountains to command someone else. A
cleansing rain began to patter down on the balcony outside
with the indescribable rich smell a good rain brought to a
fine moment.

"Whoosh! Enough to make you believe in God," he
said.

"Or that we and the weather are geared together."

"Same thing."

It *wasn't all* about sex, either.

She firmly believed that people had, as a species, an in-
nate drive to mesh with others—that the sense of self
emerged from a web of intimate relations. The Supras
seemed to feel all humans were the outcome of impersonal
drives like sex and envy; plus others they could not speak
about very well. Maybe they didn't want to reveal too
much. Kurani sometimes shrugged, that most hallowed of
gestures, as if to convey the gulf between them.

She clung to the precipice of that gulf, and sometimes
threw herself across. Or tried.

Yet she knew already that love could fade. Not so
much on its own, but from efforts of the people experiencing it—so intensely as to, well, to kill it. Love made
many naked, unsettled by longing. The pressure was always there. And oppositely, some felt too safe in a relationship and fantasized about something more racy. It
was terribly confusing.

Famously, Naturals longed for the touch of Arts, the
earliest artificial forms. She felt some of this herself. The
earliest human artifice lay in self-decoration—the attrac-
tion of the human assembly. Kurani termed this the lure of
simple skin: parts fitting together under a fleshy wrap that
served all the chores of clothes but renewed itself. She had
always been tantalized by the externals, but rumour had it
among her Meta that the internals were the truly amazing
portion of Art anatomy.

Well, maybe she would get around to them. There were very few humans recreated from the eras when human organs were shaped for artistic ends; only two in the Library. That variety had been quickly supplanted with better designs. Not of the Supra grade, but superior. Still, most such experimental forms after the earliest Arts were extinct. Fashion had its role to play, as well.

The longest-running human game lay not in self-ornamentation, but relationships. Kurani taught her a calmer way of looking at these things. This was his way of explaining what Dawn and he were about, under the covers.

In his view, the true deep human fantasy was the conviction of safety. Men believed their women were devoted, wives that their men were dependable. Both ignored contrary evidence. Both acted to fulfil the other's belief. When the whole collusive contrivance collapsed, each cried, "This is not the person I thought!" They had merely gotten trapped in the quicksand of protective grey each laid to trim the rampaging velocity of romantic love.

Even sex could develop this deadening, out of self-defence. Without a dull patina it was too vivid to sustain for long, dragging one into surrenders, losses of self, immersion in the rhythms and sensations of another. "Same reverse twist for aggression," he added cryptically.

She nodded. Love scared anyone. We primates reacted to threat with anger, so we got into fights without knowing why.

Dawn countered this with her simple sense that the Other should be an ideal mate. She felt better when she let herself see Kurani as more handsome and valuable than others thought him to be. Her dream man, personified in Kurani, would not let time or routine lessen the intensity of authentic experience. "You keep building sand castles even though you know the tide's coming in."

Their days were simple: work, study, love, sleep, then back to work. Sometimes love came right after work, even before dinner. And sometimes she thought that her need for love was really a mask over her desire for, well, sex.

But when she was in that moment, it was not so much like lust as it was like worship. Maybe what she sought in love was only symbolized by sex, and at the same time made real—something far more powerful: completion.

He had done this many times, she was sure of it. People routinely lived several centuries, and Kurani was even older. He had literally forgotten more than she knew.

One day he took her by the hand and led her into a disused corridor of the Library. He stood at one end far away, a tiny figure—and whispered words of unexpected tenderness that roared along the walls, amplified somehow by ancient acoustics. Into her ears came cherished phrases, ones she was sure she would remember all her life. The secret of these acoustic amplifiers had been long lost. But he knew just how to use it.

He was vast, yet he loved her, too—she knew this with granite conviction. She knew also that to him she must be a familiar type. Electrically primitive, but exhausting. She used that. She seduced him with her intensity, her one-plus-some personality. But she also unnerved him with the instant intimacy she offered, able to turn it on in the pivot of a second.

Their days were electric for her, in the vast Library, labouring in the long dry valley rimmed by snowcapped peaks. Her world was crisp and sure for the first time. Intoxicating, just to breathe the cutting air.

First loves were the fiercest, she realized. So it couldn't last. Fair enough. But there was nothing stopping her working on that.

And she was, right up until the attack.

The furies came in a savage, fire-bright moment.

It began with strange droplets coasting on the air, shimmering, murmuring. Floodlights had ringed a grey, chipped slab, where she worked with Kurani. They were opening out a repository of relicts from a time when interdimensional transport was possible. How, nobody knew.

The repository was described in a curious string of phrases from a long-dead language. There were spherical iso-boxes, too-long-duration containers from a society, Kurani said, that had reached the peak of mathematical wisdom—or so the meta-historians said.

The floating, humming motes distracted her. Unlike the familiar micro tech that pervaded the Library, performing tasks, these shifted and scintillated in the hard spotlight glare.

Kurani ignored them. His powers of concentration were vast and pointed. He had just discovered that these ancient people had used numbers not as nouns or adjectives, but to modify verbs, words of action. Instead of "see those three trees," they would say something like, "the living things manifesting treeness here act visibly as a collection divided to the extent of four."

And somehow this referred to the iso-boxes. Which brimmed with an odd glow.

She studied Kurani's furrowed brow as he struggled with this conceptual gulf. These ancients had used number systems that recognized three bases—10, 12, and 5—and were rooted in the body, with its five toes and six fingers. So grounded in the flesh, what insights did the ancients reach in far more rarefied pursuits? Scholars had already found a deep fathoming of the extra dimensions known to exist in the universe. The slab before Dawn and Kurani spoke of experiments in dimensional transport, all rendered in a strangely canted manner.

But the motes . . . As she recalled the fracturing moment, suddenly she looked up at a new source of light. The motes were tumbling in a field of amber glitter. Sharp blue shards of brilliance lanced into her eyes. The motes were not micro tech but *windows* into another place, where hard radiance rumbled and fought.

It all came from the iso-boxes. They contained some link to higher dimensions, she guessed, and when opened unleashed them.

She had turned to Kurani to warn him—

—and the world was sliced. Cut into thin parallel sheets, each showing a different part of Kurani, sectioned neatly by a mad geometer.

But this was not illusion, not a mere refraction in the air. He was divided, slashed crosswise. She could see into his red interior, organs working, pulsing. She stepped toward him—

Then came the fire, hot pain, and screaming. She remembered running. The motes swept after her, and she was trying to get away from the terrible screams. Only when she gasped for breath did she realize that the screams had come from her.

She had turned then, looking back down a long stony corridor that tapered to infinity—and Kurani was at the other end, not running. Impaled on a blade of light. Sliced. Writhing.

And to her shame, she had turned and run away. Without a backward glance. Terrified.

A*fter, the memory* always came sharply into her. The bare fossil outlines of later events swelled up, filling her throat, the past pressing to get out.

Finding a dozen of a neighbouring Meta cowering in a passageway, fidgeting with fear. They had to shout themselves hoarse in the thundering violence.

Then the booming eased away. Crackling energies came instead.

The other Originals said the dimensional attacks raged through all the valleys of the Library. They were being pursued by things beyond comprehension. Let the Supras fight it if they could.

They would be hunted like rats here. She agreed—they had to get out, into the forest.

The seething air in the passageway became prickly. A sound like fat frying grew near. No one could stand and wait for it.

She went down a side tunnel. The other Originals fled

toward the main passage. Better to run and hide alone, than in a straggling rabble. But the tunnel ceiling got lower as she trotted, then walked, finally duck-walked.

She cowered far back in the tunnel, alone in blackness. Stabs of virulent lightning forked in the distance and splashed the tunnel walls with an ivory glow. Getting closer. In one of the flashes she saw tiny designs in the tunnel wall. Her fingers found the pattern. Ancient, a two-tiered language. A . . . combination? Plan?

She extruded a finger into a tool wedge and tracked along the grooves. It was telling a tale of architectural detail she could not follow very well, reading at high speed through the tool. A sense-phrase in the middle of an extended brag about the design referred to a inlet or maybe outlet (a two-valence, anyway). Where?

More snapping flashes, emerald now. Nearer. Could they *hear* her?

She inched further into the tunnel. Her head bumped the ceiling; the rough bore was narrowing. In another quick glimmer, followed by an electrical snarl, she saw a web of symbol-tracks, impossible to follow. *So damn much history! Where's the door?*

She scrunched further in. The web tapered down into a shallow track and she got her finger wedge in. *Ah! Codes.* She twisted, probed—and the wall flopped open into another tunnel.

She crawled through, trying to be quiet. A glowing brown snake was coming down the tunnel. She slammed the curved hatch in its face.

Pitch black. At least the lightning had shown her what was going on. She sat absolutely still. Faint thunder and a trembling in the floor. This tunnel was round and—a soft breeze.

She crawled toward it. Not even height to duck-walk. The slight wind got stronger. Cool to her fevered brow.

Smells: dust, leaves? A dull thump behind her. She hurried, banging her knees—

—and spilled halfway out into clear air. Above, stars. A

drop of about her height, onto dirt. She reversed and dropped to the ground. Dirt. Flashes to the left. She went right.

She ran. Snapping crashes behind her. Dun shapes up ahead. Trees? A rising sucking sound behind. A brittle thrust of amber fire rushed over her left shoulder and shattered into a bush—exploding it into flames.

Trees—she dodged left. Faint screams somewhere.

The sucking sound again.

Into the trees, heels digging in hard. On the horizon the very sky was being sliced, veins opened. She could see into something red and sullen beyond, the sky of a world.

Another amber bolt, this time roasting the air near her. It veered up and ignited a crackling bower of fronds.

Screams getting louder. Up ahead? Glows there. She went right, down a gully, splashing across a stream. Not deep enough to cover her.

A spark sizzled down from the air into the trees up ahead. She went left and found a wall of brambles. Distant flickering gave her enough light to pick her way along, gasping. Around the brambles, into thick trees. She crossed the stream again. Deeper here. Downstream went back toward the open, toward the Library. She ran upstream. The sucking rush came stealing up behind. She dodged, ducked, dodged. *Stay near the stream.* If the water got deeper—

The pain swarmed over her and pushed her into blackness.

Later, she set out to search the forest further for bodies. This gave her strength despite what she dreaded finding.

She had enjoyed no steady lover, male or female, but she knew the other Originals who had worked in the Library. They had sported an ironic humour about their roles as Originals among the Supras, playing the role of the least gifted but well honoured surviving strains of primordial humans. There had been many wry jokes between them.

Not that she had been immune, of course. She had gloried in her affair with Kurani, been whispered about and envied and criticized, even insulted. Enormous fun.

The anonymous charred remains she found were a blessing, in a way. The fury was quite thorough. None had been left to rot. She could not identify them.

She searched systematically through the afternoon, finding only more scorched bodies. Even as she worked, she knew this was helping her. Better to act, not think.

Finally she stood looking down into a broad valley, tired, job done, planning where to go next. Alone.

"I trust you are all right," a deep voice said behind her.

Dawn whirled. A tall, blocky man stood on the outer deck of a brass-coloured craft that balanced silently in the air.

He had come upon her from behind without her noticing and this, more than his size and the silent power of his craft, told Dawn that she had no chance of getting away. Blinking against the sun glare, she saw that this was a Supra.

Another. It all came rushing up into her again, the smothered pain. Kurani.

And she put it away. There would be a time to feel it and that time was not now. The longing and passion had been part of becoming a young woman, a time she would treasure. Wondrous. That was over and she knew with a leaden suddenness that it would not come again. She could not let it.

And this Supra—why did he survive? When my love died?

Her head spun with wild emotions. She hated this Supra, she needed him, she wanted him to fold her in his long arms and take away the anguish.

Then she made herself put all that away, as well. Concentrate, the way Kurani did. *See what is before you.*

He carried all the advanced signatures: Big glossy eyes. Scalloped ears that could turn to capture sound. Enlarged trachea to help food bypass the windpipe better. Forward-tilted upper torso, lessening pressure on the spine. Backward-

curved neck with bigger vertebrae, counter-balancing the
close-ribbed chest. His casual amble along the deck of the
flyer told her that his knees could bend backward, muting
the grind of bones in sockets. Heavier bones, thicker skull,
an angular, glinting intelligence in the face.

The sight of him brought rushing back her memories of
Kurani. This man was slightly different, muscles lean and
planar, but of the same design-era. She gazed at him, the
yearning welling in her, and she forced it down. And after
what seemed to her like forever, forced out some words.
"I . . . yes, I am."

He smiled affably "One of our scouts finally admitted
that it was not sure all the bodies it saw were dead. I am
happy I decided to check its work."

·   As he spoke his ship settled gently near Dawn and he
stepped off without glancing at the ground. Despite his
bulk he moved with unconscious, springy lightness. She
noted abstractly that he used *I*, which Kurani seldom did.
Until now she had never wondered why.

She gestured behind her. "You came to bury my kind?"

"If necessary. I would rather save them."

"Too late for that."

He nodded as several emotions flickered across his
face—sadness, regret, firm resolve. "The scouts reported
some bodies, but all had been burned. You are all I have
found—delightfully alive."

Delightfully? The word was almost flirtatious. His calm
mildness was maddening. "Where *were* you Supras?
They—it, something from another dimension—hounded
us! Tracked us! Killed us all!"

Again his face showed a quick succession of emotions,
each too fleeting for her to read before the next crowded
in. Still he said nothing, though his mouth became a tight
line and his eyes moistened. He gestured at a pall of smoke
that still climbed on the far horizon.

Dawn followed his movement and said severely, "I
guessed you had to defend your own, but couldn't you
have, have . . ."

Her voice trailed away when she saw the pained twinge
constricting his face as her words struck home.

Then his mouth thinned again and he nodded. "All
along the Library valleys the dimensional cut destroyed.
One cannot tell whether the effect was a true attack, or a
left-over from antiquity."

Her anger, stilled for a moment by his vulnerability, returned like an acrid burn in the back of her throat. "We had
nothing to defend ourselves!"

"Did you think we had weapons?"

"Supras have everything!"

He sighed. "Few were useful. We protect through our
valiantly labouring machines, through the genius of our
past. These failed."

She felt an abyss between herself and this man. As a
Supra he had probably lived centuries; disaster was not
news any more, apparently.

"I am Fanak," he said, as though anyone would know
who he was. His casual confidence told her even more than
the name, for he was well known. She responded to his
questions about the last few days with short, precise answers. She had rarely seen Supras, growing up. Kurani had
come as a revelation. Apparently he had been unusual; this
one was not winning her over.

But as they rose with smooth acceleration Dawn
gaped, not attempting to hide her surprise. Within moments she saw the lands where she had lived and
laboured reduced to a mere spot in a vastly larger canvas.
As a young girl she had flown this high, but now the
magnitude of the Supras' latest labours became obvious.
She watched the mountains she had admired as a girl reduced to foot soldiers in an army that marched around the
curve of the world.

Her Meta had known well the green complexity of the
forests, but now many fresh, thin brown rivers flowed
through narrow canyons, cutting. These gave the mountain
range the look of a knobby spine from which many nerves
trailed into the tan deserts beyond. A planetary spinal axis,

as though the Earth itself had a mind. She wondered if in some sense this could be so.

Brilliant snowcaps crowned the tallest peaks, but these were not, she saw, the source of the countless rivers. Each muddy rivulet began abruptly high in a canyon, swelling as it ran through rough slopes. The many waterfalls and deep gullies told her that each was busily digging itself in deeper, fresh and energetic.

Dawn pointed and before she could ask Fanak said, "We feed them from tunnels. The great Millennium Lakes lie far underground here."

This land sculpting was only millennia old, but already moist wealth had reclaimed much of the planet's dry mid-continent. Fanak sat back as he silently ordered his ship to perform a long turn, showing them the expanses. She caught a brilliant spark of polished metal far away on the very curve of the planet.

"We will rebuild. Replacing you Originals will be the most difficult part."

"Just so nothing like that ever gets out again," she said.

Below them the Earth sprawled large with many places to hide. But perhaps not, for humans.

The day labour of reconstruction at least tired her muscles, though not her mind. She had several sleepless nights. Then Fanak invited her to a festivity—a "fratuung," implying restrained revelry; Dawn had to look up the word.

The invitation came out of nowhere, a message on her inboards. Phrased more like a summons than an invitation, but thrilling all the same. A Supra event! She felt a quickening in herself and did not quite know why.

It was in an ornate structure that rose from the valley floor like a luminous wave about to break. Electro-lifts took her up into it, past ascending slabs, precise parabolas of arcing orange fountains, a welter of buttresses and columns, some invisible but sensed. Sculptures she recognized as vastly ancient hovered in illuminated spaces.

Some were empire-style, with noble brows eyeing infinite prospects, while others evoked landscapes that could not be Earthly. Colossal battles were caught frozen at their climax, a huge holocrystal showing the later phases of the era in contrast. This was time-sculpture, she recalled, a craft sometimes confused with real history. Propaganda of sufficient age became art.

Fanak greeted her with an embrace, signalling that this was Not Work, in case an Original did not grasp the concept. She gave him a twist of a smile in return, and caught from him a musk that told her more than she wanted to know just now.

Frowning, she put the moment aside. They were alone—easy to do in the labyrinth of cool columns and moist recesses—and she saw that the building knew him but not her. A steady glow followed Fanak, an attendant glow that enhanced him in a ruddy nimbus. It drew him subtly out of the surrounding gloom as the embedded intelligences here tracked his eye movements. Answering light sprang forth to illuminate whatever interested him. At the moment, that was her. This radiance, she saw, framed him for her as well, making him loom masterfully.

All intended for her. She would have to disregard it.

He showed her the view from a wall that seemed to ooze away . . . showing the plain below, the sprawling devastation of the Library, ramparts of mountains rising to an azure sky. "Here," he said, and in a twinkling the floor, too, seeped away under her feet. Despite herself and her resolve to Not Be Impressed, she gave a quiet gasp.

The plain worked with patterns—shot with light, humming with purpose, alive beneath the sands. She was seeing the dumb physical world above, and beneath, the living intelligences that lay embedded in this ancient valley. All of it was aware, sentient in some sense. And—

"Beautiful," she sighed. "So much . . ."

"This is how I think of the far past," Fanak said with a studied, casual air.

"Buried . . ."

"Yes. Patterns laid down long ago, giving forth a view of the world we cannot fully comprehend. Beyond the mere slabs and indices we study. Huge."

"To know it . . . how can we?"

"I thought to show it to you, just to make plain that there is much the Ancients"—he made the capital obvious with his tone—"gave us. Things large and subtle."

"If they could make this, then . . ."

"It is all we can know of them."

"Another recording."

"Perhaps. Or an intelligence we cannot grasp."

She turned to him, close now, feeling his presence like an aroma. "Do we *know* that?"

He smiled, slow and ambiguous. "Of course not. Nothing at such a remove, across hundreds of millions of years, can be sure."

He led her across a plaza and directly into a pond of water. He did not hesitate and the water firmed up under his step. She had jerked back, and now hastened to catch up, her shoes finding a cushioned surface almost like skin. They crossed this and stepped off onto stone, and the pond reverted to water behind them. She looked back at it, but of course Fanak did not.

And here came the Supra crowd. As they entered a long hall a frisson went through the stately figures that were dining from floating tables. Fanak stopped to survey the room, opened his jacket and put his hands on his hips. She had seen this in her own kind, making the silhouette loom suddenly larger and more forbidding; or so it had been in the forest.

The effect seemed the same here. Fanak was a man of social stature and lesser Supras, she noted, lingered around the periphery. She immediately guessed why: they were hoping to renew alliances and gain new friends, without challenging the Fanaks at the centre of the room.

And they were at the centre, socially and geometrically. She felt a flush of pleasure at the attention she got, merely as his companion. Frank speculation worked in the sur-

rounding faces. Pursed lips on the women, especially.
Dawn was unique, but still an Original. Some faces plainly
said that, after all, peacocks do not show their feathers for
dogs.

Passing a couple, she heard, "What I cannot create I do
not understand." A laugh. "This I know; someone cooked
up an Original soup, I'm told."

Followed immediately by, "Isn't it always that way?"

Then, "Can't let them out without supervision, can
we?"

And, "Domesticated, they are quite nice."

Dawn wheeled on them. "What I do not create I do not
appreciate," she spat back. And stalked away. Not a bad
exit, she thought.

She turned to the food—a welcome escape. Meat without bones, skin, gristle or fat—because it was made somewhere from elemental compounds, not grown in nature.
Eggs innocent of the belly of a bird. She ate a bit, trying to
suppress the anxiety seeping up in her. No help—she cast
aside a delicacy, took a sip of fogwine, fumed, turned back
into the crowd.

"Let's . . . let's go back out," she implored Fanak.

He instantly caught her embarrassment. "Of course."

In the darkness above the valley she sighed with relief.
"I'm really not up to all this."

He slid his arms around her, while still looking outward
at the view. "You can be."

The pulse of him was immediate. She looked into his
face and could not get her breath. Only moments before
she had seen the Supras as much like her kind, but now the
difference between them welled up in her, pulse quickening from both fear and desire in equal measures. She remembered Kurani and the leaping, sudden passion, wanted
it to be that way again, to be caught up and carried downstream, sweaty and joyful and possessed by something
greater—

—and she pushed him away. "I . . . I can't."

He hid his feelings behind a formal, "I see. I am sorry"

"No, don't be, it's me, really." Hands in the air, trying to express something beyond words.

"I assumed . . ."

"Maybe I'm not . . . ready." That wasn't right, there was something worse brewing in her, but she could not say what it was.

"I am sorry."

He turned away and she bolted for the safety of the Supra crowd within. Her heels clicked anxiously, echoes from the high stone walls taunting her. She hurried into the long hall, steps ahead of Fanak, and abruptly stopped at the entrance.

And she could not say why.

So she stepped without thinking into a crowd of them—immersed in a pale yellow mist. It clung to her as she passed through them and felt in the air a ghostly silence. It clung to her and she moved among the Supras—who were saying things aloud and in Talent-talk, but somehow distantly, as though she was at the other end of the room from them in a fashion she could not quite fathom. They did not look directly at her but knew she was there. She breathed in the yellow fog and felt a gathering tension. So she . . . yawned.

This caught their attention. They looked at her for a long moment as she felt suddenly vulnerable, her jaw wide and mouth gaping like a fool.

Had she ever seen a Supra yawn? No. In school hadn't she read somewhere?—and here came the inboard reference-seeker, which whispered that *yawning seemed to be a way of communicating changing environmental or internal conditions to others, possibly as a way to synchronize behaviour, most likely a vestigial mechanism that has lost its significance in selection. Supras have omitted the reflex*—and she shut it off, sharp, for now those near her were smiling, some with hands held over mouths, not wanting to laugh.

She turned and fled from the obliging yellow fog, from the ripple of stifled laughter that followed her out of the crowd like a wave.

She breathed in the air, laced with something she had

never savoured before. All about her, the party swirled.
Supras, Ur-humans, many variants in between—all from
different eras in the aeon-long explorations of evolution.
She escaped onto a parapet. Below stretched the eroded
valley, ancient beyond measure.

She felt it come rushing up at her. This desert plain was
a baked-dry display table covered with historical curiosi-
ties. What vexed currents worked, when different ages
sought to conspire! And she was pinned here, firmly
spiked by the bland, all-powerful, infuriating, unthinkingly
condescending *reasonableness* of the Supras.

Dawn pressed her palms to her ears. The din of Talent-
talk drummed on. Some point was in contention, laced in
logics she could not follow. As soon as they got through
with their labyrinthine logic, they would notice her again.

Notice. And talk down to her. Reassure her. Treat her
like a vaguely remembered pet.

No wonder they had not recalled the many varieties of
dogs and cats, she thought bitterly. Ur-humans had served
that purpose quite nicely.

There was no one here who was . . . her. Her people . . .
Hard River Meta and all the others. All gone. They had
laboured for the Supras since far, time-shrouded antiquity,
tending the flowering biosphere. The Supras had known
enough to let them form tribes, to work their own small
will upon the forest. But drawn out of that fragile matrix,
Dawn gasped like a beached fish.

The Talent-talk drummed, drummed, drummed.

She staggered away, anger clouding her vision. Con-
flicts that had been building in her burst forth, and she
hoped the blizzard of Talent-talk hid them. But she could
avoid them no longer herself.

Even Kurani—she had felt with him a near-equality,
yes. And that had made her earlier passion possible—born,
she saw now, of her innocence. And her ignorance of their
differences. An innocence, an ignorance she had lost now.

She was like a bug here, scuttling at the feet of these
distracted supermen. They were kind enough in their cool,

lopsided fashion, but their effort to damp their abilities down to her level was visible—and galling. Longing for her own kind brimmed in her.

—drummed-drummed-drummed—

Her only hope of seeing her kind again lay in these Supras. But a clammy fear clasped her when she tried to think what fresh Ur-humans would be like.

Laboratory-made. Bodies decanted from some chilly crucible. Her relatives, yes, even clones of her. But strangers. Unmarked by life, unreared. They would be her people only in the narrow genetic sense.

And she would be bound to them in a kind of genetic slavery. She and all of her kind would be kindly, politely *owned* by the Supras.

She saw suddenly that her Meta, her Mom, her mysterious father who might yet be alive somewhere—they had all been kept in benign ignorance. The Supras clearly felt that Originals could not be actors on the interstellar stage.

And maybe they were right. But she resented the idea. In her gut she felt that Originals could matter, if they had a chance.

And somewhere, maybe some Ur-humans lived. Maybe her father. They would know the tribal intimacies, the shared culture she longed for.

If they existed, she had to find them.

Yet every nuance of the Supras' talk suggested that they would not let her go. *Domesticated, they are quite nice.*

Could she . . . ?

They were not all-powerful—she had to keep reminding herself of that. Yet their very attainments gave them vulnerabilities. Immortals were enormously cautious; accident could still destroy them. Caution could err.

And they could have missed some of her kind in the dense woods.

She sucked in a chilly breath. Things slid into place, deep inside.

Very well, then. She would escape.

So began the next great human age.

Osmund Considers

Timons Esaias

*Here's a story of a distant future, far beyond Singularity,
where humans have dwindled to a coddled few; one that
demonstrates that the human race may end with a sigh or
a whimper, but definitely not with a bang . . .*

Timons Esaias made his first sale to Interzone *in 1993
and has since become a frequent contributor to that magazine, as well as making sales to* Strange Horizons, Future Orbits, Sherwood, The Age of Reason, Alien Worlds,
*and other markets. He is also one of SF's most prolific
poets, placing poems frequently with* Asimov's Science
Fiction Magazine, The Magazine of Speculative Poetry,
Star*line, Mythic Delirium, Tales of the Unanticipated,
Full Unit Hookup, *and elsewhere. He lives in Pittsburgh,
Pennsylvania.*

Osmund was reading a book, a book of high adventure on
deep oceans in times gone by. The book failed to hold his
entire attention so that his senses wandered—taking in
the comfort of the leather wingback chair in which he
lounged, the aroma of his rare Turkmani cigars, the love-
liness of the woodwork which decorated the library from
floor to ceiling where it yielded to a magnificent fresco of
Thor trying to wrest the double-headed axe from the
grasp of the strange Oriental deities of the Minoans. For
a moment his attention returned to the voice of his lector,
and the hero's struggle between his deepest urges and his
bounden duty.

For the first time in a while, in weeks and weeks, Osmund had a thought.

"Duty?" he said.

"Your Grace?" the lector replied, breaking off the narration.

"Duty. It's very important. Yet what *is* duty? Exactly?"

"Duty, your Grace, is that obligation which an individual owes to others, and the acting upon that obligation." The lector seemed to pause for emphasis. "Duty, in the final analysis, is the structural steel upon which the Nation depends for its stability."

Osmund took a cigar from the box at his elbow; placed the end into the cutter, which made a satisfying *snick;* then held it out for the lighter to focus its beam on the other end. "But what, to be specific, is *my* duty?" A luscious cloud of blue smoke rose from the cigar, and the lighter's beam cut out.

The lector's tone grew slightly unctuous. "Duty, your Grace, is essentially a one-way obligation. Duty is owed by the lesser to the greater; it is owed upward. All the servitors here at the Club, for instance, owe to your Grace the duties of instant obedience, courteous service, and careful planning. Your Grace, however, has no superiors, and therefore has no duties."

Some hours later, as the waitdroids were clearing away the pheasant d'orange and bringing in the cold soup, he asked the chandelier the question he had been trying to formulate all afternoon. "The books sometimes speak of people having duties to themselves. What duties have I, to myself?"

"None," the chandelier replied, its voice high and crystal clear and grace-noted with a tinkling like that of chimes. "Before humans were perfected they sometimes felt themselves to have a higher and a lower self. It must have been very difficult. With that understanding, they would therefore feel that the lower selves owed duties to the higher selves. When the lower selves failed in their duty in small ways there would be comedy. When the failures were large, there would often be tragedy."

Osmund spooned his soup quietly, but the chandelier did not continue. Finally he asked, "But in my case . . . ?"

"Perfected humans, your Grace, have just one self. There can be no duty where there is no discrepancy of caste."

The soup was magnificent.

"**W**omen!" *Osmund exclaimed,* echoing the line the lector had just pronounced. The lector did not reply, in deference to the billiard shot that Osmund seemed on the verge of making. He put his cue at rest, though, and slid one hip onto the rail of the table. "They are great objects of desire, are they not?"

"Yes, your Grace. When humans were subject to inordinate desire, women frequently gave rise to it—most generally among unneutered males. Equally, female humans found some men desir . . ."

"Have I ever seen a woman?"

"Outside of sensoria and of static artworks, I assume you mean? No, your Grace has never actually seen a woman in person."

Osmund scratched the side of his head with the end of the cue, leaving a trail of blue chalk in his hair. "And why not?"

"Contact between humans can lead to procreation."

"And that would be bad, would it?"

"Very bad, your Grace. It is my duty, and the duty of everything here at the Club, to prevent it."

Osmund took a rare turn on the Club's gallery, with its exceptional views of the City. The thick windows prevented any unpleasant chemicals or drafts, and the volume had been turned very low so that he heard the outside noises only as a murmur, for the Club knew that Osmund did not care for clatter.

He stood for a time watching the traffic on the Avenue upon which the Club fronted, an Avenue whose name escaped him. He did not ask it. A steady stream of androids and other servitors bustled about their business, some on the sidewalk wearing great hats and flowing cloaks to protect them from all the things in the environment. Most, however, travelled in vehicles: open chariots, automobiles, one-horse hansom cabs, drayage wagons, helicars and trucks. There was a steam locomotive and small Pullman car, though without rails, chugging its way from the east. Osmund knew from his books that these vehicles would never have been seen together, not before modern times. He felt a surge of almost pain, a deep pity, for the bleak lives people had led in the past, surrounded by the artifacts of only one era at a time.

Perhaps, he reminded himself quickly, *they did not mind it as I would.* After all, the lesson he had been taught in childhood about the old times was that irrational humankind, imperfected humankind, had been uncomfortable with, and intolerant of, difference.

He strode down to the end of the North gallery, turned along the West gallery and paced its full length, and finally turned into the observation bay at the corner for the view of the canal and river. Just 30 metres away a two-masted Viking longship sat outside the canal lock, waiting for the gates to open. The servitor at the steering oar seemed heavily tarnished from exposure, almost etched. Osmund wondered briefly where the ship had come from, and whither it was bound, but he did not inquire. A gentleman, he knew, did not pester the staff with too many questions, and he had already asked several this week.

Out on the river a three-masted, barque-rigged submarine was making sail and steering for the estuary channel and the sea. Gaslights twinkled through the windows all along the Texas deck, suggesting both gaiety and elegant comfort. Were it at all polite, perhaps he would have inquired as to what individual was aboard, but he only imagined himself there, cruising among the islands of the Skagerrak, or creeping through schools of giant squid.

"I believe I would like to take a trip," he announced. "By train, perhaps." He took out a cigarillo which he fitted into his most ornate meerschaum holder, paused to admire the way the oils from the tobacco had coloured it a faint rose, and then held it out for a lighter. "Into the mountains."

Osmund watched with some fascination as the servitors hustled several trunks through the Club doors into the enclosed porte-cochere, and then took shelter inside while the outer door was lifted, in portcullis fashion, to allow a magnificent team of three matching cream horses and grey-black offside outrider to draw in a sky-blue coach with brilliant brass trim.

The portcullis lowered into place, and again the servitors bustled about, loading the trunks on top and behind the carriage, and setting up a small gangway so that Osmund would not even need to descend the stairs and then step up into the coach, but could walk directly into it. A maidroid scurried up, silk and taffeta rustling, and handed a breast-pocket cigar box to the butler, who stepped forward, bowed precisely, and presented it to Osmund with the brief words, "for the road, your Grace."

As the carriage trundled smartly along the Avenue, turning in the Square and partly circling the monuments, Osmund busied himself with pouring a demitasse of espresso. He had experienced these same streets in a variety of sensoria, but could not be sure how long it had been since he had actually, personally, travelled them. A question on this subject formed in his mind, though it came forth with an alteration.

"How old am I?"

"As your Grace will no doubt remember, it is considered improper for servants to remind one."

"Yes. Yes, indeed." Osmund sank back into the cushions and realized, with surprise, that he must be very old in the terms that animals and earlier humans had used. Really, really quite old. "Of course."

At the entrance to the Underway he was bustled into an

elevator, and his trunks into another, and disgorged directly into the observation room of the canal boat which would carry him to the train station. He actually experienced a delay before the elevators disconnected from the boat and it began to motor along the dark tunnel of the subterranean canal. He remembered the dark tunnel and its suggestion of dankness from previous journeys, but had forgotten the murals and the mosaics. On the port side there were elaborate, and highly metaphorical, interpretations of the Stations of the Invention of the True Telephone. On the starboard, in reverse, were realistic portrayals of the great confrontations of non-violence, and interspersed among them were elegant collage and shadow-box pieces commemorating many of the notable Peaces in human history.

He noted that the explanatory voice in his inner ear for the series of Stations was that of a child, and for the other side was an authoritative male. He remembered how, as a very young person, he had often strained to get one eye on one set of paintings and the other on a different set so that the inner voices would overlap and give him the illusion of being in a party or slightly crowded room.

The memory amused him, but he did not repeat the experiment.

After dining on lentils, squab, and medallions of mastodon, with an extremely cunning claret, Osmund entered the forward car of his train and sprawled in the observation bay to watch the hills crawl by. He was enjoying travel, and congratulating himself on getting out of the Club for a few days.

For some reason, perhaps his recent reading, perhaps in reaction to the futurism of the newest sensoria, he found himself dwelling on the past. Much of the countryside was wild, with full-grown trees that formed an impenetrable green wall on each side of the right-of-way for several miles at a stretch. There were many farms, but they were not nearly so densely situated as they once had been, when this whole land had been lumbered clear and fenced and closely cultivated or grazed. He saw barns and crofts here and there, even the occasional house or small village, but knew that such things were kept up for aesthetic reasons now. Storage and stalls would all be underground, along with whatever closets and repair bays the servitors needed.

Not much of what these farms produced could be safely used, in any case. That would change, of course. Over time.

He had begun to nod off when the train turned into a fairly tight bend, overlooking a dell filled with ornamental gardens and graciously bordered ponds. As they drew further into the bend Osmund realized that there was a second set of three private cars toward the rear of the train, behind a series of fiat-cars stacked with great slabs of limestone. Someone else must be taking a trip into the hills.

For a moment he thought he saw a flash, a merest glimpse, of auburn hair in one of the observation bays, and he quickly motioned for the curtains to block the view. One must not be rude.

The display cases along the credenzas of the smoking lounge were filled with a marvellous collection of dress swords, presentation dirks and several incredibly beautiful boxes of duelling pistols—representing every era of weaponry from matchlock to fusion torch. Near the ceiling were ornately decorated hunting muskets, with Persian and Mughal stocks. These were nothing, however, compared to the various cuffs and locking sleeves that had been used for passive resistance and so beautifully decorated that trying to cut or break them would be reprehensible, regardless of the cause being promoted by the protesters.

"Excuse me, your Grace."

"Yes?" Osmund turned from his examination of the display to find the valet proffering a tray bearing a gift-wrapped cube. There was, unaccountably, a scent of sandalwood in the room.

"A gift, a souvenir of a chance encounter." The valet

remained in its proffering posture, but slid the tray onto the
nearest table. "Another citizen, whose cars were attached
to this train, sent it to you with her compliments."

Osmund stared at the present, quite astounded. He had
not had a gift in so long he barely knew what to do. " '*Were*
attached,' I understood you to say?"

"Indeed. The citizen's cars diverted at the last switch."

"Well. Be sure and see that something appropriate is
sent along to her with my compliments."

"Certainly."

The *gift, when* he finally brought himself to destroy the
wrapping, proved to be a solid topaz statue of a hip-
pogryph. The talons were beryl, the hooves ruby, the feathers mother-of-pearl, the mustachios emerald and the eyes
inset with obsidian. He knew that he would treasure it for
the rest of his life, a memorial to the link that binds humankind.

"Good thing we didn't procreate," he muttered.

"Your Grace?" the centrepiece replied.

"Nothing. A joke."

He did not go to his sleeping compartment that evening,
but spent the night smoking and wondering about the
woman in the other cars. What her life had been like. What
other travels she might have taken.

Hours later, in the small hours of the morning, he realized that he had decided that the servitors were wrong
about duty. He could not phrase it precisely, even to himself; and to speak it aloud would be to invite argument and
correction from the staff. But he did have some kind of
duty, an important one, if somewhat vague. He owed a
duty to the time when the world would be less threatening,
and its wounds had healed. A duty to a time—he felt certain it would be a *time* more than a *place*—when humans
might again be trusted to meet face to face; when humans
would begin to take another step in their history.

He had not the vaguest idea what that step might be. He

did feel, however, that even a perfected human might act wrongly, or somehow, thoughtlessly, delay the healing. It would be his duty to consider the situation. His duty to act for the best.

"In the morning," he said to the ashtray. "I would like to return to my Club."

Coelacanths

Robert Reed

Here's as strange and distant a far-future as you're ever likely to see, even in today's science fiction, a world far beyond Singularity that has become so alien to the few remaining humans who scuttle like cockroaches through its interstices that they have given up all hope of understanding it and concentrate all their energies and ingenuity just on the daily battle to survive.

Robert Reed sold his first story in 1986 and quickly established himself as a frequent contributor to The Magazine of Fantasy & Science Fiction *and* Asimov's Science Fiction Magazine, *as well as selling many stories to* Science Fiction Age, Universe, New Destinies, Tomorrow, Synergy, Starlight, *and elsewhere. Reed may be one of the most prolific of today's young writers, particularly at short fiction lengths, seriously rivaled for that position only by authors such as Stephen Baxter and Brian Stableford. And—also like Baxter and Stableford—he manages to keep up a very high standard of quality while being prolific, something that is not at all easy to do. Reed's stories such as "Sister Alice," "Brother Perfect," "Decency," "Savior," "The Remoras," "Chrysalis," "Whiptail," "The Utility Man," "Marrow," "Birth Day," "Blind," "The Toad of Heaven," "Stride," "The Shape of Everything," "Guest of Honor," "Waging Good," "Killing the Morrow," and at least a half dozen others equally as strong, count as among some of the best short work produced by anyone in the '80s and '90s; many of his best stories were assembled in his first collection,* The Dragons of Springplace. *Nor is he non-prolific as a novelist, having turned out eight novels since the end of the '80s, including* The Lee Shore, The Hormone Jungle, Black Milk, The Remarkables, Down the Bright Way, Beyond the Veil of Stars, An Exaltation of*

Larks, Beneath the Gated Sky, Marrow, *and* Sister Alice. *His most recent book is a novella chapbook,* Mere. *Coming up is a new novel,* The Well of Stars. *Reed lives in Lincoln, Nebraska.*

THE SPEAKER

He stalks the wide stage, a brilliant beam of hot blue light fixed squarely upon him. "We are great! We are glorious!" the man calls out. His voice is pleasantly, effortlessly loud. With a face handsome to the brink of lovely and a collage of smooth, passionate mannerisms, he performs for an audience that sits in the surrounding darkness. Flinging long arms overhead, hands reaching for the distant light, his booming voice proclaims, "We have never been as numerous as we are today. We have never been this happy. And we have never known the prosperity that is ours at this golden moment. This golden now!" Athletic legs carry him across the stage, bare feet slapping against planks of waxed maple. "Our species is thriving," he can declare with a seamless ease. "By every conceivable measure, we are a magnificent, irresistible tide sweeping across the universe!"

Transfixed by the blue beam, his naked body is shamelessly young, rippling with hard muscles over hard bone. A long fat penis dangles and dances, accenting every sweeping gesture, every bold word. The living image of a small but potent god, he surely is a creature worthy of admiration, a soul deserving every esteem and emulation. With a laugh, he promises the darkness, "We have never been so powerful, we humans." Yet in the next breath, with a faintly apologetic smile, he must add, "Yet still, as surely as tomorrow comes, our glories today will seem small and quaint in the future, and what looks golden now will turn to the yellow dust upon which our magnificent children will tread!"

PROCYON

Study your history. It tells you that travel always brings its
share of hazards; that's a basic, impatient law of the universe. Leaving the security and familiarity of home is
never easy. But every person needs to make the occasional
journey, embracing the risks to improve his station, his
worth and self-esteem. Procyon explains why this day is a
good day to wander. She refers to intelligence reports as
well as the astrological tables. Then by a dozen means, she
maps out their intricate course, describing what she hopes
to find and everything that she wants to avoid.

She has twin sons. They were born four months ago,
and they are mostly grown now. "Keep alert," she tells the
man-children, leading them out through a series of rein-
forced and powerfully camouflaged doorways. "No naps,
no distractions," she warns them. Then with a backward
glance, she asks again, "What do we want?"

"Whatever we can use," the boys reply in a sloppy
chorus.

"Quiet," she warns. Then she nods and shows a caring
smile, reminding them, "A lot of things can be used. But
their trash is sweetest."

Mother and sons look alike: They are short, strong people with closely cropped hair and white-gray eyes. They
wear simple clothes and three fashions of camouflage, plus
a stew of mental add-ons and microchine helpers as well as
an array of sensors that never blink, watching what human
eyes cannot see. Standing motionless, they vanish into the
convoluted, ever-shifting background. But walking makes
them into three transient blurs—dancing wisps that are no-
ticeably simpler than the enormous world around them.
They can creep ahead only so far before their camouflage
falls apart, and then they have to stop, waiting patiently or
otherwise, allowing the machinery to find new ways to
help make them invisible.

"I'm confused," one son admits. "That thing up ahead—"

"Did you update your perception menu?"

"I thought I did."

Procyon makes no sound. Her diamond-bright glare is enough. She remains rigidly, effortlessly still, allowing her lazy son to finish his preparations. Dense, heavily encoded signals have to be whispered, the local net downloading the most recent topological cues, teaching a three-dimensional creature how to navigate through this shifting, highly intricate environment.

The universe is fat with dimensions.

Procyon knows as much theory as anyone. Yet despite a long life rich with experience, she has to fight to decipher what her eyes and sensors tell her. She doesn't even bother learning the tricks that coax these extra dimensions out of hiding. Let her add-ons guide her. That's all a person can do, slipping in close to one of *them*. In this place, up is three things and sideways is five others. Why bother counting? What matters is that when they walk again, the three of them move through the best combination of dimensions, passing into a little bubble of old-fashioned up and down. She knows this place. Rising up beside them is a trusted landmark—a red granite bowl that cradles what looks like a forest of tall sticks, the sticks leaking a warm light that Procyon ignores, stepping again, moving along on her tiptoes.

One son leads the way. He lacks the experience to be first, but in another few weeks, his flesh and sprint-grown brain will force him into the world alone. He needs his practice, and more important, he needs confidence, learning to trust his add-ons and his careful preparations, and his breeding, and his own good luck.

Procyon's other son lingers near the granite bowl. He's the son who didn't update his menu. This is her dreamy child, whom she loves dearly. Of course she adores him. But there's no escaping the fact that he is easily distracted, and that his adult life will be, at its very best, difficult. Study your biology. Since life began, mothers have made hard decisions about their children, and they have made the deadliest decisions with the tiniest of gestures.

Procyon lets her lazy son fall behind.

Her other son takes two careful steps and stops abruptly, standing before what looks like a great black cylinder set on its side. The shape is a fiction; The cylinder is round in one fashion but incomprehensible in many others. Her add-ons and sensors have built this very simple geometry to represent something far more elaborate. This is a standard disposal unit. Various openings appear as a single slot near the rim of the cylinder, just enough room showing for a hand and forearm to reach through, touching whatever garbage waits inside.

Her son's thick body has more grace than any dancer of old, more strength than a platoon of ancient athletes. His IQ is enormous. His reaction times have been enhanced by every available means. His father was a great old soul who survived into his tenth year, which is almost forever. But when the boy drifts sideways, he betrays his incxperience. His sensors attack the cylinder by every means, telling him that it's a low-grade trash receptacle secured by what looks like a standard locking device, AI-managed and obsolete for days, if not weeks. And inside the receptacle is a mangled piece of hardware worth a near-fortune on the open market.

The boy drifts sideways, and he glimmers.

Procyon says, "No," too loudly.

But he feels excited, invulnerable. Grinning over his shoulder now, he winks and lifts one hand with a smooth, blurring motion—

Instincts old as blood come bubbling up. Procyon leaps, shoving her son off his feet and saving him. And in the next horrible instant, she feels herself engulfed, a dry cold hand grabbing her, then stuffing her inside a hole that by any geometry feels nothing but bottomless.

ABLE

Near the lip of the City, inside the emerald green ring of Park, waits a secret place where the moss and horsetail and tree fern forest plunges into a deep crystalline pool of warm spring water. No public map tells of the pool, and no trail leads the casual walker near it. But the pool is exactly the sort of place that young boys always discover, and it is exactly the kind of treasure that remains unmentioned to parents or any other adult with suspicious or troublesome natures.

Able Quotient likes to believe that he was first to stumble across this tiny corner of Creation. And if he isn't first, at least no one before him has ever truly seen the water's beauty, and nobody after him will appreciate the charms of this elegant, timeless place.

Sometimes Able brings others to the pooi, but only his best friends and a few boys whom he wants to impress. Not for a long time does he even consider bringing a girl, and then it takes forever to find a worthy candidate, then muster the courage to ask her to join him. Her name is Mish. She's younger than Able by a little ways, but like all girls, she acts older and much wiser than he will ever be. They have been classmates from the beginning. They live three floors apart in The Tower Of Gracious Good, which makes them close neighbors. Mish is pretty, and her beauty is the sort that will only grow as she becomes a woman. Her face is narrow and serious. Her eyes watch everything. She wears flowing dresses and jeweled sandals, and she goes everywhere with a clouded leopard named Mr. Stuff-and-Nonsense. "If my cat can come along," she says after hearing Able's generous offer. "Are there any birds at this pond of yours?"

Able should be horrified by the question. The life around the pool knows him and has grown to trust him. But he is so enamored by Mish that he blurts out, "Yes, hundreds of birds. Fat, slow birds. Mr. Stuff can eat himself sick."

"But that wouldn't be right," Mish replies with a disapproving smirk. "I'll lock down his appetite. And if we see any wounded birds . . . any animal that's suffering . . . we can unlock him right away . . . !"

"Oh, sure," Able replies, almost sick with nerves. "I guess that's fine, too."

People rarely travel any distance. City is thoroughly modern, every apartment supplied by conduits and meshed with every web and channel, shareline and gossip run. But even with most of its citizens happily sitting at home, the streets are jammed with millions of walking bodies. Every seat on the train is filled all the way to the last stop. Able momentarily loses track of Mish when the cabin walls evaporate. But thankfully, he finds her waiting at Park's edge. She and her little leopard are standing in the narrow shade of a horsetail. She teases him, observing, "You look lost." Then she laughs, perhaps at him, before abruptly changing the subject. With a nod and sweeping gesture, she asks, "Have you noticed? Our towers look like these trees."

To a point, yes. The towers are tall and thin and rounded like the horsetails, and the hanging porches make them appear rough-skinned. But there are obvious and important differences between trees and towers, and if she were a boy, Able would make fun of her now. Fighting his nature, Able forces himself to smile. "Oh, my," he says as he turns, looking back over a shoulder. "They do look like horsetails, don't they?"

Now the three adventurers set off into the forest. Able takes the lead. Walking with boys is a quick business that often turns into a race. But girls are different, particularly when their fat, unhungry cats are dragging along behind them. It takes forever to reach the rim of the world. Then it takes another two forevers to follow the rim to where they can almost see the secret pool. But that's where Mish announces, "I'm tired!" To the world, she says, "I want to stop and eat. I want to rest here."

Able nearly tells her, "No."

Instead he decides to coax her, promising, "It's just a little farther."

But she doesn't seem to hear him, leaping up on the pink polished rim, sitting where the granite is smooth and flat, legs dangling and her bony knees exposed. She opens the little pack that has floated on her back from the beginning, pulling out a hot lunch that she keeps and a cold lunch that she hands to Able. "This is all I could take," she explains, "without my parents asking questions." She is reminding Able that she never quite got permission to make this little journey. "If you don't like the cold lunch," she promises, "then we can trade. I mean, if you really don't."

He says, "I like it fine," without opening the insulated box. Then he looks inside, discovering a single wedge of spiced sap, and it takes all of his poise not to say, "Ugh!"

Mr. Stuff collapses into a puddle of towerlight, instantly falling asleep.

The two children eat quietly and slowly. Mish makes the occasional noise about favorite teachers and mutual friends. She acts serious and ordinary, and disappointment starts gnawing at Able. He isn't old enough to sense that the girl is nervous. He can't imagine that Mish wants to delay the moment when they'll reach the secret pool, or that she sees possibilities waiting there—wicked possibilities that only a wicked boy should be able to foresee.

Finished with her meal, Mish runs her hands along the hem of her dress, and she kicks at the air, and then, hunting for any distraction, she happens to glance over her shoulder.

Where the granite ends, the world ends. Normally nothing of substance can be seen out past the pink stone—nothing but a confused, ever-shifting grayness that extends on forever. Able hasn't bothered to look out there. He is much too busy trying to finish his awful meal, concentrating on his little frustrations and his depraved little daydreams.

"Oh, goodness," the young girl exclaims. "Look at that!"

Able has no expectations. What could possibly be worth the trouble of turning around? But it's an excuse to give up on his lunch, and after setting it aside, he turns slowly, eyes jumping wide open and a surprised grunt leaking out of him as he tumbles off the granite, landing squarely on top of poor Mr. Stuff.

ESCHER

She has a clear, persistent memory of flesh, but the flesh isn't hers. Like manners and like knowledge, what a person remembers can be bequeathed by her ancestors. That's what is happening now. Limbs and heads; penises and vaginas. In the midst of some unrelated business, she remembers having feet and the endless need to protect those feet with sandals or boots or ostrich skin or spiked shoes that will lend a person even more height. She remembers wearing clothes that gave color and bulk to what was already bright and enormous. At this particular instant, what she sees is a distant, long-dead relative sitting on a white porcelain bowl, bare feet dangling, his orifices voiding mountains of waste and an ocean of water.

Her oldest ancestors were giants. They were built from skin and muscle, wet air and great slabs of fat. Without question, they were an astonishing excess of matter, vast beyond all reason, yet fueled by slow, inefficient chemical fires.

Nothing about Escher is inefficient. No flesh clings to her. Not a drop of water or one glistening pearl of fat. It's always smart to be built from structure light and tested, efficient instructions. It's best to be tinier than a single cell and as swift as electricity, slipping unseen through places that won't even notice your presence.

Escher is a glimmer, a perfect and enduring whisper of light. Of life. Lovely in her own fashion, yet fierce beyond all measure.

She needs her fierceness.

When cooperation fails, as it always does, a person has to throw her rage at the world and her countless enemies.

But in this place, for this moment, cooperation holds sway.

Manners rule.

Escher is eating. Even as tiny and efficient as she is, she needs an occasional sip of raw power. Everyone does. And it seems as if half of everyone has gathered around what can only be described as a tiny, delicious wound. She can't count the citizens gathered at the feast. Millions and millions, surely. All those weak glimmers join into a soft glow. Everyone is bathed in a joyous light. It is a boastful, wasteful show, but Escher won't waste her energy with warnings. Better to sip at the wound, absorbing the free current, building up her reserves for the next breeding cycle. It is best to let others make the mistakes for you: Escher believes nothing else quite so fervently.

A pair of sisters float past. The familial resemblance is obvious, and so are the tiny differences. Mutations as well as tailored changes have created two loud gossips who speak and giggle in a rush of words and raw data, exchanging secrets about the multitude around them.

Escher ignores their prattle, gulping down the last of what she can possibly hold, and then pausing, considering where she might hide a few nanojoules of extra juice, keeping them safe for some desperate occasion.

Escher begins to hunt for that unlikely hiding place.

And then her sisters abruptly change topics. Gossip turns to trading memories stolen from The World. Most of it is picoweight stuff, useless and boring. An astonishing fraction of His thoughts are banal. Like the giants of old, He can afford to be sloppy. To be a spendthrift. Here is a pointed example of why Escher is happy to be herself. She is smart in her own fashion, and imaginative, and almost everything about her is important, and when a problem confronts her, she can cut through the muddle, seeing the blessing wrapped up snug inside the measurable risks.

Quietly, with a puzzled tone, one sister announces, "The World is alarmed."

"About?" says the other.

"A situation," says the first. "Yes, He is alarmed now. Moral questions are begging for His attention."

"What questions?"

The first sister tells a brief, strange story.

"You know all this?" asks another. Asks Escher. "Is this daydream or hard fact?"

"I know, and it is fact." The sister feels insulted by the doubting tone, but she puts on a mannerly voice, explaining the history of this sudden crisis.

Escher listens.

And suddenly the multitude is talking about nothing else. What is happening has never happened before, not in this fashion . . . not in any genuine memory of any of the millions here, it hasn't . . . and some very dim possibilities begin to show themselves. Benefits wrapped inside some awful dangers. And one or two of these benefits wink at Escher, and smile. . . .

The multitude panics, and evaporates.

Escher remains behind, deliberating on these possibilities. The landscape beneath her is far more sophisticated than flesh, and stronger, but it has an ugly appearance that reminds her of a flesh-born memory. A lesion; a pimple. A tiny unsightly ruin standing in what is normally seamless, and beautiful, and perfect.

She flees, but only so far.

Then she hunkers down and waits, knowing that eventually, in one fashion or another, He will scratch at this tiny irritation.

THE SPEAKER

"You cannot count human accomplishments," he boasts to his audience, strutting and wagging his way to the edge of the stage. Bare toes curl over the sharp edge, and he grins jauntily, admitting, "And I cannot count them, either. There are simply too many successes, in too many far-flung places, to nail up a number that you can believe. But allow me, if you will, this chance to list a few important marvels."

Long hands grab bony hips, and he gazes out into the watching darkness. "The conquest of our cradle conti-nent," he begins, "which was quickly followed by the con-quest of our cradle world. Then after a gathering pause, we swiftly and thoroughly occupied most of our neighbor-

ing worlds, too. It was during those millennia when we learned how to split flint and atoms and DNA and our own restless psyches. With these apish hands, we fashioned great machines that worked for us as our willing, eager slaves. And with our slaves' more delicate hands, we fabricated machines that could think for us." A knowing wink, a mischievous shrug. "Like any child, of course, our thinking machines eventually learned to think for themselves. Which was a dangerous, foolish business, said some. Said fools. But my list of our marvels only begins with that business. This is what I believe, and I challenge anyone to say otherwise."

There is a sound—a stern little murmur—and perhaps it implies dissent. Or perhaps the speaker made the noise himself, fostering a tension that he is building with his words and body.

His penis grows erect, drawing the eye.

Then with a wide and bright and unabashedly smug grin, he roars out, "Say this with me. Tell me what great things we have done. Boast to Creation about the wonders that we have taken part in . . . !"

PROCYON

Torture is what this is: She feels her body plunging from a high place, head before feet. A frantic wind roars past. Outstretched hands refuse to slow her fall. Then Procyon makes herself spin, putting her feet beneath her body, and gravity instantly reverses itself. She screams, and screams, and the distant walls reflect her terror, needles jabbed into her wounded ears. Finally, she grows quiet, wrapping her arms around her eyes and ears, forcing herself to do nothing, hanging limp in space while her body falls in one awful direction.

A voice whimpers.

A son's worried voice says, "Mother, are you there? Mother?"

Some of her add-ons have been peeled away, but not all
of them. The brave son uses a whisper-channel, saying,
"I'm sorry," with a genuine anguish. He sounds sick and
sorry, and exceptionally angry, too. "I was careless," he admits. He says, "Thank you for saving me." Then to someone else, he says, "She can't hear me."

"I hear you," she whispers.

"Listen," says her other son. The lazy one. "Did you
hear something?"

She starts to say, "Boys," with a stern voice. But then
the trap vibrates, a piercing white screech nearly deafening
Procyon. Someone physically strikes the trap. Two some-
ones. She feels the walls turning around her, the trap making perhaps a quarter-turn toward home.

Again, she calls out, "Boys."

They stop rolling her. Did they hear her? No, they found
a hidden restraint, the trap secured at one or two or ten
ends.

One last time, she says, "Boys."

"I hear her," her dreamy son blurts.

"Don't give up, Mother," says her brave son. "We'll get
you out. I see the locks, I can beat them—"

"You can't," she promises.

He pretends not to have heard her. A shaped explosive
detonates, making a cold ringing sound, faraway and useless. Then the boy growls, "Damn," and kicks the trap, ac-
complishing nothing at all.

"It's too tough," says her dreamy son. "We're not doing
any good—"

"Shut up," his brother shouts.

Procyon tells them, "Quiet now. Be quiet."

The trap is probably tied to an alarm. Time is short, or
it has run out already. Either way, there's a decision to be
made, and the decision has a single, inescapable answer.
With a careful and firm voice, she tells her sons, "Leave
me. Now. Go!"

"I won't," the brave son declares. "Never!"

"Now," she says.

"It's my fault," says the dreamy son. "I should have been keeping up—"

"Both of you are to blame," Procyon calls out. "And I am, too. And there's bad luck here, but there's some good, too. You're still free. You can still get away. Now, before you get yourself seen and caught—"

"You're going to die," the brave son complains.

"One day or the next, I will," she agrees. "Absolutely."

"We'll find help," he promises.

"From where?" she asks.

"From who?" says her dreamy son in the same instant. "We aren't close to anyone—"

"Shut up," his brother snaps. "Just shut up!"

"Run away," their mother repeats.

"I won't," the brave son tells her. Or himself. Then with a serious, tight little voice, he says, "I can fight. We'll both fight."

Her dreamy son says nothing.

Procyon peels her arms away from her face, opening her eyes, focusing on the blurring cylindrical walls of the trap. It seems that she was wrong about her sons. The brave one is just a fool, and the dreamy one has the good sense. She listens to her dreamy son saying nothing, and then the other boy says, "Of course you're going to fight. Together, we can do some real damage—"

"I love you both," she declares.

That wins a silence.

Then again, one last time, she says, "Run."

"I'm not a coward," one son growls.

While her good son says nothing, running now, and he needs his breath for things more essential than pride and bluster.

ABLE

The face stares at them for the longest while. It is a great wide face, heavily bearded with smoke-colored eyes and a

long nose perched above the cavernous mouth that hangs
open, revealing teeth and things more amazing than teeth.
Set between the bone-white enamel are little machines
made of fancy stuff. Able can only guess what the add-on
machines are doing. This is a wild man, powerful and free.
People like him are scarce and strange, their bodies reengineered in countless ways. Like his eyes: Able stares into
those giant gray eyes, noticing fleets of tiny machines
floating on the tears. Those machines are probably delicate
sensors. Then with a jolt of amazement, he realizes that
those machines and sparkling eyes are staring into their
world with what seems to be a genuine fascination.

"He's watching us," Able mutters.

"No, he isn't," Mish argues. "He can't see into our
realm."

"We can't see into his either," the boy replies. "But just
the same, I can make him out just fine."

"It must be. . . ." Her voice falls silent while she ac-
cesses City's library. Then with a dismissive shrug of her
shoulders, she announces, "We're caught in his topological
hardware. That's all. He has to simplify his surroundings to
navigate, and we just happen to be close enough and
aligned right."

Able had already assumed all that.

Mish starts to speak again, probably wanting to add to
her explanation. She can sure be a know-everything sort of
girl. But then the great face abruptly turns away, and they
watch the man run away from their world.

"I told you," Mish sings out. "He couldn't see us."

"I think he could have," Able replies, his voice finding
a distinct sharpness.

The girl straightens her back. "You're wrong," she says
with an obstinate tone. Then she turns away from the edge
of the world, announcing, "I'm ready to go on now."

"I'm not," says Able.

She doesn't look back at him. She seems to be talking
to her leopard, asking, "Why aren't you ready?"

"I see two of them now," Able tells her.

"You can't."

"I can." The hardware trickery is keeping the outside realms sensible. A tunnel of simple space leads to two men standing beside an iron-black cylinder. The men wear camouflage, but they are moving too fast to let it work. They look small now. Distant, or tiny. Once you leave the world, size and distance are impossible to measure. How many times have teachers told him that? Able watches the tiny men kicking at the cylinder. They beat on its heavy sides with their fists and forearms, managing to roll it for almost a quarter turn. Then one of the men pulls a fist-sized device from what looks like a cloth sack, fixing it to what looks like a sealed slot, and both men hurry to the far end of the cylinder.

"What are they doing?" asks Mish with a grumpy interest.

A feeling warns Able, but too late. He starts to say, "Look away—"

The explosion is brilliant and swift, the blast reflected off the cylinder and up along the tunnel of ordinary space, a clap of thunder making the giant horsetails sway and nearly knocking the two of them onto the forest floor.

"They're criminals," Mish mutters with a nervous hatred.

"How do you know?" the boy asks.

"People like that just are," she remarks. "Living like they do. Alone like that, and wild. You know how they make their living."

"They take what they need—"

"They steal!" she interrupts.

Able doesn't even glance at her. He watches as the two men work frantically, trying to pry open the still-sealed doorway. He can't guess why they would want the doorway opened. Or rather, he can think of too many reasons. But when he looks at their anguished, helpless faces, he realizes that whatever is inside, it's driving these wild men very close to panic.

"Criminals," Mish repeats.

"I heard you," Able mutters.

Then before she can offer another hard opinion, he turns to her and admits, "I've always liked them. They live by their wits, and mostly alone, and they have all these sweeping powers—"

"Powers that they've stolen," she whines.

"From garbage, maybe." There is no point in mentioning whose garbage. He stares at Mish's face, pretty but twisted with fury, and something sad and inevitable occurs to Able. He shakes his head and sighs, telling her, "I don't like you very much."

Mish is taken by surprise. Probably no other boy has said those awful words to her, and she doesn't know how to react, except to sputter ugly little sounds as she turns, looking back over the edge of the world.

Able does the same.

One of the wild men abruptly turns and runs. In a supersonic flash, he races past the children, vanishing into the swirling grayness, leaving his companion to stand alone beside the mysterious black cylinder. Obviously weeping, the last man wipes the tears from his whiskered face with a trembling hand, while his other hand begins to yank a string of wondrous machines from what seems to be a bottomless sack of treasures.

ESCHER

She consumes all of her carefully stockpiled energies, and for the first time in her life, she weaves a body for herself: A distinct physical shell composed of diamond dust and keratin and discarded rare earths and a dozen subtle glues meant to bind to every surface without being felt. To a busy eye, she is dust. She is insubstantial and useless and forgettable. To a careful eye and an inquisitive touch, she is the tiniest soul imaginable, frail beyond words, forever perched on the brink of extermination. Surely she poses no threat to any creature, least of all the great ones. Lying on the edge of the little wound, passive and vulnerable, she waits for Chance to carry her where she needs to be. Probably others are doing the same. Perhaps thousands of sisters and daughters are hiding nearby, each snug inside her own spore case. The temptation to whisper, "Hello," is easily ignored. The odds are awful as it is; any noise could turn this into a suicide. What matters is silence and watchfulness, thinking hard about the great goal while keeping ready for anything that might happen, as well as everything that will not.

The little wound begins to heal, causing a trickling pain to flow.

The World feels the irritation, and in reflex, touches His discomfort by several means, delicate and less so.

Escher misses her first opportunity. A great swift shape presses its way across her hiding place, but she activates her glues too late. Dabs of glue cure against air, wasted. So she cuts the glue loose and watches again. A second touch is unlikely, but it comes, and she manages to heave a sticky tendril into a likely crevice, letting the irresistible force yank her into a brilliant, endless sky.

She will probably die now.

For a little while, Escher allows herself to look back across her life, counting daughters and other successes, taking warm comfort in her many accomplishments.

Someone hangs in the distance, dangling from a similar tendril. Escher recognizes the shape and intricate glint of her neighbor's spore case; she is one of Escher's daughters. There is a strong temptation to signal her, trading information, helping each other—

But a purge-ball attacks suddenly, and the daughter evaporates, nothing remaining of her but ions and a flash of incoherent light.

Escher pulls herself toward the crevice, and hesitates. Her tendril is anchored on a fleshy surface. A minor neuron—a thread of warm optical cable—lies buried inside the wet cells. She launches a second tendril at her new target. By chance, the purge-ball sweeps the wrong terrain, giving her that little instant. The tendril makes a sloppy connection with the neuron. Without time to test its integrity, all she can do is shout, "Don't kill me! Or my daughters! Don't murder us, Great World!"

Nothing changes. The purge-ball works its way across the deeply folded fleshscape, moving toward Escher again, distant flashes announcing the deaths of another two daughters or sisters.

"Great World!" she cries out.

He will not reply. Escher is like the hum of a single angry electron, and she can only hope that he notices the hum.

"I am vile," she promises. "I am loathsome and sneaky, and you should hate me. What I am is an illness lurking inside you. A disease that steals exactly what I can steal without bringing your wrath."

The purge-ball appears, following a tall reddish ridge of flesh, bearing down on her hiding place.

She says, "Kill me, if you want. Or spare me, and I will do this for you." Then she unleashes a series of vivid images, precise and simple, meant to be compelling to any mind.

The purge-ball slows, its sterilizing lasers taking careful aim.

She repeats herself, knowing that thought travels only so quickly and The World is too vast to see her thoughts and react soon enough to save her. But if she can help . . . if she saves just a few hundred daughters . . . ?

Lasers aim, and do nothing. Nothing. And after an instant of inactivity, the machine changes its shape and nature. It hovers above Escher, sending out its own tendrils. A careless strength yanks her free of her hiding place. Her tendrils and glues are ripped from her aching body. A scaffolding of carbon is built around her, and she is shoved inside the retooled purge-ball, held in a perfect darkness, waiting alone until an identical scaffold is stacked beside her.

A hard, angry voice boasts, "I did this."

"What did you do?" asks Escher.

"I made the World listen to reason." It sounds like Escher's voice, except for the delusions of power. "I made a promise, and that's why He saved us."

With a sarcastic tone, she says, "Thank you ever so much. But now where are we going?"

"I won't tell you," her fellow prisoner responds.

"Because you don't know where," says Escher.

"I know everything I need to know."

"Then you're the first person ever," she giggles, winning a brief, delicious silence from her companion.

Other prisoners arrive, each slammed into the empty spaces between their sisters and daughters. Eventually the purge-ball is a prison-ball, swollen to vast proportions, and no one else is being captured. Nothing changes for a long while. There is nothing to be done now but wait, speaking when the urge hits and listening to whichever voice sounds less than tedious.

Gossip is the common currency. People are desperate to hear the smallest glimmer of news. Where the final rumor comes from, nobody knows if it's true. But the woman who was captured moments after Escher claims, "It comes from the world Himself. He's going to put us where we can do the most good."

"Where?" Escher inquires.

"On a tooth," her companion says. "The right incisor, as it happens." Then with that boasting voice, she adds, "Which is exactly what I told Him to do. This is all because of me."

"What isn't?" Escher grumbles.

"Very little," the tiny prisoner promises. "Very, very little."

THE SPEAKER

"We walk today on a thousand worlds, and I mean 'walk' in all manners of speaking." He manages a few comical steps before shifting into a graceful turn, arms held firmly around the wide waist of an invisible and equally graceful

partner. "A hundred alien suns bake us with their perfect light. And between the suns, in the cold and dark, we survive, and thrive, by every worthy means.

Now he pauses, hands forgetting the unseen partner. A look of calculated confusion sweeps across his face. Fingers rise to his thick black hair, stabbing it and yanking backward, leaving furrows in the unruly mass.

"Our numbers," he says. "Our population. It made us sick with worry when we were ten billion standing on the surface of one enormous world. 'Where will our children stand?' we asked ourselves. But then in the next little while, we became ten trillion people, and we had split into a thousand species of humanity, and the new complaint was that we were still too scarce and spread too far apart. 'How could we matter to the universe?' we asked ourselves. 'How could so few souls endure another day in our immeasurable, uncaring universe?'"

His erect penis makes a little leap, a fat and vivid white drop of semen striking the wooden stage with an audible plop.

"Our numbers," he repeats. "Our legions." Then with a wide, garish smile, he confesses, "I don't know our numbers today. No authority does. You make estimates. You extrapolate off data that went stale long ago. You build a hundred models and fashion every kind of vast number. Ten raised to the twentieth power. The thirtieth power. Or more." He giggles and skips backward, and with the giddy, careless energy of a child, he dances where he stands, singing to lights overhead, "If you are as common as sand and as unique as snowflakes, how can you be anything but a wild, wonderful success?"

ABLE

The wild man is enormous and powerful, and surely brilliant beyond anything that Able can comprehend—as smart as City as a whole—but despite his gifts, the man is

obviously terrified. That he can even manage to stand his
ground astonishes Able. He says as much to Mish, and then
he glances at her, adding, "He must be very devoted to
whoever's inside."

"Whoever's inside what?" she asks.

"That trap." He looks straight ahead again, telling himself not to waste time with the girl. She is foolish and bad-
tempered, and he couldn't be any more tired of her. "I
think that's what the cylinder is," he whispers. "A trap of
some kind. And someone's been caught in it."

"Well, I don't care who," she snarls.

He pretends not to notice her.

"What was that?" she blurts. "Did you hear that—?"

"No," Able blurts. But then he notices a distant rumble,
deep and faintly rhythmic, and with every breath, growing.
When he listens carefully, it resembles nothing normal. It
isn't thunder, and it can't be a voice. He feels the sound as
much as he hears it, as if some great mass were being dis-
placed. But he knows better. In school, teachers like to explain what must be happening now, employing tortuous
mathematics and magical sleights of hand. Matter and energy are being rapidly and brutally manipulated. The universe's obscure dimensions are being twisted like bands of
warm rubber. Able knows all this. But still, he understands
none of it. Words without comprehension; froth without
substance. All that he knows for certain is that behind that
deep, unknowable throbbing lies something even farther
beyond human description.

The wild man looks up, gray eyes staring at that something.

He cries out, that tiny sound lost between his mouth and
Able. Then he produces what seems to be a spear—no, an
elaborate missile—that launches itself with a bolt of fire,
lifting a sophisticated warhead up into a vague gray space
that swallows the weapon without sound, or complaint.

Next the man aims a sturdy laser, and fires. But the
weapon simply melts at its tip, collapsing into a smolder-
ing, useless mass at his feet.

Again, the wild man cries out.

His language could be a million generations removed from City-speech, but Able hears the desperate, furious sound of his voice. He doesn't need words to know that the man is cursing. Then the swirling grayness slows itself, and parts, and stupidly, in reflex, Able turns to Mish, wanting to tell her, "Watch. You're going to see one of *Them*."

But Mish has vanished. Sometime in the last few moments, she jumped off the world's rim and ran away, and save for the fat old leopard sleeping between the horsetails, Able is entirely alone now.

"Good," he mutters.

Almost too late, he turns and runs to the very edge of the granite rim.

The wild man stands motionless now. His bowels and bladder have emptied themselves. His handsome, godly face is twisted from every flavor of misery. Eyes as big as windows stare up into what only they can see, and to that great, unknowable something, the man says two simple words.

"Fuck you," Able hears.

And then the wild man opens his mouth, baring his white apish teeth, and just as Able wonders what's going to happen, the man's body explodes, the dull black burst of a shaped charge sending chunks of his face skyward.

PROCYON

One last time, she whispers her son's name.

She whispers it and closes her mouth and listens to the brief, sharp silence that comes after the awful explosion. What must have happened, she tells herself, is that her boy found his good sense and fled. How can a mother think anything else? And then the ominous deep rumbling begins again, begins and gradually swells until the walls of the trap are shuddering and twisting again. But this time the monster is slower. It approaches the trap more cautiously, summoning new courage. She can nearly taste its courage now, and with her intuition, she senses emotions that might be curiosity and might be a kind of reflexive admiration. Or do those eternal human emotions have any relationship for what *It* feels . . . ?

What she feels, after everything, is numbness. A terrible deep weariness hangs on her like a new skin. Procyon seems to be falling faster now, accelerating down through the bottomless trap. But she doesn't care anymore. In place of courage, she wields a muscular apathy. Death looms, but when hasn't it been her dearest companion? And in place of fear, she is astonished to discover an incurious little pride about what is about to happen: How many people—wild free people like herself—have ever found themselves so near one of *Them*?

Quietly, with a calm smooth and slow voice, Procyon says, "I feel you there, you. I can taste you."

Nothing changes.

Less quietly, she says, "Show yourself."

A wide parabolic floor appears, gleaming and black and agonizingly close. But just before she slams into the floor, a wrenching force peels it away. A brilliant violet light rises to meet her, turning into a thick sweet syrup. What may or may not be a hand curls around her body, and squeezes. Procyon fights every urge to struggle. She wrestles with her body, wrestles with her will, forcing both to lie still while the hand tightens its grip and grows comfortable. Then using a voice that betrays nothing tentative or small, she tells what holds her, "I made you, you know."

She says, "You can do what you want to me."

Then with a natural, deep joy, she cries out, "But you're an ungrateful glory . . . and you'll always belong to me . . . !"

ESCHER

The prison-ball has been reengineered, slathered with camouflage and armor and the best immune-suppressors on the

market, and its navigation system has been adapted from
add-ons stolen from the finest trashcans. Now it is a battle-
phage riding on the sharp incisor as far as it dares, then
leaping free. A thousand similar phages leap and lose their
way, or they are killed. Only Escher's phage reaches the
target, impacting on what passes for flesh and launching its
cargo with a microscopic railgun, punching her and a thousand sisters and daughters through immeasurable distances
of senseless, twisted nothing.

How many survive the attack?

She can't guess how many. Can't even care. What matters is to make herself survive inside this strange new
world. An enormous world, yes. Escher feels a vastness
that reaches out across ten or twelve or maybe a thousand
dimensions. How do I know where to go? she asks herself.
And instantly, an assortment of possible routes appear in
her consciousness, drawn in the simplest imaginable fashion, waiting and eager to help her find her way around.

This is a last gift from Him, she realizes. Unless there
are more gifts waiting, of course.

She thanks nobody.

On the equivalent of tiptoes, Escher creeps her way into
a tiny conduit that moves something stranger than any
blood across five dimensions. She becomes passive, aiming for invisibility. She drifts and spins, watching her surroundings turn from a senseless glow into a landscape that
occasionally seems a little bit reasonable. A little bit real.
Slowly, she learns how to see in this new world. Eventually she spies a little peak that may or may not be ordinary
matter. The peak is pink and flexible and sticks out into the
great artery, and flinging her last tendril, Escher grabs hold
and pulls in snug, knowing that the chances are lousy that
she will ever find anything nourishing here, much less
delicious.

But her reserves have been filled again, she notes. If she
is careful—and when hasn't she been—her energies will
keep her alive for centuries.

She thinks of the World, and thanks nobody.

"Watch and learn," she whispers to herself.

That was the first human thought. She remembers that odd fact suddenly. People were just a bunch of grubbing apes moving blindly through their tiny lives until one said to a companion, "Watch and learn."

An inherited memory, or another gift from Him?

Silently, she thanks Luck, and she thanks Him, and once again, she thanks Luck.

"Patience and planning," she tells herself.

Which is another wise thought of the conscious, enduring ape.

THE LAST SON

The locked gates and various doorways know him—recognize him at a glance—but they have to taste him anyway. They have to test him. Three people were expected, and he can't explain in words what has happened. He just says, "The others will be coming later," and leaves that lie hanging in the air. Then as he passes through the final doorway, he says, "Let no one through. Not without my permission first."

"This is your mother's house," says the door's AI.

"Not anymore," he remarks.

The machine grows quiet, and sad.

During any other age, his home would be a mansion. There are endless rooms, rooms beyond counting, and each is enormous and richly furnished and lovely and jammed full of games and art and distractions and flourishes that even the least aesthetic soul would find lovely. He sees none of that now. Alone, he walks to what has always been his room, and he sits on a leather recliner, and the house brings him a soothing drink and an intoxicating drink and an assortment of treats that sit on the platter, untouched.

For a long while, the boy stares off at the distant ceiling, replaying everything with his near-perfect memory.

Everything. Then he forgets everything, stupidly calling
out, "Mother," with a voice that sounds ridiculously
young. Then again, he calls, "Mother." And he starts to rise
from his chair, starts to ask the great empty house, "Where
is she?"

And he remembers.

As if his legs have been sawed off, he collapses. His
chair twists itself to catch him, and an army of AIs brings
their talents to bear. They are loyal, limited machines.
They are empathetic, and on occasion, even sweet. They
want to help him in any fashion, just name the way . . . but
their appeals and their smart suggestions are just so much
noise. The boy acts deaf; and he obviously can't see anything with his fists jabbed into his eyes like that, slouched
forward in his favorite chair, begging an invisible someone
for forgiveness. . . .

THE SPEAKER

*He squats and uses the tip of a forefinger to dab at the pud-
dle of semen, and he rubs the finger against his thumb,
saying, "Think of cells. Individual, self-reliant cells. For
most of Earth's great history, they ruled. First as bacteria,
and then as composites built from cooperative bacteria.
They were everywhere and ruled everything, and then the
wild cells learned how to dance together, in one enormous
body, and the living world was transformed for the next
seven hundred million years."*

*Thumb and finger wipe themselves dry against a hairy
thigh, and he rises again, grinning in that relentless and
smug, yet somehow charming fashion. "Everything was
changed, and nothing had changed," he says. Then he
says, "Scaling," with an important tone, as if that single
word should erase all confusion. "The bacteria and green
algae and the carnivorous amoebae weren't swept away by
any revolution. Honestly, I doubt if their numbers fell ap-
preciably or for long." And again, he says, "Scaling," and*

sighs with a rich appreciation. "Life evolves. Adapts.
Spreads and grows, constantly utilizing new energies and
novel genetics. But wherever something large can live, a
thousand small things can thrive just as well, or better.
Wherever something enormous survives, a trillion bacteria
hang on for the ride."

For a moment, the speaker hesitates.

*A slippery half-instant passes where an audience might
believe that he has finally lost his concentration, that he is
about to stumble over his own tongue. But then he licks at
the air, tasting something delicious. And three times, he
clicks his tongue against the roof of his mouth.*

*Then he says what he has planned to say from the be-
ginning.*

"I never know whom I'm speaking to," he admits. "I've
never actually seen my audience. But I know you're great
and good. I know that however you appear, and however
you make your living, you deserve to hear this:

"Humans have always lived in terror. Rainstorms and
the eclipsing moon and earthquakes and the ominous guts
of some disemboweled goat—all have preyed upon our
fears and defeated our fragile optimisms. But what we fear
today—what shapes and reshapes the universe around
us—is a child of our own imaginations.

"A whirlwind that owes its very existence to glorious,
endless us!"

ABLE

The boy stops walking once or twice, letting the fat leopard keep pace. Then he pushes his way through a last wall
of emerald ferns, stepping out into the bright damp air
above the rounded pool. A splashing takes him by surprise.
He looks down at his secret pool, and he squints, watching
what seems to be a woman pulling her way through the
clear water with thick, strong arms. She is naked. Astonishingly, wonderfully naked. A stubby hand grabs an

overhanging limb, and she stands on the rocky shore, moving as if exhausted, picking her way up the slippery slope until she finds an open patch of halfway flattened earth where she can collapse, rolling onto her back, her smooth flesh glistening and her hard breasts shining up at Able, making him sick with joy.

Then she starts to cry, quietly, with a deep sadness.

Lust vanishes, replaced by simple embarrassment. Able flinches and starts to step back, and that's when he first looks at her face.

He recognizes its features.

Intrigued, the boy picks his way down to the shoreline, practically standing beside the crying woman.

She looks at him, and she sniffs.

"I saw two of them," he reports. "And I saw you, too. You were inside that cylinder, weren't you?"

She watches him, saying nothing.

"I saw something pull you out of that trap. And then I couldn't see you. *It* must have put you here, I guess. Out of its way." Able nods, and smiles. He can't help but stare at her breasts, but at least he keeps his eyes halfway closed, pretending to look out over the water instead. "*It* took pity on you, I guess."

A good-sized fish breaks on the water.

The woman seems to watch the creature as it swims past, big blue scales catching the light, heavy fins lazily shoving their way through the warm water. The fish eyes are huge and black, and they are stupid eyes. The mind behind them sees nothing but vague shapes and sudden motions. Able knows from experience: If he stands quite still, the creature will come close enough to touch.

"They're called coelacanths," he explains.

Maybe the woman reacts to his voice. Some sound other than crying now leaks from her.

So Able continues, explaining, "They were rare, once. I've studied them quite a bit. They're old and primitive, and they were almost extinct when we found them. But when *they* got loose, got free, and took apart the Earth . . .

and took everything and everyone with them up into the sky . . ."

The woman gazes up at the towering horsetails.

Able stares at her legs and what lies between them.

"Anyway," he mutters, "there's more coelacanths now than ever. They live in a million oceans, and they've never been more successful, really." He hesitates, and then adds, "Kind of like us, I think. Like people. You know?"

The woman turns, staring at him with gray-white eyes. And with a quiet hard voice, she says, "No."

She says, "That's an idiot's opinion."

And then with a grace that belies her strong frame, she dives back into the water, kicking hard and chasing that ancient and stupid fish all the way back to the bottom.

The Dog Said Bow-Wow

Michael Swanwick

Michael Swanwick made his debut in 1980, and in the twenty-five years that have followed he has established himself as one of SF's most prolific and consistently excellent writers at short lengths, as well as one of the premier novelists of his generation. He has won the Theodore Sturgeon Award and the Asimov's *Readers Award poll. In 1991, his novel* Stations of the Tide *won him a Nebula Award as well, and in 1995 he won the World Fantasy Award for his story "Radio Waves." He's won the Hugo Award four times between 1999 and 2003, for his stories "The Very Pulse of the Machine," "Scherzo with Tyrannosaur," "The Dog Said Bow-Wow," and "Slow Life." His other books include the novels* In The Drift, Vacuum Flowers, The Iron Dragon's Daughter *(which was a finalist for the World Fantasy Award and the Arthur C. Clarke Award, a rare distinction!),* Jack Faust, *and, most recently,* Bones of the Earth, *plus a novella-length book,* Griffin's Egg. *His short fiction has been assembled in* Gravity's Angels, A Geography of Unknown Lands, Slow Dancing Through Time *(a collection of his collaborative short work with other writers),* Moon Dogs, Puck Aleshire's Abecedary, *and* Tales of Old Earth. *He's also published a collection of critical articles,* The Postmodern Archipelago, *and a book-length interview,* Being Gardner Dozois. *His most recent books are the collections* Cigar-Box Faust and Other Miniatures, The Periodic Table of SF, *and* Michael Swanwick's Field Guide to the Mesozoic Megafauna. *Swanwick lives in Philadelphia with his wife, Marianne Porter. He has a website at www.michaelswanwick.com.*

Here he takes us to a colorful, curious, and eccentric future on the far side of a worldwide Singularity, to spin a swashbuckling, slyly entertaining adventure explaining why there really are some things that Mankind Was Not Meant To Know and that they certainly shouldn't tamper with.

The dog looked as if he had just stepped out of a children's book. There must have been a hundred physical adaptations required to allow him to walk upright. The pelvis, of course, had been entirely reshaped. The feet alone would have needed dozens of changes. He had knees, and knees were tricky.

To say nothing of the neurological enhancements.

But what Darger found himself most fascinated by was the creature's costume. His suit fit him perfectly, with a slit in the back for the tail, and—again—a hundred invisible adaptations that caused it to hang on his body in a way that looked perfectly natural.

"You must have an extraordinary tailor," Darger said.

The dog shifted his cane from one paw to the other, so they could shake, and in the least affected manner imaginable replied, "That is a common observation, sir."

"You're from the States?" It was a safe assumption, given where they stood—on the docks—and that the schooner *Yankee Dreamer* had sailed up the Thames with the morning tide. Darger had seen its bubble sails over the rooftops, like so many rainbows. "Have you found lodgings yet?"

"Indeed I am, and no I have not. If you could recommend a tavern of the cleaner sort?"

"No need for that. I would be only too happy to put you up for a few days in my own rooms." And, lowering his voice, Darger said, "I have a business proposition to put to you."

"Then lead on, sir, and I shall follow you with a right good will."

•   •   •

• • •

The dog's name was Sir Blackthorpe Ravenscairn de Plus Precieux, but "Call me Sir Plus," he said with a self-denigrating smile, and "Surplus" he was ever after.

Surplus was, as Darger had at first glance suspected and by conversation confirmed, a bit of a rogue—something more than mischievous and less than a cut-throat. A dog, in fine, after Darger's own heart.

Over drinks in a public house, Darger displayed his box and explained his intentions for it. Surplus warily touched the intricately carved teak housing, and then drew away from it. "You outline an intriguing scheme, Master Darger—"

"Please. Call me Aubrey."

"Aubrey, then. Yet here we have a delicate point. How shall we divide up the . . . ah, *spoils* of this enterprise? I hesitate to mention this, but many a promising partnership has foundered on precisely such shoals."

Darger unscrewed the salt cellar and poured its contents onto the table. With his dagger, he drew a fine line down the middle of the heap. "I divide—you choose. Or the other way around, if you please. From self-interest, you'll not find a grain's difference between the two."

"Excellent!" cried Surplus and, dropping a pinch of salt in his beer, drank to the bargain.

It was raining when they left for Buckingham Labyrinth. Darger stared out the carriage window at the drear streets and worn buildings gliding by and sighed. "Poor, weary old London! History is a grinding-wheel that has been applied too many a time to thy face."

"It is also," Surplus reminded him, "to be the making of our fortunes. Raise your eyes to the Labyrinth, sir, with its soaring towers and bright surfaces rising above these shops and flats like a crystal mountain rearing up out of a ramshackle wooden sea, and be comforted."

"That is fine advice," Darger agreed. "But it cannot comfort a lover of cities, nor one of a melancholic turn of mind."

"Pah!" cried Surplus, and said no more until they arrived at their destination.

At the portal into Buckingham, the sergeant-interface strode forward as they stepped down from the carriage. He blinked at the sight of Surplus, but said only, "Papers?"

Surplus presented the man with his passport and the credentials Darger had spent the morning forging, then added with a negligent wave of his paw, "And this is my autistic."

The sergeant-interface glanced once at Darger. and forgot about him completely. Darger had the gift, priceless to one in his profession, of a face so nondescript that once someone looked away, it disappeared from that person's consciousness forever. "This way, sir. The officer of protocol will want to examine these himself."

A dwarf savant was produced to lead them through the outer circle of the Labyrinth. They passed by ladies in bioluminescent gowns and gentlemen with boots and gloves cut from leathers cloned from their own skin. Both women and men were extravagantly bejeweled—for the ostentatious display of wealth was yet again in fashion—and the halls were lushly clad and pillared in marble, porphyry, and jasper. Yet Darger could not help noticing how worn the carpets were, how chipped and sooted the oil lamps. His sharp eye espied the remains of an antique electrical system, and traces as well of telephone lines and fiber optic cables from an age when those technologies were yet workable.

These last he viewed with particular pleasure.

The dwarf savant stopped before a heavy black door carved over with gilt griffins, locomotives, and fleurs-de-lis. "This is a door," he said. "The wood is ebony. Its binomial is *Diospyros ebenum.* It was harvested in Serendip. The gilding is of gold. Gold has an atomic weight of 197.2."

He knocked on the door and opened it.

The officer of protocol was a dark-browed man of imposing mass. He did not stand for them. "I am Lord Coherence-Hamilton, and this—" he indicated the slender, clear-eyed woman who stood beside him—"is my sister, Pamela."

Surplus bowed deeply to the Lady, who dimpled and dipped a slight curtsey in return.

The protocol officer quickly scanned the credentials. "Explain these fraudulent papers, sirrah. The Demesne of Western Vermont! Damn me if I have ever heard of such a place."

"Then you have missed much," Surplus said haughtily. "It is true we are a young nation, created only seventy-five years ago during the Partition of New England. But there is much of note to commend our fair land. The glorious beauty of Lake Champlain. The gene-mills of Winooski, that ancient seat of learning the *Universitas Vridis Montis* of Burlington, the Technarchaeological Institute of—" He stopped. "We have much to be proud of, sir, and nothing of which to be ashamed."

The bearlike official glared suspiciously at him, then said, "What brings you to London? Why do you desire an audience with the queen?"

"My mission and destination lie in Russia. However, England being on my itinerary and I a diplomat, I was charged to extend the compliments of my nation to your monarch." Surplus did not quite shrug. "There is no more to it than that. In three days I shall be in France, and you will have forgotten about me completely."

Scornfully the officer tossed his credentials to the savant, who glanced at and politely returned them to Surplus. The small fellow sat down at a little desk scaled to his own size and swiftly made out a copy. "Your papers will be taken to Whitechapel and examined there. If everything goes well—which I doubt—and there's an opening—not likely—you'll be presented to the queen sometime between a week and ten days hence."

"Ten days! Sir, I am on a very strict schedule!"

"Then you wish to withdraw your petition?"

Surplus hesitated. "I . . . I shall have to think on't, sir."

Lady Pamela watched coolly as the dwarf savant led them away.

The room they were shown to had massively framed mirrors and oil paintings dark with age upon the walls, and a generous log fire in the hearth. When their small guide had gone, Darger carefully locked and bolted the door. Then he tossed the box onto the bed, and bounced down alongside it. Lying flat on his back, staring up at the ceiling, he said, "The Lady Pamela is a strikingly beautiful woman. I'll be damned if she's not."

Ignoring him, Surplus locked paws behind his back, and proceeded to pace up and down the room. He was full of nervous energy. At last, he expostulated, "This is a deep game you have gotten me into, Darger! Lord Coherence-Hamilton suspects us of all manner of blackguardry."

"Well, and what of that?"

"I repeat myself: We have not even begun our play yet, and he suspects us already! I trust neither him nor his genetically remade dwarf."

"You are in no position to be displaying such vulgar prejudice."

"I am not *bigoted* about the creature, Darger, I *fear* him! Once you let suspicion of us into that macroencephalic head of his, and he will worry at it until he has found out our every secret."

"Get a grip on yourself, Surplus! Be a man! We are in this too deep already to back out. Questions would be asked, and investigations made."

"I am anything but a man, thank God," Surplus replied. "Still, you are right. In for a penny, in for a pound. For now, I might as well sleep. Get off the bed. You can have the hearth-rug."

"I! The rug!"

"I am groggy of mornings. Were someone to knock, and I to unthinkingly open the door, it would hardly do to have you found sharing a bed with your master."

The next day, Surplus returned to the Office of Protocol to declare that he was authorized to wait as long as two weeks for an audience with the queen, though not a day more.

"You have received new orders from your government?" Lord Coherence-Hamilton asked suspiciously. "I hardly see how."

"I have searched my conscience, and reflected on certain subtleties of phrasing in my original instructions," Surplus said. "That is all."

He emerged from the office to discover Lady Pamela waiting outside. When she offered to show him the Labyrinth, he agreed happily to her plan. Followed by Darger, they strolled inward, first to witness the changing of the guard in the forecourt vestibule, before the great pillared wall that was the front of Buckingham Palace before it was swallowed up in the expansion of architecture during the mad, glorious years of Utopia. Following which, they proceeded toward the viewers' gallery above the chamber of state.

"I see from your repeated glances that you are interested in my diamonds, 'Sieur Plus Precieux!" Lady Pamela said. "Well might you be. They are a family treasure, centuries old and manufactured to order, each stone flawless and perfectly matched. The indentures of a hundred autistics would not buy the like."

Surplus smiled down again at the necklace, draped about her lovely throat and above her perfect breasts. "I assure you, madame, it was not your necklace that held me so enthralled."

She colored delicately, pleased. Lightly, she said, "And that box your man carries with him wherever you go? What is in it?"

"That? A trifle. A gift for the Duke of Muscovy, who is the ultimate object of my journey," Surplus said. "I assure you, it is of no interest whatsoever."

"You were talking to someone last night," Lady Pamela said. "In your room."

"You were listening at my door? I am astonished and flattered."

She blushed. "No, no, my brother . . . it is his job, you see, surveillance."

"Possibly I was talking in my sleep. I have been told I do that occasionally."

"In accents? My brother said he heard two voices."

Surplus looked away. "In that, he was mistaken."

England's queen was a sight to rival any in that ancient land. She was as large as the lorry of ancient legend, and surrounded by attendants who hurried back and forth, fetching food and advice and carrying away dirty plates and signed legislation. From the gallery, she reminded Darger of a queen bee, but unlike the bee, this queen did not copulate, but remained proudly virgin.

Her name was Gloriana the First, and she was a hundred years old and still growing.

Lord Campbell-Supercollider, a friend of Lady Pamela's met by chance, who had insisted on accompanying them to the gallery leaned close to Surplus and murmured, "You are impressed, of course, by our queen's magnificence." The warning in his voice was impossible to miss. "Foreigners invariably are."

"I am dazzled," Surplus said.

"Well might you be. For scattered through her majesty's great body are thirty-six brains, connected with thick ropes of ganglia in a hypercube configuration. Her processing capacity is the equal of many of the great computers from Utopian times."

Lady Pamela stifled a yawn. "Darling Rory," she said, touching the Lord Campbell-Supercollider's sleeve. "Duty calls me. Would you be so kind as to show my American friend the way back to the outer circle?"

"Of course, my dear." He and Surplus stood (Darger was,

of course, already standing) and paid their compliments.
Then, when Lady Pamela was gone and Surplus started to
turn toward the exit, "Not that way. Those stairs are for com-
moners. You and I may leave by the gentlemen's staircase."

The narrow stairs twisted downward beneath clouds of
gilt cherubs-and-airships, and debouched into a marble-
floored hallway. Surplus and Darger stepped out of the
stairway and found their arms abruptly seized by baboons.

There were five baboons all told, with red uniforms and
matching choke collars with leashes that gathered in the
hand of an ornately mustached officer whose gold piping
identified him as a master of apes. The fifth baboon bared
his teeth and hissed savagely.

Instantly, the master of apes yanked back on his leash
and said, "There, Hercules! There, sirrah! What do you do?
What do you say?"

The baboon drew himself up and bowed curtly. "Please
come with us," he said with difficulty. The master of apes
cleared his throat. Sullenly, the baboon added, "Sir."

"This is outrageous!" Surplus cried. "I am a diplomat,
and under international law immune to arrest."

"Ordinarily, sir, this is true," said the master of apes
courteously. "However, you have entered the inner circle
without her majesty's invitation and are thus subject to
stricter standards of security."

"I had no idea these stairs went inward. I was led here
by—" Surplus looked about helplessly. Lord Campbell-
Supercollider was nowhere to be seen.

So, once again, Surplus and Darger found themselves
escorted to the Office of Protocol.

"The wood is teak. Its binomial is Tectonia grandis. Teak is
native to Burma, Hind, and Siam. The box is carved elabo-
rately but without refinement." The dwarf savant opened it.
"Within the casing is an archaic device for electronic inter-
communication. The instrument chip is a gallium-arsenide

ceramic. The chip weighs six ounces. The device is a product of the Utopian end-times."

"A modem!" The protocol officer's eyes bugged out. "You dared bring a *modem* into the inner circle and almost into the presence of the queen?" His chair stood and walked around the table. Its six insectile legs looked too slender to carry his great, legless mass. Yet it moved nimbly and well.

"It is harmless, sir. Merely something our technarchaeologists unearthed and thought would amuse the Duke of Muscovy, who is well-known for his love of all things antiquarian. It is, apparently, of some cultural or historical significance, though without re-reading my instructions, I would be hard pressed to tell you what."

Lord Coherence-Hamilton raised his chair so that he loomed over Surplus, looking dangerous and domineering. "*Here* is the historic significance of your modem: The Utopians filled the world with their computer webs and nets, burying cables and nodes so deeply and plentifully that they shall never be entirely rooted out. They then released into that virtual universe demons and mad gods. These intelligences destroyed Utopia and almost destroyed humanity as well. Only the valiant worldwide destruction of all modes of interface saved us from annihilation!" He glared.

"Oh, you lackwit! Have you no history? These creatures hate us because our ancestors created them. They are still alive, though confined to their electronic netherworld, and want only a modem to extend themselves into the physical realm. Can you wonder, then, that the penalty for possessing such a device is—" he smiled menacingly—"death?"

"No, sir, it is not. Possession of a *working* modem is a mortal crime. This device is harmless. Ask your savant."

"Well?" the big man growled at his dwarf. "Is it functional?"

"No. It—"

"Silence." Lord Coherence-Hamilton turned back to Surplus. "You are a fortunate cur. You will not be charged with any crimes. However, while you are here, I will keep this filthy device locked away and under my control. Is that understood, Sir Bow-Wow?"

Surplus sighed. "Very well," he said. "It is only for a week, after all."

That night, the Lady Pamela Coherence-Hamilton came by Surplus's room to apologize for the indignity of his arrest, of which, she assured him, she had just now learned. He invited her in. In short order they somehow found themselves kneeling face-to-face on the bed, unbuttoning each other's clothing.

Lady Pamela's breasts had just spilled delightfully from her dress when she drew back, clutching the bodice closed again, and said, "Your man is watching us."

"And what concern is that to us?" Surplus said jovially. "The poor fellow's an autistic. Nothing he sees or hears matters to him. You might as well be embarrassed by the presence of a chair."

"Even were he a wooden carving, I would his eyes were not on me."

"As you wish " Surplus clapped his paws. "Sirrah! Turn around."

Obediently, Darger turned his back. This was his first experience with his friend's astonishing success with women. How many sexual adventuresses, he wondered, might one tumble, if one's form were unique? On reflection, the question answered itself.

Behind him, he heard the Lady Pamela giggle. Then, in a voice low with passion, Surplus said, "No, leave the diamonds on."

With a silent sigh, Darger resigned himself to a long night. Since he was bored and yet could not turn to watch the pair cavorting on the bed without giving himself away, he was perforce required to settle for watching them in the mirror.

They began, of course, by doing it doggy-style.

•   •   •

The next day, Surplus fell sick. Hearing of his indisposition, Lady Pamela sent one of her autistics with a bowl of broth and then followed herself in a surgical mask.

Surplus smiled weakly to see her. "You have no need of that mask," he said. "By my life, I swear that what ails me is not communicable. As you doubtless know, we who have been remade are prone to endocrinological imbalance."

"Is that all?" Lady Pamela spooned some broth into his mouth, then dabbed at a speck of it with a napkin. "Then fix it. You have been very wicked to frighten me over such a trifle."

"Alas," Surplus said sadly, "I am a unique creation, and my table of endocrine balances was lost in an accident at sea. There are copies in Vermont, of course. But by the time even the swiftest schooner can cross the Atlantic twice, I fear me I shall be gone."

"Oh, dearest Surplus!" The Lady caught up his paws in her hands. "Surely there is some measure, however desperate, to be taken?"

"Well . . ." Surplus turned to the wall in thought. After a very long time, he turned back and said, "I have a confession to make. The modem your brother holds for me? It is functional."

"Sir!" Lady Pamela stood, gathering her skirts, and stepped away from the bed in horror. "Surely not!"

"My darling and delight, you must listen to me." Surplus glanced weakly toward the door, then lowered his voice. "Come close and I shall whisper."

She obeyed.

"In the waning days of Utopia, during the war between men and their electronic creations, scientists and engineers bent their efforts toward the creation of a modem that could be safely employed by humans. One immune from the attack of demons. One that could, indeed, compel their obedience. Perhaps you have heard of this project."

"There are rumors, but . . . no such device was ever built."

"Say rather that no such device was built *in time*. It had just barely been perfected when the mobs came rampaging through the laboratories, and the Age of the Machine was over. Some few, however, were hidden away before the last technicians were killed. Centuries later, brave researchers at the Technarchaeological Institute of Shelburne recovered six such devices and mastered the art of their use. One device was destroyed in the process. Two are kept in Burlington. The others were given to trusted couriers and sent to the three most powerful allies of the Demesne—one of which is, of course, Russia."

"This is hard to believe," Lady Pamela said wonderingly. "Can such marvels be?"

"Madame, I employed it two nights ago in this very room! Those voices your brother heard? I was speaking with my principals in Vermont. They gave me permission to extend my stay here to a fortnight."

He gazed imploringly at her. "If you were to bring me the device, I could then employ it to save my life."

Lady Coherence-Hamilton resolutely stood. "Fear nothing, then. I swear by my soul, the modem shall be yours tonight."

The room was lit by a single lamp that cast wild shadows whenever anyone moved, as if of illicit spirits at a witch's Sabbath.

It was an eerie sight. Darger, motionless, held the modem in his hands. Lady Pamela, who had a sense of occasion, had changed to a low-cut gown of clinging silks, dark-red as human blood. It swirled about her as she hunted through the wainscoting for a jack left unused for centuries. Surplus sat up weakly in bed, eyes half-closed, directing her. It might have been, Darger thought, an allegorical tableau of the human body being directed by its sick animal passions, while the intellect stood by, paralyzed by lack of will.

"There!" Lady Pamela triumphantly straightened, her necklace scattering tiny rainbows in the dim light.

Darger stiffened. He stood perfectly still for the length of three long breaths, then shook and shivered like one undergoing seizure. His eyes rolled back in his head.

In hollow, unworldly tones, he said, "What man calls me up from the vasty deep?" It was a voice totally unlike his own, one harsh and savage and eager for unholy sport. "Who dares risk my wrath?"

"You must convey my words to the autistic's ears," Surplus murmured. "For he is become an integral part of the modem—not merely its operator, but its voice."

"I stand ready," Lady Pamela replied.

"Good girl. Tell it who I am."

"It is Sir Blackthorpe Ravenscairn de Plus Precieux who speaks, and who wishes to talk to . . ." She paused.

"To his most august and socialist honor, the mayor of Burlington."

"His most august and socialist honor," Lady Pamela began. She turned toward the bed and said quizzically, "The mayor of Burlington?"

"'Tis but an official title, much like your brother's, for he who is in fact the spy-master for the Demesne of Western Vermont," Surplus said weakly. "Now repeat to it: I compel thee on threat of dissolution to carry my message. Use those exact words."

Lady Pamela repeated the words into Darger's ear.

He screamed. It was a wild and unholy sound that sent the Lady skittering away from him in a momentary panic. Then, in mid-cry, he ceased.

"Who is this?" Darger said in an entirely new voice, this one human. "You have the voice of a woman. Is one of my agents in trouble?"

"Speak to him now, as you would to any man: forthrightly, directly, and without evasion." Surplus sank his head back on his pillow and closed his eyes.

So (as it seemed to her) the Lady Coherence-Hamilton explained Surplus's plight to his distant master, and from him received both condolences and the needed information to return Surplus's endocrine levels to a functioning harmony. After proper courtesies, then, she thanked the American spy-master and unjacked the modem. Darger returned to passivity.

The leather-cased endocrine kit lay open on a small table by the bed. At Lady Pamela's direction, Darger began applying the proper patches to various places on Surplus's body. It was not long before Surplus opened his eyes.

"Am I to be well?" he asked and, when the Lady nodded, "Then I fear I must be gone in the morning. Your brother has spies everywhere. If he gets the least whiff of what this device can do, he'll want it for himself."

Smiling, Lady Pamela hoisted the box in her hand. "Indeed, who can blame him? With such a toy, great things could be accomplished."

"So he will assuredly think. I pray you, return it to me."

She did not. "This is more than just a communication device, sir," she said. "Though in that mode it is of incalculable value. You have shown that it can enforce obedience on the creatures that dwell in the forgotten nerves of the ancient world. Ergo, they can be compelled to do our calculations for us."

"Indeed, so our technarchaeologists tell us. You must . . ."

"We have created monstrosities to perform the duties that were once done by machines. But with *this*, there would be no necessity to do so. We have allowed ourselves to be ruled by an icosahexadexal-brained freak. Now we have no need for Gloriana the Gross, Gloriana the Fat and Grotesque, Gloriana the Maggot Queen!"

"Madame!"

"It is time, I believe, that England had a new queen. A human queen."

"Think of my honor!"

Lady Pamela paused in the doorway. "You are a very pretty fellow indeed. But with this, I can have the monarchy and keep such a harem as will reduce your memory to that of a passing and trivial fancy."

With a rustle of skirts, she spun away.

"Then I am undone!" Surplus cried, and fainted onto the bed.

Quietly, Darger closed the door. Surplus raised himself from the pillows, began removing the patches from his body, and said, "Now what?"

"Now we get some sleep," Darger said. "Tomorrow will be a busy day."

The master of apes came for them after breakfast, and marched them to their usual destination. By now, Darger was beginning to lose track of exactly how many times he had been in the Office of Protocol. They entered to find Lord Coherence-Hamilton in a towering rage, and his sister, calm and knowing, standing in a corner with her arms crossed, watching. Looking at them both now, Darger wondered how he could ever have imagined that the brother outranked his sister.

The modem lay opened on the dwarf savant's desk. The little fellow leaned over the device, studying it minutely.

Nobody said anything until the master of apes and his baboons had left. Then Lord Coherence-Hamilton roared, "Your modem refuses to work for us!"

"As I told you, sir," Surplus said coolly, "it is inoperative."

"That's a bold-arsed fraud and a goat-buggering lie!" In his wrath, the Lord's chair rose up on its spindly legs so high that his head almost bumped against the ceiling. "I know of your activities"—he nodded toward his sister—"and demand that you show us how this whoreson device works!"

"Never!" Surplus cried stoutly. "I have my honor, sir."

"Your honor, too scrupulously insisted upon, may well lead to your death, sir."

Surplus threw back his head. "Then I die for Vermont!"

At this moment of impasse, Lady Hamilton stepped forward between the two antagonists to restore peace. "I know what might change your mind." With a knowing smile, she raised a hand to her throat and denuded herself of her diamonds. "I saw how you rubbed them against your face the other night. How you licked and fondled them. How ecstatically you took them into your mouth."

She closed his paws about them. "They are yours, sweet 'Sieur Precieux, for a word."

"You would give them up?" Surplus said, as if amazed at the very idea. In fact, the necklace had been his and Darger's target from the moment they'd seen it. The only barrier that now stood between them and the merchants of Amsterdam was the problem of freeing themselves from the Labyrinth before their marks finally realized that the modem was indeed a cheat. And to this end they had the invaluable tool of a thinking man whom all believed to be an autistic, and a plan that would give them almost twenty hours in which to escape.

"Only think, dear Surplus." Lady Pamela stroked his head and then scratched him behind one ear, while he stared down at the precious stones. "Imagine the life of wealth and ease you could lead, the women, the power. It all lies in your hands. All you need do is close them."

Surplus took a deep breath. "Very well," he said. "The secret lies in the condenser, which takes a full day to re-charge. Wait but—"

"Here's the problem," the savant said unexpectedly. He poked at the interior of the modem. "There was a wire loose."

He jacked the device into the wall.

"Oh, dear God," Darger said.

A savage look of raw delight filled the dwarf savant's face, and he seemed to swell before them.

"I am free!" he cried in a voice so loud it seemed impossible that it could arise from such a slight source. He shook as if an enormous electrical current were surging through him. The stench of ozone filled the room.

He burst into flames and advanced on the English spy-master and her brother.

While all stood aghast and paralyzed, Darger seized Surplus by the collar and hauled him out into the hallway, slamming the door shut as he did.

• • •

They had not run twenty paces down the hall when the door to the Office of Protocol exploded outward, sending flaming splinters of wood down the hallway.

Satanic laughter boomed behind them.

Glancing over his shoulder, Darger saw the burning dwarf, now blackened to a cinder, emerge from a room engulfed in flames, capering and dancing. The modem, though disconnected, was now tucked under one arm, as if it were exceedingly valuable to him. His eyes were round and white and lidless. Seeing them, he gave chase.

"Aubrey!" Surplus cried. "We are headed the *wrong way!*"

It was true. They were running deeper into the Labyrinth, toward its heart, rather than outward. But it was impossible to turn back now. They plunged through scattering crowds of nobles and servitors, trailing fire and supernatural terror in their wake.

The scampering grotesque set fire to the carpets with every footfall. A wave of flame tracked him down the hall, incinerating tapestries and wallpaper and wood trim. No matter how they dodged, it ran straight toward them. Clearly, in the programmatic literalness of its kind, the demon from the web had determined that having early seen them, it must early kill them as well.

Darger and Surplus raced through dining rooms and salons, along balconies and down servants' passages. To no avail. Dogged by their hyper-natural nemesis, they found themselves running down a passage, straight toward two massive bronze doors, one of which had been left just barely ajar. So fearful were they that they hardly noticed the guards.

"Hold, sirs!"

The mustachioed master of apes stood before the doorway, his baboons straining against their leashes. His eyes widened with recognition. "By gad, it's you!" he cried in astonishment.

"Lemme kill 'em!" one of the baboons cried. "The lousy bastards!" The others growled agreement.

Surplus would have tried to reason with them, but when he started to slow his pace, Darger put a broad hand on his back and shoved. "Dive!" he commanded. So of necessity the dog of rationality had to bow to the man of action. He tobagganed wildly across the polished marble floor between two baboons, straight at the master of apes, and then between his legs.

The man stumbled, dropping the leashes as he did.

The baboons screamed and attacked.

For an instant, all five apes were upon Darger, seizing his limbs, snapping at his face and neck. Then the burning dwarf arrived, and, finding his target obstructed, seized the nearest baboon. The animal shrieked as its uniform burst into flames.

As one, the other baboons abandoned their original quarry to fight this newcomer who had dared attack one of their own.

In a trice, Darger leaped over the fallen master of apes, and was through the door. He and Surplus threw their shoulders against its metal surface and pushed. He had one brief glimpse of the fight, with the baboons aflame, and their master's body flying through the air. Then the door slammed shut. Internal bars and bolts, operated by smoothly oiled mechanisms, automatically latched themselves.

For the moment, they were safe.

Surplus slumped against the smooth bronze, and wearily asked, "Where did you *get* that modem?"

"From a dealer of antiquities." Darger wiped his brow with his kerchief. "It was transparently worthless. Whoever would dream it could be repaired?"

Outside, the screaming ceased. There was a very brief silence. Then the creature flung itself against one of the metal doors. It rang with the impact.

A delicate girlish voice wearily said, "What is this noise?"

They turned in surprise and found themselves looking up at the enormous corpus of Queen Gloriana. She lay upon her pallet, swaddled in satin and lace, and abandoned by all, save her valiant (though doomed) guardian apes. A pervasive yeasty smell emanated from her flesh. Within the tremendous folds of chins by the dozens and scores was a small human face. Its mouth moved delicately and asked, "What is trying to get in?"

The door rang again. One of its great hinges gave.

Darger bowed. "I fear, madame, it is your death."

"Indeed?" Blue eyes opened wide and, unexpectedly, Gloriana laughed. "If so, that is excellent good news. I have been praying for death an extremely long time."

"Can any of God's creations truly pray for death and mean it?" asked Darger, who had his philosophical side. "I have known unhappiness myself, yet even so life is precious to me."

"Look at me!" Far up to one side of the body, a tiny arm—though truly no tinier than any woman's arm—waved feebly. "I am not God's creation, but Man's. Who would trade ten minutes of their own life for a century of mine? Who, having mine, would not trade it all for death?"

A second hinge popped. The doors began to shiver. Their metal surfaces radiated heat.

"Darger, we must leave!" Surplus cried. "There is a time for learned conversation, but it is not now."

"Your friend is right," Gloriana said. "There is a small archway hidden behind yon tapestry. Go through it. Place your hand on the left wall and run. If you turn whichever way you must to keep from letting go of the wall, it will lead you outside. You are both rogues, I see, and doubtless deserve punishment, yet I can find nothing in my heart for you but friendship."

"Madame . . ." Darger began, deeply moved.

"Go! My bridegroom enters."

The door began to fall inward. With a final cry of "Farewell!" from Darger and "Come *on!*" from Surplus, they sped away.

By the time they had found their way outside, all of Buckingham Labyrinth was in flames. The demon, however, did not emerge from the flames, encouraging them to believe that when the modem it carried finally melted down, it had been forced to return to that unholy realm from whence it came.

The sky was red with flames as the sloop set sail for Calais. Leaning against the rail, watching, Surplus shook his head. "What a terrible sight! I cannot help feeling, in part, responsible."

"Come! Come!" Darger said. "This dyspepsia ill becomes you. We are both rich fellows, now! The Lady Pamela's diamonds will maintain us lavishly for years to come. As for London, this is far from the first fire it has had to endure. Nor will it be the last. Life is short, and so, while we live, let us be jolly!"

"These are strange words for a melancholiac," Surplus said wonderingly.

"In triumph, my mind turns its face to the sun. Dwell not on the past, dear friend, but on the future that lies glittering before us."

"The necklace is worthless," Surplus said. "Now that I have the leisure to examine it, free of the distracting flesh of Lady Pamela, I see that these are not diamonds, but mere imitations." He made to cast the necklace into the Thames.

Before he could, though, Darger snatched away the stones from him and studied them closely. Then he threw back his head and laughed. "The biters bit! Well, it may be paste, but it looks valuable still. We shall find good use for it in Paris."

"We are going to Paris?"

"We are partners, are we not? Remember that antique wisdom that whenever a door closes, another opens? For every city that burns, another beckons. To France, then, and adventure! After which, Italy, the Vatican Empire, Austro-Hungary, perhaps even Russia! Never forget that you have yet to present your credentials to the Duke of Muscovy."

"Very well," Surplus said. "But when we do, *I'll* pick out the modem."

Barry Westphall Crashes the Singularity

James Patrick Kelly

Here's a sly little tale that suggests that if you get tired of waiting for the Singularity to arrive, you can always go to it.

James Patrick Kelly made his first sale in 1975, and has since gone on to become one of the most respected and popular writers to enter the field in the last twenty years. Although Kelly has had some success with novels, especially with Wildlife, *he has perhaps had more impact to date as a writer of short fiction, with stories such as "Solstice," "The Prisoner of Chillon," "Glass Cloud," "Mr. Boy," "Pogrom," "Home Front," "Undone," and "Bernardo's House," and he is often ranked among the best short story writers in the business. His story "Think Like a Dinosaur" won him a Hugo Award in 1996, as did the story, "10^{16} to 1" in 2000. Kelly's first solo novel, the mostly ignored* Planet of Whispers, *came out in 1984. It was followed by* Freedom Beach, *a mosaic novel written in collaboration with John Kessel, and then by another solo novel,* Look Into the Sun. *His short work has been collected in* Think Like a Dinosaur, *and, most recently, in the collection* Strange But Not a Stranger. *Born in Mineola, New York, Kelly now lives with his family in Nottingham, New Hampshire. He has a website at www.JimKelly.net and reviews Internet-related matters for* Asimov's Science Fiction Magazine.

"In the name of the Holy Coffee and the Blessed Shot of Cuervo, amen." Barry Westphall waves the sign of the cross over the steaming cup, then sips. It is his third refill.

The bartender of the Armadillo Lodge is too busy washing glasses to pay attention, even though Westphall is his only customer.

"So anyway," Westphall says, "the brain is a quantum device." He licks a brown dribble from the corner of his mouth. "Capable of accessing the entire field of space-time by folding the empty dimensions." Westphall has had the headache for almost eight hours now. "You may be wondering how I know this." It feels like bees stinging his brain. "I haven't a clue." The tequila helps a little.

The phone rings in the kitchen; the bartender leaves Westphall to answer it.

"Of course, these dimensions aren't easily folded," says Westphall. "Takes an unusual combination of intense physical stimulation and careful neurotransmitter suppression to access a time line." He peers into the mirror behind the bar.

> **"I mean it," says the medbot's *N* partition. "He wouldn't be talking to no one. I think he sees us."**
> **"He sees nothing," says the medbot's *D* partition. Its *N* has always been excitable.**

Westphall rests his elbow on the bar and points at his reflection. "Something's wrong," he says to the mirror. "I know that much for sure. What the hell are you doing to me?"

> **"Unpack his next major memory cluster." The *D* partition invokes a priority glyph.**
> **In 2196, the medbot's *V* partition retracts the needle array from the brain of Barry Westphall's cryogenically frozen corpse, repositions it and inserts. A rosette of neurons fires and dies. Stills of twenty minutes Westphall's life on the night of July 22, 2002 tile across the medbot's sensorium.**

/Skip/

A woman wearing a black halter-top and jeans with the knees out surveys the nearly empty room.

/Skip/

She moves from the end of the bar to the seat next to Westphall.

/Skip/

She is too white by half to be living in the desert.

/Skip/

He watches her rattle ice in her empty glass.

/Skip/

Westphall lays a twenty dollar bill on the check.

/Skip/

Room Seven is a nightmare of knotty pine. There are cigarette burns in the wheat-colored carpet and a black halter top on the bureau.

"What can I do for you?" says the woman.

Westphall rubs a finger along his eyebrow. "Intense physical stimulation?"

"Whatever." The blue-green edge of a tattoo peeks from the waistband of her panties. She hitches both thumbs under the elastic. "You like?"

Westphall whistles like wind on a screen door.

The tattoo is of a rose that looks like a skull. Her hands are busy as she brushes her lips down his chest. "Did you know," says Westphall, "that quantum non-locality means that photons can communicate instantaneously over vast stretches of space-time?"

"Sure."

He lifts his hips. She bounces his Dockers off the closet door. She climbs on top of him and giggles as he counts vertebrae to the strap of her bra. He turns from her sloppy kiss to the mirror over the bureau.

"Ever feel like you were in two places at once?" he asks the future.

D partition proclaims a network resource alert.

The woman nibbles the lobe of his ear. "I'm right here, hotshot. Where are you?"

All the medbot's partitions repurpose non-essential functions to assist in the dissection of Westphall's memory. Even A partition breaks away from the daily memory synchronization to monitor the anomaly.

"Sorry," he says to her. "Wasn't talking to you." He licks the tip of her nose.

The medbot's A partition intervenes in the procedure. "What is he doing?" It invokes the emergency glyph. "Next memory cluster!" Nearby bots join the session.

The V partition retracts and repositions the needle; neurons fire and die. Stills tile across the sensorium.

/Skip/

Her naked back arches, pale as moonlight.

/Skip/

Westphall fills a plastic cup with tequila.

/Skip/

The pale woman sprawls in a nest of sheets.

/Skip/

An older woman in a blue uniform strips bedding into her laundry cart.

"Where is he?" says the medbot, as all its partitions but *V* freeze on the anomalous images. "Back, go back." By now most of the world's intelligence collective has joined the session. *V* continues to manipulate the needles sunk in Westphall's exposed cerebrum as the sensorium shows him putting an empty plastic glass on the bedstand of Room Seven at the Armadillo Lodge at 11:36PM.

A nanosecond later, he disappears from 2002. And instantly reappears in 2196.

"Excuse me," said Westphall, "but that's my brain you're destroying."

The medbot is just beginning to turn as Westphall yanks its sensorium module backward, breaking it off at the stalk and resulting in a catastrophic failure. Since most of the intelligence collective is following the session with an attention quotient of 98%, over six thousand nodes crash with the medbot.

Westphall pulls needles out of his frozen cerebrum. "*You* sent for me," he tells himself, "when they started dissecting you." He finishes, steps back and takes a good look at his dead body. He aged well. He makes a good-looking corpse, even with the top of his skull sawed off. It gives him a reason to live. "Why did you do this to yourself?"

He hears himself whisper over the medbot's brain-dead speakers. His voice sounds old. Raspy. Apologetic. "I thought they might revive me."

"Doesn't look like it."

"No." His corpse does not open his eyes.

"I always wanted to see the future."

"Me too." Westphall glances at the stack of frozen corpses waiting to have their memories un-packed. "Too bad I can't stay."

The pale woman blinks in the morning light. The sec-ond thing she notices is that the quart of Cuervo is empty. Westphall flushes the toilet and emerges from the bath-room of Room Seven.

"Come here, hotshot." She pats his side of the bed. "How's that headache?"

Barry Westphall settles next to her. "It's over," he says.

Flowers From Alice

Charles Stross & Cory Doctorow

Cory Doctorow is the coeditor of the popular Boing Boing *website (boingboing.net) and the outreach coordinator for the Electronic Frontier Foundation (www.eff.org). In 2001, he also won the John W. Campbell Award as the year's Best New Writer. His stories have appeared in* Asimov's Science Fiction Magazine, Science Fiction Age, On Spec, *and elsewhere, and were recently collected in* A Place So Foreign and Eight More. *His well-received first novel,* Down and Out in the Magic Kingdom, *won the* Locus Award *as Best First Novel. His most recent book is the novel* Eastern Standard Tribe. *He has a website at www.craphound.com.*

Charles Stross's bio notes appear with his solo story in this anthology on page 45.

Here they join their considerable talents to demonstrate that even deep in a Singularity, a wedding is always going to be a stressful occasion . . .

I don't know why I invited Al to my wedding. Nostalgia, maybe. Residual lust. She was the first girl I ever kissed, after all. You never forget your first. I couldn't help but turn my head when round-hipped, tall girls with pageboy hair walked by, hunched over their own breasts in terminal pubescent embarrassment, awkward and athletic at the same time. You don't get much of that these days outside of Amish country, no parent would choose to have a kid who was quite so visibly strange as Al had been as a teenager, but there were still examples of the genre to be had, if you looked hard enough, and they stirred something within me.

I couldn't forget Al, though it had been twenty years
since that sweet and sloppy kiss on the beach, ten years
since I'd run into her last, so severely post- that I hardly
recognized her. Wasn't a week went by that she didn't
wander through my imagination, evoking a lip-quirk that
wasn't a smile by about three notches. My to-be recognized it; it drove her up the wall, and she let me know
about it during post-coital self-criticism sessions.

It was a very wrong idea to invite Al to the wedding, but
the wedding itself was a bad idea, to be perfectly frank.
And I won't take all the blame for it, since Al decided to
show up, after all—if "decided" can be applied to someone
as post- as she (s/he?) (they?) [(s | t)/he(y)?] was by then.
But one morning as we sat at our prenuptial breakfast
table, my to-be and me, and spooned marmalade on our
muffins and watched the hummingbirds visit the feeder
outside our nook's window, one morning as we sat naked
and sated and sticky with marmalade and other fluids, one
morning I looked into my fiancée's eyes, I prodded at the
phone tattooed on my wrist and dialed a directory server
and began to recite the facts of Al's life into my hollow
tooth in full earshot of my lovely, lovely intended until the
directory had enough information to identify Al from
among all the billions of humans and trillions of multiplic-
itous post-humans that it knew about and the phone rang in
my hollow tooth and I was talking to Al.

"Al," I said, "Alice? Is that you? It's Cyd!"

There was no sound on the end of the line because when
you're as self-consciously post- as Al, you don't make un-
intentional sound, so there was no sharp intake of breath or
other cue of her reaction to this voice from her past, but
she answered finally and said, "Cyd, wonderful, it's been
too long," and the voice was warm and nuanced and rich
as any human voice but more so, tailored for the strengths
and acoustics of my skull and mouth which she had no
doubt induced from the characteristics of the other end of
the conversation. "You're getting married, huh? She
sounds wonderful. And you, you're doing well too? Well!

I should say so. Cyd, it's good to hear from you. Of course
one of me will come to your wedding. Can we help? Say
we can! I, oh, the caterer, no, you don't want to use that
caterer, she's booked for another wedding the day before
and a wedding *and* a Bar Mitzvah the day after, you know,
so, please, let me help! I'm sending over a logistics plan
now, I just evolved it for you, it's very optimal, you don't
have to use it, of course, though you should really."

And my to-be shook her head and answered *her* phone
and said, "Why hello, Alice! No, Cyd sprang this on me
without warning—one of his little surprises. Yes, I can see
you're talking to him, too. Of course, I'd love to see the
plans; it was so good of you to come up with them. Yes,
yes, of course. And you'll bring a date, won't you?"

Meanwhile, in my tooth, Al's still nattering on, "You
don't mind, do you? I respawned and put in a call to your
beautiful lady. I'm resynching with the copy every couple
instants, so I can tell you we're getting along famously,
Cyd, you always did have such great taste but you're *hope-
less* with logistics. I see the job is going well, I knew you'd
be an excellent polemicist, and it's such a vital function in
your social milieu!"

I didn't get more than ten more words in, but the society of Al kept up the conversation for me. I never got
bored, of course, because she had a trillion instances of me
simulated somewhere in her being, and she tried a trillion
different conversational gambits on all of them and chose
the ones that evoked the optimal response, fine-tuning as
she monitored my breathing and vitals over the phone. She
had access to every nuance of my life, of course, there's no
privacy with the post-humans, so there was hardly any
catching up to do.

I didn't expect her to show up on my door that afternoon.

My betrothed took it very well. She was working in her
study on her latest morph porn, down on the ground floor,

and I was upstairs with my neurofeedback machine, working up a suitable head of bile before writing my column. She beat me to the door.

"Who is it?" I called irritably, responding more to the draft around my ankles than to any conscious stimulus. No reply. I unplugged myself, swore quietly, then closed my eyes and began to ramp down the anger. I found people responded all wrong to me when I was mad. "Who?" I called again.

"Cyd! How cozy, what a great office!" A flock of silver lighter-than-air golf balls caromed off the doorframe and ricocheted around me—one softly pinged me on the end of the nose with a warm, tingling shock. It smelled utterly unlike a machine: human and slightly flowery—

"Al?" I asked.

The ball inflated, stretching its endoskeleton into a transducer surface. The others homed in on it, merging almost instantly into an inflatabubble that suddenly flashed into a hologram of Al as I'd last seen her in the flesh—only slightly tuned, her back straight and proud, her breasts fetchingly exposed by a Cretan-style dress that had been in fashion around the time we split up. "Hiya, Cydonia!" That grin, those sturdy, well-engineered teeth, and a sudden flashback to a meeting in a mall all those years ago. "Don't worry, I'm downstairs talking to your love wearing the real primary-me body, this is just a remote, *hey*, I *love* the antique render farm but isn't it a bit out of tune? Please, let me to fix it!"

"Ung," I said, shivering with fright, guts turning to jelly and hackles rising—exactly the wrong reaction and deeply embarrassing, but there's a *reason* I work behind a locked door most of the time. "Gimme five."

"How kawaii!" Al burst apart into half a dozen beachball-sized balloons and bounced out onto the landing. "See you downstairs!"

I just stood there, muscles twitching in an adrenalin-induced haze, as I wrestled to get my artificially induced anger under control. It took almost a minute, during which time I forced myself to listen as a series of loud thumping noises came from the hall downstairs, and I heard the sound of voices, indistinct, through the open doors: my fiancee's low and calm, and Al as enthusiastic and full of laughter as a puppy in a mid-belly rub. Al had left an afterscent behind, one that gave me dizzying flashbacks to teenage sexual experimentation—my first sex change, Al's first tongue job—and left me weak at the knees in an aftershock of memories. It's funny how after the fire's burned down all you can remember are the ashes of conflict, the arguments that drove you apart, until your ex shows up and reminds you what you've lost. Although knowing Al it might just as well be a joke as accidental.

Presently I went downstairs, to find the door open and a couple of huge crates sitting in the front yard—too big to come through the door without telling the house to grow a service entrance. I followed the voices to the living room, where my fiancée was curled up on our kidney-shaped sofa, opposite Al, who had somehow draped herself across the valuable antique tube TV and was reminiscing about nothing in particular at length. Her main incarnation looked alarmingly substantial, nothing like the soap-bubbles except for a slightly pearlescent luster to her skin. "You're so lucky with Cyd! So to speak. He's such a stable, consistent, unassuming primal male pre-post-! I won't say I envy you but you really need to make more of your big day together, I promise you, you won't regret it. I remember when we spoofed out from under our teachers one day and we blew a month's allowance at the distraction center and he said, Al, if I ever get—"

"Hello there," I said, nodding to Al, civil enough now my autonomic nervous system wasn't convinced I was under attack. "Do you metabolize? If so, can I offer you anything? Coffee, perhaps? What have you been up to all this time?" I barely registered my fiancée's fixed, glassy-eyed stare, which was glued to Al's left nipple ring like a target designator, or the way she was twitching her left index finger as if it was balanced on the hi-hat of a sidearm controller. These were normally bad signs, but right then, I was still reeling from the shocking smell of Al's skin. I know it was all part of her self-rep, but how could I possibly have forgotten it?

"Cyd!" She was off the television and across the room like the spirit of electricity, and grabbed me in a very physical bear hug. The nipple ring was hard, and even though her body wasn't made of CHON anymore she felt startlingly real. She grinned at me with insane joy. "Whee! Three hundred and twenty-seven million eight hundred and ninety-six thousand one hundred and four, five, six, seconds, and you *still* feel good to grab!" Over her shoulder, "You're a *very lucky person* to be marrying him, you know. Have you made up your mind what you are doing about the catering? Did you like my suggestion for the after-banquet orgy? What about the switch fetish session? You are going to be so good together!"

My affianced had a strained smile that I recognized as the mirror image of my own bared-teeth snarl when someone interrupted my work. As usual, her face was reflecting my own mood, and I stared at her tits until I had the rhythm of her breath down, and then matched it with my own, slowing down, bringing her down to the calm that I was forcing on myself. "Hey, Al," I said, patting her shoulder awkwardly.

"Oh, I'm doing it again, aren't I? Hang on, let me underclock a little." She closed her eyes and slowly touched her index finger to her nose. "Muuuuuch better," she said. "Sorry, I'm not really fit for human company these days. I've been running at very high clockspeed. Order makes order, you know—I'm going to wind up faster than entropy winds down and overtake thermodynamics if I can. I'm about a week away from entangling enough particles in Alpha Centauri to instantiate there, then I'm going to eat the star and, whee, look out chaos!"

"Ambitious," my betrothed said. I liked her absence of ambition, usually—so refreshing amid the grandiose schemes of the fucking post-s. "You're certainly *very* kind to have done so much thinking about our wedding, but we were planning to keep it all simple, you know. Just friends and family, a little dancing. Rather retro, but . . ." She trailed off, with a meaningful glance at me.

"But that's how we want it," I finished, taking my cue. I moved over to the sofa and sat by my promised and rubbed her tiny little feet, the way she liked. Human-human contact. Who needs any more than this?

She jerked her feet away and sat up. "You two haven't seen each other in so long, why don't I leave you to catch up?" she said, in a tone that let me know that I had better object.

"No, no, no," I said. "No. Work to do, too much work to do. Deadlines, deadlines, deadlines." I was uncomfortably aware of the heat radiating off Al's avatar, a quintillion smart motes clustered together, pliable, fuckable computation, the grinding microfriction of which was keeping her at about three degrees over blood-temp. "So good to see you, Al. What we'll do, we'll look over these plans and suggestions and whatnot, such very good stuff, I'm so sure, and we'll get in touch with you about helping out, right?"

She beamed and wedged herself onto the sofa between us, arms draped over our shoulders. "Of course, of course. You two, oh, I'm so happy for you. Perfect for each other!" She gave my intended a kiss on the cheek, and then gave me one that landed close enough to my earlobe to tickle the little hairs there. The kiss was fragrant, and wet as the first one, and I heard faint, crashing surf. It was only after she'd moved back (having darted her tongue out and squirmed it to the skin under my beard) that I realized she'd been generating it. I crossed my legs and furiously tried to think my erection away.

She bounded out the door and then stood on our lawn, amidst the crates. She gestured at them; "They're a wedding present!" she called, loud enough to rattle the picture window. Our neighbor across the street scowled at her from his attic, where he painted still lives of decaying fruit ten hours a day. "Enjoy!"

"Well, she hasn't changed," my love said, scowling. "You seemed very happy to see her again."

"Yes," I said, awkwardly, jiggling my crossed foot. "Well. I guess I'll try to get her gifts inside before it rains or something, right? Why don't you go back to work?"

"Yes," she said. "I'll go back to work. I'm sure the gifts are lovely. Call me once they're unpacked, all right?"

"Sure," I said, and jiggled my foot.

I considered ordering the house to carve a service door, but decided at length that peristalsis was the optimal solution—otherwise, I'd still have to find a way to drag the goddamned crates into the house. I shoved all our living room furniture into a corner and went down to the cellar to scoop up the endless meters of the house trunk that we'd fabbed to help us move in but hadn't had a use for since. I spread it out along the lawn, stretching its mouth-membrane overtop of the largest of the three crates, then pulled the other end through the picture window. I retreated to the living room and used a broom handle to tickle the gag-reflex at the near end of the tube and then leapt clear as the tube shudderingly vomited a gush of dust over the floor. I hit the scrubber-plate with my fist and escaped out the front door before I'd gotten more than a lungful of crud, chased by convection currents that cycled all the room's air toward the filters in the baseboards.

Out on the lawn, the house trunk was slowly digesting the crate, gorging it upwards to the picture-window. Once there was enough slack on the lawn end, I stretched the twitching membrane overtop of the second crate, and then the third. The house trunk's muscular digestion slowed, but continued, inexorably, moving the trunks living-room-ward.

I met the first trunk with a crowbar and set to work on it, surprised as ever at the fabulous working order of my biceps and back muscles. Sedentary life will never get the best of me, not so long as I am master of my own flesh, ordering it to stay limber and strong.

The crate was ready to fall to pieces just as the second box was eructing onto the living room floor. I guided number two to a clear spot, then knocked out the last fasteners on number one and slid the panels aside.

It was a dining room table, handsome and spare, made from black oak, with a fine grain that was brought out by a clear varnish. It had an air of antiquity, but it was light enough to move with one hand. Subsequent boxes disgorged four matching chairs and a sideboard.

I reversed the house trunk and evacuated the crate remnants back onto the lawn, where I decided I'd deal with them later.

I dialed my fiancée's number and waited for her to answer. "I've unpacked," I said. "Come out and see."

A couple of minutes later she poked her head round the door and sniffed. "Smells like trouble," she remarked. "That's a lot of furniture. What does she do, breed the stuff?"

"I don't know." I rubbed the sideboard. "Hey, you. Wake up. Tell me about yourself."

"Cyd?" said the table, hesitantly. "Is it lunchtime already?" It spoke with Al's voice.

The chairs began to climb out of their crates and shake off the packing fuzz; one by one they gathered around the table and hunkered down. "What do you feel like today?" asked Al-the-table. "How about a light Mediterranean salad, rocket and tomatoes and mozarella with a drizzle of balsamic vinegar and extra-virgin olive oil? Or maybe my special wasabi and eggplant nori?"

Herself yanked one of the chairs out from the table and sat on it, hard. "I'll have a plate of tacos and salsa," she said, glaring at the sideboard. "And make it snappish."

The table extruded cutlery—dumb, old-fashioned silver, no less—and the sideboard sidled up to her and offered a plate. She took it with poor grace and began to pick at her food. "I don't like the style," she declared. "This old antique shit went out with the history of the month club. Gimme some Nazi kitsch any day of the week."

"Sure!" trilled Al's instantiation, and the table sprouted swastikas.

"I can do without lunch," I said. "I'm not really feeling hungry."

"Oh, for fuck's sake." My fiancée looked disgusted and shoved the plate away. "You like this furniture so much, *you* do the washing up." She took a deep breath. "Been meaning to talk to you, anyway."

"Anything in particular, love?" I asked.

"Yeah." She stood up abruptly. "It can wait. I was just thinking about a little recreational surgery, is all."

Recreational surgery? "Uh, what kind?" I asked. "We're getting married in just six days, now. Will it take long? You can't do anything substantial like a set of extra arms—you'd need to alter your dress, wouldn't you?"

"Oh, nothing much." She mimed an elaborate yawn. "I'm just thinking it's been too long since I wore the balls in this household."

"Hey, I'm keeping mine!" I said. "Anyway, isn't it traditional for a bride to be female at the altar?"

"Oh yes," she agreed, nodding brightly. "The bride's supposed to be a young female virgin if she's going to wear white! That's me all over." She giggled alarmingly, jumped up onto the tabletop, and spread her legs wide. "Fuck it, come here, Cyd. Right now, on the table. See this? Young? Virgin? You be the judge!"

Afterwards, as we lay in the accommodating depressions Al-table had generated for us, my fiancée trailed a lazy tongue along my throat. "All right, then," she said. "If you want a girl-bride, I'll stay female. It's only a week, after all."

I propped myself up on one elbow. "Thanks, honey," I said, gently cupping one of her breasts. "It's just, you know. This wedding's going to be complicated enough as it is. We don't need more changes at the last minute."

"I know," she said. "Well, back to work."

• • •

The *writing went* well that afternoon. I worked up a really good head of rage and ranted into my phone for three hours, watching the words scroll along the ticker at the bottom of my field of vision. When I was done, I did an hour of yoga, feeling the anger ease out of my muscles as I moved slowly from posture to posture.

I did a fullscreen display of the text, read it back, tweaked a few phrases, and fired it off to my blog. Another week's work finished.

I headed down to the living room. The Al-dinette had neatly arranged itself. "Good column," it said to me. "You've really found a niche."

"How are you powering yourself?" I said.

"You'd be surprised at how little draw an instantiation pulls. Your romp with your girl generated enough kinetic to power me for a month. If I need more, there's always photovoltaic and a little fusion—I don't like to use nuclear, though. Splitting my atoms reducing my computational capacity; enough of that and I'd be too stupid to talk in a couple centuries."

"Jesus," I said. "Well, it was a very . . . *thoughtful* . . . gift, Al, thank you."

"Oh, don't thank me! Just keep recharging me the way you just did and we'll call it even."

"Well then," I said. "Well."

"I've made you uncomfortable. I'm sorry, Cyd. Seems like I'm always weirding you out, huh?"

My chuckle was more bitter than I'd intended. "Goes with the territory, I suppose."

"Don't be coy," the table said with mock sternness, and the chair under my bum wiggled flirtatiously. "You know that you were attracted to the weirdness."

And I had been. On the beach, as she leaned in and sank her teeth gently into the skin below the corner of my jaw, worrying at it with her tongue before grabbing me by the back of my head and kissing me with a ferocity that made my pulse roar in my ears. I'd only been, what, twelve, and she thirteen, but I was smitten then and there and, I feared, always and forever.

The chair contrived to give my ass a friendly squeeze. "There, you see—you're just one of those fellas who can't help but be infatuated with the post-human condition."

My betrothed didn't show up for dinner that night. I ate alone at the AI-table, eschewing our kitchenette for the light conversation and companionship of the AI-furnishings. I knocked on the woman's studio door before heading to bed and she hollered a muffled admonishment about virgin brides and her intention to sleep separate until the Day. I swore I heard the dining room table giggle as it digested my dirty dishes.

She was gone when I rose the next morning. AI-table, AI-chair, and I had a companionable breakfast together. AI-table said, as I was drinking my second cup of coffee, "You're certainly taking it very well."

"Taking what?"

"Gender reassignment. Honestly! And after you agreed last night that the wedding was too imminent to contemplate any major replumbing. Poor Cyd, always being tempest tossed by the women in his life."

The coffee burned north from my gut along the back of my throat. I tapped my palm until her phone was ringing in my ear.

"Hello," she said. Her voice was deeper, the mirror of my own.

"God *damn* it," I shouted without preamble. "You *promised!*"

"Oh, come on, hysterics never help. It's just for a day or two."

"No it *isn't*," I said. "You're stopping right now and beginning the reversal. This is completely unfair, you've got no right to be changing things around now."

"Don't you tell me what to do, Cydonia. This is supposed to be a partnership of equals."

"Look," I said, trying some of my deep-breathing juju. "Look. Okay. Fine. If you want to do this, do it. Fine. It's your body. I love you whatever shape it's in."

"Oh, Cyd," she said, and I actually heard her face crumple up preparatory to a good cry. "I'm sorry, I just wanted a change, you know. Just a mood. I would have changed back, but you didn't know that. Don't worry, I'll change back."

Thank you. "Great—I'm sorry if I blew up there. Just wound a little tight is all. I'm always like this the day after I turn in a column."

True to her word, my fiancée returned with the same gonads she'd been wearing the night before. She pointed this out to me in the living room. "You were right. Cyd," she explained contritely, sitting on one of the chairs in the improvised upstairs dining room with her legs splayed to show me what she had. "I'm really sorry it took me so long to figure it out, but you were absolutely *completely* right. I don't know what I was thinking! A young female virgin is exactly what you're going to get at the altar. See, I went for the complete genital reconstruction? I even have a hymen again." She showed me it—then picked up a medieval-looking piece of steel underwear and locked herself into it with a solid *clunk* before I figured out what was going on. "See, look what a pretty chastity belt I found!" She looked thoughtful, and for a moment I wondered if she was merely bluffing—but then she stood up, took an experimental step, winced, and smiled at me, and I realized with a sinking heart that she meant to go through with this whatever the cost. "You're going to have a virgin bride. Isn't tradition wonderful?"

"Ah," I said faintly. "I take it that oral sex is out, too?"

"What's sauce for the goose is sauce for the gander," she said. "You get my key at the altar, and not a millisecond before!"

"Oh." I checked my countdown timer: fifty-two hours and sixteen minutes before I could have sex again. Well, sex with *her*—Al-table maybe had other ideas. "This isn't quite what I had in mind," I said tiredly.

"Fine. Go fuck yourself—if you can," she said sharply, then turned and hobbled out of the living room, muttering under her breath.

When my fiancée got into one of these moods there was no reasoning with her. Not that I'm very reasonable myself when I get a wild hair up my ass, but this, this passive-aggressive sexual torture, this was really low. In addition to winding me up—for she refused to so much as let me touch her, never mind share a bed or bodily fluids—this was putting *her* in a foul mood.

"At *least* I could masturbate if I wanted to," I told my couch as I lay in it, staring miserably at the ceiling.

"You could do more than masturbate," the couch replied in sultry tones. "Don't you think you're doing this to yourself?" I'd woken that morning to discover that Al was colonizing every stick of furniture in the house, converting it into computronium to back up the instances in the living room. The floorboards weren't floorboards any more, but warm computational matter that looked like floorboards but captured the kinetic energy of every foot that trod them and converted it straightaway to computation on behalf of my damned dinette set.

"Myself—" I closed my eyes and counted to twenty "Al. Al. Let's get one thing straight. I am a human being. I am marrying *another* human being. You are a piece of furniture—at least in this instance."

"But I'm not just furniture!" She sounded so hurt that I apologized immediately. "I'm a thinking-feeling-person with a self-image and a warm heart and a whole functional range of emotional responses to share with you. Why do you keep rejecting me?"

"Because—" I stopped. "No offense, but there's a lot of shit I need to get straight before I can answer that question, Al." And indeed there was.

"Was it something I did?" she asked.

"Yes. No." I felt something and opened my eyes. The couch was reaching around me, gently stroking—"Stop that."

"Stop what?"

"Don't pretend. Al! All I wanted was a bitch session."

"I think you want something else," said Al-sofa. "I can give it to you."

"Can you?" I asked. "*Can* you?" I sat up and looked around the room, feeling a strong urge to throw something. "You had to go post-!" Break something. "You left me behind!" Scream. "I'm not ready!" Stamp.

"I still love you," said one of the chairs, peeping out timidly from behind a thankfully still sub-sentient bookcase. "Please stop doing this to yourself."

"You're dead!" I burst out before I could stop myself.

"Am not! If anyone here's dead it's you—dead between the ears!" The psychiatric couch spiked up in hostile black rubbery cones, like a fetishist's dream of hedgehog skin. "You're afraid!"

"Yeah, afraid of discovering I'm just buggy software," I said. "Like you."

"Human code is *good* code," Al said.

"Yeah, but you still asked them to upload you." I looked away, out the window, out across the desolate cityscape—anywhere but at Cyd's furnishings. "That's not exactly a survival trait, is it?"

"You could join me," she said.

There, that was it.

"I'm getting married tomorrow," I said. "I haven't even had my fucking stagette. I'm wearing a *fucking chastity belt*. And you're already proposing I should break my vows?"

"You haven't made them yet," she said, a trifle smugly. The couch sprouted hair-thin pseudopods that worked their way between the chastity belt and my skin, silky warm computation invading my groin, touching my nipples, pulling my hair, sucking at my toes. I writhed in place and stifled a groan. and then there was another pod slithering throatwise, filling my nose, oxygenating my lungs, oozing sensation-intensifiers directly into my alveoli and up to my brain. I screamed without making a sound, jackknifing.

It had always been like this with Al, whether I was a boy and she was a girl, or vice-versa, or any permutation thereof, except for this one, and now this one. Al, who'd taken my first virginity, taking another one now. Al, who I'd always been able to talk with, tell anything, be understood by. She was in my optic nerve now, shimmering above me like an angel, limned with digitally white light, scissoring her legs round me.

"I do love you, Cyd," she said. "Both of you. All of you. Can't you all love me, too?"

"No," I moaned, around the pseudopod. "No, not ready to go post, not ready for it." I was thrashing now, enveloped in Al, losing myself in ecstasy, my oldest friend within and without me.

"You don't need to be," Al-pod and Al-vision and Al-sofa whispered to and through my bones. "Marry me, both of you. A meat-marriage, a pre- post- marriage. All of my instances and all of yours, in holy matrimony."

The pleasure was incredible, the safety and the warmth. Cyd and I couldn't marry, shouldn't marry. He wouldn't *name* me, called me those stupid pet-names, wouldn't acknowledge his self-created mirror-self, his first step en route to post-. Al understood, understood me and Cyd, two instances of the same person. I couldn't marry Cyd, but we could marry Alice.

*S*ince I *was* twelve and Al bit my jaw before tumbling me to the sand and changing my world forever, since that night and that day and that long road that Al and I have walked, I have always known, in my heart, that I was meant for Al and she for me.

I can't be a vast society like her, not yet: two are quite enough for me. Quite enough for her, too. She's colonized both of me for computation, out of raw reflex, and so my body-temp is a little higher than normal, but my column is better than it's ever been and I've thrown away the neuro-feedback toy—my wife (my wife!) (wives?) (husbands?) (wives/husbands?) takes care of any neurotweaking I need these days.

I don't see my ex-fiancée much; she stayed in Al-house and I moved into a treehouse that Al grew me in our old back yard. But of an evening I sometimes hear my voice coming from the attic room where I'd kept my study, pas-sionate howls and heated whisper hisses, and I smile and lean back into Al-tree's bough and revel in wedded bliss.

Tracker

Mary Rosenblum

One of the most popular and prolific of the new writers of the '90s, Mary Rosenblum made her first sale to Asimov's Science Fiction Magazine *in 1990 and has since become a mainstay of that magazine and one of its most frequent contributors, with almost thirty sales there to her credit. She has also sold to* The Magazine of Fantasy and Science Fiction, Science Fiction Age, Pulphouse, New Legends, *and elsewhere.*

Rosenblum produced some of the most colorful, exciting, and emotionally powerful stories of the '90s, earning her a large and devoted following of readers. Her linked series of Drylands stories have proved to be one of Asimov's *most popular series, but she has also published memorable stories such as "The Stone Garden," "Synthesis," "Flight," "California Dreamer," "Casting at Pegasus," "Entrada," "Rat," "The Centaur Garden," "Skin Deep," "Songs the Sirens Sing," and many, many others. Her novella "Gas Fish" won the* Asimov's *Readers Award Poll in 1996, and was a Finalist for that year's Nebula Award. Her first novel,* The Drylands, *appeared in 1993 to wide critical acclaim, winning the prestigious Compton Crook Award for Best First Novel of the year; it was followed in short order by her second novel,* Chimera, *and her third,* The Stone Garden. *Her first short story collection,* Synthesis and Other Stories, *was widely hailed by critics as one of the best collections of 1996. Her most recent books are a trilogy of mystery novels written under the pen name Mary Freeman, and she is now at work on more science fiction novels. A graduate of Clarion West, Mary Rosenblum lives with her family in Portland, Oregon.*

Here she takes us to a future that's forgotten that there ever was *a time before Singularity—but which hasn't for-*

*gotten the great gulf that exists (and possibly always will
exist) between the rich and the poor. And between owner
and owned.*

The City Man was calling him.

Tracker lifted his head from his garden, distracted from
the small fears and satisfactions of the black beetles sucking juice from the ruffled cabbages beneath his fingers.
The scent of that calling came to him on the soft westerly
winds that also carried molecules of ocean, fish, and sea-
gull shit, dying shelled-things, and hungry water-living
mammals. It blew across City, too, and the scents it carried
from that place bore images, but few names, to Tracker's
mind. Only City Man's calling carried a name.

But City Man was not really a name. His name was a
complex of scent and touch, of not touching, tone of voice,
and the small sharp veerings of emotion—a thread that
strung Tracker's days and nights and more days of remembered history into a contiguous thread.

City Man had created Tracker.

Jesse whined, and nudged his leg with her nose, her canine eyes on his face. She couldn't hear City Man's calling, but she knew that Tracker heard him, because her
engineered brain let her know. Since she stared at him, he
saw himself briefly through her eyes, a long face with
planes and slopes like the cliff faces above the cove beach,
his hair the tawny red of the clay soil beneath the winter
rains. He caught a glimpse of his cabbages, fat and green
and round at the edges of her vision. Their smooth green
roundness filled him brief satisfaction. These were old
genes, unaltered, the same cabbages an old-days human
might have grown, a thousand years ago, when their genes
were equally innocent.

Jesse nudged him again. Conscience. Friend. Eyes.

"All right," he said aloud. "Let's find out what he wants."
He put out his hand, felt the hair-warmth-duty of her pres-

ence come up against his palm. She showed him the dirt path
between the irregular boundaries of his garden beds with her
sight, tugged him along with her silent urgency.

"He's only going to want to play," he said to her gruffly.
"Show off one of his little creations."

Jesse didn't answer, marching firmly along, showing
him the path she knew that he should take. She was good
at that—keeping his feet from stumbling. Tracker felt a
birdwing shadow of fear and thought back quickly. How
old was she? City Man had made her for him, and he had
no idea what lifespan he had built into her genes. Had
never thought to ask. His step faltered, as he contemplated
the cabbages and old-days plants with lost names, swept
by her eyes. Smelled earth, and the tickling lifethought of
small squirming things. His world.

She nipped at him. Impatient.

"Coming." Beyond the tall wall of his garden, City
waited. He gathered his senses tightly into himself as he
absently admired the paving of white marble inlaid with
abstract patterns of green jasper and blue lapis in front of
Jesse's paws. Too bright, he thought, but that would
change, as soon as one of the City got bored. For awhile—
years or decades—it had been paved in mother of pearl. He
had liked that, liked the subtle opalescent gleam that Jesse
had showed him and the memory-song of the shells that had
once held life. They walked a lot then. It had been a cloudy
cool time, before someone turned up the sun. They passed
a few folk on the wide street, but no City people. You
rarely saw City people. Few that they were, they didn't
spend much time in City unless someone had made it new.
No one had made it new for some time now.

They reached the City Man's gate. Jesse would never
look wholly at it. She looked aside, studying the thin-
sliced agate that tiled the wall. He knew the gate by its feel
beneath his palms. It was made of bones. He wasn't sure
whose bones they were, but they were delicate—a flying
creature. They murmured to him of wind as a solid living
thing as he pushed the gate open.

He was right. City Man had a visitor. Woman, he smelled, hormones in balance, full of life, unshadowed by death. He could always smell it—that lack of Death's shadow. It shaded all the City creations, a hint of darkness on a sunny day. Not so, for City's Residents. Death could not shadow them. They summoned it only at will, their servant, no master. Jesse wouldn't look at the Woman or at City Man, so he stood still, admiring the raked sand and small perfect shells that she showed him. It occurred to him that he had never really looked at City Man. Jesse wouldn't do it.

"Of course, he's blind," City Man was saying to the Woman. "He doesn't need eyes. If I asked him to find you, he would feel you on the far side of the planet. Or on the orbital. On the Moon Garden. He's that aware."

"Oh, you're so sure you're the top Creator in the solar system." The Woman sounded bored, but it was an act. He could feel her interest prickling his skin, mixed with a sharp edge of jealousy. Tracker studied the tight spiral of a shell the color of a rainy morning. A creature had made that, without thought or intent. City Man had made a tribe of men and women who built endless sand sculptures on the beach below his garden—sculptures that the tide daily washed away. Like the shell maker.

Slowly, he realized that the Woman had left the garden and that City Man was contemplating him. Jesse was leaning against his knee, wanting hard to be gone.

"Tracker." City Man came close enough that the clove-and-sweat scent of him, and that hard clean lack of Death's shadow, filled Tracker's senses.

"I want you to find someone." He put a hand on Tracker's shoulder.

Jesse flinched.

"One of my creations. She ran away once before, and I found her. This time . . . I don't feel like going. I have better things to do."

The jagged edge of his lie brushed Tracker's mind, and he stifled a wince. Jesse growled, so low and soft that City

Man didn't hear her. Tracker put a hand down on her silken head. Shushed her.

"Here she is." He moved away. Something rustled, and then City Man thrust a spider-silk bag against Tracker's chest.

He took it, felt softness and small bits of hardness within the folds of silk.

"She probably went to find the kite flyers again." Burning like bee stings filled his words. "She stayed with them a long time, last time. Go find her." He turned away, his scent and presence diminishing. "She's mine, and I want her back, Tracker."

Jesse nudged at him, panting with eagerness to be gone from this place. He wound his fingers in her silky coat, feeling her fear. "Why are you afraid?" he asked her softly as she pulled him through the bone-barred gate and back out into City's white marble and lapis. "He won't hurt you. He doesn't care."

Jesse licked his hand, and then—deliberately—nipped the soft pad of flesh between his thumb and forefinger.

Tracker sucked in his breath at the sting of pain, pressed his hand to his mouth, tasting the coppery note of blood on his tongue.

Twilight shrouded the fat cabbages with their innocent genes by the time he and Jesse reached the garden. They went inside and he told Jesse to go play. He didn't need her here. His house existed as scents of comfort, curving walls, cushions and tables that held his echo and Jesse's, static and welcoming. He crossed the thick carpet to run his hands along a sculpture of wave-polished wood, crafted by a young man who helped carve the sand sculptures that the waves erased with each tide.

Mindless and innocent, like the shell maker.

He fingered the complex twine of wood with polished wood and shook his head, frowning. Then he sat at his table with its not-quite-satiny grain and opened the slick folds of spider silk. It held a rumpled wad of fabric. He lifted it to his face, inhaling the scents of dust, wind, and longing. A picture flickered in his mind—a melon-colored kite diving through a cloudless sky. *She probably went to find the kite flyers again.* The small hard things were freshwater pearls, lumpy and irregular, that filled his mind with the timeless passage of slow watery days. Gold wires had been threaded through them, as if they had been used for earrings once. The nip on his hand had scabbed over, and he touched the grainy roughness of scab, wondering what had upset Jesse. After awhile, he got up and went out into the garden, to harvest lettuce, leaf by crisp leaf, and pull tiny sweet carrots from the loose soil. He ended beside his trellis of peas, face to the gentle breeze that was blowing fish scent and the evening-smoke of the sand sculptors in from the shore. Each carrot root and tiny sphere of peagerm was a small death. Tracker tossed the last empty pod into the compost bin at the edge of the garden. Life lived on death, he thought. Until City and the people who lived here came to be.

They had defied Death.

The cooking fires on the beach were burning out. The distant scent of orcas came to Tracker. They were playing out in the dark bay, not hungry right now, just playing. He went into his house, comforted by the familiar textures and contours, and lay down on the cushions in the corner. After a few minutes, Jesse crept in beside him. She licked his hand where she had nipped it, turned around twice, and lay down with a sigh.

They left City in the morning, walking face-on into the warmth of the rising sun. Jesse frisked like a puppy. The land outside City's walls was desert. That surprised Tracker a little. It had been prairie last time he had been out here, full of flowers. How long ago? He tried to fix the time, gave up. Someone had decided that the land should be desert so . . . it was desert. One of City's residents

sculpted the land with glaciers. Tracker remembered City
Man saying so.

They had time to sculpt a landscape with glaciers.

Away from the shore, the wind blew hot from the center
of the land, and Tracker lifted his head, his hand on Jesse's
head, not bothering to look through her eyes. He could taste
her. The one City Man wanted. Out there. The melon-colored
kite dove and rose in the cloudless sky, and he scented that
hint of dust and longing, mingled with . . . joy.

They walked, living off the dried vegetables and meat
in his pack, sleeping in the hottest part of the day, walking
beneath the waxing moon. One of City's members had
sculpted the face of the moon. Dark lines and spaces
crossed it, Tracker saw, as Jesse raised her nose to howl at
it; stark against its white disk, a stain of crimson spread
like a tortured rose near the center. He wondered who had
made that stain.

On the morning after the full moon, on the day they
shared the last of their water, they found her.

Her scent had been strong in his face all night, and an
eager restlessness kept him striding on through the darkness, patient Jesse uncomplaining at his side. He stumbled
on rocks, sometimes, and fell once, but he didn't care. The
wind was soft now, a desert breath against his face,
stroking his cheeks like gentle fingers.

In the first faint warmth of morning, he halted. Ahead,
he sensed life, bright with flesh scent and laughter, and the
joy of being alive in the warmth of a new day. The kiters.
It must be. Then, Jesse looked, and saw the bright greens
and blues, yellows and oranges of the kites as they soared
and spiraled into the bright air, forming tightly only to
break apart into explosions of color and reform once more,
tails writing cryptic glyphs against the sky. A single melon-
colored kite soared suddenly, briefly, circling the twined
and ordered mass of the kites, a rogue dancing to its own
tune.

She was there.

Tracker let his breath out slowly, and, as if it had heard

him, the kite veered suddenly, soaring away from the dancing spiral, straining toward him briefly before it settled lightly to earth.

Tracker slung the near-empty pack over his shoulder and strode forward. Jesse took her place at his side, her eyes showing him the rocks and scrub and small scuttling insects in front of them. He wanted her to look up again, to watch the kites, but she kept her eyes stubbornly on the ground. Then, abruptly, she stopped, and finally, she looked up. Tracker looked with her eyes, ready to see *her*, the melon kite in her hands, smelling of dust and longing.

It shocked him a little, as Jesse's vision showed him his quarry. Golden hair tumbled around her face, and over her shoulders. Her eyes, the color of spring grass, laughed at him, and she smiled, the kite in her hands, the curves of her body hidden by a loose shift of kite-fabric. Two polished horns sprang from her temples, curving gracefully to deadly points. Two more horns, smaller, also curved, sprang one from each hip. The shift had slitted sides so that the curved spurs could protrude, and the hemmed edges revealed a flash of tanned and muscular thigh. She smiled, and the laughter in her eyes was familiar, as if they were old friends.

"I've been waiting for you," she said, and held out one slender hand.

He took it. Jesse growled and fixed her eyes on the woman's leg, as if contemplating a bite. "Quiet." Tracker no longer needed her eyes. The woman's presence filled his senses so that vision would have been a distraction only. Life, he thought absently. She was life itself, a flame of vitality that radiated energy into the universe around her like a burning fire. Her fingers curved around his, *holding* his hand in a way that defined the casual phrase, as aware of the texture of his flesh, the tension of his bones, and the pulse of blood and neural synapses, as he was.

She was so aware.

It disturbed him that City Man had made her, good though he was.

Jesse growled again, softly, uncertainty shivering through her.

"My name is Yolanda." Her voice was low, and as intimate as if they were lying side by side in a tumbled bed. "Donai sent you."

He nodded, comprehending that "Donai" was her name for the City Man, attuned for her reaction. Anger, fear, flight, attack?

She laughed again, and he felt only sadness woven with silver threads of amusement. And . . . love. "He came himself, last time. But Donai never does anything the same way twice."

Jesse growled again, sharply this time, pressing forward between them, her head forward, ears pricked. Tracker realized that the kiters had come, forming a shifting vortex of curiosity, hostility, and fear around them. Jesse's eyes roved from form to form, tension knotting her body as they drew closer, reading threat in their wary stares. He put his hand on her, not bothering to look, because he didn't need to see their faces. She quieted instantly, but her tension shivered through the skin of his palm and up his arm.

"Stranger." One came close, radiating vitality and health, although the shadow of Death suggested that he was not young. Jesse tensed, attack hormones torturing her. "I am Karin." He was the source of the hostility Tracker had scented, although it was under tight control. "This is Sairee," his tone indicated gesture. "She is Mayor. I am Center. We would like to know what we can do for you?"

They knew. Tracker kept his restraining hand on Jesse's shoulders as he bowed slightly. "I came to speak with . . . Yolanda." It impressed them that he told the truth. Certainly the Center—whatever that was—Karin, expected him to lie, and Tracker's small truth cracked his armor of hostility Roiling tensions seeped through the cracks. "You have been in City," he said.

"Yes." The Center's sweat went acrid with suspicion. "If Yolanda wishes to speak with you, she may," he said flatly "If she wishes to go with you she may. If she does not, she will stay. Is your dog going to attack? She wants to."

"She is only afraid that you threaten me." Tracker stroked Jesse's head, impressed again by this creation's awareness. "She only wants to protect me."

"There are wild dog packs out here. They kill straying humans. I wonder where they came from."

The Center was staring at his face. Tracker felt the pressure of his eyes, shrugged. "They were created," he said. "As you were. And I. And Yolanda. I don't know why they were put here."

For a moment, everyone was silent. Then a hand touched his arm, and Jesse whined with his flinch. A soft gray presence, a woman heavy with knowledge and authority, stood close to him. "Come have water," she said. "And food. The flight wind is past, and it's time to eat." She took his hand, and Tracker felt an odd sense of déjà vu, as if this had happened before. She tugged him forward—guiding him, he realized with a small twinge of surprise. She had guessed that he was blind. He let her steer him around the scrubby tufts of thorn and ancient, worn stones. As Jesse fell reluctantly in at his heel—still growling—he realized that the sense of déjà vu was *hers*, not his.

She had done this before, and the memory was so strong in her that, for an instant, a circle of vans wavered into being in his mind's eye. Once, long ago, this woman had led Yolanda down to the vans, he realized.

They crested a low ridge and moved slowly down into a wide flat channel that faintly remembered long-gone flowing water. A dusty scent of slow-living plants and small furry and scaled lives colored the wind. Jesse showed him a circle of colorful wooden vans, topped by canopies of neon bright kite fabric. Sails, he thought. The roof could be raised to the wind, to drive the vans. Carvings of leaves and kite shapes decorated the painted sides. A cluster of small, wiry children watched from the shadow of the vans, their curiosity a brightness pricking at his

senses. None of them were older than ten or eleven,
Tracker guessed, and wondered where the older children
were. Everyone scattered to a van, in small groups of three
or four, stooping to greet the children who ran to them,
glancing over their shoulders at Tracker and Jesse. They
did not point, Tracker noticed. One did not point, among
this tribe of creations. The Center, Karin, had joined them,
his hostility a low simmer now, as the woman guided
Tracker toward a yellow van with a green and orange
canopy/sail.

He gestured to Jesse to remain outside, and felt his way
up the broad steps and into the close, life-scented interior.
He felt a bench beneath his groping hands, eased himself
onto it. It felt good to sit like this. The edge of a table or
counter brushed his arm and he listened to the disciplined
choreography of the three creations moving within the
confined space. They had shared this space for a long time
to move with such comfort. Small thumps told of containers being set onto the table top beside him. He smelled
water and cooking food. He groped for them, aware of the
man, Karin's, sudden intense scrutiny, closed his hand
around an earthenware mug full of sweet water. He drained
it, thirsty.

"You are blind?" Karin's surprise brightened the space.

"The dog is his eyes." Yolanda's voice, rich with certainty

"Is that true?" Sairee, concerned. "You can bring it in
here."

Tracker shook his head. "It's not important." The van's
interior was taking shape around him, the dimensions defined by scent, the bounce of sound, pockets of stagnant
air, and the casual movements of the three. Bed over there
and another above. Food space beyond where he sat. All
else would be cupboards for storage. He felt a finely
crafted cabinet door behind his legs. The kiters had skill
with wood, too. Sairee pushed an earthenware bowl gently
into his hands. He found a carved wooden spoon, scooped
up some kind of cooked grain, sweetened with berries that

tasted of summer sun. For a time, they ate silently, the
sound of spoon against bowl and the warm comfort of
swallowed food filling the van. Tracker finished the grain
and set the bowl down on the table.

"You understand that if Yolanda doesn't want to go
back with you, you can't force her." Karin spoke immediately, as if he had been waiting for Tracker to finish, his
voice edged with challenge and threat.

He had been in love with her. Tracker tilted his head, savoring the subtle play of chemical conversation. Not any
more, but the echo was there, a duet with Sairee's gentle
sadness. She knew that Yolanda would choose to leave, he
thought. As she had known immediately that he was blind.
Aware, these creations, yes. Very.

"I'm going to go with him." The air rippled as Yolanda
reached to touch Karin. "It's time."

Karin didn't speak, but the air moved with his abrupt
gesture of denial. Sairee said nothing, but her sadness
deepened. Tracker expected Karin to argue and protest, but
it was Sairee who spoke, thoughtful. "How does your dog
see for you?"

Tracker frowned, wondering what would make sense to
these people with their kites and carved wood. "City Man
engineered her," he said slowly "He changed the part of
her brain that sees. It talks to me."

A small hot brightness woke in Sairee, like a tiny bright
flower unfolding. "You know about City tech," she said.
"Is there a . . . disease that kills children?"

Tracker frowned, feeling the depth of their listening,
and the bright desperate flower of Sairee's hope.

"I mean . . . our children have begun to die. By their
thirteenth summer. You saw them outside. It's a sickness.
Maybe City people know how to cure it."

"Hush, Sairee." Karin's voice was rough and hard with
old anger. "They wouldn't share a cure with us anyway."

How to say to these people that disease did not exist,
not even out here? "I'm sorry," Tracker said at last. "I
don't know."

"Ah well." The hope flower withered, leaving grayness in its wake. "I'm sorry."

Tracker felt the stir of her rising. "We'll let you rest, stranger." She paused for an instant. "Will you share your name with us?"

Names were important here. "Tracker," he said and felt their instant of hesitation. "That is my name," he said.

They didn't believe him, but they were polite about it and left, taking Sairee's grief and Karin's anger with them. He turned to face Yolanda, feeling the glow of her like sunlight on his flesh.

"These are gentle people, Tracker." Yolanda touched his face with her fingertips. "Someone created them to be finite, and this is how they are ending."

"City Man—Donai—created them."

She took her fingers away, her sudden anger like the flick of a sharp nail against his cheek. "How do you know that?"

He shrugged, because the silver music of their origin was written in their scent. "I just do."

"He never told me that. I don't believe you."

She was lying, and angry grief edged the lie. Tracker shrugged and stood. He went outside to the nervously waiting Jesse and squatted beside her, squeezing one silken ear, sorry for her anxiety. She thumped her tail and licked his face, telling him it was okay, even though it wasn't. Climbing back into the van, he followed water-scent to a clay pitcher and returned to fill her small bowl and open a package of dried meat from his pack for her.

"Welcome to The Caravan." One of the children, a bright flare of life and youthful joy-in-living, squatted beside him, earning a wary stare from Jesse. Her eyes showed him red hair and freckles, and long legs like a horse-colt. "Did you have something to eat and drink?" she asked with a grownup reserve and a carefully restrained impatience that suggested the words were important custom.

Tracker nodded as he set the full water bowl down for Jesse. "Thank you."

"Are you really from City?" Social necessity taken care
of, the words burst forth, gleaming silver with curiosity.
"What's it like? Are there really all kinds of weird mon-
sters there? And are the streets really paved with gems and
polished agate? What is so awful there that Karin won't
talk about it?"

Tracker smiled, amused at the girl's burning enthusiasm. "I don't know why your Center won't talk about it."

"Silly not to." The girl made a face. "It just makes me
wonder about it more than if he told me everything."

Wise child. Tracker smiled. "My name is Tracker."

"Is that really a name?" Doubting.

"I don't have any other." He poured the dried meat out
for Jesse. The girl burned like Yolanda, in a different way.
Like a spring sun versus a summer sun, he thought.

She had been considering his statement. "My name is
Karda." She had decided he was telling the truth.

Karin's daughter. Tracker scented it. And Sairee's? "Do
you want to go see City?" he asked, his hand on Jesse's
silken coat.

"Yes." Her nod stirred the air. "Just to see why Karin
won't say anything. It can't be that horrible. But I don't
think I want to live there." Thoughtful. "I like this life.
What does City have? I mean, all those people stuck in one
place. Do they Fly?"

She meant kites. Tracker shrugged. "Perhaps some. I've
never heard of it, but anything can be done." People with
millennia to live did everything eventually.

"Are you going to take Yolanda away?" Hard tone this
time, warning him that she didn't want to be lied to.

"She chooses to come with me."

The girl's sudden stabbing grief surprised him. He
turned toward her, but Jesse's attention was on her food, so
he groped toward her spring-sun warmth, his fingers finding her shoulder, sensing the quivering control that kept
back the tears. "I'm sorry," he said, meaning it, because it
was such an intense pain for someone this young. "I'm not
forcing her," he said gently.

"I know." Karda swallowed, fighting with her pain and her tears. "She said she wouldn't, but I knew she would some day. She . . . lies about things like that. Sometimes . . . she lies to herself, I think."

Tracker frowned, feeling truth in the texture of her words. She knew that Yolanda lied. He wondered if the kiters had been created to know truth. He had thought that he was the only one. Perhaps City Man had sculpted it into other creations, too. Not Yolanda. Jesse had finished, and now looked up into the girl's face, her tail wagging, not worried about this one. Tracker saw the gleam of tears on her tawny cheeks, watched his fingers brush them away. "I'm sorry," he said.

"I'm not angry at you." Karda rose gracefully to her feet. "She would have gone when she was ready anyway."

Eleven, he thought. If the kiter children were dying at puberty . . . he sensed it ripening in her, that rich change from child to woman, felt a sudden deep pang of regret. Jesse whined and nudged his hand.

"Tracker, I'm ready to go." Yolanda's shadow fell across Jesse, the curve of her hip-spurs elongated curves on the ochre soil, the shadow of her head crowed with twin curves.

"Right now?" Karda's voice quivered.

Through Jesse's eyes, Tracker watched Yolanda cross swiftly to the girl, cup her face in her long-fingered hands, and kiss her gently on the forehead and cheeks. "Right now, my love," she said softly. For a moment her fingers lingered on the girl's golden hair, then she turned swiftly away to face Tracker. "I brought food and water."

Tracker hesitated. Now that he had found her, he had only to speak to City Man and he would send a flyer for them. He felt oddly reluctant to do so, and wasn't sure why.

"Give me your water bottles." Karda held her sorrow in a tight net of anger now. She seized them and hurried off, toward a distant van. Jesse growled and swung her head to show him Karin approaching, his expression grim.

Oh, yes, Karda's father. You could see it in the shape of his face.

"Catch up with me," Yolanda said. Fabric rustled as she swung a pack lightly to her shoulder and strode away, her scent trailing behind her.

Karin stopped, all churning emotion. "How did you know I was in City?" His voice was harsh.

Tracker shrugged. "It changes you. I felt it."

"I went back with him—the man who came for Yolanda. He let her stay here. I . . . didn't belong there." Karin's eyes narrowed, and for a moment a hint of fear gleamed on their surface. "What else do you feel?" he asked softly.

Your fear for your daughter, Tracker thought and didn't say. The death that waits in her with her womanhood. Your knowledge of the twisted sculpture in your cells that sends your kites into the sky. Yes, kite-flyer, you felt it when you walked through those City gates. That you are a sculpture and not a human. "Many things," he said aloud. He felt Karda approaching with the filled bottles. Again Karin's fear surfaced, bright as the flash of an ocean fish. He heard the kiter get heavily to his feet and move to take the dripping water bottles from his daughter and send her brusquely away. He thrust the bottles, cool and dripping, against Tracker's chest.

"Good-bye, stranger," he said, his voice hard. "I don't think we'll meet again."

In a small handful of years, they would all be dead, with no children to replace them. Tracker bowed his head, seeing the vans in the old woman's memory, bright and beautiful, their sails fluttering in the hot breeze. He turned away and Jesse bounded along next to him, very happy to be leaving this place. Yolanda had covered a lot of ground and led him now, a beacon far ahead, against the distant murmur of City and sea. He didn't try to catch up to her, content to follow, not needing Jesse's eyes to find Yolanda's trail in the breeze. He could open his link to City Man any time and the flyer would come.

He didn't open it.

They walked, separated by a space that grew neither wider nor narrower, until the sun's heat faded from his face and small creatures began to stir in their hiding places from the sun. As the last of the sun's heat faded, replaced by night's chill, Yolanda finally halted. Her eyes on the scatter of diamond stars overhead, she didn't move as Jesse led Tracker up to her. The moon was up, the red stain like a rose on its pale face, as Jesse lifted her nose to it. She wanted to howl, but did not. Yolanda took Jesse's face in her hands, her own face large in Tracker's shared sight. "I'm sorry," she murmured, stroking the dog's ears. "We were both cruel to you today."

Jesse thumped her tail wearily and flopped onto the still-warm sand, her tongue lolling. It was all sand here, white as snow beneath their feet, radiating away the day's heat as the air cooled. Water scented the air sweetly, and Yolanda pressed a bottle into Tracker's hand. The water had been flavored by her mouth, and he tasted her as he drank. Thick fabric whispered, and Tracker guessed that she had pulled a blanket from her pack. It popped softly as she shook it out, then hissed against the sand. "Look at me." She spoke to Jesse, and they both looked.

She lay back on a yellow quilt made of kite fabric filled with soft plant fibers. Her shift slid up her long thigh, baring it to the polished curve of her hip-spur as she tilted her head to the sky. Her hair tumbled down over her shoulders, parted by the horns springing from her forehead. Silver moonlight gleamed like water on the polished curve of those horns.

"Do you know why Donai made me?" she asked at last, her voice dreamy.

Tracker, squatting by his pack, feeding meat to Jesse, didn't answer.

"He made me to love him. He made me to kill him one day."

She was speaking truth. Tracker looked up, his eyes narrowing. City people could die. It didn't happen often, but they could. No disease could touch them, they did not age. They could heal nearly any injury.

But . . . they could die.

If they chose to.

"I don't want to go back." Sorrow shivered in her words like the silver light, cold and beautiful. "But I have to." She rose to her feet suddenly, the twin moons above her head like a crown of light as she came to stand over him. Jesse whined, and lowered her head to her paws, tail thumping uncertainly as she banished Yolanda's face. "Do you know why I'm leaving, Tracker?"

"No." He didn't need Jesse's eyes. She filled his senses, as if the moon hovered before him, blazing with silver light and animal heat.

"I'm killing them. The children." Her voice was low and full of pain. "He must have done it when he came to get me and I wouldn't go. He changed me so that I poisoned them." Her resignation held a bitter note. "He always gets what he wants." She reached down, taking his hands and pulling him to his feet. His toe caught the kite fabric quilt. "Come sit with me," she said, a mix of command and plea.

He sat on the soft slickness of the quilt that smelled of her. And of Karin. She knelt beside him to unlace his boots, burning like the spring sun, warming him, filling his senses with images of sun on bright fabric and clouds and blue sky. He felt her gaze on his face, and, suddenly, he understood. It was there, written like a silvery thread in the scent of her. Karda. Karin's daughter, but not Sairee's.

Yolanda's.

She stood suddenly and kite fabric rustled. Her shift pooled on the quilt beside him and he felt her spring-sun heat as she slid her leg across his waist to straddle him. He wanted to protest, but her heat drowned him, and as she pushed him back, he groped for memory of another moment like this, found shadows like slippery fish in the depths of his memory. Her mouth found his and her taut

muscular body moved against his, and the shadow fish of
memory fled.

He woke to the faint chill whisper of breeze that pre-
saged the sun's warmth. The scent of dew on dry leaves
and stone filled his nostrils, and the night-scurry of tiny
lives all around. For a moment, he had no idea of where he
was or when, simply floated in a limbo of cool air and
scent. Jesse was a furry warmth against his leg and head on
his chest, Yolanda slept deeply. He felt the polished curve
of her hip spur against his side. A small pain drew his fingers and he felt a crust of dried blood scabbing a shallow
gash in his thigh. He had no memory of her spur tearing his
skin.

A small uneasiness crept through him, something . . .
wrong. He sharpened his senses, gathering them, shutting
out the scurrying insect lives that filled the space around
him and opening himself to the rush of blood through her
veins, the spiral dance of her cells. Yes. His skin tightened,
although not from the morning chill. As Yolanda stirred, he
sat up, newly aware, feeling Jesse's flicker of wakening,
her tail-thump of inquiry. He looked through her eyes to
watch Yolanda toss the tangled gold of her hair back from
her face, her eyes full of sleep and the memories of pleasure. Tracker swallowed against a sudden sharp ache in his
chest.

"What's wrong?" She touched his face. "Your skin is
the color of desert flower honey when the sun hits it, you
know."

The invitation in her touch made him shiver again, and
Jesse whined. Yolanda withdrew her hand. "Something *is*
wrong."

"You're City" The words came out in a hushed tone,
almost a whisper. He couldn't speak them aloud out here.

"I was born there." Yolanda considered, thoughtful.
"The woman I called Mother lived with me in a garden.
There were huge flowers and some of them moved their
petals, like butterflies bound to a vine. That was his hobby
then. Plants. But that's not what you mean."

"No." His throat was too dry, he had to swallow again to get the words out. "You *are* City. Like him. City Man. Donai. I can . . . I know it." It was there, that bright absence of Death.

She was shaking her head, sadness deepening.

"Not possible, Tracker. I . . . have a daughter, remember? City people can't breed with the beings they create. That has always been true."

And it was, and it was true, he had sensed her relationship to Karda, had forgotten in the shock of his discovery. He groped for her hand, lifted the palm to his face, tasting that absence on her skin. She had to be City. Yolanda made no effort to pull her hand away.

"You scared me when I first saw you, blind Tracker. It's as if I live on the surface of the world that you inhabit. You see things, sense things, that I can't perceive and that scares me."

Jesse was looking at his own face now, carved with strain, but he could feel the emerald pressure of her eyes on him.

"And you scared me," she went on softly, "because I thought you were City, here to claim me, not someone sent by Donai." She paused, her stare warm against his skin. "At night, years ago, Karin would come to my bed. And in the morning, after he had gone back to sleep with Sairee, I would smell him on my hair and skin, as if his spirit was still lying in my arms. What are you sensing, Tracker? I am dying a little with every passing day, ticking off a finite life. What about you? Tell me about the woman who carried you, Tracker. I remember mine. I called her Mother, and she sang to me in the sun of the garden."

"No." It was sigh more than whisper. He wanted to tell her that he remembered, describe this woman for her.

He could not.

Grope as he might, all he found was a chain of days that disappeared into a far distance, endlessly. Before Jesse, another creature, lithe and furry, and before that one, before that one?

"City people don't just breed." Yolanda went on relent-lessly. "They select genotypes, they match carefully. There are only so many who can live in City, only so many who can be admitted to share the universe. Donai told me about this, about the rules. That is the only rule they may not break, Tracker. To breed without consensus, without per-mission. I remember when he told me, Tracker. It was not long after I had left the garden, when I was his lover. And his words were bitter, but his tone was not, and I wondered about that."

He felt her smile, sharp and cold as a blade edge against his skin. "I think you are City, Tracker. Didn't you ever no-tice? Were you too close to see it? I think you are Donai's own son."

She was right, oh yes, the memory was there, opening now, unrolling like an endless carpet, drawing his mind's eye back though a storm of days and nights and days, faces, voices, hands touching, animal fur and cold noses, summers and winters. . . . Drowning. All the time, City Man's face, everywhere, in all the seasons. City Man. Donai. Drowning. Tracker sank silently beneath the end-less, bottomless sea of yesterdays, weighed down by his sudden understanding of . . . what he was.

H*e woke to* nighttime cold, to the rough-wet caress of Jesse's tongue punctuated by the cold thrust of her nose. He was lying on the fabric quilt and the crackle of flame and scent of smoke suggested a fire nearby. Jesse nudged him again. He reached out, patted her, dizzy briefly as the deep sea of past threatened to suck him down once more. For an instant, a hundred Jesses with different fur and form and faces nudged him. Treading water in those depths, he focused until he was aware of only *this one,* and sat up.

"I was getting worried." Yolanda sat on the corner of the quilt, Jesse showing him her knees drawn up, her shift pulled down over her legs for warmth. "We're nearly out of water. I didn't find any communication device in your pack, so I assume you need to call Donai yourself. And the Caravan is heading east, not west. So we're on our own." But no trace of worry colored her words. "You've been unconscious for two days. I gave the dog the rest of the food."

He might not ever have waked up. For a long time, he had been lost in the depths of that huge chaotic sea. He might never have found his way back to *this* moment, *this* time. Slowly, Tracker reached out to touch her arm. She accepted his touch, even put her hand on his with a gentle sympathy.

That acceptance was the same acceptance that Jesse offered him.

Tracker summoned City Man through his link. Then they waited for the flyer, which arrived as the day's heat grew. City Man was not on board, and Tracker felt a moment of piercing gratitude for that. They climbed the ramp, Yolanda first, her cool composure tinged with sorrow, then Tracker, and last Jesse, panting in the noonday heat. The cushioned interior was cool, and Tracker got Jesse a bowl of water from the refreshment wall. A tiled shower cabinet drew Yolanda to strip and step inside, turning so that the jets of warm water scoured every square centimeter of her lithe body. He looked through Jesse's eyes at the sleek curves of her flesh, momentarily swept away by the memory of the night spent with her on the kite fabric blanket beneath the ancient and weary sky.

He grieved for it.

She emerged, dry, naked, and glowing. She didn't invite him to make love to her. She would surely accept if he asked, would no more refuse than Jesse would refuse his summons. That had been built into her, lay there as real as the shadow of Death.

He didn't ask.

He could feel the swift approach of City. Beyond it, the sand people would be working on the sculptures that the waves would erase. The flyer skimmed above City's silent clamor, settled into the quiet lawn behind City Man's resi-

dence. Grass like living velvet gave beneath Tracker's feet
as he stepped out. Yolanda leaped lightly down beside him,
but her sorrow clouded the air around them. Jesse kept her
eyes low, tail down, afraid. He closed his fingers in her fur,
tugging gently, and he felt her tail move briefly.

City Man was in the garden. Jesse showed him blue-
flowered twining plants. The snaky shoots wove about his
legs, not touching him, their blue flowers like eyes. As he
and Yolanda and Jesse approached, the vines lifted and
pointed in their direction. Jesse shouldered into Yolanda
and planted her feet, refusing to move farther. Yolanda
stood still, her knees against the furry barricade that was
Jesse. Tracker felt her gaze fixed on City Man.

Tracker walked up to him, not needing Jesse's eyes. The
vine things twined briefly around his calves and then released him, retreating as if he poisoned them. They knew
City when they felt it. Like Yolanda. "Donai," Tracker
said.

City Man's attention focused sharply on Tracker. The
plants cowered away from both of them, and City Man finally shifted his attention to them. "Waste of time," he
said. "I'll have to start over. I never doubted you'd find
her."

"She's not yours anymore," Tracker said gently.
"Donai."

City Man's attention was on him fully, now. "I can go
to the City Council." Tracker enunciated each syllable precisely. "I can tell them what you did. What I am."

Stillness. A spike of caution, quickly extinguished.
"What I did?" City Man put on a good-humored tolerance
that was as translucent as gauze. "And what *are* you, besides a very well-created tracking dog?"

"I'll go to the Council and tell them that I am . . . your
son. Father." The word made him sway, and the dark, bottomless sea beneath his feet nearly rose to swallow him
again. But the effect on City Man was visible. He went
still, and Tracker tasted his . . . vulnerability

This was new. Never before.

"Yolanda couldn't know," City Man whispered.

"Oh no." Tracker shook his head, demons shrieking inside his skull. "She doesn't know. I simply . . . remembered."

"You can't," City Man said calmly. "You don't have the ability. I made sure of that."

It was an admission, and they both realized it at the same instant. City Man swallowed, an audible, dry sound. "They'll destroy you, if you tell them."

Tracker bent his head, wishing he could cry, but that ability had slipped away from him as he drowned in that vast sea. "They'll destroy us both, Father." Again. The name burned them both equally.

"They denied my petition for offspring." City Man breathed the words. "My DNA contains too many flaws. But it also contains vast talent. I can twist that ladder to create people and tribes, plants and animals, that no one has ever been able to rival. I can do things that nobody else can do, no matter how much they copy me. So what if you can sculpt glaciers, mountains, the face of the moon? I can sculpt races!" He turned to face Tracker, filled with a depthless calm. "They'll destroy you. Think about that. You have forever."

It was a weapon, those three sentences. Oh, he felt it, that tug of cells. *Live forever.* It weakened his knees, called to him with a Siren's voice to go back to his garden, pet Jesse, and make love to Yolanda. He could do that. City Man would reward him for doing that. He would help him to pretend, and, after awhile, Tracker would . . . forget. The promise was there. And real. "Let's walk," he said, and it was the first command he had ever uttered.

City Man complied, and that was another admission. They strolled away from the cowering vines, through a garden of growing green things, sweet with the scents of plant sex. Behind them, Jesse and Yolanda waited, and Tracker felt a clench of sorrow for the similarity of their waiting. Tracker finally stopped, feeling the silence between them like a pair of crossed swords, a silent struggle.

Tracker shrugged suddenly, fingers groping to find a fleshy blossom humming with a summer's joy. He fingered the petals gently, did not pick it. "Who was my mother?" he asked.

"You don't remember." A silver thread of triumph wove City Man's words together.

Tracker shook his head. "I just can't find her." She was there somewhere, lost in that sea. "I would like to know." And he wasn't challenging, wasn't threatening, was merely . . . asking.

City Man walked on and Tracker followed, waiting.

"There was no other." The words came slowly. "I used my DNA, recombined it to grow, and implanted it in a . . . creation." He was silent for a long time. "I . . . sculpted you." He spoke slowly, thoughtfully. "If I wasn't good enough for them, then I could make *you* into whatever I wanted. I gave you a gift."

Tracker felt his stare as City Man pivoted to face him, like desert sunlight on his skin.

"You can't remember. Not for more than a few decades. Tell me about your last lover? Your last dog?" Sly triumph shaded his words. "I made you immortal, but I gave you a mortal memory"

And by that, he could own Tracker forever. Tracker lifted his head, feeling the early starlight on his face, remembering the wide, bright eyes of the kiter girl. "You failed," he said gently. He reached out to touch his father's face, felt the hard edge of his disbelief. "I could wish you had succeeded."

"You belong to me. If you tell, we both die," Donai whispered. "Life forever. It's not so easy to give up."

"No," Tracker said. "It's not." Then he turned and walked away, not needing eyes, back to where Jesse and Yolanda waited beneath the silver moon.

The sun was barely peeking up over the horizon as Tracker crested the desert rise and spied through Jesse's eyes the

circle of kite-roofed wagons below. He halted, and
Yolanda came up to stand beside him, still and silent, her
awareness of his City flesh a thin and impenetrable wall
between them, one that would always be there.

Her scent tickled him, overlaid with dust and the bright,
spiraling joy of the kiters' morning flight as their kites
twined the dry sky. It had changed, her scent, richer now,
tinged with tentative new life. He groped, touched the polished curve of her hip spur, felt the texture of her joy. It
matched the kiters's.

With a sigh, he stepped forward, making his way with
Jesse's guidance down the gentle slope of the sage-covered
hill that had once been a roving dune, but was now netted
to the earth with roots. Before they reached the bottom, a
figure emerged from one of the wagons and ran to meet
them.

"I knew you were coming." Karda halted breathless in
front of them. "I knew you were coming back!"

Yolanda stepped forward, arms outstretched, enfolding
the child to her. The girl winced slightly as one hip spur
scratched her arm lightly, but barely noticed the tiny trickle
of blood.

And so she was inoculated with the antidote to City
Man's lethal virus. And Yolanda would free the rest of the
kiters from City Man's vengeance. That had been part of
Tracker's bargain with City Man. He looked through
Jesse's eyes and found Karda standing in front of him,
looking up at him. "Are you going to stay here, too? Forever?"

"Yes," he said.

She frowned, because she could sense truth, and this
was not truth, but it was not a lie, either. "For as long as
you live," he said, and that truth she heard.

"I'm a lot younger than you," she said, with a child's
forthrightness.

"You are." He smiled, because for the kiters, he was
like them. Not City. Yolanda might know, but she would
not say, and here he would be . . . not alone. And that

tentative silver note of life in Yolanda would grow and
strengthen, and, in a space of time, would be born as a
child. His child, and Yolanda's. You made me too much
like them, Tracker thought. Enough to do this. Enough not
to fear Death. He groped for Karda's hand and she closed
her small, slender fingers around his. For awhile, this
would be an island, where he would learn to swim in the
dark sea that lurked in his head. And when the child was
old enough, they would leave. Because there were others
like them. He felt them. Behind him, he felt the distant forever murmur of City rising beside the patient sea. Beginning and end, he thought. My gift to you. Father.

With Karda guiding his feet, they walked through the
sage as the first kite spiraled upward to meet the rising sun,
and, for the first time, Tracker felt a sense of peace.

Steps Along the Way

Eric Brown

New British writer Eric Brown, with more than fifty short story sales to his credit, is one of the most prolific authors at shorter lengths currently working in the field. He's become one of Interzone*'s most frequent contributors and also appears in markets such as* Spectrum SF, Science Fiction Age, Aboriginal SF, Moon Shots, *and many others. His first book was the collection* The Time-Lapsed Man and Other Stories, *which appeared in 1990; his first novel,* Meridian Days, *appeared in 1992, soon followed by* Penumbra *and* New York Nights. *His most recent book is the novel* Bengal Station. *He lives in Haworth, England.*

Here he shows us that no matter how high up the ladder of evolution we might climb, we should never get so high as to lose sight of those coming up behind . . .

On the eve of my five-hundredth rebirthday, as I strolled the gardens of my manse, a messenger appeared and informed me that I had a visitor.

"Severnius wishes to consult you on a matter of urgency," said the ball of light. "Shall I make an appointment?"

"Severnius? How long has it been? No—I'll see him now."

The light disappeared.

It was the end of a long autumn afternoon, and a low sun was filling the garden with a rich and hazy light. I had been contemplating my immediate future, quite how I should approach the next century. I am a man methodical and naturally circumspect: not for me the grand announcements of intent detailing how I might spend my *next* five hundred years. I prefer to plan ahead one hundred years at a time, ever hopeful of the possibility of change, within myself and without. For the past week I had considered many avenues of inquiry and pursuit, but none had appealed to me. I had awoken early that morning, struck with an idea like a revelation: Quietus.

I composed myself on a marble bench beneath an arbor entwined with fragrant roses. The swollen sun sank amid bright tangerine strata, and on the other side of the sky, the moon rose, full yet insubstantial, above the manse.

Severnius stepped from the converter and crossed the glade. He always wore his primary soma-form when we met, as a gesture of respect: that of a wise man of yore, with flowing silver-gray hair and beard. He was a Fellow some two thousand years old, garbed in the magenta robes of the Academy.

We embraced in silence, a short communion in which I reacquainted myself with his humanity.

"Fifty years ?" I asked.

He smiled. "More like eighty," he said, and then gave the customary greeting of these times: "To your knowledge."

"Your knowledge," I responded.

We sat and I gestured, and wine and glasses appeared upon the bench between us.

"Let me see, the last time we met, you were still researching the Consensus of Rao."

"I concluded that it was an unworkable proposition, superseded by the latest theories." I smiled. "But worth the investigation."

Severnius sipped his wine. "And now?"

"I wound down my investigations ten years ago, and since then I've been exploring the Out-there. Seeking the new . . ."

He smiled, something almost condescending in his expression. He was my patron and teacher; he was disdainful of the concept of the new.

"Where are you now?" he asked. "What have you found?"

"Much as ever, permutations of what has been and what is known . . ." I closed my eyes, and made contact. "I^2 is on Pharia, in the Nilakantha Stardrift, taking in the ways of the natives there; I^3 is in love with a quasi-human on a nameless moon half a galaxy away; I^4 is climbing Selerious Mons on Titan."

"It appears that you are . . . *waiting?*" he said. "Biding your time with meaningless pursuits. Considering your options for the next century."

I hesitated. It occurred to me then how propitious was his arrival. I would never have gone ahead with Quietus without consulting him.

"A thought came to me this morning, Severnius. Five hundred years is a long time. With your tutelage and my inquiries . . ." I gestured, "I have learned much, dare I say everything? I was contemplating a period of Quietus."

He nodded, considering my words. "A possibility," he agreed. "Might I inquire as to the duration?"

"It really only occurred to me at dawn. I don't know— perhaps a thousand years."

"I once enjoyed Quietus for five hundred," said Severnius. "I was reinvigorated upon awakening—the thrill of change, the knowledge of the learning to be caught up with."

"Precisely my thoughts."

"There is an alternative, of course."

I stared at him. "There is?"

He hesitated, marshaling his words. "My Fellows at the Academy last week Enstated and Enabled an Early," he said. "The process, though wholly successful physiologically, was far from psychologically fulfilled. We had to wipe his memories of the initial awakening and instruction. We are ready to try again."

I stared at him. The Enstating and Enabling of an Early was a rare occurrence indeed. I said as much.

"You," Severnius said, "were the last."

Even though I had been considered a success, my rehabilitation had required his prolonged patronage. I thought through what he had told me so far, the "urgency" of his presence here.

He was smiling. "I have been watching your progress closely these past eighty years," he said. "I submitted your name to the Academy. We agreed that you should be made a Fellow, subject to the successful completion of a certain test."

"And that is?" I asked, aware of my heartbeat. All thought of Quietus fled at the prospect of becoming a Fellow.

"The patronage and stewardship of the Early we Enstated and Enabled last week," Severnius said.

It was a while before I could bring myself to reply. Awareness of the great honor of being considered by the Academy was offset by my understanding of the difficulty of patronage. "But you said that the subject was psychologically damaged."

Severnius gestured. "You studied advanced psychohealing in your second century. We have confidence in your abilities."

"It will be a considerable undertaking. A hundred years, more?"

"When we Enstated and Enabled you, I was your steward for almost fifty years. We think that perhaps a hundred years might suffice in this case."

"Perhaps," I said, "before I make a decision, might I meet the subject?"

Severnius nodded. "By all means," he replied, and while he gave me the details of the Early, his history, I closed my eyes and made contact. I recalled I^2 from his studies on Pharia, and I^4 from Titan. I^3 I gave a little time to conclude his affair with the alien.

Minutes later I^2 and I^4 followed each other from the converter and stepped across the glade, calling greetings to Severnius. They appeared as younger, more carefree versions of myself, before age and wisdom had cured me of vanity. I stood and reached out, and we merged.

Their thoughts, their respective experiences on Pharia and Titan, became mine—and while I^2 and I^4 had reveled in their experiences, to me they were the antics of children, and I learned nothing new. I resolved to edit the memories when an opportune moment arose.

Severnius, with the etiquette of the time, had averted his gaze during the process of merging. Now he looked up and smiled. "You are ready?"

I stood. We crossed to the converter, and then, before stepping upon the plate, both paused to look up at our destination.

The Moon, riding higher now, and more substantial against the darker sky, gazed down on us with a face altered littlè since time immemorial. The fact of its immutability, in an age passé with the boundless possibilities of change, filled me with awe.

We converted.

The Halls of the Fellowship of the Academy occupied the Sea of Tranquillity, an agglomeration of domes scintillating in the sunlight against the absolute black of the Luna night.

We stepped from the converter and crossed the regolith toward the Academy. Severnius led me into the cool, hushed shade of the domes and through the hallowed halls. He explained that if I agreed to steward the Early, then the ceremony of acceptance to the Fellowship would follow immediately. I glanced at him. He clearly assumed that I would accept without question.

The idea of ministering to the psychological well-being of an Early, for an indefinite duration, filled me with apprehension.

We came to the interior dome. The sight of the subject within the silver hemisphere, trapped like some insect for inspection, brought forth in me a rush of memories and emotions. Five hundred years ago, I, too, had awoken to find myself within a similar dome. Five hundred years ago,

I presume, I had looked just as frightened and bewildered as this Early.

A gathering of Fellows—Academics, Scientists, Philosophers—stood in a semicircle around the dome, watching with interest and occasionally addressing comments to their colleagues. Upon the arrival of Severnius and myself, they made discreet gestures of acknowledgment and departed, some vanishing within their own converters, others choosing to walk.

I approached the skin of the dome and stared.

The Early was seated upon the edge of a low foam-form, his elbows lodged upon his knees, his head in his hands. From time to time he looked up and stared about him, his clasped hands a knotted symbol of the fear in his eyes.

I felt an immediate empathy, a kinship.

Severnius had told me that he had died at the age of ninety, but they had restored him to a soma-type approximately half that age. His physique was lean and well-muscled, but his most striking attribute was his eyes, piercingly blue and intelligent.

I glanced at Severnius, who nodded. I walked around the dome, so that I would be before the Early when I entered, and stepped through the skin of the hemisphere. Even then, my sudden arrival startled him. He looked up, his hands gripping his knees, and the fear in his eyes intensified.

He spoke, but in an accented English so primitive that it was some seconds before I could understand his words.

"Who the hell are you?" he said. "What's happening to me?"

I held up a reassuring hand and emitted pheromones to calm his nerves. In his own tongue, I said, "Please, do not be afraid. I am a friend."

Despite the pheromones and my reassurances, he was still nervous. He stood quickly and stared at me. "What the hell's happening here?"

His agitation brought back memories. I recalled my own awakening, my first meeting with Sevemius. He had seemed a hostile figure, then. Humankind had changed over the course of thirty thousand years, become taller and more considerate in the expenditure of motion. He had appeared to me like some impossibly calm, otherworldly creature.

As I must have appeared to this Early.

"Please," I said, "sit down."

He did so, and I sat beside him, a hand on his arm. The touch eased him slightly.

"I'd like to know what's happening," he said, fixing me with his intense, sapphire stare. "I know this sounds crazy, but the last I remember . . . I was dying. I know I was dying. I'd been ill for a while, and then the hospitalization . . ."

He shook his head, tears appearing in his eyes as he gazed at his hand—the hand of a man half the age of the person he had been. I reached out and touched his arm, calming him.

"And then I woke up here, in this body. Christ, you don't know what it's like, to inhabit the body of a crippled ninety-year-old, and then to wake up suddenly . . . suddenly *young* again."

I smiled. I said nothing, but I could well recall the feeling, the wonder, the disbelief, the doubt and then the joy of apprehending the reality of renewal.

He looked up at me, quickly, something very much like terror in his eyes. "I'm alive, aren't I? This isn't some dream?"

"I assure you that what you are experiencing is no dream,"

"So this is . . . Afterlife?"

"You could say that," I ventured. "Certainly, for you, this is an Afterlife." I emitted pheromones strong enough to forestall his disbelief.

He merely shook his head. "Where am I?" he asked in little more than a whisper.

"The time is more than thirty thousand years after the century of your birth."

"Thirty thousand years?" He enunciated each word separately, slowly.

"To you it might seem like a miracle beyond comprehension," I said, "but the very fact that you are here implies that the science of this age can accomplish what in your time would be considered magic. Imagine the reaction of a Stone Age man, say, to the wonders of twentieth-century space flight."

He looked at me. "So . . . to you I'm nothing more than a primitive—"

"Not at all," I said. "We deem you capable of understanding the concepts behind our world, though it might take a little time." This was a lie—there were many things that would be beyond his grasp for many years, even decades.

Severnius had told me that the subject had evinced signs of mental distress upon learning the disparity between his ability to understand and the facts as they were presented. I would have to be very careful with this subject—if, that was, I accepted the Fellowship.

"So," he said, staring at me. "Answer my question. How did you bring me here?"

I nodded. "Very well . . ." I proceeded to explain, in terms he might understand, the scientific miracle of Enstating and Enabling. It was a ludicrously simplistic description of the complex process, of course, but it would suffice.

His eyes bored into me. His left cheek had developed a quick, nervous tic. "I don't believe it . . ."

I touched his arm, the contact calming him. "Please . . . why would I lie?"

"But how could you possibly recover my memories, my feelings?"

"Think of your childhood," I said, "your earliest memories. Think of your greatest joy, your greatest fear. Tell me, have we succeeded?"

His expression was anguished. "Christ," he whispered. "I can remember everything . . . everything. My childhood, college." He shook his head in slow amazement. "But . . . but my understanding of the way the universe works . . . it tells me this can't be happening."

I laughed at this, "Come! You are a man of science, a rationalist. Things change: what was taken as written in stone is overturned; theory gives way to established fact, which in turn evolves yet more fundamental theory, which is then verified . . . and so proceeds the advance of scientific enlightenment."

"I understand what you're saying," he said. "It's just that I'm finding it hard to believe."

"In time," I said, "you will come to accept the miracles of this age."

Without warning, he stood and strode toward the concave skin of the dome. He stared at his reflection, and then turned to face me.

"In time, you say? Just how long have I got?" He lifted his hand and stared at it. "Am I some laboratory animal you'll get rid of once your experiment's through?" He stopped and considered something. "If you built this body, then you must be able to keep it indefinitely—"

He stopped again, this time at something in my expression. I nodded. "You are immortal," I said.

I could see that he was shaken. The tight skin of his face colored as he nodded, trying to come to terms with my casual pronouncement of his new status.

"Thirty thousand years in the future," he whispered to himself, "the world is inhabited by immortals . . ."

"The galaxy," I corrected him. "Humankind has spread throughout the stars, inhabiting those planets amenable to life, adapting others, sharing worlds with intelligent beings."

Tears welled in his eyes. He fought not to let them spill, typical masculine product of the twentieth century that he was.

"If you did this for me," he said, "then it's within your capability to bring back to life the people I loved, my wife and family—"

"And where would we stop?" I asked. "Would we En-state and Enable the loved ones of everyone we brought forward?" I smiled. "Where would it end? Soon, everyone who had ever lived would live again."

He failed to see the humor of my words. "You don't know how cruel that is," he said.

"I understand how cruel it seems," I said. "But it is the cruelty of necessity." I paused. I judged that the time was right to share my secret. "You see, I, too, was once like you, plucked from my deathbed, brought forward to this strange and wondrous age, fearful and little comprehending the miracles around me. I stand before you as testament to the fact that you will survive this ordeal, and come to understand."

He stared at me, suspicious. At last he said, "But why . . . ? Why you and me?"

"They, the people of this age, considered us men of importance in our time—men whose contributions to history were steps along the way to the position of preeminence that humankind now occupies. Ours is not to wonder, but to accept."

"So that's all I am—a curiosity? A specimen in some damned museum?"

"Not at all! They will be curious, of course; they'll want to know all about your time . . . but you are free to learn, to explore, to do with your limitless future what you will— with the guidance and stewardship of a patron, as I, too, was once guided."

The Early walked around the periphery of the dome. He completed a circuit, and then halted and stared at me. "Explore," he said at last, tasting the word. "You said explore? I want to explore the worlds beyond Earth! No—not only the worlds beyond Earth, the worlds *beyond* the worlds you've already explored. I want to break new ground, discover new worlds . . ." He stopped and looked at me. "I take it that you haven't charted *all* the universe?"

I hesitated. "There are places still beyond the known expanses of space," I said.

"Then I want to go there!"

I smiled, taken by his naïve enthusiasm. "There will be time enough for exploration," I said. "First, you must be copied, so that you can send your other selves out to explore the unexplored. There are dangers—"

He was staring at me in disbelief, but his disbelief was not for what I thought. "Dangers?" he almost scoffed. "What's the merit of exploration if there's no risk?"

I opened my mouth, but this time I had no answer. Something of his primitivism, his heedless, reckless thirst for life which discounted peril and hardship, reminded me of the person I had once been, an age ago.

I considered the next one hundred years, and beyond. I had reached that time of my life when all experience seemed jejune and passé; I had come to the point, after all, where I had even considered Quietus.

To go beyond the uncharted, to endanger oneself in the quest for knowledge, to think the unthinkable . . .

It was ridiculous—but why, then, did the notion bring tears to my eyes?

I hurried across the dome and took his arm. "Come," I said, leading him toward the skin of the hemisphere.

"Where—?" he began.

But we were already outside the dome, and then through the skin of another, and walking across the silver-gray regolith of the lunar surface.

He stopped and gazed about in wonder. "Christ," he whispered. "Oh, Christ, I never thought . . ."

"Over here," I said, leading him.

We crossed the plain toward the display, unchanged in thirty thousand years. He stared at the lunar module, stark beneath the unremitting light of the Sun. We stood on the platform encircling the display and stared down at the footprints the first astronauts had laid upon the surface of another world.

He looked at me, his expression beatific. "I often dreamed," he said, "but I never thought I'd ever return."

I smiled. I shared the emotions he experienced then. I

knew what it was to return. I recalled the time, not long after my rebirth in this miraculous age, when I had made the pilgrimage to Earth and looked again upon the cell where over thirty thousand years ago, I, Galileo Galilei, had been imprisoned for my beliefs.

Haltingly, I told Armstrong who I was. We stared up into the dark sky, past the earth and the brilliant Sun, to the wonders awaiting us in the uncharted universe beyond.

We embraced for a long minute, and then turned and retraced our steps across the surface of the Moon toward the domes of the Academy, where Severnius would be awaiting my decision.

The Millennium Party

Walter Jon Williams

Walter Jon Williams was born in Minnesota and now lives in Albuquerque, New Mexico. His short fiction has appeared frequently in Asimov's Science Fiction Magazine, *as well as in* The Magazine of Fantasy & Science Fiction, Wheel of Fortune, Global Dispatches, Alternate Outlaws, *and other markets and has been gathered in the collections* Facets *and* Frankensteins and Other Foreign Devils. *His novels include* Ambassador of Progress, Knight Moves, Hardwired, The Crown Jewels, Voice of the Whirlwind, House of Shards, Days of Atonement, Aristoi, Metropolitan, *and* City on Fire, *as well as the huge disaster thriller* The Rift *and a* Star Trek *novel,* Destiny's Way. *His most recent books are the first two novels in his acclaimed Modern Space Opera epic,* Dread Empire's Fall, Dread Empire's Fall: The Praxis *and* Dread Empire's Fall: The Sundering. *He won a long-overdue Nebula Award in 2001 for his story "Daddy's World."*

Here he gives us a short, sharp look at life on the far side of a Singularity, a future where there's a place for everything, and everything's in its place . . .

Darien was making another annotation to his lengthy commentary on the Tenjou Cycle when his Marshal reminded him that his wedding anniversary would soon be upon him. This was the thousandth anniversary—a full millennium with Clarisse!—and he knew the celebration would have to be a special one.

He finished his annotation and then de-slotted the savant brain that contained the cross-referenced database that allowed him to manage his work. In its place he slotted the brain labeled **Clarisse/Passion**, the brain that contained memories of his time with his wife. Not all memories, however: the contents had been carefully purged of any of the last thousand years' disagreements, arguments, disappointments, infidelities, and misconnections. . . . The memories were only those of love, ardor, obsession, passion, and release, all the most intense and glorious moments of their thousand years together, all the times when Darien was drunk on Clarisse, intoxicated with her scent, her brilliance, her wit.

The other moments, the less-than-perfect ones, he had stored elsewhere, in one brain or another, but he rarely reviewed them. Darien saw no reason why his mind should contain anything that was less than perfect.

Flushed with the sensations that now poured through his mind, overwhelmed by the delirium of love, Darien began to work on his present for his wife.

When the day came, Darien and Clarisse met in an environment that she had designed. This was an arrangement that had existed for centuries, ever since they both realized that Clarisse's sense of spacial relationships was better than his. The environment was a masterpiece, an apartment built on several levels, like little terraces, that broke the space up into smaller areas that created intimacy without sacrificing the sense of spaciousness. All of the furniture was designed for no more than two people. Darien recognized on the walls a picture he'd given Clarisse on her four hundredth birthday, an elaborate, antique dial telephone from their honeymoon apartment in Paris, and a Japanese paper doll of a woman in an antique kimono, a present he had given her early in their acquaintance, when they'd haunted antique stores together.

It was Darien's task to complete the arrangement. He added an abstract bronze sculpture of a horse and jockey that Clarisse had given him for his birthday, a puzzle made of wire and butter-smooth old wood, and a view from the terrace, a view of Rio de Janeiro at night. Because his sense of taste and smell were more subtle than Clarisse's, he by standing arrangement populated the apartment with scents, lilac for the parlor, sweet magnolia and bracing cypress on the terrace, a combination of sandalwood and spice for the bedroom, and a mixture of vanilla and cardamom for the dining room, a scent subtle enough so that it wouldn't interfere with the meal.

When Clarisse entered he was dressed in a tailcoat, white tie, waistcoat, and diamond studs. She had matched his period elan with a Worth gown of shining blue satin, tiny boots that buttoned up the ankles, and a dashing fall of silk about her throat. Her tawny hair was pinned up, inviting him to kiss the nape of her neck, an indulgence which he permitted himself almost immediately.

Darien seated Clarisse on the cushions and mixed cocktails. He asked her about her work: a duplicate of one of her brains was on the mission to 55 Cancri, sharing piloting missions with other duplicates: if a habitable planet was discovered, then a new Clarisse would be built on site to pioneer the new world.

Darien had created the meal in consultation with Clarisse's Marshal. They began with mussels steamed open in white wine and herbs, then went on to a salad of fennel, orange, and red cranberry. Next came roasted green beans served alongside a chicken cooked simply in the oven, flamed in cognac, then served in a creamy port wine reduction sauce. At the end was a raspberry Bavarian cream. Each dish was one that Darien had experienced at another time in his long life, considered perfect, stored in one brain or another, and now recreated down to the last scent and sensation.

After coffee and conversation on the terrace, Clarisse led Darien to the bedroom. He enjoyed kneeling at her feet and unlacing every single button of those damned Victorian boots. His heart brimmed with passion and lust, and he rose from his knees to embrace her. Wrapped in the sandalwood-scented silence of their suite, they feasted till dawn on one another's flesh.

Their life together, Darien reflected, was perfection itself: one enchanted jewel after another, hanging side-by-side on a thousand-year string.

After juice and shirred eggs in the morning, Darien kissed the inside of Clarisse's wrist, and saw her to the door. His brain had recorded every single rapturous instant of their time together.

And then, returning to his work, Darien de-slotted **Clarisse/Passion**, and put it on the shelf for another year.

The Voluntary State

Christopher Rowe

Here's a fascinating look at a society in the process of being swallowed and transformed by a strange and potent Singularity—and the story of what happens to those few who get stuck in its throat on the way down . . .

New writer Christopher Rowe was born in Kentucky and lives there still. With Gwenda Bond, he operates a small press and edits the critically acclaimed magazine Say. *His stories have appeared in* SCI Fiction, Realms of Fantasy, Electric Velocipede, Idomancer, Swan Sister, Trampoline, The Infinite Matrix, The Journal of Pulse-Pounding Narratives, *and elsewhere and have recently been collected in* Bittersweet Creek.

Soma had parked his car in the trailhead lot above Governor's Beach. A safe place, usually, checked regularly by the Tennessee Highway Patrol and surrounded on three sides by the limestone cliffs that plunged down into the Gulf of Mexico.

But today, after his struggle up the trail from the beach, he saw that his car had been attacked. The driver's side window had been kicked in.

Soma dropped his pack and rushed to his car's side. The car shied away from him, backed to the limit of its tether before it recognized him and turned, let out a low, pitiful moan.

"Oh, car," said Soma, stroking the roof and opening the passenger door, "Oh, car, you're hurt." Then Soma was rummaging through the emergency kit, tossing aside flares and bandages, finally, *finally* finding the glass salve. Only after he'd spread the ointment over the shattered window and brushed the glass shards out onto the gravel, only after he'd sprayed the whole door down with analgesic aero, only then did he close his eyes, access call signs, drop shields. He opened his head and used it to call the police.

In the scant minutes before he saw the cadre of blue and white bicycles angling in from sunward, their bubblewings pumping furiously, he gazed down the beach at Nashville. The cranes the Governor had ordered grown to dredge the harbor would go dormant for the winter soon—already their acres-broad leaves were tinged with orange and gold.

"Soma-With-The-Paintbox-In-Printer's-Alley," said voices from above. Soma turned to watch the policemen land. They all spoke simultaneously in the sing-song chant of law enforcement. "Your car will be healed at taxpayers' expense." Then the ritual words, "And the wicked will be brought to justice."

Efficiency and order took over the afternoon as the threatened rain began to fall. One of the 144 Detectives manifested, Soma and the policemen all looking about as they felt the weight of the Governors servant inside their heads. It brushed aside the thoughts of one of the Highway Patrolmen and rode him, the man's movements becoming slightly less fluid as he was mounted and steered. The Detective filmed Soma's statement.

"I came to sketch the children in the surf," said Soma. He opened his daypack for the soapbubble lens, laid out the charcoal and pencils, the sketchbook of boughten paper bound between the rusting metal plates he'd scavenged along the middenmouth of the Cumberland River.

"Show us, show us," sang the Detective.

Soma flipped through the sketches. In black and gray, he'd drawn the floating lures that crowded the shallows this time of year. Tiny, naked babies most of them, but also some little girls in one-piece bathing suits and even one fat prepubescent boy clinging desperately to a deflating beach ball and turning horrified, pleading eyes on the viewer.

"Tssk, tssk," sang the Detective, percussive. "Draw filaments on those babies, Soma Painter. Show the lines at their heels."

Soma was tempted to show the Detective the artistic licenses tattooed around his wrists in delicate salmon inks, to remind the intelligence which authorities had purview over which aspects of civic life, but bit his tongue, fearful of a For-the-Safety-of-the-Public proscription. As if there were a living soul in all of Tennessee who didn't know that the children who splashed in the surf were nothing but extremities, nothing but lures growing from the snouts of alligators crouching on the sandy bottoms.

The Detective summarized. "You were here at your work, you parked legally, you paid the appropriate fee to the meter, you saw nothing, you informed the authorities in a timely fashion. Soma-With-The-Paintbox-In-Printer's-Alley, the Tennessee Highway Patrol applauds your citizenship."

The policemen had spread around the parking lot, casting cluenets and staring back through time. But they all heard their cue, stopped what they were doing, and broke into a raucous cheer for Soma. He accepted their adulation graciously.

Then the Detective popped the soapbubble camera and plucked the film from the air before it could fall. It rolled up the film, chewed it up thoughtfully, then dismounted the policeman, who shuddered and fell against Soma. So Soma did not at first hear what the others had begun to chant, didn't decipher it until he saw what they were encircling. Something was caught on the wispy thorns of a nodding thistle growing at the edge of the lot.

"Crow's feather," the policemen chanted. "Crow's feather Crow's feather Crow's feather."

And even Soma, licensed for art instead of justice, knew what the fluttering bit of black signified. His car had been assaulted by Kentuckians.

Soma had never, so far as he recalled, painted a self-portrait. But his disposition was melancholy, so he might have taken a few visual notes of his trudge back to Nashville if he'd thought he could have shielded the paper from the rain.

Soma Between the Sea and the City, he could call a painting like that. Or, if he'd decided to choose that one clear moment when the sun had shown through the towering slate clouds, *Soma Between Storms*.

Either image would have shown a tall young man in a broad-brimmed hat, black pants cut off at the calf, yellow jersey unsealed to show a thin chest. A young man, sure, but not a young man used to long walks. No helping that; his car would stay in the trailhead lot for at least three days.

The mechanic had arrived as the policemen were leaving, galloping up the gravel road on a white mare marked with red crosses. She'd swung from the saddle and made sympathetic clucking noises at the car even before she greeted Soma, endearing herself to auto and owner simultaneously.

Scratching the car at the base of its aerial, sussing out the very spot the car best liked attention, she'd introduced herself. "I am Jenny-With-Grease-Beneath-Her-Fingernails," she'd said, but didn't seem to be worried about it because she ran her free hand through unfashionably short cropped blond hair as she spoke.

She'd whistled for her horse and began unpacking the saddlebags. "I have to build a larger garage than normal for your car, Soma Painter, for it must house me and my horse during the convalescence. But don't worry, my licenses are in good order. I'm bonded by the city and the state. This is all at taxpayers' expense."

Which was a very great relief to Soma, poor as he was. With friends even poorer, none of them with cars, and so no one to hail out of the Alley to his rescue, and now this long, wet trudge back to the city.

Soma and his friends did not live uncomfortable lives,

of course. They had dry spaces to sleep above their studios, warm or cool in response to the season and even clean if that was the proclivity of the individual artist, as was the case with Soma. A clean, warm or cool, dry space to sleep. A good space to work and a more than ample opportunity to sell his paintings and drawings, the Alley being one of the *other* things the provincials did when they visited Nashville. Before they went to the great vaulted Opera House or after.

All that and even a car, sure, freedom of the road. Even if it wasn't so free because the car was not *really* his, gift of his family, product of their ranch. Both of them, car and artist, product of that ranching life Soma did his best to forget.

If he'd been a little closer in time to that ranching youth, his legs might not have ached so. He might not have been quite so miserable to be lurching down the gravel road toward the city, might have been sharp-eyed enough to still *see* a city so lost in the fog, maybe sharp-eared enough to have heard the low hoots and caws that his assailants used to organize themselves before they sprang from all around him—down from tree branches, up from ditches, out from the undergrowth.

And there was a Crow raiding party, the sight stunning Soma motionless. "This only happens on television," he said.

The caves and hills these Kentuckians haunted unopposed were a hundred miles and more north and east, across the shifting skirmish line of a border. Kentuckians couldn't be here, so far from the frontier stockades at Fort Clarksville and Barren Green.

But here they definitely were, hopping and calling, scratching the gravel with their clawed boots, blinking away the rain when it trickled down behind their masks and into their eyes.

A Crow clicked his tongue twice and suddenly Soma was the center of much activity. Muddy hands forced his mouth open and a paste that first stung then numbed was swabbed around his mouth and nose. His wrists were bound before him with rough hemp twine. Even frightened as he was, Soma couldn't contain his astonishment. "Smoke rope!" he said.

The squad leader grimaced, shook his head in disgust and disbelief. "Rope and cigarettes come from two completely different varieties of plants," he said, his accent barely decipherable. "Vols are so fucking stupid."

Then Soma was struggling through the undergrowth himself, alternately dragged and pushed and even half-carried by a succession of Crow Brothers. The boys were running hard, and if he was a burden to them, then their normal speed must have been terrifying. Someone finally called a halt, and Soma collapsed.

The leader approached, pulling his mask up and wiping his face. Deep red lines angled down from his temples, across his cheekbones, ending at his snub nose. Soma would have guessed the man was forty if he'd seen him in the Alley dressed like a normal person in jersey and shorts.

Even so exhausted, Soma wished he could dig his notebook and a bit of charcoal out of the daypack he still wore, so that he could capture some of the savage countenances around him.

The leader was just staring at Soma, not speaking, so Soma broke the silence. "Those scars"—the painter brought up his bound hands, traced angles down either side of his own face—"are they ceremonial? Do they indicate your rank?"

The Kentuckians close enough to hear snorted and laughed. The man before Soma went through a quick, exaggerated pantomime of disgust. He spread his hands, why-me-lording, then took the beaked mask off the top of his head and showed Soma its back. Two leather bands crisscrossed its interior, supporting the elaborate superstructure of the mask and preventing the full weight of it, Soma saw, from bearing down on the wearer's nose. He looked at the leader again, saw him rubbing at the fading marks.

"Sorry," said the painter.

"It's okay," said the Crow. "It's the fate of the noble savage to be misunderstood by effete city dwellers."

Soma stared at the man for a minute. He said, "You guys must watch a lot of the same TV programs as me."

The leader was looking around, counting his boys. He lowered his mask and pulled Soma to his feet. "That could be. We need to go."

It *developed that* the leader's name was Japheth Sapp. At least that's what the other Crow Brothers called out to him from where they loped along ahead or behind, circled farther out in the brush, scrambled from limb to branch to trunk high above.

Soma descended into a reverie space, sing-songing subvocally and supervocally (and being hushed down by Japheth hard then). He guessed in a lucid moment that the paste the Kentuckians had dosed him with must have some sort of will-sapping effect. He didn't feel like he could open his head and call for help; he didn't even want to. But "*I will take care of you,*" Athena was always promising. He held onto that and believed that he wasn't panicking because of the Crows' drugs, sure, but also because he would be rescued by the police soon. "*I will take care of you.*" After all, wasn't that one of the Governor's slogans, clarifying out of the advertising flocks in the skies over Nashville during Campaign?

It was good to think of these things. It was good to think of the sane capital and forget that he was being kidnapped by aliens, by Indians, by toughs in the employ of a rival Veronese merchant family.

But then the warchief of the marauding band was throwing him into a gully, whistling and gesturing, calling in all his boys to dive into the wash, to gather close and throw their cloaks up and over their huddle.

"What's up, boss?" asked the blue-eyed boy Soma had noticed earlier, crouched in the mud with one elbow somehow dug into Soma's ribs.

Japheth Sapp didn't answer but another of the younger Crow Brothers hissed, "THP even got a bear in the air!"

Soma wondered if a bear meant rescue from this improbable aside. Not that parts of the experience weren't enjoyable. It didn't occur to Soma to fear for his health, even when Japheth knocked him down with a light kick to the back of the knees after the painter stood and brushed aside feathered cloaks for a glimpse of the sky.

There *was* a bear up there. And yes, it was wearing the blue and white.

"I want to see the bear, Japheth," said a young Crow. Japheth shook his head, said, "I'll take you to Willow Ridge and show you the black bears that live above the Green River when we get back home, Lowell. That bear up there is just a robot made out of balloons and possessed by a demon, not worth looking at unless you're close enough to cut her."

With all his captors concentrating on their leader or on the sky, Soma wondered if he might be able to open his head. As soon as he thought it, Japheth Sapp wheeled on him, stared him down.

Not looking at any one of them, Japheth addressed his whole merry band. "Give this one some more paste. But be careful with him; we'll still need this vol's head to get across the Cumberland, even after we bribe the bundle bugs."

Soma spoke around the viscous stuff the owl-feathered endomorph was spackling over the lower half of his face. "Bundle bugs work for the city and are above reproach. Your plans are ill-laid if they depend on corrupting the servants of the Governor."

More hoots, more hushings, then Japheth said, "If bundle bugs had mothers, they'd sell them to me for half a cask of Kentucky bourbon. And we brought more than half a cask."

Soma knew Japheth was lying—this was a known tactic of neo-anarchist agitator hero figures. "I know you're lying," said Soma. "It's a known tactic of—"

"Hush hush, Soma Painter. I like you—this you—but we've all read the Governor's curricula. You'll see that we're too sophisticated for your models." Japheth gestured and the group broke huddle. Outrunners ran out and the main body shook off cramps. "And I'm not an anarchist agitator. I'm a lot of things, but not that."

"Singer!" said a young Crow, scampering past.

"I play out some weekends, he means; I don't have a record contract or anything," Japheth said, pushing Soma along himself now.

"Welder!" said another man.

"Union-certified," said Japbeth. "That's my day job, working at the border."

More lies, knew Soma. "I suppose Kentuckians built the Girding Wall, then?"

Everything he said amused these people greatly. "Not just Kentuckians, vol, the whole rest of the world. Only we call it the containment field."

"Agitator, singer, welder," said the painter, the numbness spreading deeper than it had before, affecting the way he said words and the way he chose them.

"Assassin," rumbled the Owl, the first thing Soma had heard the burly man say.

Japheth was scrambling up a bank before Soma. He stopped and twisted. His foot corkscrewed through the leaf mat and released a humid smell. He looked at the Owl, then hard at Soma, reading him.

"You're doped up good now, Soma Painter. No way to open that head until we open it for you. So, sure, here's some truth for you. We're not just here to steal her things. We're here to break into her mansion. We're here to kill Athena Parthenus, Queen of Logic and Governor of the Voluntary State of Tennessee."

• • •

Jenny-With-Grease-Beneath-Her-Fingernails spread fronds
across the parking lot, letting the high green fern leaves
dry out before she used the mass to make her bed. Her
horse watched from above the half-door of its stall. Inside
the main body of the garage, Soma's car slept, lightly anes-
thetized.

"Just enough for a soft cot, horse," said Jenny. "All of
us will sleep well after this hard day."

Then she saw that little flutter. One of the fronds had a
bit of feather caught between some leaves, and yes, it was
coal black, midnight blue, reeking of the north. Jenny
sighed, because her citizenship was less faultless than
Soma's, and policemen disturbed her. But she opened her
head and stared at the feather.

A telephone leapt off a tulip poplar a little ways down
the road to Nashville. It squawked through its brief flight
and landed with inelegant weight in front of Jenny. It
turned its beady eyes on her.

"Ring," said the telephone.

"Hello," said Jenny.

Jenny's Operator sounded just like Jenny, something
else that secretly disturbed her. Other people's Operators
sounded like television stars or famous Legislators or like
happy cartoon characters, but Jenny was in that minority of
people whose Operators and Teachers always sounded like
themselves. Jenny remembered a slogan from Campaign,
"My voice is yours."

"The Tennessee Highway Patrol has plucked one already, Jenny Healer." The voice from the telephone thickened around Jenny and began pouring through her ears like
cold syrup. "But we want a sample of this one as well.
Hold that feather, Jenny, and open your head a little
wider."

•　　•　　•

Now, here's the secret of those feathers. The one Jenny gave to the police and the one the cluenets had caught already. The secret of those feathers, and the feathers strung like look-here flags along the trails down from the Girding Wall, and even of the Owl feathers that had pushed through that fence and let the outside in. All of them were oily with intrigue. Each had been dipped in potent *math*, the autonomous software developed by the Owls of the Bluegrass.

Those feathers were hacks. They were lures and false attacks. Those feathers marked the way the Kentuckians didn't go.

The math kept quiet and still as it floated through Jenny's head, through the ignorable defenses of the telephone and the more considerable, but still avoidable, rings of barbed wire around Jenny's Operator. The math went looking for a Detective or even a Legislator if one were to be found not braying in a pack of its brethren, an unlikely event.

The math stayed well clear of the Commodores in the Great Salt Lick ringing the Parthenon. It was sly math. Its goals were limited, realizable. It marked the way they didn't go.

The Crows made Soma carry things. "You're stronger than you think," one said and loaded him up with a sloshing keg made from white oak staves. A lot of the Crows carried such, Soma saw, and others carried damp, muddy burlap bags flecked with old root matter and smelling of poor people's meals.

Japheth Sapp carried only a piece of paper. He referred to it as he huddled with the Owl and the blue-eyed boy, crouched in a dry stream bed a few yards from where the rest of the crew were hauling out their goods.

Soma had no idea where they were at this point, though he had a vague idea that they'd described an arc above the northern suburbs and the conversations indicated that they were now heading toward the capital, unlikely as that sounded. His head was still numb and soft inside, not an unpleasant situation, but not one that helped his already shaky geographical sense.

He knew what time it was, though, when the green fall of light speckling the hollow they rested in shifted toward pink. Dull as his mind was, he recognized that and smiled.

The clouds sounded the pitch note, then suddenly a great deal was happening around him. For the first time that day, the Crows' reaction to what they perceived to be a crisis didn't involve Soma being poked somewhere or shoved under something. So he was free to sing the anthem while the Crows went mad with activity.

The instant the rising bell tone fell out of the sky, Japheth flung his mask to the ground, glared at a rangy redheaded man, and bellowed, "Where's my timekeeper? You were supposed to remind us!"

The man didn't have time to answer though, because like all of them he was digging through his pack, wrapping an elaborate crenellated set of earmuffs around his head.

The music struck up, and Soma began.

"Tonight we'll remake Tennessee, every night we re-make Tennessee . . ."

It was powerfully odd that the Kentuckians didn't join in the singing, and that none of them were moving into the roundel lines that a group this size would normally be forming during the anthem.

Still, it might have been stranger if they had joined in.

"Tonight we'll remake Tennessee, every night we re-make Tennessee . . ."

There was a thicket of trumpet flowers tucked amongst a stand of willow trees across the dry creek, so the brass was louder than Soma was used to. Maybe they were farther from the city than he thought. Aficionados of different musical sections tended to find places like this and frequent them during anthem.

*"Tonight we'll remake Tennessee, every night we re-
make Tennessee . . ."*

Soma was happily shuffling through a solo dance, keeping one eye on a fat raccoon that was bobbing its head in
time with the music as it turned over stones in the stream
bed, when he saw that the young Crow who wanted to see
a bear had started keeping time as well, raising and lowering a clawed boot. The Owl was the first of the outlanders
who spied the tapping foot.

*"Tonight we'll remake Tennessee, every night we re-
make Tennessee . . ."*

Soma didn't feel the real connection with the citizenry
that anthem usually provided on a daily basis, didn't feel
his confidence and vigor improve, but he blamed that on
the drugs the Kentuckians had given him. He wondered if
those were the same drugs they were using on the Crow
who now feebly twitched beneath the weight of the Owl,
who had wrestled him to the ground. Others pinned down
the dancing Crow's arms and legs and Japheth brought
out a needle and injected the poor soul with a vast syringe
full of some milky brown substance that had the consis-
tency of honey. Soma remembered that he knew the dancing Crow's name. Japheth Sapp had called the boy
Lowell.

*"Tonight we'll remake Tennessee, every night we re-
make Tennessee . . ."*

The pink light faded. The raccoon waddled into the
woods. The trumpet flowers fell quiet and Soma completed the execution of a pirouette.

The redheaded man stood before Japheth wearing a
stricken and haunted look. He kept glancing to one side,
where the Owl stood over the Crow who had danced.
"Japheth, I just lost track," he said. "It's so hard here, to
keep track of things."

Japheth's face flashed from anger through disappointment to something approaching forgiveness. "It is. It's
hard to keep track. Everybody fucks up sometime. And I
think we got the dampeners in him in time."

Then the Owl said, "Second shift now, Japheth. Have to wait for the second round of garbage drops to catch our bundle bug."

Japheth grimaced, but nodded. "We can't move anyway, not until we know what's going to happen with Lowell," he said, glancing at the unconscious boy. "Get the whiskey and the food back into the cache. Set up the netting. We're staying here for the night."

Japheth stalked over to Soma, fists clenched white.

"Things are getting clearer and clearer to you, Soma Painter, even if you think things are getting harder and harder to understand. Our motivations will open up things inside you."

He took Soma's chin in his left hand and tilted Soma's face up. He waved his hand to indicate Lowell.

"There's one of mine. There's one of my motivations for all of this."

Slowly, but with loud lactic cracks, Japheth spread his fingers wide.

"I fight her, Soma, in the hope that she'll not clench up another mind. I fight her so that minds already bound might come unbound."

In the morning, the dancing Crow boy was dead.

Jenny woke near dark, damp and cold, curled up in the gravel of the parking lot. Her horse nickered. She was dimly aware that the horse had been neighing and otherwise emanating concern for some time now, and it was this that had brought her up to consciousness.

She rolled over and climbed to her feet, spitting to rid her mouth of the metal Operator taste. A dried froth of blood coated her nostrils and upper lip, and she could feel the flaky stuff in her ears as well. She looked toward the garage and saw that she wasn't the only one rousing.

"Now, you get back to bed," she told the car.

Soma's car had risen up on its back wheels and was

peering out the open window, its weight resting against the force-grown wall, bulging it outward.

Jenny made a clucking noise, hoping to reassure her horse, and walked up to the car. She was touched by its confusion and concern.

She reached for the aerial. "You should sleep some more," she said, "and not worry about me. The Operators can tell when you're being uncooperative is all, even when *you* didn't know you were being uncooperative. Then they have to root about a bit more than's comfortable to find the answers they want."

Jenny coaxed the car down from the window, wincing a little at the sharp echo pains that flashed in her head and ears. "Don't tell your owner, but this isn't the first time I've been called to question. Now, to bed."

The car looked doubtful, but obediently rolled back to the repair bed that grew from the garage floor. It settled in, grumbled a bit, then switched off its headlights.

Jenny walked around to the door and entered. She found that the water sacs were full and chilled and drew a long drink. The water tasted faintly of salt. She took another swallow, then dampened a rag with a bit more of the tangy stuff to wipe away the dried blood. Then she went to work.

The bundle bugs crawled out of the city, crossed Distinguished Opposition Bridge beneath the watching eye of bears floating overhead, then described a right-angle turn along the levy to their dumping grounds. Soma and the Kentuckians lay hidden in the brushy wasteland at the edge of the grounds, waiting.

The Owl placed a hand on Japheth's shoulder, pointing at a bundle bug just entering the grounds. Then the Owl rose to his knees and began worming his way between the bushes and dead appliances.

"Soma Painter," whispered Japheth. "I'm going to have to break your jaw in a few minutes and cut out as many of

her tentacles as we can get at, but we'll knit it back up as
soon as we cross the river."

Soma was too far gone in the paste to hold both of the
threats in his mind at the same time. A broken jaw, Crows
in the capital. He concentrated on the second.

"The bears will scoop you up and drop you in the Salt
Lick," Soma said. "Children will climb on you during
Campaign and Legislators will stand on your shoulders to
make their stump speeches."

"The bears will not see us, Soma."

"The bears watch the river and the bridges, and—"

"'—and their eyes never close,'" finished Japheth.
"Yes, we've seen the commercials."

A bundle bug, a large one at forty meters in length,
reared up over them, precariously balanced on its rearmost
set of legs. Soma said, "They're very good commercials,"
and the bug crashed down over them all.

Athena's data realm mirrored her physical realm. One-to-
one constructs mimicked the buildings and the citizenry,
showed who was riding and who was being ridden.

In that numerical space, the Kentuckians' math found the
bridge. The harsh light of the bears floated above. Any bear
represented a statistically significant portion of the Governor
herself, and from the point of view of the math, the pair
above Distinguished Opposition Bridge looked like minia-
ture suns, casting probing rays at the marching bundle bugs,
the barges floating along the Cumberland, and even into the
waters of the river itself, illuminating the numerical analogs
of the dangerous things that lived in the muddy bottom.

Bundle bugs came out of the city, their capacious abdomens distended with the waste they'd ingested along
their routes. The math could see that the bug crossing
through the bears' probes right now had a lot of restaurants
on its itinerary. The beams pierced the dun-colored cara-
pace and showed a riot of uneaten jellies, crumpled cups,
soiled napkins.

The bugs marching in the opposite direction, emptied and ready for reloading, were scanned even more carefully than their outward-bound kin. The beam scans were withering, complete, and exceedingly precise.

The math knew that precision and accuracy are not the same thing.

"*Lowell's death has* set us back further than we thought," said Japheth, talking to the four Crows, the Owl, and, Soma guessed, to the bundle bug they inhabited. Japheth had detailed off the rest of the raiding party to carry the dead boy back north, so there was plenty of room where they crouched.

The interior of the bug's abdomen was larger than Soma's apartment by a factor of two and smelled of flowers instead of paint thinner. Soma's apartment, however, was not an alcoholic.

"This is good, though, good good." The bug's voice rang from every direction at once. "I'm scheduled down for a rest shift. You-uns was late and missed my last run, and now we can all rest and drink good whiskey. Good good."

But none of the Kentuckians drank any of the whiskey from the casks they'd cracked once they'd crawled down the bug's gullet. Instead, every half hour or so, they poured another gallon into one of the damp fissures that ran all through the interior. Bundle bugs abdomens weren't designed for digestion, just evacuation, and it was the circulatory system that was doing the work of carrying the bourbon to the bug's brain.

Soma dipped a finger into an open cask and touched finger to tongue. "Bourbon burns!" he said, pulling his finger from his mouth.

"Burns good!" said the bug. "Good good."

"We knew that not all of us were going to be able to actually enter the city—we don't have enough outfits, for one thing—but six is a bare minimum. And since we're running behind, we'll have to wait out tonight's anthem in our host's apartment."

"Printer's Alley is two miles from the Parthenon," said the Owl, nodding at Soma.

Japheth nodded. "I know. And I know that those might be the two longest miles in the world. But we expected hard walking."

He banged the curving gray wall he leaned against with his elbow. "Hey! Bundle bug! How long until you start your shift?"

A vast and disappointed sigh shuddered through the abdomen. "Two more hours, bourbon man," said the bug.

"Get out your gear, cousin," Japheth said to the Owl. He stood and stretched, motioned for the rest of the Crows to do the same. He turned toward Soma. "The rest of us will hold him down."

Jenny had gone out midmorning, when the last of the fog was still burning off the bluffs, searching for low moisture organics to feed the garage. She'd run its reserves very low, working on one thing and another until quite late in the night.

As she suspected from the salty taste of the water supply, the filters in the housings between the tap roots and the garage's plumbing array were clogged with silt. She'd blown them out with pressurized air—no need to replace what you can fix—and reinstalled them one, two, three. But while she was blowing out the filters, she'd heard a whine she didn't like in the air compressor, and when she'd gone to check it she found it panting with effort, tongue hanging out onto the workbench top where it sat.

And then things went as these things go, and she moved happily from minor maintenance problem to minor maintenance problem—wiping away the air compressor's crocodile tears while she stoned the motor brushes in its A/C motor, then replacing the fusible link in the garage itself. "Links are so easily fusible," she joked to her horse when she rubbed it down with handfuls of the sweet-smelling fern fronds she'd intended for her own bed.

And all the while, of course, she watched the little car, monitoring the temperatures at its core points and doing what she could to coax the broken window to reknit in a smooth, steady fashion. Once, when the car awoke in the middle of the night making colicky noises, Jenny had to pop the hood, where she found that the points needed to be pulled and regapped. They were fouled with the viscous residue of the analgesic aero the owner had spread about so liberally.

She tsked. The directions on the labels clearly stated that the nozzle was to be pointed *away* from the engine compartment. Still, hard to fault Soma Painter's good-hearted efforts. It was an easy fix, and she would have pulled the plugs during the tune-up she had planned for the morning anyway.

So, repairings and healings, lights burning and tools turning, and when she awoke to the morning tide sounds the garage immediately began flashing amber lights at her wherever she turned. The belly-grumble noises it floated from the speakers worried the horse, so she set out looking for something to put in the hoppers of the hungry garage.

When she came back, bearing a string-tied bundle of dried wood and a half bucket of old walnuts some gatherer had wedged beneath an overhang and forgotten at least a double handful of autumns past, the car was gone.

Jenny hurried to the edge of the parking lot and looked down the road, though she couldn't see much. This time of year the morning fog turned directly into the midday haze. She could see the city, and bits of road between trees and bluff line, but no sign of the car.

The garage pinged at her, and she shoved its breakfast into the closest intake. She didn't open her head to call the police—she hadn't yet fully recovered from yesterday afternoon's interview. She was even hesitant to open her head the little bit she needed to access her own garage's security tapes. But she'd built the garage, and either built or rebuilt everything in it, so she risked it.

She stood at her workbench, rubbing her temple, as a see-through Jenny and a see-through car built themselves up out of twisted light. Light Jenny put on a light rucksack, scratched the light car absently on the roof as she walked by, and headed out the door. Light Jenny did not tether the car. Light Jenny did not lock the door.

"Silly light Jenny," said Jenny.

As soon as light Jenny was gone, the little light car rolled over to the big open windows. It popped a funny little wheelie and caught itself on the sash, the way it had yesterday when it had watched real Jenny swim up out of her government dream.

The light car kept one headlight just above the sash for a few minutes, then lowered itself back to the floor with a bounce (real Jenny had aired up the tires first thing, even before she grew the garage).

The light car revved its motor excitedly. Then, just a gentle tap on the door, and it was out in the parking lot. It drove over to the steps leading down to the beach, hunching its grill down to the ground. It circled the lot a bit, snuffling here and there, until it found whatever it was looking for. Before it zipped down the road toward Nashville, it circled back round and stopped outside the horse's stall. The light car opened its passenger door and waggled it back and forth a time or two. The real horse neighed and tossed its head at the light car in a friendly fashion.

Jenny-With-Grease-Beneath-Her-Fingernails visited her horse with the meanest look that a mechanic can give a horse. The horse snickered. "You laugh, horse," she said, opening the tack locker, "but we still have to go after it."

Inside the bundle bug, there was some unpleasantness with a large glass-and-pewter contraption of the Owl's. The Crow Brothers held Soma as motionless as they could, and Japheth seemed genuinely sorry when he forced the painter's mouth open much wider than Soma had previously thought possible. "You should have drunk more of the whiskey," said Japheth. There was a loud, wet, popping sound, and Soma shuddered, stiffened, fainted.

"Well, that'll work best for all of us," said Japheth. He looked up at the Owl, who was peering through a lens polished out of a semiprecious gemstone, staring down into the painter's gullet.

"Have you got access?"

The Owl nodded.

"Talk to your math," said the Crow.

The math had been circling beneath the bridge, occasionally dragging a curiosity-begat string of numbers into the water. Always low-test numbers, because invariably whatever lived beneath the water snatched at the lines and sucked them down.

The input the math was waiting for finally arrived in the form of a low hooting sound rising up from the dumping grounds. It was important that the math not know which bundle bug the sound emanated from. There were certain techniques the bears had developed for teasing information out of recalcitrant math.

No matter. The math knew the processes. It had the input. It spread itself out over the long line of imagery the bundle bugs yielded up to the bears. It affected its changes. It lent clarity.

Above, the bears did their work with great precision.

Below, the Kentuckians slipped into Nashville undetected.

Soma woke to find the Kentuckians doing something terrible. When he tried to speak, he found that his face was immobilized by a mask of something that smelled of the docks but felt soft and gauzy.

The four younger Crows were dressed in a gamut of jer-

seys and shorts colored in the hotter hues of the spectrum.
Japheth was struggling into a long, jangly coat hung with
seashells and old capacitors. But it was the Owl that frightened Soma the most. The broad-chested man was dappled
with opal stones from collar bones to ankles and wore
nothing else save a breech cloth cut from an old newspa-
per. Soma moaned, trying to attract their attention again.

The blue-eyed boy said, "Your painter stirs, Japheth."

But it was the Owl who leaned over Soma, placed his
hand on Soma's chin and turned his head back and forth
with surprising gentleness. The Owl nodded, to himself
Soma guessed, for none of the Crows reacted, then peeled
the bandages off Soma's face.

Soma took a deep breath, then said, "Nobody's worn
opals for months! And those shorts," he gestured at the
others, "Too much orange! Too much orange!"

Japheth laughed. "Well, we'll be tourists in from the
provinces, then, not princes of Printer's Alley. Do *I* of-
fend?" He wriggled his shoulders, set the shells and cir-
cuits to clacking.

Soma pursed his lips, shook his head. "Seashells and
capacitors are timeless," he said.

Japheth nodded. "That's what it said on the box." Then,
"Hey! Bug! Are we to market yet?"

"It's hard to say, whiskey man," came the reply. "My
eyes are funny."

"Close enough. Open up."

The rear of the beast's abdomen cracked, and yawned
wide. Japheth turned to his charges. "You boys ready to
play like vols?"

The younger Crows started gathering burlap bundles.
The Owl hoisted a heavy rucksack, adjusted the flowers in
his hat, and said, "Wacka wacka ho."

In a low place, horizon bounded by trees in every direction, Jenny and her horse came on the sobbing car. From
the ruts it had churned up in the mud, Jenny guessed it had

been there for some time, driving back and forth along the northern verge.

"Now what have you done to yourself?" she asked, dismounting. The car turned to her and shuddered. Its front left fender was badly dented, and its hood and windshield were a mess of leaves and small branches.

"Trying to get into the woods? Cars are for roads, car." She brushed some muck off the damaged fender.

"Well, that's not too bad, though. This is all cosmetic. Why would a car try to go where trees are? See what happens?"

The horse called. It had wandered a little way into the woods and was standing at the base of a vast poplar. Jenny reached in through the passenger's window of the car, avoiding the glassy knitting blanket on the other side, and set the parking brake. "You wait here."

She trotted out to join her horse. It was pawing at a small patch of ground. Jenny was a mechanic and had no woodscraft, but she could see the outline of a cleft-toed sandal. Who would be in the woods with such impractical footwear?

"The owner's an artist. An artist looking for a shortcut to the Alley, I reckon," said Jenny. "Wearing funny artist shoes."

She walked back to the car, considering. The car was pining. Not unheard of, but not common. It made her think better of Soma Painter that his car missed him so.

"Say, horse. Melancholy slows car repair. I think this car will convalesce better in its own parking space."

The car revved.

"But there's the garage still back at the beach," said Jenny.

She turned things over and over. "Horse," she said, "you're due three more personal days this month. If I release you for them now, will you go fold up the garage and bring it to me in the city?"

The horse tossed its head enthusiastically.

"Good. I'll drive with this car back to the Alley, then—"
But the horse was already rubbing its flanks against her.

"Okay, okay." She drew a tin of salve from her tool belt,
dipped her fingers in it, then ran her hands across the
horse's back. The red crosses came away in her hands,
wriggling. "The cases for these are in my cabinet," she
said, and then inspiration came.

"Here, car," she said, and laid the crosses on its hood.
They wriggled around until they were at statute-specified
points along the doors and roof. "Now you're an ambu-
lance! Not a hundred percent legal, maybe, but this way
you can drive fast and whistle siren-like."

The car spun its rear wheels but couldn't overcome the
parking brake. Jenny laughed. "Just a minute more. I need
you to give me a ride into town."

She turned to speak to the horse, only to see it already
galloping along the coast road. "Don't forget to drain the
water tanks before you fold it up!" she shouted.

The bundles that were flecked with root matter, Soma discovered, were filled with roots. Carrots and turnips, a half
dozen varieties of potatoes, beets. The Kentuckians spread
out through the Farmer's Market, trading them by the arm-
load for the juices and gels that the rock monkeys brought
in from their gardens.

"This is our secondary objective," said Japheth. "We do
this all the time, trading doped potatoes for that shit y'all
eat."

"You're poisoning us?" Soma was climbing out of the
paste a little, or something. His thoughts were shifting
around some.

"Doped with nutrients, friend. Forty ain't old outside
Tennessee. Athena doesn't seem to know any more about
human nutrition than she does human psychology. Hey,
we're trying to *help* you people."

Then they were in the very center of the market, and the
roar of the crowds drowned out any reply Soma might make.

Japheth kept a grip on Soma's arm as he spoke to a gray old monkey. "Ten pounds, right?" The monkey was weighing a bundle of carrots on a scale.

"Okay," grunted the monkey. "Okay, man. Ten pounds I give you . . . four blue jellies."

Soma was incredulous. He'd never developed a taste for them himself, but he knew that carrots were popular. Four blue jellies was an insulting trade. But Japheth said, "Fair enough," and pocketed the plastic tubes the monkey handed over.

"You're no trader," said Soma, or started to, but heard the words slur out of him in an unintelligible mess of vowels. *One spring semester, when he'd already been a TA for a year, he was tapped to work on the interface. No more need for scholarships.*

"Painter!" shouted Japheth.

Soma looked up. There was a Crow dressed in Alley haute couture standing in front of him. He tried to open his head to call the Tennessee Highway Patrol. He couldn't find his head.

"Give him one of these yellow ones," said a monkey. "They're good for fugues."

"Painter!" shouted Japheth again. The grip on Soma's shoulder was like a vise.

Soma struggled to stand under his own power. "I'm forgetting something."

"Hah!" said Japheth, "You're remembering. Too soon for my needs, though. Listen to me. Rock monkeys are full voluntary citizens of Tennessee."

The outlandishness of the statement shocked Soma out of his reverie and brought the vendor up short.

"Fuck you, man!" said the monkey.

"No, no," said Soma, then said by rote, "Tennessee is a fully realized postcolonial state. The land of the rock monkeys is an autonomous partner-principality within our borders, and while the monkeys are our staunch allies, their allegiance is not to our Governor, but to their king."

"Yah," said the monkey. "Long as we get our licenses

and pay the tax machine. Plus, who the jelly cubes going to listen to besides the monkey king, huh?"

Japheth marched Soma to the next stall. "Lot left in there to wash out yet," Japheth said.

"I wash every day," said Soma, then fell against a sloshing tray of juice containers. *The earliest results were remarkable.*

A squat man covered with black gems came up to them. The man who'd insulted the monkey said, "You might have killed too much of it; he's getting kind of wonky."

The squat man looked into Soma's eyes. "We can stabilize him easy enough. There are televisions in the food court."

Then Soma and Japheth were drinking hot rum punches and watching a newsfeed. There was a battle out over the Gulf somewhere, Commodores mounted on bears darted through the clouds, lancing Cuban zeppelins.

"The Cubans will never achieve air superiority," said Soma, and it felt right saying it.

Japheth eyed him wearily. "I need you to keep thinking that for now, Soma Painter," he said quietly. "But I hope sometime soon you'll know that Cubans don't live in a place called the Appalachian Archipelago, and that the salty reach out there isn't the Gulf of Mexico."

The bicycle race results were on then, and Soma scanned the lists, hoping to see his favorites' names near the top of the general classifications.

"That's the Tennessee River, dammed up by your Governor's hubris."

Soma saw that his drink was nearly empty and heard that his friend Japheth was still talking. "What?" he asked, smiling.

"I asked if you're ready to go to the Alley," said Japheth.

"Good good," said Soma.

•   •   •

The math was moving along minor avenues, siphoning data from secondary and tertiary ports when it sensed her looming up. It researched ten thousand thousand escapes but rejected them all when it perceived that it had been subverted, that it was inside her now, becoming part of her, that it *is primitive in materials but clever clever in architecture and there have been blindings times not seen places to root out root out all of it check again check one thousand more times all told all told eat it all up all the little bluegrass math is absorbed*

"*The Alley* at night!" shouted Soma. "Not like where you're from, eh, boys?"

A lamplighter's stalk legs eased through the little group. Soma saw that his friends were staring up at the civil servant's welding mask head, gaping openmouthed as it turned a spigot at the top of a tree and lit the gas with a flick of its tongue.

"Let's go to my place!" said Soma. "When it's time for anthem we can watch the parade from my balcony. I live in one of the lofts above the Tyranny of the Anecdote."

"Above what?" asked Japheth.

"It's a tavern. They're my landlords," said Soma. "Vols are so fucking stupid."

But that wasn't right.

Japheth's Owl friend fell to his knees and vomited right in the street. Soma stared at the jiggling spheres in the gutter as the man choked some words out. "She's taken the feathers. She's looking for us now."

Too much rum punch, thought Soma, thought it about the Owl man and himself and about all of Japheth's crazy friends.

"Soma, how far now?" asked Japheth.

Soma remembered his manners. "Not far," he said.

And it wasn't, just a few more struggling yards, Soma

leading the way and Japheth's friends half-carrying, half-dragging their drunken friend down the Alley. Nothing unusual there. Every night in the Alley was Carnival.

Then a wave at the bouncer outside the Anecdote, then up the steps, then sing "Let me in, let me in!" to the door, and finally all of them packed into the cramped space.

"There," said the sick man, pointing at the industrial sink Soma had installed himself to make brush cleaning easier. *Brushes . . . where were his brushes, his pencils, his notes for the complexity seminar?*

"Towels, Soma?"

"What? Oh, here let me get them." Soma bustled around, finding towels, pulling out stools for the now silent men who filled his room.

He handed the towels to Japheth. "Was it something he ate?" Soma asked.

Japheth shrugged. "Ate a long time ago, you could say. Owls are as much numbers as they are meat. He's divesting himself. Those are ones and zeroes washing down your drain."

The broad man—hadn't he been broad?—the scrawny man with opals falling off him said, "We can only take a few minutes. There are unmounted Detectives swarming the whole city now. What I've left in me is too deep for their little minds, but the whole sphere is roused and things will only get tighter. Just let me—" He turned and retched into the sink again. "Just a few minutes more until the singing."

Japheth moved to block Soma's view of the Owl. He nodded at the drawings on the wall. "Yours?"

The blue-eyed boy moved over to the sink, helped the Owl ease to the floor. Soma looked at the pictures. "Yes, mostly. I traded for a few."

Japheth was studying one charcoal piece carefully, a portrait. "What's this one?"

The drawing showed a tall, thin young man dressed in a period costume, leaning against a mechanical of some kind, staring intently out at the viewer. Soma didn't remember drawing it, specifically, but knew what it must be.

"That's a caricature. I do them during Campaign for the provincials who come into the city to vote. Someone must have asked me to draw him and then never come back to claim it."

And he remembered trying to remember. He remembered asking his hand to remember when his head wouldn't.

"I'm . . . what did you put in me?" Soma asked. There was moisture on his cheeks, and he hoped it was tears.

The Owl was struggling up to his feet. A bell tone sounded from the sky and he said, "Now, Japheth. There's no time."

"Just a minute more," snapped the Crow. "What did we put in you? You . . ." Japheth spat. "While you're remembering, try and remember this. You *chose* this! All of you chose it!"

The angry man wouldn't have heard any reply Soma might have made, because it was then that all of the Kentuckians clamped their ears shut with their odd muffs. To his surprise, they forced a pair onto Soma as well.

Jenny finally convinced the car to stop wailing out its hee-haw pitch when they entered the maze of streets leading to Printer's Alley. The drive back had been long, the car taking every northern side road, backtracking, looping, even trying to enter the dumping grounds at one point before the bundle bugs growled them away. During anthem, while Jenny drummed her fingers and forced out the words, the car still kept up its search, not even pretending to dance.

So Jenny had grown more and more fascinated by the car's behavior. She had known cars that were slavishly attached to their owners before, and she had known cars that were smart—almost as smart as bundle bugs, some of them—but the two traits never seemed to go together. "Cars are dogs or cars are cats," her Teacher had said to ex-

plain the phenomenon, another of the long roll of enig-
matic statements that constituted formal education in the
Voluntary State.

But here, now, here was a bundle bug that didn't seem
to live up to those creatures' reputations for craftiness. The
car had been following the bug for a few blocks—Jenny
only realized that after the car, for the first time since they
entered the city proper, made a turn *away* from the address
painted on its name tag.

The bug was a big one, and was describing a gentle ca-
reer down Commerce Street, drifting from side to side and
clearly ignoring the traffic signals that flocked around its
head in an agitated cloud.

"Car, we'd better get off this street. Rogue bugs are too
much for the THP. If it doesn't self-correct, a Commodore
is likely to be rousted out from the Parthenon." Jenny
sometimes had nightmares about Commodores.

The car didn't listen—though it was normally an excellent listener—but accelerated toward the bug. The bug,
Jenny now saw, had stopped in front of a restaurant and
cracked its abdomen. Dumpster feelers had started creeping out of the interstices between thorax and head when the
restaurateur charged out, beating at the feelers with a
broom. "Go now!" the man shouted, face as red as his vest
and leggings, "I told you twice already! You pick up here
Chaseday! Go! I already called your supervisor, bug!"

The bug's voice echoed along the street. "No load?
Good good." Its sigh was pure contentment, but Jenny had
no time to appreciate it. The car sped up, and Jenny covered her eyes, anticipating a collision. But the car slid to a
halt with bare inches to spare, peered into the empty cav-
ern of the bug's belly, then sighed, this one not content
at all.

"Come on, car," Jenny coaxed. "He must be at home by
now. Let's just try your house, okay?"

The car beeped and executed a precise three-point turn.
As they turned off Commerce and climbed the viaduct that
arced above the Farmer's Market, Jenny caught a hint of

motion in the darkening sky. "THP bicycles, for sure," she said. "Tracking your bug friend."

At the highest point on the bridge, Jenny leaned out and looked down into the controlled riot of the Market. Several stalls were doing brisk business, and when Jenny saw why, she asked the car to stop, then let out a whistle.

"Oi! Monkey!" she shouted. "Some beets up here!"

Jenny loved beets.

Signals from the city center subsidiaries routing reports and recommendations increase percentages dedicated to observation and prediction dispatch commodore downcycle biological construct extra-parametrical lower authority

"It's funny that I don't know what it means, though, don't you think, friends?" Soma was saying this for perhaps the fifth time since they began their walk. "*Church* Street. *Church*. Have you ever heard that word anywhere else?"

"No," said the blue-eyed bov.

The Kentuckians were less and less talkative the farther the little group advanced west down Church Street. It was a long, broad avenue, but rated for pedestrians and emergency vehicles only. Less a street, really, than a linear park, for there were neither businesses nor apartments on either side, just low gray government buildings, slate-colored in the sunset.

The sunset. That was why the boulevard was crowded, as it was every night. As the sun dropped down, down, down it dropped behind the Parthenon. At the very instant the disc disappeared behind the sand-colored edifice, the Great Salt Lick self-illuminated and the flat acres of white surrounding the Parthenon shone with a vast, icy light.

The Lick itself was rich with the minerals that fueled the Legislators and Bears, but the white light emanating from it was sterile. Soma noticed that the Crows faces grew paler and paler as they all got closer to its source. *His*

*work was fascinating, and grew more so as more and more
disciplines began finding ways to integrate their fields of
study into a meta-architecture of science. His department
chair co-authored a paper with an expert in animal hus-
bandry, of all things.*

The Owl held Soma's head as the painter vomited up
the last of whatever was in his stomach.

Japheth and the others were making reassuring noises to
passersby. "Too much monkey wine!" they said, and,
"We're in from the provinces, he's not used to such rich
food!" and, "He's overcome by the sight of the Parthenon!"

Japheth leaned over next to the Owl. "Why's it hitting
him so much harder than the others?"

The Owl said, "Well, we've always taken them back
north of the border. This poor fool we're dragging ever
closer to the glory of his owner. I couldn't even guess
what's trying to fill up the empty spaces I left in him—but
I'm pretty sure whatever's rushing in isn't all from her."

Japheth cocked an eyebrow at his lieutenant. "I think
that's the most words I've ever heard you say all together
at once."

The Owl smiled, another first, if that sad little half grin
counted as a smile. "Not a lot of time left for talking. Get
up now, friend painter."

The Owl and Japheth pulled Soma to his feet. "What
did you mean," Soma asked, wiping his mouth with the
back of his hand, " 'the glory of his owner'?"

"Governor," said Japheth. "He said, 'the glory of his
Governor,' " and Japheth swept his arm across, and yes,
there it was, the glory of the Governor.

Church Street had a slight downward grade in its last
few hundred yards. From where they stood, they could see
that the street ended at the spectacularly defined border of
the Great Salt Lick, which served as legislative chambers
in the Voluntary State. At the center of the lick stood the
Parthenon, and while no normal citizens walked the salt
just then, there was plenty of motion and color.

Two bears were laying face down in the Lick, bobbing

their heads as they took in sustenance from the ground. A dozen or more Legislators slowly unambulated, their great slimy bodies leaving trails of gold or silver depending on their party affiliation. One was engulfing one of the many salt-white statues that dotted the grounds, gaining a few feet of height to warble its slogan songs from. And, unmoving at the corners of the rectangular palace in the center of it all, four Commodores stood.

They were tangled giants of rust, alike in their towering height and in the oily bathyspheres encasing the scant meat of them deep in their torsos, but otherwise each a different silhouette of sensor suites and blades, each with a different complement of articulated limbs or wings or wheels.

"Can you tell which ones they are?" Japheth asked the blue-eyed boy, who had begun murmuring to himself under his breath, eyes darting from Commodore to Commodore.

> *"Ruby-eyed Sutcliffe, stomper, smasher,*
> *Tempting Nguyen, whispering, lying,*
> *Burroughs burrows, up from the*
> *underground . . ."*

The boy hesitated, shaking his head. "Northeast corner looks kind of like Praxis Dale, but she's supposed to be away West, fighting the Federals. Saint Sandalwood's physical presence had the same profile as Dale's, but we believe he's gone, consumed by Athena after their last sortie against the containment field cost her so much."

"I'll never understand why she plays at politics with her subordinates when she *is* her subordinates," said Japheth.

The Owl said, "That's not as true with the Commodores as with a lot of the . . . inhabitants. I think it *is* Saint Sandalwood; she must have reconstituted him, or part of him. And remember his mnemonic?"

"*Sandalwood staring,*" sang the blue-eyed boy.

"*Inside and outside*," finished Japheth, looking the Owl in the eye. "Time then?"

"Once we're on the Lick I'd do anything she told me, even empty as I am," said the Owl. "Bind me."

Then the blue-eyed boy took Soma by the arm, kept encouraging him to take in the sights of the Parthenon, turning his head away from where the Crows were wrapping the Owl in grapevines. They took the Owl's helmet from a rucksack and seated it, cinching the cork seals at the neck maybe tighter than Soma would have thought was comfortable.

Two of the Crows hoisted the Owl between them, his feet stumbling some. Soma saw that the eyeholes of the mask had been blocked with highly reflective tape.

Japheth spoke to the others. "The bears won't be in this; they'll take too long to stand up from their meal. Avoid the Legislators, even their trails. The THP will be on the ground, but won't give you any trouble. You boys know why you're here."

The two Crows holding the Owl led him over to Japheth, who took him by the hand. The blue-eyed boy said, "We know why we're here, Japheth. We know why we were born."

And suddenly as that, the four younger Crows were gone, fleeing in every direction except back up Church Street.

"Soma Painter," said Japheth. "Will you help me lead this man on?"

Soma was taken aback. While he knew of no regulation specifically prohibiting it, traditionally no one actually trod the Lick except during Campaign.

"We're going into the Salt Lick?" Soma asked.

"We're going into the Parthenon," Japheth answered.

A*s they crossed* Church Street from the south, the car suddenly stopped.

"Now what, car?" said Jenny. Church Street was her least favorite thoroughfare in the capital.

The car snuffled around on the ground for a moment, then, without warning, took a hard left and accelerated, siren screeching. Tourists and sunset gazers scattered to either side as the car and Jenny roared toward the glowing white horizon.

The Owl only managed a few yards under his own power. He slowed, then stumbled, and then the Crow and the painter were carrying him.

"What's wrong with him?" asked Soma.

They crossed the verge onto the salt. They'd left the bravest sightseers a half-block back.

"He's gone inside himself," said Japheth.

"Why?" asked Soma.

Japheth half laughed. "You'd know better than me, friend."

It was then that the Commodore closest to them took a single step forward with its right foot, dragged the left a dozen yards in the same direction, and then, twisting, fell to the ground with a thunderous crash.

"Whoo!" shouted Japheth. "The harder they fall! We'd better start running now, Soma!"

Soma was disappointed, but unsurprised, to see that Japheth did not mean run *away*.

There was only one bear near the slightly curved route that Japheth picked for them through the harsh glare. Even light as he was, purged of his math, the Owl was still a burden and Soma couldn't take much time to marvel at the swirling colors in the bear's plastic hide.

"Keep up, Soma!" shouted the Crow. Ahead of them, two of the Commodores had suddenly turned on one another and were landing terrible blows. Soma saw a tiny figure clinging to one of the giants' shoulders, saw it lose its grip, fall, and disappear beneath an ironshod boot the size of a bundle bug.

Then Soma slipped and fell himself, sending all three of them to the glowing ground and sending a cloud of the biting crystal salt into the air. One of his sandaled feet, he saw, was coated in gold slime. They'd been trying to out-flank one Legislator only to stumble on the trail of another.

Japheth picked up the Owl, now limp as a rag doll, and with a grunt heaved the man across his shoulders. "Soma, you should come on. We might make it." *It's not a hard decision to make at all. How can you not make it? At first he'd needed convincing, but then he'd been one of those who'd gone out into the world to convince others. It's not just history; it's after history.*

"Soma!"

Japheth ran directly at the unmoving painter, the dead-weight of the Owl across his shoulders slowing him. He barreled into Soma, knocking him to the ground again, all of them just missing the unknowing Legislator as it slid slowly past.

"Up, up!" said Japheth. "Stay behind it, so long as it's moving in the right direction. I think my boys missed a Commodore." His voice was very sad.

The Legislator stopped and let out a bellowing noise. Fetid steam began rising from it. Japheth took Soma by the hand and pulled him along, through chaos. One of the Commodores, the first to fall, was motionless on the ground, two or three Legislators making their way along its length. The two who'd fought lay locked in one another's grasp, barely moving and glowing hotter and hotter. The only standing Commodore, eyes like red suns, seemed to be staring just behind them.

As it began to sweep its gaze closer, Soma heard Japheth say, "We got closer than I would have bet."

Then Soma's car, mysteriously covered with red crosses and wailing at the top of its voice, came to a sliding, crunching stop in the salt in front of them.

Soma didn't hesitate, but threw open the closest rear door and pulled Japheth in behind him. When the three of them—painter, Crow, Owl—were stuffed into the rear door, Soma shouted, "Up those stairs, car!"

In the front seat, there was a woman whose eyes seemed as large as saucers.

commodores faulting headless people in the lick protocols compel reeling in, strengthening, temporarily abandoning telepresence locate an asset with a head asset with a head located

Jenny-With-Grease-Beneath-Her-Fingernails was trying not to go crazy. Something was pounding at her head, even though she hadn't tried to open it herself. Yesterday, she had been working a remote repair job on the beach, fixing a smashed window. Tonight, she was hurtling across the Great Salt Lick, Legislators and bears and *Commodores* acting in ways she'd never seen or heard of.

Jenny herself acting in ways she'd never heard of. Why didn't she just pull the emergency brake, roll out of the car, wait for the THP? Why did she just hold on tighter and pull down the sunscreen so she could use the mirror to look into the backseat?

It *was* three men. She hadn't been sure at first. One appeared to be unconscious and was dressed in some strange getup, a helmet of some kind completely encasing his head. She didn't know the man in the capacitor jacket, who was craning his head out the window, trying to see something above them. The other one though, she recognized.

"Soma Painter," she said. "Your car is much better, though it has missed you terribly."

The owner just looked at her glaze-eyed. The other one pulled himself back in through the window, a wild glee on his face. He rapped the helmet of the prone man and shouted, "Did you hear that? The unpredictable you prophesied! And it fell in our favor!"

•   •   •

S*oma worried about* his car's suspension, not to mention
the tires, when it slalomed through the legs of the last
standing Commodore and bounced up the steeply cut steps
of the Parthenon. *He hadn't had a direct hand in the sub-*
systems design—by the time he'd begun to develop the
cars, Athena was already beginning to take over a lot of
the details. Not all of them, though; he couldn't blame her
for the guilt he felt over twisting his animal subjects into
something like onboard components.

But the car made it onto the platform inside the outer set
of columns, seemingly no worse for wear. The man next to
him—Japheth, his name was Japheth and he was from
Kentucky—jumped out of the car and ran to the vast,
closed counterweighted bronze doors.

"It's because of the crosses. We're in an emergency vehicle according to their protocols." That was the mechanic,
Jenny, sitting in the front seat and trying to staunch a nose-
bleed with a greasy rag. "I can hear the Governor," she said.

Soma could hear Japheth raging and cursing. He
stretched the Owl out along the back seat and climbed out
of the car. Japheth was pounding on the doors in futility,
beating his fists bloody, spinning, spitting. He caught sight
of Soma.

"*These* weren't here before!" he said, pointing to two
silver columns that angled up from the platform's floor,
ending in flanges on the doors themselves. "The doors
aren't locked, they're just sealed by these fucking cylinders!" Japheth was shaking. "Caw!" he cried. "Caw!"

"What's he trying to do?" asked the woman in the car.

Soma brushed his fingers against his temple, trying to
remember.

"I think he's trying to remake Tennessee," he said.

T*he weight of* a thousand cars on her skull, the hoofbeats of
a thousand horses throbbing inside her eyes, Jenny was in-

capable of making any rational decision. So, irrationally, she left the car. She stumbled over to the base of one of the silver columns. When she tried to catch herself on it, her hand slid off.

"Oil," she said. "These are just hydraulic cylinders." She looked around the metal sheeting where the cylinder disappeared into the platform, saw the access plate. She pulled a screwdriver from her belt and used it to removed the plate.

The owner was whispering to his car, but the crazy man had come over to her. "What are you doing?" he asked.

"I don't know," she said, but she meant it only in the largest sense. Immediately, she was thrusting her wrists into the access plate, playing the licenses and government bonds at her wrists under a spray of light, murmuring a quick apology to the machinery. Then she opened a long vertical cut down as much of the length of the hydraulic hose as she could with her utility blade.

Fluid exploded out of the hole, coating Jenny in the slick, dirty green stuff. The cylinders collapsed.

The man next to Jenny looked at her. He turned and looked at Soma-With-The-Paintbox-In-Printer's-Alley and at Soma's car.

"We must have had a pretty bad plan," he said, then rushed over to pull the helmeted figure from the backseat.

breached come home all you commodores come home cancel emergency designation on identified vehicle and downcycle now jump in jump in jump in

Jenny could not help Soma and his friend drag their burden through the doors of the temple, but she staggered through the doors. She had only seen Athena in tiny parts, in the mannequin shrines that contained tiny fractions of the Governor.

Here was the true and awesome thing, here was the forty-foot-tall sculpture—armed and armored—attended by the broken remains of her frozen marble enemies. Jenny managed to lift her head and look past sandaled feet, up cold golden raiment, past tart painted cheeks to the lapis lazuli eyes.

Athena looked back at her. Athena leapt.

Inside Jenny's head, inside so small an architecture, there was no more room for Jenny-With-Grease-Beneath-Her-Fingernails. Jenny fled.

S*oma saw the* mechanic, the woman who'd been so kind to his car, fall to her knees, blood gushing from her nose and ears. He saw Japheth laying out the Owl like a sacrifice before the Governor. *He'd been among the detractors, scoffing at the idea of housing the main armature in such a symbol-potent place.*

Behind him, his car beeped. The noise was barely audible above the screaming metal sounds out in the Lick. The standing Commodore was swiveling its torso, turning its upper half toward the Parthenon. Superheated salt melted in a line slowly tracking toward the steps.

Soma trotted back to his car. He leaned in and *remembered the back door, the Easter egg he hadn't documented.* A twist on the ignition housing, then press in, and the key sank into the column. The car shivered.

"Run home as fast you can, car. Back to the ranch with your kin. Be fast, car, be clever."

The car woke up. It shook off Soma's ownership and closed its little head. It let out a surprised beep and then fled with blazing speed, leaping down the steps, over the molten salt, and through the storm, bubblewinged bicycles descending all around. The Commodore began another slow turn, trying to track it.

Soma turned back to the relative calm inside the Parthenon. Athena's gaze was baleful, but he couldn't feel it. The Owl had ripped the ability from him. The Owl lying before Japheth, defenseless against the knife Japheth held high.

"Why?" shouted Soma.

But Japheth didn't answer him, instead diving over the

Owl in a somersault roll, narrowly avoiding the flurry of kicks and roundhouse blows being thrown by Jenny. Her eyes bugged and bled. More blood flowed from her ears and nostrils, but still she attacked Japheth with relentless fury.

Japheth came up in a crouch. The answer to Soma's question came in a slurred voice from Jenny. Not Jenny, though. Soma knew the voice, remembered it from somewhere, and it wasn't Jenny's.

"there is a bomb in that meat soma-friend a knife a threat an eraser"

Japheth shouted at Soma. "You get to decide again! Cut the truth out of him!" He gestured at the Owl with his knife.

Soma took in a shuddery breath. "So free with lives. One of the reasons we climbed up."

Jenny's body lurched at Japheth, but the Crow dropped onto the polished floor. Jenny's body slipped when it landed, the soles of its shoes coated with the same oil as its jumpsuit.

"My Owl cousin died of asphyxiation at least ten minutes ago, Soma," said Japheth. "Died imperfect and uncontrolled." Then, dancing backward before the scratching thing in front of him, Japheth tossed the blade in a gentle underhanded arc. It clattered to the floor at Soma's feet.

All of the same arguments.

All of the same arguments.

Soma picked up the knife and looked down at the Owl. The fight before him, between a dead woman versus a man certain to die soon, spun on. Japheth said no more, only looked at Soma with pleading eyes.

Jenny's body's eyes followed the gaze, saw the knife in Soma's hand.

"you are due upgrade soma-friend swell the ranks of commodores you were 96th percentile now 99th soma-with-the-paintbox-in-printer's-alley the voluntary state of tennessee applauds your citizenship"

But it wasn't the early slight, the denial of entry to the circle of highest minds. Memories of before *and* after, decisions made by him and for him, sentiences and upgrades decided by fewer and fewer and then one; one who'd been a *product*, not a builder.

Soma plunged the knife into the Owl's unmoving chest and sawed downward through the belly with what strength he could muster. The skin and fat fell away along a seam straighter than he could ever cut. The bomb—the knife, the eraser, the threat—looked like a tiny white balloon. He pierced it with the killing tip of the Kentuckian's blade.

A *nova erupted* at the center of the space where math and Detectives live. A wave of scouring numbers washed outward, spreading all across Nashville, all across the Voluntary State to fill all the space within the containment field.

The 144 Detectives evaporated. The King of the Rock Monkeys, nothing but twisted light, fell into shadow. The Commodores fell immobile, the ruined biology seated in their chests went blind, then deaf, then died.

And singing Nashville fell quiet. Ten thousand thousand heads slammed shut and ten thousand thousand souls fell insensate, unsupported, in need of revival.

North of the Girding Wall, alarms began to sound.

At the Parthenon, Japheth Sapp gently placed the tips of his index and ring fingers on Jenny's eyelids and pulled them closed.

Then the ragged Crow pushed past Soma and hurried out into the night. The Great Salt Lick glowed no more, and even the lights of the city were dimmed, so Soma quickly lost sight of the man. But then the cawing voice rang out once more. "We only hurt the car because we had to."

Soma thought for a moment, then said, "So did I."

But the Crow was gone, and then Soma had nothing to do but wait. He had made the only decision he had left in him. He idly watched as burning bears floated down into the sea. A striking image, but he had somewhere misplaced his paints.

Glimpse the future with collections edited by
Jack Dann
and
Gardner Dozois

A.I.s
0-441-01216-7
Ten masters of speculative fiction explore
the future of computerized intelligence, and
how humanity interacts with machines that
can outthink them—and are learning
to outsmart them.

Future Crimes
0-441-01118-7
An anthology of classic and critically
acclaimed stories about the felonies and
offenses law enforcement authorities will
face in a future that's closer than we realize.

Available wherever books are sold or at
penguin.com

a814

Fantasy that Goes to the
Next Millennium and Beyond

Flights
edited by Al Sarrantonio
0-451-46036-7

This daring, all-new anthology showcases some
of the genre's biggest names and hottest
newcomers. Setting the standard for the
twenty-first century, this collection presents
fantasy that rocks the field of
science fiction.

Includes new stories from:
Neil Gaiman
Harry Turtledove
Dennis L. McKiernan
Joyce Carol Oates
Orson Scott Card
And others

**Available wherever books are sold or at
penguin.com**

A444

New in Hardcover from Ace

Accelerando
by Charles Stross

The expansion of the award-winning short story
cycle first published in *Asimov's*.

For three generations, the Macz family has
struggled to cope with the rampant technology
advancements that have made humans nearly
obsolete. And mankind's end is coming ever closer
as something starts to dismantle the solar system.

"A NEW KIND OF FUTURE REQUIRES A NEW BREED
OF GUIDE—SOMEONE LIKE STROSS."
—*POPULAR SCIENCE*

"WHERE CHARLES STROSS GOES TODAY, THE REST
OF SCIENCE FICTION WILL FOLLOW TOMORROW."
—GARDNER DOZOIS

0-441-01284-1

Available wherever books are sold or at
penguin.com

Jack McDevitt's hero from *A Talent for War*,
Alex Benedict, returns to solve a riddle that leads him
to the very edge of known space.

Jack
McDevitt

"The logical heir to Isaac Asimov and Arthur C. Clarke."
—Stephen King

SEEKER

Author of *Polaris*

An Ace Hardcover
0-441-01329-5